"This book works! Romanus' enthusiasm jumps off every page. Not only will y~~ou be~~ inspired and motivated, you'll see how quickly your desires turn into results. I keep this book handy at all times—it's like having your own private business coach."

—SHERRY RICKERT BELUL, THE CELEBRATION LADY, MAD MOON CREATIONS

"A fabulous book chock full of practical, step-by-step guidance on how to start a business based on your passion! *Kick Start Your Dream Business* is useful for an entrepreneurial lifetime."

—VIVIAN DAI, CO-FOUNDER, ARTAXCESS

"Empowering to anyone who wants to start a business! Opens the door to endless possibilities."

—ALAN AURICH. PRESIDENT, ALLIANCE BUSINESS COACHING & CONSULTING

"*Kick Start Your Dream Business* filled me with a renewed joy and motivation for turning my dream business into a reality."

—JULIANA GALLIN, INVENTOR AND GRAPHIC ARTIST, JULIANA GALLIN DESIGN

"Fun to read and easy to implement. Romanus' enthusiasm is contagious enough to make you pull out a pen and notebook and start implementing your ideas right now."

—SUSANNE PAYNOVICH, AQUATIC SPECIALIST AND INVENTOR, WATERGYM

"Eye-opening and contagious. *Kick Start Your Dream Business* saved me from making costly mistakes."

—DAWN FRY, CHILDCARE ADVOCATE, DAWN TALK CHILDREN'S CD SERIES

"It's not a jungle out there when you have *Kick Start* as your guide. I never doubted my direction—only my steps towards it. The steps in this book gave me a map that used my dreams as markers and kept me on a magnificent course."

—DEBORAH PARDES, PRODUCER AND SINGER, MENTL MUSIC
AND MEDIA PRODUCTION

"Passionately practical! This book helped me translate my passion (yoga) into a structure (my business) through which I can share it with the world."

—MICHAEL NEWMAN, R.Y.T., FOUNDER, INNER FLOW YOGA

"*Kick Start Your Dream Business* has given me confidence that people will indeed buy something I have created from my heart."

—CARLA CALETTI, ARTIST

"Until I read this book, I had a vision of what I wanted to do professionally, but didn't know how to make it happen. *Kick Start Your Dream Business* showed me that my dreams were possible and also outlined the efforts I needed to make them a reality."

—ROBERT GRAHAM, COMMUNICATION SPECIALIST, GRAHAMCOMM

"Romanus is an inspiration. Pick up this book and make your dream a reality!"

—DAVINA CHESSID, PERSONAL AND BUSINESS COACH

"Wow! We would not have progressed to the corporation we are today without *Kick Start*'s lessons on the creative process. Romanus helps people see themselves for not only who they are, but what they want to become . . . and he provides the means to get them there."

—LESLIE CHARLESWORTH AND DENISE DOLLARD, FOUNDERS,
BUSINESS INSIGHTS, INC.

"*Kick Start Your Dream Business* changed my life. It helped me uncover my true spirit—the foundation for my business."

—EMILIE NOBLE, ARTIST'S EDUCATOR, THE EMILIE NOBLE AGENCY

"I do what I love and get paid for it. I wouldn't be where I am today without this book."

—TRENT LATHROP, ANIMATOR, BRADSTINGER.COM

"Simple. Practical. Realistic. *Kick Start Your Dream Business* helped us make sure that our product worked in the marketplace—*before* we spent any money."

—MARK BUCHL AND DREW ERICKSON, THE ADVENTURE SPORTS GUIDE:
50 THINGS TO TRY BEFORE YOU DIE

"Stimulating and thought provoking. I keep referring back to the steps as I grow my business."

—TERRY SELIGMAN, THE PICASSO OF TOUR DIRECTORS, TERRYTOURS.COM
ART ADVENTURE TOURS

KICK START
YOUR DREAM
BUSINESS

KICK START
YOUR DREAM
BUSINESS

Getting It Started and Keeping You Going

BY

ROMANUS WOLTER

TEN SPEED PRESS
Berkeley/Toronto

A Kirsty Melville Book

Ten Speed Press
P.O. Box 7123
Berkeley, California 94707
www.tenspeed.com

Distributed in Australia by Simon and Schuster Australia, in Canada by Ten Speed Press Canada, in New Zealand by Southern Publishers Group, in South Africa by Real Books, in Southeast Asia by Berkeley Books, and in the United Kingdom and Europe by Airlift Book Company.

Cover and text design by Timothy Crawford and Paul Kepple @ Headcase Design
Illustrations by Jack Desrocher

Library of Congress Cataloging-in-Publication Data

Wolter, Romanus.
    Kick start your dream business : getting it started and keeping
    you going / Romanus Wolter.
        p. cm.
    Includes index.
    ISBN 1-58008-251-3 (pbk.)
    1. New business enterprises. 2. Small business—Management.
    I. Title.
    HD62.5 .W65 2001
    658.1'1—dc21   2001004435

First printing, 2001

Printed in Canada

1 2 3 4 5 6 7 8 9 10 — 05 04 03 02 01

ACKNOWLEDGMENTS

This book would not have been possible without the support of my friends, my family, and many passionate entrepreneurs. The laughter, discussions, ideas, joy, and love we shared are all part of this book.

Thanks to Keith for his support, encouragement, late nights, and inspiration. The hours he spent poring over the contents of this book helped solidify its contents and make the adventure more meaningful. Without his insight and imagination, this book would not be nearly as complete.

To my editor, Meghan, what can I say except, "Wow!" She provided patience and grounding when I just wanted to get it done. Her ideas and energy are incorporated into every word of this book. Whenever you're ready to implement your dream, I'm there with you.

Thanks to Lori whose hours of proofreading the first draft of the book provided a reality check when I needed it the most. Lori helped make sure that what was written was understood. Marie, Louis, and Alan, I also give you my thanks for taking the time to make the book a reality.

And to my parents, who provided me with a sense of adventure when I was very young. Without their love and support, I wouldn't have been able to learn from the world and share my knowledge with others.

To all of you who remember to work from your heart, listen to others and write it down—you will make a difference in the world.

TABLE OF CONTENTS

Where Do I Begin?

"Where do I begin?" is the response I inevitably hear when I tell someone what I do for a living. It's wonderful to help people realize their dreams—not just to talk about their ideas, but actually to implement them. I believe I'm successful because my heart is in what I do. I love helping people make a living from doing something they feel passionate about.

The best way to begin is to speak from your passion. When you do, others will inevitably help you. Your conversations may even stimulate other people's creative energy and move them toward implementing their own ideas. Consider the following conversation I had with a new acquaintance at a comedy club:

> After sitting down at our table, Pam turned to me and casually asked, "So what do you do for a living?"
>
> "I help turn an 'Aha!'—a dream—into a successful business."
>
> Surprised, Pam asked, "And how do you do that?"
>
> "I've developed a practical, step-by-step process that helps people kick start their dream businesses."
>
> After thinking for a moment, Pam looked at me and asked, "I have an idea, so where do I begin?"

Where do I begin? This question halts people in their tracks as their fears mount and self-doubt sets in. This question has stopped many dreams and probably some of the greatest ideas on earth. My answer to this question is always the same, just as it was with Pam.

> "You have already begun. You have taken a step, you have asked for help and are searching for answers. Congratulations! There is no stopping you now. To keep the momentum going, you have to do just three things."
>
> Pam repeated, "Three things?"
>
> "I call them the 'Rules to live by.' First, speak from your passion; it energizes you and others. Next, listen; people have experiences and knowledge

that will help you. Finally, write it down. Committing your idea to paper makes it real and allows people to discover how they can help you."

Pam's eyes focused intensely on me, oblivious of the commotion and noise around us. I sensed that she had an idea in her heart. Handing her a napkin, I said, "Write the name of your idea on the top of the paper. If you don't have a name yet, describe your idea the best you can."

Astonished, Pam said, "The thing I'm passionate about? Right now?"

"Is there ever a better time to make your dream real?"

Pam took the napkin, found a pen in her purse, and began to write.

Continuing, I told her, "After you write down the name or description of your idea, list all the reasons why you haven't implemented it yet, what's stopping you. The reasons can include: I don't have enough time, I don't have the knowledge, I need more money, or people may laugh at me. Just take a moment and write down any reasons why you haven't implemented your idea. Do it now."

Pam continued to write furiously. After about two minutes, she looked up and started to hand the paper to me, but quickly took it back and wrote some more. "Finished," Pam exclaimed soon, proudly holding up the napkin.

"Great. Now fold the napkin in half and hold it up with one hand." Pam looked a little confused but did as I suggested. Looking her in the eye I said, "Tear it up into the smallest pieces you can." Pam was uncertain what to do. She sat there with a dazed look on her face and her hand up in the air holding the napkin that contained all of her worries, troubles, and obstacles. She couldn't believe that I wanted her to tear it up.

"Tear it up," I repeated. With vigor, Pam began to tear up the napkin. The pieces flew all over the floor. When she was done, she smiled slyly.

What Pam wrote on the napkin is of little significance because as she works on her idea, she will discover solutions to each of her concerns. All she has to do is believe in herself and her idea, listen to others, and write down her idea so it becomes real. That is all you have to do, too.

This book, your friends, and people you have yet to meet are here to help you overcome obstacles and implement your dream. *Kick Start Your Dream Business* will guide you through the process with easy-to-follow steps and the information you need to succeed. You will learn the questions to ask to get the assistance you need. You have taken the first step, now get ready for the ride!

Pam decided to implement her idea. Step by step she spoke from her heart, listened to others, wrote her idea down, and asked for help when she needed it. And she launched her company with great success.

By the way, Pam still has some pieces of that napkin from the first time we met. They remind her that if you work from your heart and ask for help, your dream can come true.

Introduction

Kick Start Your Dream Business is a step-by-step guide that turns an "Aha!"—a dream—into a successful business. No matter what your experience, education, income, or knowledge, this book helps you understand your passion and manage the creative and business processes necessary to bring your idea into reality. It helps you develop an action plan to ensure your business works in the market-place *and* in your life.

Dream like a child, decide as an adult is the operating principle incorporated into every step in this book. It encourages you to allow the child inside you to dream of possibilities. Then, as an adult, you can analyze information and decide on the best actions to take.

USING THIS GUIDE

The steps in this book are divided into chapters so information is easy to find. The steps have been specifically arranged to save you time, money, and effort. However, you are in charge of making your dream real and can use the steps as you wish.

The term "product" is generically used throughout this book to describe the idea you are working on. The idea of a "product" prompts you to package your idea in a manner that is easy for others to understand. At its most fundamental level, every business (and business owner) must sell something (product or service) to someone to make a living. Artists sell paintings, restaurants sell food, sculptors sell statues, consultants sell their knowledge, and producers sell their films.

To get the most out of *Kick Start Your Dream Business*, keep the following suggestions in mind:

- **Begin at the beginning.** Read the book once to become familiar with the To Dos in each chapter. It always helps to know where you are going. Then go back to the beginning and start implementing your dream.

- **Learn something from each To Do.** Instead of skipping a step, take a moment to discover how it can help you make your business a greater success. You will be surprised at how certain information can help you build or improve your product.
- **Accomplish each step at your own pace.** This is not a race. Build the best product or service you can in the time you have available. Everyone's life is different; incorporate your business into your life your own way.
- **Ask for help.** Friends will be willing to help you. Experts enjoy sharing their experiences and ideas with people who have a dream. If you know the right questions to ask, you are sure to find the answers. Always be on the lookout for a partner in crime. You never know, a librarian might just become your best friend in this process!
- **Share information with others.** One of the most powerful and rewarding actions you can take in life is to share information. As you progress through the book, you will gather new information, and develop outrageous new marketing ideas.
- **Share your success stories, discoveries, and ideas and send them to me.** I will incorporate them into the next version of this book and into my courses. This is an uplifting way for you to share your experiences with millions of people. Send your suggestions and ideas to romanus@briia.com.

We are taught that if we follow the rules of the world, we will achieve happiness. Unfortunately, these rules do not always stimulate creativity or passion; rather they demand conformity. So get ready to break the rules, have some fun, follow your heart, and use this book to make your dream a reality!

Starting your own business is an adventure. You don't know exactly where it will lead you, but the act of achieving each step is amazing. Every step you take brings you closer to accomplishing your goal. To make the adventure fun:

- **Believe in yourself.** Know that you will make the right decisions to turn your passion into a reality. Beliefs influence reality. Believe in yourself and your idea and your energy will attract others who will help you succeed.
- **Put your idea down in writing.** If you are reading this book, there is prob-

ably an idea inside you that is waiting to be born. It's there when you wake up in the morning and when you go to sleep at night. It feels like a restless friend. Grab the nearest piece of paper, napkin, or ticket stub—and write it down. Your idea is now born and alive, ready to grow into a successful business.

- **Buy yourself time.** Pick a specific time each week in which the only thing you will do is work on your idea. Nothing will distract you—this is your special time. It can be as little as one or two hours a week. Commit yourself to this time, and you will make your dream a reality.

- **Keep an open mind and trust your instincts.** This is not the time to judge yourself or other people. Listen to others and learn from them.

- **Make a Why I Can't Do This list.** Include everything that is stopping you from implementing your idea on the list—from "I am not educated" to "I do not have enough money."

- **Tear the list up.** Realize that there is nothing on the list that can hold you back if you are willing to work hard and take chances. Kick Start will help you work through the obstacles you encounter. With conviction, tear the list up into the smallest pieces possible and throw it over your right shoulder for luck. As you do this, tell yourself, "The only barrier to achieving my goal is me."

- **Starting tonight, create a To Do list every night.** Keep this list in a book so you can review your accomplishments whenever you need to. If you are supposed to contact someone, list their telephone number and address with each To Do so you don't have to look them up again later.

- **Starting tomorrow—do the list you created.** Prioritize your list by putting the tasks that immediately affect your business first. Some ideas to make it easier to get through your To Do list are:
    - Do the most irritating or hardest task first—it frees up your mind and time to do other things. (It will be in the back of your mind irritating you anyway!)
    - Check off the tasks as you accomplish them.
    - Celebrate with a mental "congratulations"; it only takes a few seconds.
    - Do not beat yourself over the head. Remember that it is difficult to obtain your dream, and you are taking positive steps forward.

- **Keep your word.** Keep your word to others and yourself, because your reputation can take you places or bar you from them. If you say you will do something, do it! And if you can't do it, don't promise it.
- **Create a work space.** Set up a comfortable space where you can spend time achieving, even if it is in the kitchen or the basement. As time goes on, you will gather the tools and information you need. Your space might have: a large table for you to work on with enough room (hopefully) for a computer, a comfortable chair to sit in, storage space, a special place for this book, good lighting, a dedicated telephone line, and a huge trash can.
- **Don't delay.** Start today. There is nothing you "need" except this book and your imagination. You don't need a computer, a specialist, or $10,000 to get started. If you wait for these things to come, your idea will not manifest. As you go through this guide, you will discover the resources you truly require.

ONE

Grounding Your Idea

Making your dream a reality starts with your heart and your passion. Chapter 1 helps you identify your heart's motivation and build a solid foundation under your dream. That foundation is your intent, remaining constant and providing firm support as you kick start your dream business.

STEP 1

THE PROFILE

INTRODUCTION

Step 1 helps bring your idea to fruition. You have listened to your inner self and your dreams; now you can take steps to change your life. Your profile is a written statement that describes your business and the problem it helps solve. This step lessens the frustration you and those around you may feel when you try to describe your idea. Once you put your idea down in writing, it takes on a life of its own.

This is a difficult step because as you focus your idea, your dream changes, becoming a reality. As it becomes real, you may feel as if you have lost part of it. It may even seem that your idea is becoming small and limited.

These are natural feelings. Before you could change your idea at will, making it anything you wanted it to be. Now you are defining your ideas in words that can never fully express your imagination.

Luckily, when you record your idea something magical happens—your frustration disappears. Writing down your idea establishes a connection between you and the rest of the world. All of a sudden, the world begins to support your goal rather than put up roadblocks. People (including yourself) begin to really understand what you are trying to achieve: friends begin to offer ideas that will help you progress, and contacts who can help you establish your dream business appear out of thin air. By clearly defining your idea, the imagination and heart of others join you to grow and expand your idea beyond your expectations.

As you work through this step, don't worry about becoming too focused. The more specifically you develop your idea now, the freer you will be to get carried away in subsequent steps. So use this step to build a firm foundation from which your idea can grow into something fantastic.

Life is about adventure, and establishing your own business is the most fantastic adventure you can undertake. Every adventure needs a launching point, and

THUMBS UP

Accomplish something every day. Your momentum will carry you forward faster than you ever imagined.

INSPIRATION

Speak from your heart, listen to others, write down your idea, and the world will encourage you to implement your dreams.

your Profile is a perfect place to start. Remember, no one can help you implement your idea unless they know what you are trying to achieve. And once they understand, their help will be limitless.

Imagine your idea is a seed being cupped tightly in your hand with nowhere to grow. You can tell everyone what it is—a rose, an orange tree, a field of wildflowers. However, a seed without soil, sun, water, or a little nurturing will never grow. People can imagine what the seed would become, but no one will experience or share its beauty unless you open your hand, plant it in the ground, and create an environment for it to prosper.

❋ SUPPORT FROM HOME

A client of mine, Heather, had an idea for starting her own script reading and film development company. She loved helping people turn their writing into films that would surprise the audience. Heather had a very close relationship with her parents and decided to tell them about her passion. They freaked out. The questioned her endlessly: "How will you make money?" "Don't people in Hollywood just use people and throw them away?" "Do you have the talent?"

Heather was devastated. The people she needed support from the most had turned on her. She was at a loss as to what to do.

Heather came to see me after one of my workshops and explained her situation to me. I simply asked her what she had learned in the workshop that could help her. She thought and then said, "I guess I wasn't clear when I explained it. I'll write it down, get it more focused, and ask them to support me." I nodded and said, "After all, didn't they raise you and help make you who you are today? So aren't they part of every decision you make?" Heather smiled brightly and hugged me.

Heather wrote her letter to her parents and guess what—she's now helping her father develop an idea he's always had for a story. That's all it takes, letting people know your true intent and asking for their help, not their fears.

Just like the seed, your idea needs a great environment and the help of others to grow. So take the time to clearly define your idea now. By the time you actually launch your business, your idea will be shaped and molded by your research, customer input, friendly suggestions, costs, and other information you discover along the way.

Our families, friends, and school system emphasize end results rather than the discovery of what we are meant to do. People may react negatively to your idea because they worry about your future or the heartache you may have to endure to achieve your dreams. They weren't taught to react positively to passion. It is almost as if society teaches us only to worry about the consequences rather than to dream and achieve.

Society lacks a method for recognizing, validating, and implementing passion. *Kick Start Your Dream Business* helps you define, trust in, and implement your passion. *Kick Start* helps make dreams a reality.

GOAL

To define your dream and share it with the people who are important to you.

TO DO

1. **Obtain a Product Notebook to record all your thoughts, ideas, drawings, and worksheets you develop while reading this book.**

   Your Product Notebook will help you stay focused and organized. It is your personal workspace—you can use it to do a brain dump, draw packaging ideas, or write down words that you feel describe your product.

   Your Product Notebook can be any size or color. I recommend a spiral-bound notebook to my clients because it is easier to keep specific pages open. A lined notebook will help you keep your notes neater—especially if you have horrible handwriting like I do!

   If you make notes on a separate piece of paper (e.g., a napkin) or find interesting articles, keep them and staple them (or copy what you wrote) into your Product Notebook later. Some of my clients have found it helpful to supplement their Product Notebooks with a 3-ring binder. This binder gives them a place to hold any loose pages (such as articles, pictures, flyers, or marketing samples).

OUTCOME

A foundation upon which to build your dream business.

You will achieve what you write down. And you will not achieve what you don't write down.

Carry your Product Notebook with you at all times so you can write down any observations or ideas you develop. Your Product Notebook serves three purposes. First, it is a central place to keep your ideas, thoughts, bits of wisdom, and To Dos from this book. Second, it is a record of when and how you developed your business idea. This documentation may become important to you someday if you become involved in any litigation. Third, it will calm your mind and relieve stress because you will no longer worry about losing any of your ideas; they will be preserved in your Product Notebook.

Your notebook can serve many other purposes. A client of mine, Keith, used it to answer people who were skeptical of his idea. When he was meeting with a potential distributor, partner, or investor, he would always set his Product Notebook on the table in front of him. If the person questioned whether or not his idea would be a success, Keith would flip through his Product Notebook explaining all the work he had completed to date.

By using his notebook as a shield, Keith was able to speak about his passion rather than automatically defend his idea. Keith's enthusiasm calmed his potential partners—after all, if someone is passionate enough about their idea to keep a Product Notebook, they will surely find a way to make their dream a reality.

2. **Write down a brief description of your idea.**

Don't spend a lot of time worrying about finding the right words, just get your idea down on paper. The rest of the steps in the book will help you clearly define your idea. An example description is: A new eating utensil that makes cutting and eating tomatoes easier.

3. **Define the problem that your idea solves and describe how the problem is solved.**

By solving a problem, you establish a need (a reason why someone would want to buy your idea) or a benefit. For example, the new utensil mentioned above can help people save time by safely and quickly slicing tomatoes for salads. A book can help people realize that their dreams can come true.

BRAINSTORM

Name: What potential names reflect your idea?

Customers: Who do you think would be interested in buying your idea?

Distribution: Where could you sell this idea?

Promotion: How would you tell people about your idea?

4. **Recreate the chart on page 11 in your Product Notebook. Use the chart to list all your ideas about your product.**

Do not discount or analyze any ideas. Just write down anything that comes into your mind. This exercise gets you thinking positively and helps build a foundation from which you can create your business.

5. **Explain how you came up with your idea.**

By telling people how you developed your idea, you involve them in the process. This can also help you defend your idea if someone else tries to steal it from you. (*Note:* See the movie *Working Girl*; it's fun, it's inspiring, and the elevator scene near the end shows the importance of documenting how you came up with your idea.) For example: I kept slicing myself while cutting vegetables and decided it was time for a new knife that will slice vegetables but not fingers.

6. **Describe how developing this idea will change you, your life, and your relationships with people who are important to you.**

Explain who you are now and who you will become in the process of achieving your goal. Once you incorporate your dream into your life, there is no stopping it. You and the people in your life will be changed as your dreams expand and your life flourishes.

7. **Set your work aside for one day.**

These steps are exhausting. They challenge you to open your heart and mind. You will uncover feelings, thoughts, fears, hopes, and anxieties associated with your idea. Set it all aside, take a breath, and go do something fun. I love going to the ice cream parlor, looking at all the flavors, and realizing the endless combinations. Stretch your imagination by ordering two scoops that you have never ordered before. Sit in your favorite easy chair and enjoy!

8. **Look over your answers and absorb what you have written.**

Do your words reflect what is in your heart and mind? If so, congratulations. You have set a clear goal for yourself. If not, change your answers so they reflect what is in your heart—not what society expects you to say. This is important. You have to be passionate about your goal to achieve it. It's going to be a lot of hard work, a lot of late nights, and a lot of fun.

9. **Assign dates to your goals using the Table of Contents for this book.**
Look over the Table of Contents and read the chapter descriptions of the steps you will be taking. Put a date by each chapter heading. Setting dates provides you with goals that will keep you moving forward. It familiarizes you with the process and provides you with answers to people's questions. For instance, if someone asks, "How are you going to finance your idea?" you can say, "Financing comes after I've clearly defined my idea, its market, and how I'm going to produce it." This exercise provides you with the confidence to concentrate on what needs to be accomplished right now. It also shows people you know how to accomplish your idea.

10. **Take ownership of your idea by sharing your answers to the previous questions with someone you trust and asking them to support you in the future.**
Sit down and write this person a letter, a real letter—stamp and all—not an e-mail. Tell them why it's important for you to implement this idea. Don't ask them to evaluate the idea, just ask them to listen to you as you explain it.

You may ask this person to be a mentor or sounding board for you as you progress with your business. Receiving a letter from a friend these days is rare, and it will help this person realize how important this business is to you.

You will spend a lot of time and energy making your idea real. Prepare them by telling them it will be difficult at times, and you will need their support, energy, and understanding to achieve your goals. If they understand your goals, they will become an energy field that surrounds and protects you!

Society doesn't easily welcome passion—there are no "cool" words to express it and many people lack patience with our fumbled attempts to explain it. This book will help you pursue and achieve your dreams. Its steps will help you articulate your passion so people will understand it and will honor your dream.

YOUR INTENT

INTRODUCTION

Now that you have written down what you hope to accomplish, it is time to concentrate on why you want to develop your product. Your personal intent will be the driving force for implementing your dream.

Have you ever known someone who started a project but didn't follow through with it? They worked on it for a while, struggled some, and then decided that it just was not worth their effort. Even if their idea was brilliant, they abandoned it.

I've seen this over and over again—and the missing element in each instance is clear. It is passion. Their idea was not connected to their heart. Being passionate about your product is critical for success. Some people explain the reason for business failures to be lack of financing, lack of a proper business plan, or lack of time to implement their business. Passion overcomes each and every one of these obstacles. You may also feel fear, but guess what—that means you are truly passionate. Fear is okay; don't let it stop you from moving forward.

During this step, you will identify your internal intent (how you will benefit from implementing your idea) and external intent (how your idea will benefit others). Your intent comes from your heart and your passion. By letting your heart and mind mingle, you open yourself up to the fun, joy, and excitement that comes with creating something new. Clarifying your intent also helps other people understand your idea and provides them with the opportunity to help you. This is a powerful step because your intent reflects the reason you are implementing your idea—the benefit it provides. And when you speak about benefiting others, people are often more inclined to work with you.

Louisa, a client of mine, actually warned a new client, "Watch out for the soul discussion exercise. Once you complete it, wham!—you're in business."

THUMBS UP

Focus on one idea at a time. Start with the one idea that is burning a hole in your heart, the one that will change your life.

Details about your product may change over time—its name, packaging, pricing, advertising (to name a few things)—but your intent for creating the product does not change so easily. Your intent guides you by providing an emotional foundation from which you can start and grow your own business.

This may sound easy. It isn't. When you speak from your heart, you become vulnerable. Others may attack your idea, causing you to become frustrated and hurt. Don't be. As has often been said, "We can't control the actions of others, but we can control our reaction to them." That is what I want you to practice, believing in yourself and not being worried about how others react to you and your dream.

Society has trained us to react pessimistically to new ideas, especially ones with an artistic bent. Most people point out the faults of your idea first, but given the chance they eventually turn to compliments and, more importantly, to suggestions for improvement. If you shut them up while they are criticizing or giving you their "valuable" opinion, you will miss the ideas they have to help you grow.

To avoid becoming frustrated or hurt, learn to listen. That's right—L-I-S-Ten to everyone and discover any helpful information they have to offer. The first four letters of listen are "L-I-S-T." Do not judge any ideas, thoughts, or critiques people give you, just listen and list. Write down what people have to say and thank them for their insight. You never know which ideas will work for you and which will not. Don't lose them; write them down in your Product Notebook. You are in charge of your business; you can decide whether or not to use someone else's suggestions.

The coolest thing about L-I-S-Tening is that it makes people feel as though they are part of your dream. They feel that they are contributing something to the world, and what better feeling is there? People that you L-I-S-Ten to will become part of your team, and they may bring you that contact you need some day for financing or marketing your business. Congratulations, you have now expanded your marketing team at no cost to you.

NOTE

You can deflect criticism by associating it with a future step. For example, if someone attacks the economics of your idea, say, "That's a great point to consider when I'm looking at financing my idea. Thanks."

GOAL

*To create a
foundation for
your business idea
by defining your
internal and
external intent.*

OUTCOME

*Personal focus,
energy, passion,
and commitment.*

✳ A SOUL ADVENTURE

Kristen approached me with her idea for a new tour company in San Francisco. She wanted to provide a behind-the-scenes look at the city. She knew her idea would work because tourists love visiting and exploring San Francisco.

In Step 1, Kristen stated that she wanted to start a tour company that would take people off the beaten path. She decided that her clients would be tourists and she would promote the tours by placing brochures in hotel lobbies.

As she talked about her idea, she added that she was nervous because there were already many tour companies in San Francisco (over 30 from her investigation). I told her not to worry about the competition yet because she was still defining her idea and a major portion of her idea was missing—her heart. Why was she interested in giving tours? What benefits would her tours provide?

Kristen followed the exercises outlined in Step 2 and really focused in on her internal and external intent. Her internal intent was to start a business in which she could combine her love for entertainment with her love for history. She loved exploring.

Focusing on her external intent, Kristen stated that she had been a businesswoman who traveled a great deal. And one thing that bothered her during her travels was that she never had time to experience the beauty and charm of the cities she was visiting. After writing this down, she decided that her company would target business people who wanted to experience the "real" San Francisco. Further, Kristen decided to concentrate on high technology businesses that were having a hard time recruiting new employees.

Aha! By focusing on her intent, Kristen developed a company based on what she really wanted to accomplish—a business that came from her heart. Bay Area or Bust! builds loyalty right from the start. Her customized tours convince prospective employees that her client's company and San Francisco are the places to grow their personal and professional lives. She distinguishes each company from the competition by showing how the sponsoring company has helped grow San Francisco's community, just as they help their employees succeed and prosper.

In just two steps, Kristen had developed a business that stood out from the competition. She began to tell people about her idea, and she immediately had two large companies interested in her product—a product she was still defining!

Other people started to refer customers to her, and by following the steps outlined in this book, Kristen continued to grow her idea. Now she has expanded her tours to include relocation services.

By writing her idea down and focusing on her intent, Kristen defined her company in a manner that focused on the benefits she could provide. This exercise helped her differentiate her business. You will accomplish the same thing by completing this step.

N O T E

Brainstorming is not an analytical process. In essence, it is creating and filling up a "dream junk drawer" with any ideas you or anyone else may generate. Just think, the cutesy dinosaur, Barney, could have been stopped short by people discounting the idea up front.

TO DO

1. Turn to a new a page in your Product Notebook and label it "My Internal Intent." Underneath it write, "The heart of my business," and then brainstorm on your internal intent.

Your internal intent explains why you want to develop your product. What will you gain from this endeavor personally? Write down all your ideas. Make sure that you consider everything you want to achieve. Examples include:

- To own my own business.
- To make enough money to earn a living.
- To meet different people.
- To help people appreciate paintings.
- To explore the world.

Focus on how achieving your dream will affect you personally. For example, if you stated that your internal intent was to make $1 million, restate your goal by explaining how having $1 million would benefit your life.

2. **Discuss each intent with the friend you invited to help you in Step 1, To Do number 10.**

By sharing your intent with another person, you now have someone who can remind you of why you started on the journey of owning your own business. A sounding board will make sure you are headed down the right track. Your friend will support you, but it's important for them to know why your business is so important to you. Put your heart into your words.

3. **State your internal intent in one or two sentences.**

The clearer your intent is, the greater the likelihood you will achieve it. If you cannot state your internal intent in one or two sentences, pick out key words ("develop" a product that . . .) and write two sentences using these key words. For instance, my clients have written:

"To travel the world and discover cool products. To combine my love for art and education and make money."

"To work outside. To write and have people learn from my experiences."

4. **Label a page in your Product Notebook, "My External Intent." Underneath it subtitle the page, "How It Benefits Others," then brainstorm on your external intent.**

Your external intent focuses on how your idea will benefit other people. You can express this as "This idea will enable people to . . ."

It may be hard to determine the external effects of your idea. Try this fun exercise. Close your eyes and let your imagination take you to the future; your idea is now an actual product or service that people are using. How are they using it? Are they laughing? If so, your external intent could be to make people laugh. Are they learning? If so, your external intent could be to educate.

Questions that can help you define your external intent include:

- Do I intend to inform, entertain, provoke, or educate?
- Do I want to help others make money?
- Do I want to make people laugh?
- Will this idea make people's lives easier? Will I save them time, effort, or money?

5. Discuss your external intent with your friends and write down any other brainstorms that come up.

This is a great way to get your friends involved in and excited about your business. Remember to L-I-S-Ten (just write down what they have to say without commenting on it). This is exciting because now you will be able to hear how your future customers may use your product. Keep an open mind and have fun.

6. In your Product Notebook, state your external intent in one or two clear, concise sentences.

This clarity will tell people how your business will help them achieve their goals. You can also test people's reaction to your idea by telling them your external intent and seeing whether or not they are interested in its benefits.

7. Look at both of your intents and ask yourself, "Is this idea part of my soul and my life goals?"

You're developing a small business based on your dream. To achieve your goal, it will have to be an intimate part of your life. To love that life your goal must be based on your intent—your passion.

If you are passionate about your dream, you will achieve it. If you are not, you may still achieve success, but instead of being fun, your idea may become a chore and you may give up before it hits the market. Passion will see you through the tough times.

8. In your Product Notebook label a page, "Why I Am Creating This Business." Under it write down your idea's name, your internal intent, and your external intent.

What is written on this page is really what creating your own business is about—helping yourself and others. This is the heart of your business.

To emphasize this point most of my clients draw a heart around the three items. I suggest you do too. That way whenever you are tired or discouraged, you can look at your heart and remember how your idea will benefit you and others. One glance will provide you with the energy you need to conquer the challenges that lie ahead.

Intent is a powerful foundation for your dream business; if it comes from your heart you will not falter.

SELF-CONTRACT

INTRODUCTION

This contract is for you. It defines what you will accomplish and when you hope to accomplish it, reminding you of the promises you made to yourself. By reflecting on and writing down your goals, your mind and heart will help you achieve your goals rather than worry about them. Upon signing your contract, you will really start to move forward; you are on your way.

A lot of people give up on their dreams because of the stress involved. There is no better way to manage stress than to put your worry down on paper and then ask for help. Often, telling someone else about our problems sends them away. Many of my clients include their initial worries in their contracts. Then they reserve a page in their Product Notebooks for future concerns. Once they (or a friend) find a solution (or the worry goes away), they put a big X mark through that problem.

Your contract will be an inspiration to you. When you are feeling down or think that your dream business won't ever be implemented, look over your contract and your intent and reflect on them. The contents will energize you, allowing you to continue achieving your dreams.

THUMBS UP

Don't become a queen or king of list making. Write down what you are going to do and then accomplish it.

TO DO

1. **Label a page in your Product Notebook "My Self-Contract." Below the title write your name and the date.**

Everyone has their own unique way of creating a self-contract. One client even wrote her contract on a piece of parchment paper and framed it. However you create your contract, put a copy in your Product Notebook.

2. **In the first paragraph of your contract, describe your idea and its benefits by telling a short story.**

The beginning of the story is a quick description of your product idea (your description from Step 1), the middle is the benefits it provides to people (your external intent from Step 2), and the ending is who your customers are (refer to the brainstorming exercise in Step 1).

Writing this story down helps solidify your idea. You can also use the story to tell people about your idea while you are conducting research. Stories involve people and hold their interest; use them as often as you can.

3. **In the next paragraph of your contract, search your heart (and the dates you put on the Table of Contents) and establish a date that you would like to launch your business.**

By recording this date, you establish a concrete goal for yourself. It also tells other people when you hope to launch your business. This date can change as you develop your dream. But remember, writing it down makes it real, so the more accurate your launch date, the more solid your foundation will be.

4. **In the next paragraph of your contract, write that you will enlist the help of others to grow your business.**

You will need to ask for help as you develop your idea. The biggest obstacle most people face is knowledge, and the lack of it. Other people have information and resources that we may not have access to. You don't have to know everything, but life is much simpler when you have people to call who do. Always ask for help, people love to help dreams come true.

5. **In the next paragraph of your contract, declare that this contract is between you and your future.**

This statement connects your goals to your life. After all, when you create a business from your passion, you are changing your life and the lives of others.

GOAL

To formulate a working contract with yourself that will commit you to your goals.

OUTCOME

A signed self-contract that will provide you inspiration when you need it.

You are now working from your head as well as your heart, and you will receive help when you ask for it.

6. **In the final paragraph of your contract, state that you are the only one who can void this contract.**

   The success or failure of your business is really up to you. No matter what your friends, relatives, storeowners, or the press may say (or think) about your business, they cannot void the contract. Only you can do that.

7. **Sign and date your self-contract.**

   The last step in making this contract a reality is your signature. Sign it. Commit yourself to creating a business that will change your life and the lives of others. Congratulations! You are on your way to turning your dream into a dream business!

SHARING YOUR IDEA

To help you, people only need to understand what your idea is, the benefits it provides, and who your customers are. If someone needs more detailed information, you should discuss your idea with them only after you have read Chapter 4, Protecting It.

Gathering Useful Information

Dream like a child, decide as an adult, is the theme of this chapter. Each step of the way toward making your business a reality, you will dream of the possibilities and explore what is already in the market. Then, thinking like an adult, you will analyze the information and take action. Gaining an understanding of what is already out there will strengthen the foundation you laid in Chapter 1 and help make your idea competitive.

MARKET BRAINSTORMING

INTRODUCTION

The last three steps helped you build a solid foundation for your idea. This step helps you understand the market and test your product. Keep an open mind and learn everything you can; like a child, think of everything as possible. You have planted the seed, now it is time to give it some water and sunshine so it can take root and begin to grow.

Remember that brainstorming is best described as filling up a dream junk drawer. The goal is to generate as many ideas as possible. Make sure you don't judge any ideas yet because the ideas you discover during this step will take on different meanings and uses as you develop your product. Brainstorming is just a huge brain dump.

For example, have you ever heard a song and hated it, but when you heard the song later under different circumstances (in a movie or while you were with someone you love), it took on a whole new perspective? The same thing will happen to the ideas you develop in this step.

Be vulnerable; tell people about your idea and ask for help in developing it. Then relax and just L-I-S-Ten. From my experience, I've learned most people will want to help you implement your ideas, not steal them or corrupt them. The possibility of gaining allies and resources by talking to others usually outweighs the risk of someone stealing or belittling your ideas.

Take your time to complete this step. It is a lot of hard work but is well worth it. It is one of the most beneficial steps you will accomplish. This step will help you:

- Explain your product to your friends and others who can help you.
- Create a source of future marketing ideas.

NOTE

You may be feeling overwhelmed, that you have a lot to accomplish. This is a normal feeling. To relieve anxiety, carry your Product Notebook with you at all times, write down the things you have to do, and then cross them off as you accomplish them.

GOAL

To generate marketing ideas by using your imagination, experience, and gut feelings.

OUTCOME

An outrageous list of possible products, customers, distributors, retailers, sponsors, and marketing events.

- Determine what partners can help you distribute your product or service.
- Learn to L-I-S-Ten.
- Begin developing a marketing plan that will distinguish your product from the competition.
- Create an Information Center in Step 8 by providing an initial list of product attributes. The Information Center is a reference that will assist you in quickly locating any ideas you generate and any competitive information you discover.

TO DO

1. **In your Product Notebook, put each of the following titles on a separate page: Product, Customers, Distribution, Retailers, Sponsorship, and Marketing Events.**

    These topics are the primary areas you need to develop to market your product. The ideas generated in each of these areas will help you get your product into the hands of your customers.

2. **Re-create the charts found on pages 28 to 34 in your Product Notebook.**

    You can recreate the charts in this book on the respective pages you created in To Do number 1. Use these pages to write down additional ideas throughout your brainstorming process. Keep your Product Notebook with you at all times. You never know when an idea will smack you on the side of the head.

    Note: You can photocopy the charts and paste them into your Product Notebook. You can also obtain larger copies of the charts by printing out the same charts at www.tenspeed.com/kick-start.

3. **By yourself, go through the questions asked in the charts and brainstorm on any ideas you have for each.**

    Dream like a child. This is a time to have fun. Set your imagination free and write down whatever comes to your mind. You will analyze your answers later.

4. **Bring a group of friends together (three is fine), tell them about your idea, ask them the questions asked in the charts, and write down any ideas they come up with.**

Remember to just L-I-S-Ten. Let your friends help you. This is not the time to judge. It's wonderful to laugh at outrageous ideas, but don't forget to write them down. The crazy thing about life is that seemingly poor ideas can become popular products. Imagine what people said to the person who thought of marketing a rock as a pet—the Pet Rock made millions!

This step accomplishes three things. One, it gives you additional ideas you might never have thought of. Two, it includes your friends in your dreams. Three, it helps you practice and become comfortable with asking for help. You will become so comfortable asking for help that later on, you will probably receive your best ideas from complete strangers.

Remember to write down the name(s) of anyone participating in your brainstorming session. In addition to having witnesses for your ideas, later on these people can help you remember why you put something in your Product Notebook. Just call them up and ask, "Why did I put a dozen exclamation marks after the word 'costume' in my Product Notebook?" It will give you both a good laugh and probably generate even more creative ideas.

5. **Start investigating current interest in your topic.**

Read all you can; it is a wonderful way to keep up to date with new trends and ideas for your business. Simple things like clipping newspaper articles and watching the news, talk shows, and newsmagazine shows, can make a difference in your business. Keep the articles and comments about the ideas discussed in the appropriate area of your Product Notebook or a 3-ring binder.

INSPIRATION

Have fun with this step. If you do not know an answer to a certain question, make it up. The more outrageous the better. Keep brainstorming.

INSPIRATION

At first you may not be able to think of any answers, but let your mind wander and you will be surprised where the imagination will lead you.

Market Brainstorming

PRODUCT

Product Areas	
Name: What benefit does your product provide? Some people name their product for exactly what it does (e.g., Bug-Be-Gone).	
Benefits: What will attract customers to your product? Why do people "need" your product? What problem does it solve?	
Packaging: Imagine your product's packaging and describe it. What colors are used on it? How big is it?	
Technology: Is there any special technology involved with your product or its packaging?	

Durability: How durable will your product be? Will people buy it once a year or more often?	
Equipment: Is there any special equipment required for your customers to use your product (e.g., a film projector)?	
Return policy: Will you accept product returns from your customers? Why or why not?	
Season: Will the sales of your product be affected by the seasons or other events (e.g., Valentine's Day)?	
Logo and slogan: What images represent your product (e.g., a moon or a knife and fork)? Brainstorm on a slogan for your product. The slogan should be fun, quirky, and most of all should describe your product. Try to keep your slogan to one-syllable words; they're easier to say and remember (e.g., "Just do it" or "We do it your way").	
Spin-offs: Can your product be spun off (i.e., made into a similar product or an extension of the original product)?	

CUSTOMERS

Don't discount any ideas. Simply gather all the information you can; it may be useful in the future.

Customer Areas	
Target: Which group of people does your product target? Imagine people buying your product and describe them: men or women, boys or girls, age, race and ethnic background, marital status, income, education, profession, places they live and shop.	
Not a target: Is there anyone you do not want to target (e.g., children or certain political or religious groups)?	
Organizations: What organizations or corporations would buy your product (e.g., churches or the gas company)?	
Press: What TV shows do your customers watch and what magazines and newspapers do they read?	

RETAILERS

Retailers are places that will sell your product directly to customers.

Retailer Areas	
Location: Where could you sell your product (e.g., department stores, supermarkets, novelty shops, or college bookstores)?	
Virtual locations: Could you sell your product on television, in a catalog, or on the Internet? Or do your customers have to touch, smell, or feel your product before buying it?	
Other sales channels: What other ways could you sell your product (e.g., telephone sales, direct mail, or door-to-door)?	
Nontraditional retailers: What other nontraditional retail outlets can you think of to carry your product (e.g., airplanes, bars, or late night infomercials)?	

DISTRIBUTION

Representatives ("reps") sell your product and distributors deliver it to multiple retail locations. Distributors often warehouse and fulfill orders for your product also. Reps only take orders; warehousing and fulfilling orders remains your responsibility.

Distribution Areas	
Distributors: What traditional distributors or representatives would be interested in your product (e.g., book, novelty, or film)?	
Self-distribution: Can you self-distribute your product via mail or by visiting stores?	
Nonprofits: Could nonprofit organizations sell your idea to their membership as a fundraising effort?	
Geography: What is your product's geographic scope (e.g., local, regional, or nationwide)?	

SPONSORSHIP

Sponsors are individuals or organizations that would benefit from being affiliated with your product. These sponsors can help get your product noticed. They can provide money, in-kind services, or promotional expertise.

Sponsorship Areas	
Benefit: What opportunities or benefits does your idea offer to large groups of people? Can it benefit communities, groups, or corporations that provide services to a large number of people?	
Organizations: What specific organizations would benefit from sponsoring your product? If you listed any organizations as customers, now is the time to think of them as sponsors.	

MARKETING EVENTS

Marketing is anything you do to tell people about your product.

Marketing Areas	
Unique strategies: List any unique press events or strategies you can think of for your product (e.g., paint the name of your business on your car).	
Personal direct contact: List any ideas you have for making personal contact with customers or distributors (e.g., sales demonstrations in stores).	
Promotion: List any conferences, trade shows, or other promotional events you would like to attend.	

MARKETING IDEAS THAT WILL ATTRACT ATTENTION

1. **Unusual Marketing Events**
   - Wear your product. Put your business name or logo on T-shirts, buttons, or hats.
   - Create a mascot. Dress in costume and hand out flyers about your business in your neighborhood or at a trade show. A fun mascot will help you stand out.
   - Give a percentage of your profits to a charity. This activity will provide you with access to new customers and with great free publicity in your local paper.
   - Use public access television. Start your own television show on your local public access channel (just call your cable company for information). You can host the show and invite your customers on as guests. This is a great way to develop word-of-mouth advertising, free press, and customer loyalty.
   - Create a contest. Have a contest in which your customers send you unique ways in which they use your product—the most original wins a prize. You gain a unique story that will be of interest to the press and expand your customer list.

2. **Corporate Identity**
   - Use your logo on all your marketing materials including business cards and letterhead. Consistent usage of your logo on all marketing materials will improve customer recognition.
   - The use of a consistent color can help your product stand out in the market.

3. **Personal Direct Contact**
   - Create a workshop that uses your product.
   - Attend trade shows.
   - Speak at seminars and other networking events.

NOTE

See Chapter 7, Telling the World, for more detail on these great ideas.

4. Free Press

- Write articles for your local newspaper about the life of an entrepreneur.
- Write an article about how your product helps benefit others.
- What Internet sites (e.g., e-zines or helpful sites) can you contribute a story to?

5. Paid Advertising and Direct Mail

- What publications can you advertise in?
- What organizations can you send a direct mail piece to?
- Are there any industry magazines you can advertise in?
- Can you develop a flyer that you can drop off in mailboxes around your neighborhood?

REAL-LIFE INVESTIGATION

INTRODUCTION

Your product is still developing. This step uses specific questions to help you explore the marketplace, discover similar products, and grow your idea. The coolest thing is that your investigation also provides you with a list of places where you can eventually sell your product.

Conducting a real-life investigation is like going on a field trip. You will visit different locations to gather information on existing products that other people have spent a lot of time developing and marketing. Do not make any decisions about your product yet; just write down all the ideas that come into your head.

People that have developed these products have spent time and money refining their packaging so customers will be attracted to their product. Use their research for your own product. Do not copy what they have produced. The goal of this investigation is to continue your brainstorming with real-world examples. For instance, look at the packaging of a similar product and list the colors, graphics, and words you really like.

The information you gather now will enable you to create an Information Center later (Step 8), so you can speak intelligently about your product and other comparable products in the market. By knowing what is in the market, you will be able to distinguish your product and will also gain the trust of potential partners.

When you conduct your real-life investigation, observe, ask questions, and L-I-S-Ten. Then ask some more questions. People love to talk and share their knowledge—take advantage of that.

INSPIRATION

This step saves you a lot of time and avoids reinventing the wheel. By gathering product pricing, marketing, display, and manufacturing information quickly, you will learn from the experience of others what worked well and what didn't.

L-I-S-Ten and learn. You can analyze all your ideas later!

Real-life investigation is both eye-opening and frustrating. It's eye-opening because you'll be investigating the market that you're interested in, and it's frustrating because you'll probably find a product or service that is similar to yours. Don't get overwhelmed or discouraged. Since your idea comes from your heart—your passion—it will develop into something unique. That is what this adventure is all about—discovering your passion, learning what is already in the market, then creating something that stands out from everything else.

GOAL

To gather information on real-world products, services, and contacts.

OUTCOME

A chart showing what the market looks like right now.

✳ WHAT WILL IT BE WHEN IT GROWS UP?

A client of mine had an idea for a book that provided a look inside the lives of gay people from a straight person's point of view. We went through the steps for this book, producing her profile, intent, self-contract, and market brainstorming. During the real-life investigation step, she went to a bookstore and discovered three books on the same subject. Discouraged, she nearly gave up on her idea.

However, when she looked back at her Product Notebook she remembered that her internal intent was to share her views and her sense of humor with other people. Her external intent was to provide an informative look into the life a gay person. Neither intent was to produce a book!

Rejuvenated, she continued her real-life investigation by telling storeowners about her idea and her intent. They told her that their customers have asked for and would buy a game on the subject.

She took that information to heart and produced a board game that is now distributed internationally. She did not lose any of her work; she just had to be willing to listen to other people.

Remember, if you get discouraged or feel lost, go back to your intent. Since your idea is grounded in your heart, you will develop something that will take the market by storm.

TO DO

1. **Copy the charts on the following pages into your Product Notebook.**
   You can photocopy the charts or print them out from the Internet site www.tenspeed.com/kick-start and paste them in to your Product Notebook. Feel free to add any questions to the charts that are specific to your idea. When your charts are complete, you will have a wonderful tool to compare your product to the competition.

2. **Visit local stores, offices, or places that sell products similar to yours. When you find a product that is similar to yours, fill in the real-life investigation charts.**
   Discover all you can about the similar product. First, look over the product and discover what you like and don't like about it. List your comments in your charts.

   Always talk to any front-line people (e.g., salespeople, ticket takers, and managers) about your product. These people know your customers because they deal with them every day. Describe your product to them and ask questions such as: "Do you have any packaging or pricing suggestions? Any in-store display ideas or events? How is the similar product selling? Can you share any distributors names?" You can use this information to solidify your idea.

   Don't be timid! If you see a customer buying a product like yours, ask them if you could talk to them about a new product idea. If they say yes, tell them about your product and write down any suggestions they may have. You can also ask them what they like or dislike about the product they are buying.

   Consider buying the similar product to determine how the inventors put it together, how easy it is to use, and how it can help you improve your product. If you are developing a service, get brochures on similar services and ask the same questions.

3. **If you are developing a product that is offered in a different city, call or visit the location and speak with the owner or inventor.**
   Businesses outside your immediate area may not view you as direct competition and may be more willing to share information with you. Small-business people love to talk. It is like they are boasting about one of their children.

INSPIRATION

There probably is a similar product on the market. That's OK. Your idea is your brain-child and as you work on it, it will continue to grow, change, and become unique.

INSPIRATION

Focus on benefit. Small-business people love talking about their companies, especially if someone is willing to help them expand their business. It is about give and take. Focus on benefit and help everyone win, including you.

NOTE

Do not feel the need to cement ideas, retailers, or manufacturers at this point. There is still a lot to learn.

Before visiting a business outside your area, consider how you can benefit their business. How will working with you increase their sales? If you focus on mutual benefit rather than on your needs, the other person will be more open with you. They may even be willing to discuss their internal processes and any heartache they had in starting their business.

Ask your contact about what worked and what didn't, and about suppliers, customers, and sales outlets. Be sure to ask for any materials (e.g., menus, ads, or brochures) they can send you. These items will help you speak intelligently to other business owners when you meet with them.

4. **On your calendar, mark a date to attend a trade show, gift fair, or conference that specializes in your product area.**

You can find the dates and locations of trade shows on the Internet at www.expoguide.com. Find a show about your product area and mark your calendar.

❋ NEW RECRUITS

A client of mine, Richard, was considering opening a recruiting company in Los Angeles. Richard decided to call a firm in San Francisco to find out more about the internal processes of running a recruiting business. Before calling, he focused on how he could help the other business grow.

During his brainstorming session, he discovered a trend—a number of his business acquaintances had discussed moving or had already moved to San Francisco from Los Angeles. He realized that he could help the other company grow by referring these people to their recruiting firm. When he called the San Francisco recruiting company, Richard told them about his idea and how he could help their company by referring new clients to them from Los Angeles.

It worked. Later that week, Richard drove up to San Francisco, met with the company's owner, and gained firsthand knowledge of what it takes to establish a successful recruiting company.

Trade shows are a wonderful place to conduct real-life investigations. You will see products you never thought of, meet buyers, speak with store owners, and have a great time. Be sure to get a program guide from the show. It lists the companies that attended and their contact information.

Ask questions before you attend a trade show (or visit the trade show's web site). Ask what the total attendance is expected to be, how many vendor booths will be associated with your specific area, and what trade publications are associated with the show.

Try to find a way to attend the show for free (e.g., volunteer your services). If you have to pay a fee and the show has a lot of information about your product area, it's probably worth it to attend.

5. **Continue to investigate different retail areas and record new discoveries in your Product Notebook.**

Do not just visit one retail location. The more information you can gather now, the better your product will become. Take your time, conduct your research, and make your product as unique as possible. After all, your product represents your passion.

INSPIRATION

Whenever you ask other people for information, always ask yourself: "Is there any way I can help their business grow?" Share your ideas with them; it will help you build great relationships.

Real-Life Investigation

SIMILAR PRODUCTS

Product Areas	
General information: What is the name, address, and phone number? This information is usually on the package.	
Price: How much does the product cost? Does the price seem reasonable?	
Benefits: How does the product benefit customers? What need does it fulfill? What problem does it solve?	
Features: What is the most appealing thing about the product? What makes you want to buy it?	

Packaging: Describe and/or draw the product. What are its colors, material, designs? What stands out? What is bad about it? What's the first thing that caught your eye?

Logo and slogans: What words are on the packaging? Is the logo displayed prominently: Describe and/or draw the product's logo.

Technology: What technology is involved with the product or its packaging (e.g., an electronic motor)?

Season: What season is it? Ask a salesperson whether the product sells better during certain times of the year. List those times.

Warranties: Are there any warranties (promises of quality) on the packaging? If so, list them. If not, ask a salesperson for both the product's and the store's warranties (or guarantee). List them both.

Spin-offs: Do you see any spin-off ideas near the product? Are any mentioned on the packaging?

CUSTOMERS

Customer Areas	
Target: Who buys the competitive product (e.g., men, women, boys, or girls)? Try to list age, race or ethnic background, and marital status. If you can talk to customers, ask about their income level, education, and profession. Use any words you can think of to describe your customer.	
Not a target: Is there anyone the other product does not target (e.g., minors)?	
Press: What TV shows does the customer watch and what magazines or newspapers do they read?	
Organizations: Do any organizations or corporations buy or sponsor the product?	
Nonprofits: Do any nonprofits buy or sponsor the product?	

RETAILERS

Retailer Areas	
Locations: What physical locations sell the product? List store name, contact name, phone and fax numbers, and address. Often store clerks and cashiers will give you the names and addresses of their corporate or "central" buyers. These are the people you will contact in the future to buy your product!	
Additional sales channels: Ask one of the store helpers or managers whether they know any other places (e.g., stores, catalogs, or Internet sites) where the product is sold.	
Product placement: Where was the product physically located in the store? Ask the front-line person whether its location ever changes and why.	
Promotion: Does it have a special container or is it just on the shelf? Does the store conduct special in-store events for new products? Describe any displays or advertising the product uses.	

DISTRIBUTION

Distribution Areas	
How does the store buy the product (e.g., reps, distributor, or catalog)?	
What is the contact information for the distribution company or sales representative? What percentages do they take?	
Does the store accept products from independent manufacturers? (If so, contact these stores directly.)	
What is the similar product's geographic scope? If it's limited, ask why.	
Representatives: Ask the salesperson or manager if they know any appropriate sales representatives. If so, ask them for contact information for representatives that would be interested in your product.	
Distribution: Is a distributor's or representative's name and contact information listed on the product's packaging. If it is, write it down.	

SPONSORSHIP

Sponsorship Areas

Organizations: Do any specific organizations or corporations endorse the product? (An endorsement means that the company recognizes the benefit of the product and is willing to be associated with it, not necessarily that they buy it.)

Charities: Are any charities associated with the product? Charities have large, powerful mailing lists.

MARKETING IDEAS

Marketing Areas	
Unique strategies: Do the front-line personnel mention any unique press events or strategies (e.g., in-store displays or rebates)?	
Personal direct contact: Does the salesperson have any ideas for making direct contact with customers (e.g., in-store demonstrations)?	
Advertisements: Does the salesperson have any advertisements for the similar product? Ask for a copy.	
Promotional events: Ask the salesperson if there have been any special promotions. Do they know of any conferences, trade shows, or other promotional events for the product?	

RESEARCHING THE FOUNDATION

INTRODUCTION

This step helps you discover information that will save you time and effort. Researching the foundation means investigating historical data that can help you grow your business. It is as simple as taking a local field trip.

Someone has probably written about a product similar to yours, telling who its customers are, where it is sold, and how much it costs. This information will help you develop your press, manufacturing, and distribution lists, expand your client list, and provide you with valuable marketing ideas. Spending one or two days now will save you weeks of researching, correcting mistakes, and developing marketing materials from scratch later.

You can complete this step with a trip to the library. By using the technology available there, you will find a great deal of information quickly. Don't be afraid to use new research methods (e.g., a computer, the Internet, or electronic databases). Experts are available to assist you.

The more you research, the more solid your idea will become. The more solid your idea, the more time you will save in producing and marketing your product. Time spent now will save you from running around in circles or adjusting your product later. For example, you may discover ideas on how to correctly price your product, find experienced manufacturers, or even unearth an article about what features consumers expect from a product similar to yours. You can use this information to change your product now, rather than after your product fails to sell.

THUMBS UP

Do this research now. You will build a foundation for your business that will save you time, money, and frustration in the future.

1. **Label a page in your Product Notebook "Researching the Foundation" and re-create the charts on pages 53 to 63 on it and the pages that follow.**
Photocopy the charts or download them at www.tenspeed.com/kick-start and paste them in your Product Notebook. Keeping the charts in your Product Notebook makes it easy for you to locate them when you need them.

2. **Visit your local public or college library and ask for help finding the information you need to fill in your charts.**
Use reference materials, the Internet, a news clipping service, or other sources to research articles that have been written about the products you found in Step 5, Real-life Investigation. A librarian's job (and, likely, passion) is to help people discover unique information. Ask the librarian for help if you need it.
Resources you can use in your investigation include:
   - **Reference materials.** Ask the librarian to point you to books (or use the library's card file system) that provide information on your product area or industry. Find titles that relate to your product, skim through the books, and write down any information you discover in your Product Notebook charts. Industry-specific reference books such as Dun & Bradstreet reports (which you can use to research your competition) and the yellow pages (which can direct you to manufacturers, legal help, and other professional firms) are helpful. Two great resource books are *The Small Business Sourcebook: The Entrepreneur's Resource,* which lists over 25,000 sources of information from statistical resources to trade shows, and *The Encyclopedia of Associations* which lists organizations you can contact to obtain industry information.
   - **Newsclipping service.** The library has an electronic search engine that finds articles written in almost every magazine and newspaper in print. You type in key words that relate to your product, and the computer will list articles containing those key words on your screen. Read the articles and record any pertinent information in your charts. For example, you can start your press list by writing down the name and contact information of the

N O T E

There is help available, so use it. Small Business Development Centers (SBDC) 800-689-1912, can help you achieve business success by providing free or inexpensive access to one-on-one counseling, training, and loan information.

reporter who wrote the article. You may also obtain valuable pricing information and distribution contacts in various articles. If you ever need more information (e.g., contact information or phone numbers), try calling or e-mailing the reporter who wrote the article in question and ask for them.

- **The Internet.** Many libraries now have connections to the Internet. Ask for help in searching the Internet for great business information and ideas. Using different search engines will lead you to more articles, industry information, and information on similar products. Search engines on the Internet help you research the information available on the Internet. You can think of them as electronic filing systems. They search their large database of files and return any items that match the words you type in. When searching the Internet, use multiple phrases and search engines to find available sites. Each search engine investigates the Internet differently. They also present the information back to you in different formats. Think of the Internet as a huge library. Each person conducts research at the library a little differently. And when they present their information, their presentations vary depending on what they feel are the most important factors. Search engines are the same way.

- **CD-ROMs.** You can use special category CD-ROMs (electronic storage devices), to expand your search. The library should have CD-ROMs that cover specific subjects such as census data (used to investigate your target market) and information from specific industry groups.

3. **Contact or visit any other organizations or agencies you discovered and conduct further research.**
You will surely discover some associations or other groups that will have further information to help you complete the charts in your Product Notebook. Visit or contact these organizations to garner specific information about your competition and your customers, increasing your chance for success. For instance, the Bureau of Census is a wonderful place to find out more about your customers. Call the Bureau at 301-457-1305 or find more information on their Internet site at www.census.gov.

GOAL

To conduct historical research and gain detailed sales, manufacturing, and press information.

OUTCOME

A chart showing production and press contact names, marketing ideas, and trends.

✳ STYLISH INFORMATION

A designer was making a little money selling her jewelry to friends, family, and by word-of-mouth. When she spoke with me, she really wanted help. She no longer wanted to "just scratch by"; she wanted a large account to buy her jewelry so she could also make a living from her passion.

She had been trying to sell her jewelry to stores and catalogs for over two years. She would walk the streets in different neighborhoods or in cities she was visiting and invite stores to distribute her wares. She even sent out sample items to large chain stores and catalogs hoping to pique their interest.

After hearing her story, I recommended that she to go to the library. Bewildered, she looked at me and asked, "Do they buy jewelry?" I smiled and told her that while they didn't buy jewelry, they could help her locate people that do. After all, making a sale is all about locating people who are willing to pay for your product.

She reluctantly went to the library to complete this step. In less than four hours, using the library's electronic search engines and the Internet, she discovered pricing information, new sources for gems, press leads, and possible investors.

Her research also suggested a new sales outlet. She read in one article that Barney's of New York was changing its merchandising strategy. The store wanted to create a new line of merchandise geared toward young women. Her jewelry served the same audience.

Using the person's name she found in the article, she contacted Barney's and told them about her research and how her product would complement their strategy. Barney's asked for a product sample and two months later placed a large order.

Researching the Foundation

SIMILAR PRODUCTS

Product Areas	
Inventors: What information did you find on product inventors? List their names, addresses, phone numbers, and e-mail addresses.	
Price: How much does the product cost?	
Description: What words are used to describe the product? Writing specific words down helps you become familiar with the language used in the industry to describe specific products. (For example, you may use the word "curvy" and the article may say "aerodynamic.")	
Benefits: How does the product benefit customers? What problem does it solve?	

Features: What outstanding features do people mention?	
Technology: What technology is involved with the product or its packaging?	
Product information: What other product information is mentioned, such as units sold or production costs? This information will help you determine the demand for your product.	
Season: Is there any reference to the selling season for the product? This can include spin-offs of other products.	
Logo and slogan: How are the logo and any slogans displayed? Write down any slogans mentioned in the article.	
Other products: What other products are mentioned?	

CUSTOMERS

Customer Areas	
Target: Is there any mention of customers who buy the product or the audience to whom the product is targeted? List them.	
Size: What is the size of the target market, how many units have been sold, and how many are projected to be sold?	
Not a target: Are any customers mentioned to be inappropriate (e.g., minors)? List them.	
Organizations: Are any corporations, nonprofits, or organizations buying, sponsoring, or somehow affiliated with the product? List them.	
Promotional events: Are there any special promotional events?	
Other information: Are there any other intriguing comments? List them.	

RETAILERS

Retailer Areas

Locations: Are any locations mentioned?
List store names, buyers' names,
phone and fax numbers, and addresses.

Nontraditional locations: Is the product
sold in any nontraditional places
(e.g., candles in a health food store)?

Unique locations: What Internet sites,
catalogs, or television shows are
mentioned?

DISTRIBUTION

Distribution Areas	
Distributors: Are any distributors mentioned? List them. Include any mention of costs associated with distribution (e.g., distributor's pay or storage costs).	
Representatives: Are any representatives mentioned? List them. Include any mention of associated commissions (e.g., percentage of wholesale price).	
Self-distribution: Is there any information on self-distribution? Include any contact names that are mentioned for manufacturing, selling, or storing the product.	
Geography: Are any geographic areas mentioned? Include regional and international markets.	

SPONSORSHIP

Sponsorship Areas	
Organizations: Are any specific organizations or corporations sponsoring or endorsing the product? Include any organizations for or against the product. Controversy is not always bad; it can help generate publicity for your idea.	
Charities: Are any specific charities mentioned as possible partners?	

MANUFACTURERS

Manufacturer Areas	
Contact information: Are any manufacturers mentioned? Include names and any contact information.	

OUTSIDE FIRMS

Outside firms that you will hire to perform specific tasks.

Outside Firm Areas	
Experts: Are any specialty firms mentioned that helped produce the product (e.g., legal, graphics, or public relations)? These names and contact information will start your list of subject matter experts.	

MARKETING IDEAS

Here's your opportunity to come up with ideas for promotional events that will get your customers to recognize and buy your product.

Marketing Areas

Articles: What are the names of the magazine or newspaper, the article, and the reporter. Also list the reporter's contact information, if provided. This information will help develop your press list (a list of names and contact numbers that you will contact to help market your product).

Inventor contacts: What inventors' contact information did you find?

Quotes: What quotes are there from the inventor, customers, or reporter? These quotes will help you develop your press packs and future advertising.

Media section: What section of the newspaper, magazine, or other media is the article in (e.g., the arts section, the new product section, or the front page)? This will provide you with an idea of where a story on your product might be placed.

Unique strategies: What unique press events or strategies are mentioned?

Personal direct contact: What ideas do the articles have for making personal direct contact with customers (e.g., workshops or newsletters)?

Advertisements: Did you find any ads for the product? Describe the ad and list where it was found, including its location on the page (e.g., top right).

Promotional events: What conferences, trade shows, or other promotional events are mentioned?

TRENDS

A trend is defined as "a general movement" and "a current style or preference." Trends provide information that may help you sell your product. (For example, "More people are moving out West," "More couples are having babies.") However, trend reporting can be biased, so be sure the source you use is a recognized one. Don't rely solely on the opinions of others, though; always use your own knowledge and experience to determine what is going on in your market.

Trend Areas	
Target: What growth is expected in your target market (e.g., the number of teenagers is expected to grow by 10 percent next year)?	
Economic trends: Economic trends create a sense of security for your investors. What trends did you discover for your project? Include dollars spent on your type of product and the increase or decrease in disposable income (the extra dollars people spend on recreation).	
Technological trends: What trends in technology did you find (e.g., a forecast that in two years people will be able to watch movies over the Internet)?	

Social trends: What social trends might support your product (e.g., a renewed interest in spirituality, a return to nostalgia, an increase in working families, heightened environmental concerns, or a fitness craze)?

Political trends: What political trends may affect your product (e.g., senators placing a ban on importing plastic toys from China or an increase in minimum wages)?

International trends: What international trends may affect your ability to sell your product overseas (e.g., Europe considering banning the importation of clothes made in the United States)?

CONDUCTING A SURVEY

INTRODUCTION

A survey is an efficient and effective way to find out what people are thinking, to fill in any holes you may have in your research, and to determine whether there is strong interest in your product. It enables you to test your ideas before actually implementing them. Since surveys provide you with real information on what may work, they save you a lot of time and money in rework.

To conduct a successful survey, you should keep it simple, issue it to people who are likely to purchase your product, and never ignore the results. The simpler your survey, the more likely people will be to complete it and the easier it will be for you to analyze the results.

One way to ensure your survey population includes prospective customers is to go to the actual location where you will be establishing your business or selling your product. When I was working with a client who wanted to start a coffee shop, he issued the survey outside the empty storefront where he wanted to start his business. After all, the people walking by were his potential customers.

Do not ignore your survey results. They will help confirm, change, and develop your idea. Listen carefully to the people who respond to your survey. They are there to help you avoid making mistakes that could cost you a lot of time and money. The information you gather will help you define your business and avoid mistakes that you may not have foreseen. Use the results to improve your business.

THUMBS UP

Don't be discouraged by the results of a survey. Review the results and determine how the information can help you evolve your business.

TO DO

1. **Define the purpose of your survey.**

Determine the purpose of your survey by looking over your research. What do you hope to accomplish with your survey? Are there any areas that you do not have information for? Or areas you would like to explore further? If so, make those areas part of your research goals.

You can also try to obtain answers to specific questions. For example: Will people want to buy your idea? Where will they buy it? How much are they willing to pay for it?

If you already have enough information about a specific area, such as pricing (you have similar product prices, you have spoken to store owners and learned what price your product would sell at), skip that area. Keep the survey simple. You only need to survey people about the areas where you need more information.

2. **Define questions that will help you answer your research goals.**

Try to develop questions that will help you fill in missing information. Keep your questions short and simple. Never have a question that can be answered with just a "yes" or "no." Hints on creating survey questions:

- Always keep your questions to the point (your goal).
- Limit your survey to under five minutes or about ten to fifteen questions.
- Try not to use open-ended questions (questions that do not have specific answers to them). These questions can be hard to quantify because everyone may provide a different answer. Do not, for example, ask what they think the world needs. Ask instead, "Of the following new products, which do you think would be most beneficial to you?" List a number of products, including your own, and gauge the response.
- Group your questions (keeping similar questions together). For example, keep all packaging questions together and all pricing questions together.

GOAL

To augment your research with specific, real information and ideas.

OUTCOME

Action items based on customer reactions to your idea.

NOTE

Survey people who are your potential customers. It is the best way to ensure your product meets their needs.

NOTE

Be flexible and tailor your survey to a person's needs. If a person prefers to write down their answers rather than speak to you directly, let them.

3. **Develop a list of people to survey (e.g., store owners, neighbors, classmates, or professionals).**

Your list of people should include anyone who might buy or recommend your product. For instance, if you are selling a new kitchen utensil you should not only interview moms who cook and kitchen store owners, but also chefs, husbands, and cafeteria workers.

4. **Decide on your survey approach.**

Surveys can be conducted by phone, the Internet, mail, fax, or in person. In-person surveys are the best because they allow you to gauge people's physical reactions as well as their verbal ones. Sometimes body language communicates more than words do. Most of my clients conduct in-person surveys at locations where they know potential customers will be. That way, they are hitting the right target market.

5. **Issue your survey and obtain responses.**

Try to interview at least a hundred people to obtain a good sense of the marketplace. If you are issuing surveys in person, go to a place where you might find potential customers to survey. (For example, for a new toy, stand outside a toy store; for a new food product, survey chefs or hang out in your local grocery aisle.) Just as you did in Step 5, Real-Life Investigation, you may want to travel to a different city that has a similar product and survey actual customers. You can even ask a store owner whether he would mind if you surveyed his customers. Of course, you should include a couple of questions that would benefit the owner. (For example, Should his store carry your product? What two additional products would you like to see in his store?) Make sure you obtain the finished surveys so you can analyze the information.

6. **Read the completed surveys and analyze the data.**

Put any product and marketing suggestions you obtain in the appropriate areas of Step 6, Researching the Foundation. If your charts start to get full, use sticky notes. Attach the notes to your chart and record your additional survey answers on it. Or you can copy additional charts, and report the extra information in the appropriate space.

Look at the answers and see what came up most often. Look for any over-all trends. Do people say that your product is unique? Do people want to buy it? Do they like the name? Note any trends you spot in your Product Notebook.

❈ GROUNDS FOR SUCCESS

A client went through all the steps that we have discussed so far. In the profile step, he defined his idea as a coffee shop that served and sold exotic-flavored coffee. He thought people were bored with regular coffee and would flock to his store. He even thought of a name, Not Just Coffee.

Next he defined his intent. His internal intent was to own a business that allowed him to interact with customers. His external intent was to provide a fun place where people could enjoy distinctive drinks. He completed his market brainstorming, visited other coffee shops during his real-life investigation, and found some great pricing, marketing, and statistical information at the library. He was ready to go . . . or so he thought!

Using the exercises in this step, he developed his survey and issued it outside the location where he wanted to establish his shop. The results devastated him. People loved the idea of a fun place to have exotic drinks but felt that there were already too many coffee shops in the neighborhood.

Did he give up? No! Did he go ahead with his plans anyway? No! He went back and looked at his intent. To his surprise, the survey results supported his intent—people wanted a fun place to go for exotic drinks; however, they felt that the coffee market was saturated.

Coincidentally, a friend of his had just returned from a trip to the opposite coast and told him about a place he had visited called The Fruit Shake. The Fruit Shake was a fun place that served drinks made from tasty combinations of fruit juices.

Armed with this new information, he reissued his survey and discovered that passersby loved the juice joint idea. He continued down the path of developing his idea (based on his intent) and opened a wonderful juice shop that serves distinctive, healthy drinks.

INSPIRATION

Have fun issuing your survey, and people will want to help you. You might offer people instant gratification if they fill out a survey (e.g., a huge red lollipop, a smiley face sticker, a free dessert from a local restaurant, or a discount coupon for your product).

7. **Look at people's comments about your competition.**

Try and determine what features you can develop that will distinguish your product and what features you should avoid. You have not started to build your product yet, so you can always make changes that meet your customers' needs.

8. **Develop conclusions based on the information gathered, and determine an appropriate course of action (e.g., changing the name or adding a requested feature).**

Sit back and review the results of your surveys and any trends you recognized. For instance, if more than half the people surveyed would not buy your product or do not know where you would sell it, now is the time to really look at your idea and determine what changes need to be made. Listen to your potential customers.

It is a great idea to ask a friend to help you develop appropriate courses of action. Even if they only act as a sounding board. When you talk things out with another person you remain calm and focused and develop some great courses of action. Remember one course of action is to not change your idea at all. You can choose this if your survey results warrant it.

9. **If necessary, reissue the survey reflecting the new information you received from the original survey.**

The best people to tell you that you are headed down the right track are your potential customers. Generally, you will only need to issue a new survey under two circumstances. First, if you were not able to find qualified people who could answer the questions you developed. Second, if the people you interviewed suggested a new strategy (e.g., a new name or new features), and you want to determine whether other people like your new ideas or courses of action.

Giving It Life

All right! This chapter brings your idea to life. Now you will develop a real-life sample of your dream. Something you can show your friends and family. You will make your product stand out from the competition and develop a set of Rules to Live By so you can take advantage of opportunities for your product. Most importantly, you will affirm your commitment to move forward and build your idea into a thriving business.

STEP 8

INFORMATION
CENTER

INTRODUCTION

So far, you have established your intent, developed your idea through brain-storming, and obtained information about the marketplace and the competition. Now is the time to develop a reference guide so you can easily tell people about your product.

This guide is called an Information Center and holds all the information you have developed for your idea and competing products. The Information Center helps keep you organized, focused, and confidently moving forward. It is some-thing "real" that you can show to other people, enabling you to explain your idea coherently and demonstrate that your product is strong enough to succeed. It allows your idea to take on a life of its own.

TO DO

1. Copy each of the Information Center charts on the pages 75 to 86 into your Product Notebook.

These charts will help you distinguish your product from the competition. The charts will also build your confidence by providing you with specifics to describe your market in an informed manner. Don't forget you may photocopy the charts or download them from www.tenspeed.com/kick-start, print them out, and paste them in your Product Notebook.

THUMBS UP

Clearly defining the unique charac-teristics of your product will make it stand out in the market. People will use these unique characteris-tics to tell other people about your product, they'll tell others, and so on . . .

2. **Fill in the first column of each chart with the characteristics you have decided your product will incorporate.**

Look over all the ideas you generated in Step 4, Market Brainstorming; Step 5, Real-Life Investigation; Step 6, Researching the Foundation; and Step 7, Conducting a Survey. Then, using the knowledge you have gained, decide which features to incorporate into your product. Fill in the first column of each of the Information Center charts with words that describe your product and any ideas you generated.

This is an opportunity for you choose the attributes that you feel are most important to your product. Concentrate on characteristics that stand out from the competition and meet your customers' needs.

3. **Fill in the second column of charts A through F with information you discovered in your research (especially Steps 5, 6, and 7).**

This step has you put all your research information in one place. The second column of the chart gives you language to speak intelligently about your competition and what makes your product unique. Be honest and incorporate all the unique attributes of competitive products.

4. **Compare the information in column 1 and column 2 of charts A through F.**

Circle the items that make your product or the competing products unique. These circled items direct you to the differences between your product and those already in the market.

5. **In the third column of charts A through F, write down the similarities and differences between your product and the existing products.**

The information and questions associated with each topic are there to guide your thinking process. You can use the points specified in the third column to easily compare your idea to products that already exist in the market. Any unique qualities that your idea has will become your product's selling points. Now you can tell store owners and other people about your product and how it fits into the marketplace.

6. Decide whether any of the features you circled should become part of your product. If so, add them to first column in a different ink color or with a different font.

This process is about learning from others. Look over the unique features of products already on the market. The inventors that put these products out in the market have, most likely, completed a lot of customer research and know what works and what doesn't. Use their experience to improve your product. Don't just add features, be sure you have a good reason for changing your product (e.g., store owners told you it is "a must"). It is a good idea to complete this activity with a friend so you have a sounding board for your ideas.

N O T E

Some of my more technically oriented clients have created their Information Center using a database, spreadsheet, or other computer program. If you are so inclined, go for it!

✳ THE WHOLE WORLD?

A client was working with me to develop an Internet training video that explained how to use the Internet in easy-to-understand terms. Up to this step, Keith thought that everyone who owned a computer was his target market. And every time he thought about marketing to such a large group of people, he became frustrated. Very frustrated.

As he was putting all his information into his Information Center charts, I asked Keith to try to limit his target market. He didn't think it was possible until he noticed a pattern. Of all the different age groups he had researched, only older participants consistently expressed a desire for Internet training. And no one else had developed videos for the senior market.

After selecting these users as his initial target market, his frustration and fears eased considerably. He realized that if he developed a video that an elderly person with no computer experience could understand, then the product could help everyone who needed a similar tool (e.g., working mothers, children, or business people).

By focusing on a specific target market, Keith stopped being overwhelmed by the tasks ahead. Instead, he concentrated on specific outlets and began to have fun creating his business. After he implemented his idea, his target market spread the word of his services without abandon.

7. **Review the Customer chart and try to pick out three specific sets of customers you are going to target.**

By targeting a specific set of customers, you will be able to develop product features that grab their attention. And, more importantly, by defining a specific target market, you will spend time developing a great business instead of worrying about how you are going to market your idea to everyone in the world. If you develop a fantastic product for one set of customers, other customers will find out about it.

8. **Review your Information Center charts with a friend.**

Explain what makes your product unique and then L-I-S-Ten and learn from their feedback. Reviewing your Information Center charts with a friend provides you with a safe environment to talk about your product and why it will be a success. This discussion will build your confidence and give you ideas on how to make your product even better.

9. **Update your Information Center charts as you receive information or change your product.**

Your Information Center charts are something concrete you can show people. They show how your product will stand out from the competition by comparing your idea to already-existing products and highlighting your product's unique attributes. They convince people (including yourself!) that you will succeed.

This reference guide should be updated continually, so you can always speak intelligently about the market. More importantly, you will see how changes in the market affect your product or service.

10. **Congratulate yourself by doing something fun—go to a movie, have a decadent dessert.**

You have come a long way without any "physical" reward. To be successful, it is important to have fun and balance in your life. Go out and celebrate. Invite some friends along and catch up on the great things happening to everyone.

CHART A: PRODUCT

Product Areas

	Your Product	Existing Product	Comparison
Name: Is yours more fun, more descriptive?			
Price: List only the existing products' prices.			
Benefits: Does your product offer additional benefits? What differences can you promote? Does the other product offer benefits yours should?			
Features: What are each product's most appealing features?			

	Your Product	Existing Product	Comparison
Packaging: How will your product catch your customer's eye? What is the size of the competitions' packaging?			
Logo and slogan: Draw the product's logo and write down its slogan. Is yours unique?			
Warranties and return policy: Is yours similar?			
Season: Is either product seasonal?			
Spin-offs: List any spin-offs you discovered.			
Financials: How many units did the product sell?			
New entrants: List any possible new competitors.			

CHART B: CUSTOMERS

Customer Areas

	Your Product	Existing Product	Comparison
Target market: Who are the customers? What is the total possible number of customers?			
Not a target: Which customers are not a target?			
Press: List magazines, movies, TV shows, and newspapers that the products can be or were featured in.			

	Your Product	Existing Product	Comparison
Internet: Is the competition available on the Internet?			
Point-of-sale: Describe any point-of-sale displays the competition uses and any that you may use.			
Other sales: List all corporations, organizations, and nonprofits that are endorsing or may endorse either product.			

CHART C: RETAILERS

Retail Areas

	Your Product	Existing Product	Comparison
Traditional retailers: Does your list include all the places where the existing product is sold?			
Nontraditional retailers: Does your list expand upon the existing product's list?			
Specialty retailers: List all Internet sites, catalogs, and direct mail ideas you found.			
International markets: Can your product expand the existing product's geographic coverage?			

CHART D: DISTRIBUTION

Distribution Areas

	Your Product	Existing Product	Comparison
Distributors: List all distributor information, including costs. Are there methods the competition is using that you're not?			
Representatives: List the representatives you found. Does the competition have any exclusive deals that can hurt you?			
Self-distribution: Write down all self-distribution ideas you found.			

CHART E: SPONSORSHIP

Sponsorship Areas

	Your Product	Existing Product	Comparison
Public opinion: List any comments you received on your product and any comments you found on existing products.			
Organizations: List all organizations, groups, corporations, and nonprofits that sponsor existing products and could sponsor yours.			

CHART F: MARKETING IDEAS

Marketing Areas

	Your Product	Existing Product	Comparison
Articles: List the titles of any newspapers, magazines, or television shows that you believe could help promote your product.			
List and describe all the articles you found. Include the name of the newspaper or magazine, title of the article, reporter's name, telephone number of the main office, and the location of the article (e.g., the front page or the arts section).			
List any quotes from the inventors, distributors, or reporters; include quote, person's name, and their association with product.			

	Your Product	Existing Product	Comparison
Unique strategies: List any unique press events or strategies you generated or discovered.			
Marketing materials: Describe any marketing materials you found. What did they include? What ideas will you use for your product?			
Personal direct contact: List any ideas you created or found for making personal direct contact with customers.			

	Your Product	Existing Product	Comparison
Promotional events: List any conferences, trade shows, or other promotional events you found or that the articles mentioned.			
Advertisements: If you find any advertisements, describe them here and list where the advertisement was found (e.g., upper left corner, the *Chronicle*, art section).			

CHART G: OTHER CONTACT INFORMATION

Other Contact Areas

Inventors: List any inventors contact information you found.	
Manufacturers: List any manufacturing contacts you found.	
Specialty firms: List any specialty firms mentioned that could help you produce your product.	

CHART H: TRENDS

Trend Areas	
Economic trends: List any economic trends (e.g., aging population) and the source of the information.	
Target market: List any information on the expected growth in your target market.	
Technological trends: List any trends in technology that you discovered.	
Social trends: List any social trends that may affect sales or interest in your product.	
Political trends: List any political trends that may affect sales or interest in your product.	
International trends: List any international trends that may affect sales or interest in your product.	

OPPORTUNITIES AND THREATS

INTRODUCTION

In this step, you will employ your Information Center from Step 8, your gut feelings, and your friends to discover opportunities and threats that may help or limit the success of your product. An opportunity is usually an area that the competition has not discovered or marketed. A threat is not necessarily a bad thing. It is just something that you have to recognize and plan for so it won't hurt your business.

Acknowledging threats empowers you to confidently create your business, instead of constantly looking over your shoulder. It allows you to focus your energy on building your business rather than worrying about what might go wrong. In this step you will also develop strategies to counter any threats you or your friends uncover.

Opportunities are usually associated with your product's benefits, especially benefits that your competition does not offer. These benefits allow you to increase your sales, go after new customers, or fulfill an unmet need.

When creating your list of opportunities and threats, look at each situation from different angles (e.g., as a customer, as a manufacturer, as a hairdresser, or as an owner of a luxury yacht). Be honest, because if you ignore a threat now, it will haunt you in the future. If you don't recognize an opportunity, you can't take advantage of it.

THUMBS UP

Celebrate your opportunities, but do not ignore your threats. With the help of others, develop a strategy to counter every obstacle.

GOAL

To discover market opportunities and understand the impact of external threats.

OUTCOME

A plan to counter any threats and take advantage of all opportunities.

1. In your Product Notebook, make a preliminary list of opportunities and threats to your product.

You can use the Information Center charts A through F you created in Step 8 to discover possible opportunities and threats. Pay special attention to the features you circled in column 1 and column 2 of Information Center charts A through F. Your product's unique characteristics are opportunities you can use to market your product. Features that your competition has and you do not may threaten your success.

2. Expand your list by brainstorming on perceived opportunities and threats.

Be especially aware of your gut feelings; if you sense that something is an opportunity or a threat, write it down. If you have a feeling that your product has something others don't (an opportunity) or that something is missing (a threat)—list that.

You want to uncover EVERY SINGLE opportunity and threat you can. Do something silly to come up with ideas. Open your Product Notebook to its profile page (Step 1), and put it on the floor in a space free of sharp objects and sharp corners. Now stand on your head, right on top of your notebook. Can you think of any opportunities and threats? Write them down. (After returning to your feet, of course!)

3. Invite friends over to help you brainstorm on additional opportunities and threats.

We are often very hard on ourselves and may only concentrate on what could go wrong with our product. L-I-S-Ten to your friends and use common sense to add to your list of opportunities and threats (e.g., a growing number of people in your target market could be an opportunity, and unforeseen competition could be a threat). The following questions may stimulate your friends to start talking about opportunities and threats:

• **Name.** Is your name distinguishable? If so, that may be an opportunity.

• **Customer interest.** What are the characteristics of people who have expressed interest in buying your product? Going after this type of person is a great opportunity.

- **Retailers.** Have any retailers refused to carry a product similar to yours? If so, did this create an opportunity by creating controversy or is it a threat to sales? Do any retailers carry similar products? If not, this could be a threat to your distribution plans.
- **Distribution.** Through your research, have you discovered any distributors or representatives with exclusive relationships with other products? If so, this may be a threat because it limits your sales force.

✳ A DOG'S WORLD

Sarah was working on developing a coffee table book that told the history of the White House through the eyes of White House pets. She enjoyed completing the steps in this guide until she started investigating her opportunities and threats.

She had told a store owner that her book would sell because a comparable book about the Bushes' dog, Millie, had sold a large number of copies. The store owner looked at her and said, "Millie's book had Barbara Bush associated with it, and you are not Barbara Bush!"

Sarah's heart sank, and she doubted that her book would sell at all. What did she do? She wrote the threat down and then asked her friends to help her develop a strategy to counter it. And indeed they did!

They suggested that Sarah obtain historical White House stories from famous people who had worked at or visited the White House. Then she could use the White House pets to tell the stories. Instead of having the endorsement and stories of one person, Sarah is now compiling stories and interesting facts from many famous people that worked in or visited the White House.

She went back to the store owner and explained her new idea to him, the store owner became very enthusiastic. The owner was convinced that the name recognition and the following these people have will help sell many copies of her book. Sarah was in dog heaven as she continued developing her idea.

INSPIRATION

Open your mind and soul to the possibilities around you.

NOTE

Ask for help. People will be glad to help you turn your threats into opportunities.

People want to see you succeed. They are just uncertain how to help. By asking them specific questions, you open a world of possibilities.

- **Competition.** Have there been similar products in the market? Did they sell well? If you find a similar product from the past and it did not sell well, define what makes your product different enough to make people want to buy it.
- **Press.** Has the press said anything negative about a similar existing product? If so, can you turn that negative to your advantage? For example, have you improved upon a feature that people disliked?
- **Trends.** Did you discover any trends that will help or hurt the introduction and sales of your product? (For example, does your product ride on a trend like nostalgia?)

4. **Review each threat and determine its severity.**

Label each threat as:

- Avoidable: There is some way to avoid it completely. If it is avoidable, list the ways to avoid the threat.
- Not avoidable: It's there and you have to deal with it.
- Unpredictable: There's no way to know what may happen.

Now is the time to label each threat so you can decide whether it is something you can live with or whether you need to develop a strategy to counter it. Labeling each threat requires you to acknowledge its existence. It also lessens your anxiety because now you will develop strategies to counter the threats you discovered. This is another useful activity to do with friends so you have a sounding board.

5. **Brainstorm with friends and experts on how to turn your threats into opportunities.**

Everyone brings different experiences to the table. Since other people are not as emotionally involved with your idea as you are, they can be more objective about a threat and its associated risks. Ask them for possible ways to counter the threats labeled "not avoidable" or "unpredictable."

You will be surprised by the strategies they develop to help turn threats into opportunities. You never know who will come up with a great idea to avoid a potential threat. L-I-S-Ten to their ideas, write them down, and learn. Their ideas will help you create strategies that will save you a lot of heartache and rework.

6. **Mark the threats that you labeled not avoidable with a star.**

A star makes the not avoidable threats stand out. It highlights the threats that can hurt your business.

Review each unavoidable threat and ask yourself: "I see the threat ahead. Can I live with it, and will my product survive it?" If you answer yes, continue. If you answer no, you may need to change your product to avoid the threat.

A person's perception often becomes their reality. If you *think* there's no way to avoid a threat and that it will surely sink you, it very well may. To be a success you cannot be looking over your shoulder or waiting for your product to fail—you have to continue with confidence. Either dismiss the threat by saying you can live with it or develop a strategy to counter it.

7. **Take each opportunity and celebrate it! Write down ways in which you can exploit your good fortune.**

Recognize each opportunity because these are what will help your product succeed. For example, a client of mine developed a board game that a high school bought. She quickly created a High School Sales Program. She added the words "Used by High Schools to Educate Our Youth" to her sales information and received a great deal of sales and free press from expanding on this opportunity.

8. **In your Product Notebook, label the top of a page "Rules to Live By."**

Your Rules to Live By simply puts into writing the opportunities you are pursuing and the strategies you will use to counter any threats. Since this page states your unique opportunities and strategies, it acts as a reminder of what you have agreed to do. Share your Rules to Live By with others and show them how the time you spent researching paid off and why you will be successful. Your rules are a celebration of the time you took to prepare yourself for the future.

Refer to your Rules to Live By on a regular basis; they will help keep your enthusiasm alive. As new threats or opportunities appear, you can repeat the above To Dos and change your Rules to Live By as appropriate.

REALITY CHECK

INTRODUCTION

Commitment. This one word will change the way you and others view your business. Until you are committed to your project, there is always a hesitancy in your actions. However, once you are committed, your life will change. Events will occur that will help move you forward. People will come into your life with the knowledge and inspiration you need. Miracles will happen.

People are enthusiastic when they first think of an idea for their own business. Remember how happy you were when you first talked about your idea? However, after spending time developing an idea, some people begin to change their minds, to question themselves.

This is normal, human. The novelty has worn off. You are now making your dream a reality, and hard work is not always exciting. Do not confuse excitement with passion. Just because you are not giddy about your product doesn't mean that you aren't passionate—it just means that you are now grounded in a new reality. You are taking the development of your product seriously. To keep the novelty alive, remember to *Dream like a child, decide as an adult* every step of the way.

The Reality Check step affirms your commitment to implementing your idea. This step does not measure your excitement about your product, it just provides you with the opportunity to check in with your passion. To make sure that what you are working on connects your heart and your life.

Only *you* can determine whether you are passionate about your product. There are no checklists available, no one can delve into your soul and say, "Yes, you are passionate." It's up to you, so be honest with yourself. Does your idea still light a fire in your heart? If so, continue developing it because you will be successful. If it does not, revisit your intent and see how your product can fit into your passion.

THUMBS UP

Make sure you are passionate about your idea. Passion is the best foundation for success.

Don't be afraid to abandon an idea that does not fit your personal goals. Working on your idea has already changed you. So what you developed in Step 1 may no longer suit you. Focusing on your intent rather than a specific product may have altered your direction and helped you discover your true passion.

By this time, you have enlisted help from friends and family. You may feel that you owe it to all those folks to keep going. You may worry that if you stop now your friends and family will think you are lazy or a quitter. This is not true. In fact, it takes

✱ HOW DO YOU SAY THAT?

Holly approached me with an idea for a new communications model that would help companies that take phone orders, improve customer service, and close more sales. Her internal intent was to explain her communications model to people, and her external intent was to help organizations increase their telephone sales efficiency.

As she proceeded through the steps, her idea expanded and became a business that offered customer service workshops. She had three corporate clients interested in paying for her workshops.

Then came the Reality Check step. After she completed this step, Holly called me. In a sullen voice she said, "I don't want to go on with my workshops." I asked her, "Why?" and she replied, "My parents have become ill. I can no longer take the time to travel because I have to stay home and assist them."

Not missing a beat, I said, "Holly, let's look again at your intent for pursuing this idea." Without hesitation, she replied, "I still want people to learn from my model." Knowing this, I then asked her, "How can you make this happen if you can't travel and have to stay at home?" After thinking for a moment, she said, "How about developing a video or book explaining my model?"

Bingo. Holly went back to her intent, and even though her circumstances had changed, she was able to pursue her idea. Whenever you are frustrated or feel lost, take time to reflect on your intent. It will provide you with the energy, commitment, and new ideas you need to move forward.

a strong person to pursue their dreams and an even stronger person to recognize when they are going down the wrong path. If necessary, talk to others about it and start down a new path. Everything you have learned so far applies to this discussion. Contemplate your intent and implement your passion appropriately.

GOAL

To reflect upon your idea and confirm that you are following your heart.

OUTCOME

Renewed sense of commitment, direction, and energy.

❋ OWN IT ALL?

A client of mine, Jerome, had completed all the steps up till this one with great enthusiasm. He knew he loved his idea. Jerome wanted to create a business he called The Gathering. The Gathering was a place where anyone could turn his or her dream into a business.

The Gathering would have computers, a resource library, film equipment, publishing equipment, and even a stage. It would encourage and enable other people's dreams to continue. Jerome was so excited about the idea that he was ready to buy a small building he had discovered.

Jerome approached his Reality Check confidently. He looked internally and knew that he was so passionate about his idea that nothing could stop him. However, something strange happened when he shared his idea with his best friend—something that shook the very foundation of his passion.

After he enthusiastically explained his idea to his friend, he paused and L-I-S-Tened. Jerome's friend looked directly at him and asked, "I know you're passionate about this idea, but do you really want to own a building?"

Wow. Jerome had never thought of this aspect of his idea. He wanted to help others, not worry about making a mortgage payment, paying for heat, and eventually hiring employees. When would he have time to actually help others?

Jerome revisited his intent and realized that it didn't say he wanted to own a building. His intent was to help others achieve their dreams. Aha! He wanted to help others achieve their dreams!

With this realization, Jerome went on (with the help of his friend) to develop a consulting practice that did just that. Instead of owning a building, he partnered with other organizations (e.g., theaters, printing presses, and schools) that owned the resources his clients needed and was able to help many people achieve their goals.

The real challenge comes from actually implementing your idea, so be sure that you are passionate about it. That is all anyone can ask of you. As a small business owner, you will be wedded to your product. You will be constantly talking to everyone about your idea, working to interest customers, tracking shipments, and collecting money. It will be a lot of fun but a great deal of work. Make sure you are ready to move forward because the next steps in the book are a call to *action*.

TO DO

1. **Determine whether your product is a reflection of your passion.**

   Read and compare the information you developed in Step 2, Intent, to the Information Center charts you created in Step 8. Confirm that the product you are developing truly reflects your passion.

   Ask yourself: "Is the product I am developing connected to my passion? Is this idea still something I want to put my heart, soul, and mind into? Do I still believe that my idea will make a difference in the marketplace?"

   If you answer yes—great—keep going! If not, think about how you may be able to change your product so it complements your passion. Remember that you are focusing on benefits you deliver to your customers; it is OK if your product changes.

   Passion is what helps entrepreneurs succeed. It is what will keep you going when someone is late paying you, when the computers go down and a deadline is approaching, and when you are working late on a Saturday night while your friends are at a movie. Passion is what life is all about, and your business must fit with your life.

2. **Tell a friend about your idea and your passion and ask them for their thoughts about how your idea fits with your passion.**

   Ask for help. Friends are wonderful sounding boards. Share the results of the soul searching you completed in To Do number 1. L-I-S-Ten and decide what your next step will be. They will help you develop a life that incorporates your passion.

With a friend's help, verify that what you are working on truly connects to your passion. If it does, continue. If it doesn't, discuss with your friend whether or not you should continue or whether there is a way to alter your product to match your passion. If you are passionate about your product, it will be easier to succeed.

You may feel like you owe it to everyone who has helped you to continue working on your idea. Stopping work or changing the direction of your product is a very hard thing to do. That is why enlisting the help of a friend is so important right now. You need people who will support you and will help you stay on track. And guess what—if you are honest with yourself and with others, they will support your efforts.

✳ TO BE MY OWN BOSS?

A client of mine, Elizabeth, went through the steps in the book and launched her own Internet business. During the process, she kept returning to the Reality Check step to verify that she was truly passionate about her business.

Six months after launching her company, Elizabeth called me. During our conversation she spoke from her heart. She explained that while she loved the Internet and she loved her business, being an entrepreneur was not for her. She missed the teamwork and support that a larger organization provided. She wanted set hours and the opportunity to build a family. She wanted to continue to do what she was doing, but as an employee.

She asked whether or not I thought her friends and family would think she was a failure. Instead of answering her question, I simply asked her, "Would have you discovered your passion for the Internet if you hadn't started your own business?" She said, "No." I smiled.

Elizabeth called her friends and family and told them the news. She was still pursuing her passion but by different means. Guess what—one of her friends connected her with the hiring manager of an Internet company. Elizabeth's experience and passion got her the job. She loves her new life. A life based on her passion.

3. **Congratulate yourself! You have completed one of the hardest steps in this book—exploring your passion and being honest with yourself.**

This is a *huge* deal! You are now moving forward with life with a true *commitment to your passion.* Go to a rooftop or the top of a slide and shout, "I will make my dream a reality!"

Some of my clients have celebrated their reality checks by taking a loved one out to dinner, popping a couple bottles of champagne, or even taking a mini (and well-deserved) vacation. Celebrate! It is also a great idea to buy a trinket (or save the cork from the champagne bottle) that will symbolize your commitment and passion.

PRODUCT STATEMENT

INTRODUCTION

If you are reading this, then you have decided to move forward with your idea. Congratulations! You are in for the best ride of your life. Like a roller coaster, there will be ups and downs, but you will always be zooming forward.

A product statement is a written summary of your goals, your product, and your plans to market it. It concisely describes your business and explains why you will be a success. Its purpose is to help organize everything you have developed thus far so you can quickly share your idea with potential buyers, investors, reporters, and partners.

Even though you have not yet developed a real-life example of your idea, you actually have enough information to sell your product right now. You have developed a name for your idea, defined its customers, listed its benefits, compared it to the competition, discovered press leads, and even developed strategies to counter any threats that await you. You are probably more prepared than most people already in business. However, for people to really understand what your product is and the benefits it offers, you have to condense it into a concise, powerful statement.

You have approximately thirty seconds to make a lasting impression on anyone you meet. Thirty seconds, that's it. The more confident and knowledgeable you are in those first thirty seconds, the more likely people will be to listen to and believe in you.

A person also has to hear a message at least five times before they fully understand and remember it. You need to develop a simple message that you love and will make an impact on your customers.

To announce your business, you must develop a brief, powerful message that is heard over and over again. This message is what I call a "30-second commercial."

THUMBS UP

Use your 30-second commercial all the time. It is a personal, passionate way to build a solid foundation (and customers) for your business.

This commercial allows you to quickly present a clear, consistent message about your business, its customers, and its unique benefits. The commercial becomes the foundation for your marketing plan. So develop your 30-second commercial and say it to everyone you meet, because you never know who might refer you to a new store, new clients, or new investors.

A warning: You may develop such an effective 30-second commercial that people believe you are already in business. You may even ask yourself, "Why am I not selling anything yet?"

This reaction is normal. Look back at all you have accomplished so far and at all the people who have helped you accomplish it. This hard work has built a solid foundation for your business, so be sure not to jeopardize it by developing an inferior product or service because you are anxious to start. The answer to your question is simple: It's not time yet. You couldn't have come this far without building on your foundation, step by step. So enjoy the praise, keep people informed of your progress, and continue to develop a business that blows the competition away when you open your doors.

TO DO

1. **In your Product Notebook, create your own 30-second commercial.**

   A 30-second commercial is a short statement, fifty words or less, that describes your products, its benefits, and its customers. Your 30-second commercial helps you present a concise, clear message that makes a strong first impression. It helps you become known as someone who provides a specific benefit.

   You do not have to tell people everything about your business to get them to call you or purchase your product. They just need to understand the benefit your product provides. The goal of the 30-second commercial is to get people to remember your product's benefits and ask, "Where can I buy it?" or "How do you do that?" It helps you communicate your idea effectively, in terms everyone can understand, so they can easily refer even more business to you.

   Thirty seconds isn't much time, so choose your words carefully. Your 30-second commercial may evolve as you learn more about your product and people's reactions to certain words. It will soon become a habit—when people ask about your business, you will respond with your 30-second commercial.

WORKSHEET: 30-SECOND COMMERCIAL

A. Write a paragraph about your product by telling a story. The beginning of the story is about what your product does, the middle describes potential customers, and the end explains its unique benefits (the external intent you defined in Step 2, Intent). Here's an example:

> *Briia helps people start and expand their own businesses. We make dreams a reality by following a step-by-step process that takes people through the product development process. From marketing to financing, our workshops and personal coaching help turn a person's passion into a business. Every one of our clients creates an action plan that will lead to their own success.*

> *Our customers are people who have an idea for a business and want to make it a reality. These people are usually in transition, and they don't have a lot of spare time. They need a practical step-by-step process to keep them focused, organized, and moving forward. They are entrepreneurs or emerging entrepreneurs.*

> *Our unique benefit is that we use a person's passion as the foundation for their business. Our process is practical and easy to understand. We inspire people to achieve their dreams.*

B. After you are satisfied with your story, read it again. Circle any key words. Key words in the example above are: *start, expand, dreams, reality, workshops, coaching, passion, entrepreneur, business, step-by-step, moving forward, practical, action plan,* and *success.*

C. Use the circled words to develop shorter, stronger statements. Say each sentence aloud as though you were telling someone about yourself at a cocktail party. Would they understand you, your business, and its unique characteristics? If so, they're much more likely to buy your product or refer business to you.

> *Briia inspires people to start and expand their own businesses. Our workshops and personal coaching help make dreams a reality. Our work is based on a practical step-by-step process that keeps entrepreneurs moving forward as they create an action plan for business success.*

D. Rewrite the above sentences to formulate your 30-second commercial. In fifty words or less, describe your company, its customers, and the unique benefits that will distinguish your business from the competition.

> *Briia offers workshops and personal coaching that inspire and guide entrepreneurs step by step through the process of creating an action plan for success. We help people kick start and grow their dream businesses.*

E. After you develop your 30-second commercial, try putting your last sentence first. By focusing on the benefit you provide, you are able to make an instant impact with your potential new customers.

> *Briia helps people kick start their dream businesses. Step by step, our workshops and personal coaching guide entrepreneurs through the process of creating a practical action plan for success.*

INSPIRATION

Your 30-second commercial will energize your customers. A typical response to my 30-second commercial is: "How do I get started?" This makes my marketing efforts easier because my customers realize that I can help them.

2. **Define how you will achieve the goals set in your 30-second commercial.**
Take out your Product Notebook. In this To Do and the ones that follow, you will be rewriting the information you developed earlier to develop a document that tells the story of your business. You have gained greater insight into your passion, your product's attributes, and the competition. This is the time to reflect, challenge your intellect, and incorporate all you have learned.

First define how you will succeed in your business. This should be a simple statement that explains how you will achieve the business your 30-second commercial describes. For example, are you going to partner with other organizations, will you hire talented people, or will you use technology to help you achieve your goals? State how you will make your business a success.

Briia will partner with economic development organizations and corporations that serve small businesses nationwide to inform customers about how to start and expand their dream businesses. We will also offer our services on the Internet to make access to information easy.

3. **Use the information from the Trends chart in Step 8 and Opportunities and Threats in Step 9 to define your key success factors.**

   A key success factor is any single activity or advantage that must be present for your product to succeed. (For example, Is there a time frame in which the product has to come to market to succeed, such as August for the Christmas season?)

   Explain the trends affecting your market and current opportunities and how you will use them to your advantage. You can ride a trend to increase your business. For example: People are working longer hours and spending more time away from their families. They now want to start their own businesses so they can include their family in their work. This factor plus the fact that com-

❖ WHEN IS A BUSINESS A BUSINESS?

A client who started a hypnotherapy business developed such an effective 30-second commercial that she sold her service to several clients before she had her product fully developed. Kathy spoke with such clarity and confidence that people believed her service had existed for years. They were hypnotized by her energy and were ready to sign up.

What did she do? She kept potential customers apprised of the development of her company, and when she was ready, signed them up as her first clients. The fact that just talking about her business garnered interest worked miracles for her confidence and her business.

puters have made it easier to market new ideas has greatly increased the number of startup businesses in the past five years.

4. **Create your objectives.**

Objectives are specific business goals that are precise and measurable. Write down when you hope to open the doors to your business. This date gives you a goal to work toward.

Record any other objective you have discovered during your research. For instance, if your research has helped you determine how many units you hope to sell, write that down. Be realistic and always state your goals by focusing on outcome rather than on action.

> *Briia will open its doors for business in 1990. During our first year, we will see over 150 clients and conduct 50 speaking engagements.*

5. **Clearly describe your product and its environment.**

Begin by stating your product's name and its unique benefits. Use the Information Center charts you developed in Step 8 to compare your product to the competition. End this section with the top three reasons why your product will be a success. Your paragraphs should:

- Provide a brief overview of the competition, its products, and its strategies (e.g., pricing, who they are targeting, how they sell their products, their product strengths and weaknesses, any product spin-offs).
- State your product's strengths. Emphasize the differences from other products already in the market. How did analyzing the competition help you understand what customers want? What niche markets are not being served?
- Describe your current pricing by using a competitor's price since this is all the information you currently have. You will determine your real price in Chapter Eight, Setting the Price.
- Describe your product's packaging. Emphasize how it will capture the imagination of the competition's customers.
- In the last paragraph, state the top three reasons your product will be successful.

N O T E

If you do not find any similar products in the market, describe how your product is meeting an untapped customer need.

6. **Describe your customers.**

Use the information from the Customer chart in Step 8 to clearly state your target market (the customers you are seeking). Be sure to:

- Describe the people to whom you are targeting your product. Include age, income, education, occupation, and location. Report the market size. If you want to get specific, you can break your customer profile into the following areas: Who will use it? Who will make the decision to buy it? Who will actually buy it? Who will influence its purchase?

- Describe their unmet needs that your product will satisfy, making it desirable.

- Describe how your target market finds out about new products (e.g., specific newspapers, radio, or television shows).

- List any inappropriate customers, and state why you will not target your media campaign toward this market. You can describe how this group of people may actually help promote your product. (For example, If you create a controversial product and send it to an extremist group they may call for a ban of your product, which in turn can increase awareness through media coverage and word-of-mouth advertising. It may seem devious, but it can be effective.)

- List any associations, nonprofits, or charities that may benefit by using your product directly or as a premium (a gift for people who join or give support to their organization). For example, nonprofit organizations may use your product as a gift for people who donate over $50.

7. **Describe how you plan to market your product.**

Use the information from the Product Areas, Sponsorship Areas, and Marketing Areas charts in Step 8 to describe your marketing ideas. People will be interested in hearing all the ideas you have, so be sure to:

- Describe how you completed your research (e.g., using the Internet, researching press, attending trade shows, or visiting stores).

- Describe any product display ideas you have and how the display will help your product gain attention. How will it be different from what the competition is using?

- Describe or draw your logo and write down your product's slogan. The logo is a graphical representation of what your product does—make the icon memorable. It will affect how the public relates to your product.

- State how your marketing campaign will focus on the seasons if they will affect your product sales.
- List any unusual marketing events or tactics you developed.
- List your press targets and include a short explanation of why each target would be interested in your product.

8. **Mention any potential retailers that may sell your product.**
   Use the information from the Retail Areas chart in Step 8, Information Center, to describe potential retail locations. List:
   - All the traditional retailers you will approach.
   - All the nontraditional retailers you will approach.
   - All special retail outlets you will approach.

9. **Mention any distributors and reps you will approach to sell your product.**
   Use the information from the Distribution Areas chart in Step 8, Information Center, to describe potential distributors and reps you will be using. Describe:
   - The distributors with whom you hope to work. Include geographic coverage, payment percentages, and exclusivity.
   - The reps you hope to work with. Include geographic coverage, payment percentages, and exclusivity terms.
   - Any plans you have for self-distribution.

N O T E

When finalizing your logo and other marketing materials, it is a great idea to work with a design student or graphic artist.

REAL-LIFE EXAMPLE

INTRODUCTION

You have completed a written description of your product and your goals. Now it is time to develop a real-life example of your idea. Some people refer to a real-life example as a prototype or a trial version.

Your real-life example is something you can wrap your arms around. It's an actual representation of your passion. This is probably the most exciting thing you will create. Have fun!

At this point, you can still change your product at little or no cost. Your real-life example helps determine if your product will sell. You will test your idea by showing it to others, listening to their ideas, and modifying it as required.

Use your imagination to develop something that represents your product. If you are working on a new product, develop a sample version. If your idea is a service, develop a brochure that describes your services and their benefits. If you are developing a new restaurant, develop your first menu. If you are developing a Web site, sketch out what each page will look like. If you are going to open a store, draw how merchandise will be laid out on the floor.

Your real-life example is a marketing tool. You can show it to potential investors, store owners, and distributors to gauge their reactions. Listen to these professionals; they know the market and your customers.

People will always offer suggestions on how you can improve your idea. Even after your product has been in the market for years, there will be areas for improvement. (After twenty years, George Lucas changed the *Star Wars* movies and made them even more successful.)

Ask others for help to develop your real-life example. You can obtain inexpensive help from local university students, carpenters, builders, and your family.

THUMBS UP

Ask people for their input! Everyone has something unique to offer, and you never know what ideas they may generate that will improve your idea.

TO DO

1. **Draw (or have a friend draw) to the best of your ability, your product and all its components.**

You are the inventor, and no one is more qualified to represent your idea than you. So do the best you can. I promise you will be pleasantly surprised with the results. Use descriptive language and include size, color, and material information.

If you are developing a service, create a marketing piece (a draft brochure) that explains your business and the services you offer. For example, if you are starting an accounting firm, use your 30-second commercial as a foundation to develop a brochure that describes your company, the services you offer, and your fee schedule. You can include graphics or a sketch of your business sign to add visual appeal.

2. **Build a simple real-life example of your product.**

This example will solidify your idea. It will make it REAL. It will also help others understand your product and its benefits. Use as many actual materials as you can.

If you cannot build a real-life example from the materials your product will actually be made from, stop for a minute and brainstorm. Call your friends, visit a craft shop, go to a ceramics store, or visit a manufacturing facility, and ask for help. You will discover a creative solution.

Packaging is a key component in promoting your product. It is the first thing that attracts customers, and it represents you when you are not there. It must inspire people to buy it.

To make your packaging as effective as possible you should:

- Develop your packaging based on ideas you generated in earlier steps. Simplicity is sometimes the best way to go—your packaging needs to shout the benefits your product provides. If people don't know what your product does or how it benefits them, they will not buy it. Incorporate the enthusiasm and spirit of your 30-second commercial into your packaging.
- Investigate the packaging used on other products. If their ideas are not legally protected (and most packaging items are not), consider incorpo-

GOAL

To put your idea into a tangible form.

OUTCOME

A real-life example you can show potential customers, retailers, and investors.

rating the ideas you love into your own packaging. Make them your own so your product stands out in the marketplace.

• Finalize your packaging by hiring a professional graphic artist or product design student. This person can provide the finishing, winning touches.

For a service, the item that describes your business offerings (e.g., a menu, brochure, or catalog) is your most important packaging piece. Use your research and other business's marketing pieces to develop yours. Then hire a professional graphic artist to provide the finishing touches. Important information to include: the name of your business, your slogan, a brief description

INSPIRATION

Always ask people, "How can my idea be improved?" Do not ask, "Do you like it?" The first question is more open ended and also elicits more constructive responses than the second question.

✽ A FLOWER POT FOR A HAT?

A client decided to create a real-life example of a costume character he was going to develop and sell. The problem was, Chris had never sewn anything in his life and was intimidated by the idea of making a whole animal. What did he do? He went shopping.

Chris went to costume stores and asked for help but found that their sewing services were too expensive. He found a mask-making kit at a hobby store, but it wasn't exactly right. Luck struck at a craft store. He found a pattern for the body of the animal that he had envisioned. The only problem was that he had no idea how to make the animal's head.

Chris continued to pound the pavement and finally ended up at a construction store. Once there, he asked a clerk for help. The clerk shrugged his shoulders and suggested that he go to the flower department. Chris didn't think the flower department could help, but remembering that he should listen, he decided to investigate further.

At the flower shop, he asked for help again. The clerk listened to his needs, looked around her area, and suggested using a metal flower pot holder and chicken wire to form the head. Then he could sew fake fur and eyes directly onto the chicken wire. With a little patience and imaginative suggestions, Chris was able to create a real-life example of his product. Chris learned that if you need to create something and you ask for help, you will succeed.

of your company and your product based on your 30-second commercial (Step 11, Product Statement), a description of your qualifications, and testimonials from customers who love your company.

3. **Use your real-life example as a development and marketing tool.**
Test your product by showing it to friends and other people (store owners) who can help bring your idea to market. Ask for their suggestions and use any ideas that you believe will improve your product. L-I-S-Ten to people's feedback.

If someone comes up with great suggestions that will improve your product (and that you agree with), incorporate these suggestions into a new real-life example. The closer you can come to creating the "real thing," the greater your likelihood of success. Repeat this procedure as many times as you want. After all, the more you test your real-life example, the better it becomes. And right now you still have the time to alter your product before you commit a lot of money to it.

N O T E

Packaging often is more important than the actual product. Make sure your package communicates the benefits your product provides.

N O T E

Before showing your real-life example to people outside your circle of friends, it is a good idea to read Chapter 4, Protecting Your Product.

F O U R

Protecting It

Preventing something from happening is often easier than suffering unwanted consequences. An ounce of prevention is worth a pound of cure. This chapter looks at the steps you can take to protect your product. I compare this process to safely fastening a seat belt; it will reduce your stress and provide you with some insurance as you develop your product.

STEP 13

PROTECTING

YOUR IDEA

INTRODUCTION

Everyone comes up with a great idea at some time in their lives. Right now, you are that person. By working through this book, you have probably realized that starting your own business is full of surprises, discoveries, and "Ahas." It's been very unpredictable hasn't it? Wouldn't it be nice if part of the process was straightforward?

There are three specific actions you can take to protect your product, and they are very mundane—some might even say a little boring. But don't you deserve a break? Yes, you do! This chapter explains the specific steps that can protect your product.

It is very difficult to fully protect any product. The methods available will deter people from copying or stealing your product idea, but they cannot guarantee it won't happen. Even if you properly protect your product, you could still end up in court. It is best to think of these steps as an insurance policy. They will keep you ahead of the game, and you'll have the U.S. court system on your side.

Remember, insurance does not mean that something bad will happen—but it's there if you need it. In this chapter, we'll spotlight the three main methods used to protect products: Step 13a, Copyrights; Step 13b, Trademarks; and Step 13c, Patents.

The product protection process can seem very confusing. To limit your anxiety, I will start with some suggestions on how you can protect your idea right now before introducing copyrights, trademarks, and patents. The easy-to-follow question and answer format will familiarize you with the concepts before diving into the steps.

What are the best precautions I can take to prove that that my product is an original idea and that I alone own it?

- Keep your Product Notebook up to date. Make sure you keep track of any meetings you attend, including meeting dates, participants, discussion points, and decisions. Your notebook is a paper trail that can be used in court as evidence if necessary. Put your name on the cover of your Product Notebook and date each entry if you haven't already.

- Once you have developed any materials that you believe should be protected (e.g., the name of your idea or your 30-second commercial from Step 11, Product Statement), put the materials in a large envelope, sign it across the seal, and mail it to yourself. When you receive it in the mail, do

❋ WHEN IS A NAME REALLY A NAME?

Aaron appeared on the verge of a panic attack when he met me for the first time. Aaron had been in business for about three months. He'd developed brochures, business cards, signs, and other marketing collateral using a name he thought was unique. When he decided to add a web site to his marketing campaign, he received a big surprise—the name he thought was his own invention was already taken! He was at a loss as to what to do, convinced that all the money and time he had spent so far had been wasted.

Fortunately, I believe there are always alternatives. First, we checked with the U.S. Patent and Trademark Office's online search database and confirmed that the name had not yet been officially trademarked. We completed the online forms and sent in Aaron's trademark application.

Then we placed a call to the web site owner and discovered that, even though they had registered the site name, they were no longer planning on using it. Aaron was lucky. He was able to secure the web site name and use all the materials he had already developed. Just think of the time, effort, and frustration he would have saved by conducting the proper research before he spent money on developing his marketing materials.

not open it! The postmark date on the envelope acts as evidence of the date you created the materials. This will help you protect any materials you wish to copyright (Step 13a) rather than patent (Step 13c).

- I would guess that by this point you've spilled your guts to just about everyone you know. Good for you! Continue to share all the gory details with your trusted loved ones (who are required to listen to your enthusiastic ramblings over and over and over . . .). However, be careful when you start telling the details of your idea to people outside of your circle. Keep the specifics of how you will implement your idea to yourself. What should you tell people about your idea? Just the basics, such as: "What is your product, and how will it benefit my customers?" All they really need to know is in the Product Statement you developed in Step 11. At this point, they do not need to know the process you will take to develop, manufacture, and sell your product.

- When it is time to send out samples or plans, be sure to ship them via registered mail for proof that the proper party (e.g., investors, retailers, or the copyright office) receives them. This will help you track down any items you send, especially if someone says, "Oh, that? I haven't seen it. It must be lost in the mail." The registered mail receipt helps you prove that someone received the materials you sent.

- Put a Confidential stamp on everything you consider to be proprietary (things that are, as James Bond would say, "For Your Eyes Only"). This statement reminds people that the information is yours and should not be shared. The following is good example of a notice you can modify to meet your needs: "Notice: The material contained herein is confidential. It is proprietary information of [Your Company] and may not be copied or distributed without prior written approval."

- Develop a nondisclosure agreement, and have people sign it before telling them about your product. The agreement not only tells people you are serious about protecting your product but it leaves a paper trail you can use if any legal action is necessary. A sample Nondisclosure Agreement follows. Other templates are available on the Internet or in other books.

What is a copyright?

A copyright protects original works that are in a "fixed" (i.e., written, drawn, or performed) format. A copyright is usually reserved for original artistic, musical, or literary works. Ideas you have in your head are not protected, so as soon as you get an idea, write it down; now it is "fixed." Once you put your idea into a fixed form, you own it, and this protection lasts for seventy years from the date of your "departure from the earth."

Step 13a explains copyrights in further detail. Items that can be copyrighted include stories, instructions, scripts, paintings, computer programs, music, advertisements, drawings, and photographs.

What is a trademark or a service mark?

Trademarks protect items (e.g., a word, phrase, symbol, or design) that your customers believe are closely linked to your company or product, including product name, slogans, and logos. Service marks are the same as trademarks (phrases, symbols, and so on), but they protect things that represent a service rather than a product. You gain ownership of a trademark or service mark by being the first to use it on the products you sell or the services you provide. The protection for these marks is forever, as long as you continue to use them to promote your product or service and keep your registration up to date (paying a maintenance fee every ten years).

Step 13b discusses trademark issues in further detail. Items that can be trademarked include written slogans, musical slogans, logos, and product names.

What is a patent?

Patents protect inventions that create new processes, new chemical formulas, new manufacturing processes, and designs that enhance an existing process. These discoveries have to be considered "novel" (no one knowledgeable about the line of business would have thought of it). Patents do not protect an idea, suggestion, or method of doing business. Patents limit competition because they can protect your invention for up to twenty years.

Step 13c further discusses patents. Examples of patentable items are a new way to develop a microchip, a better medical device, or a new computer keyboard design.

Sample Nondisclosure Agreement

It is desirable that you obtain legal guidance from an attorney, especially for patents. You can obtain a list of recommended lawyers from your local chamber of commerce or Small Business Development Center, or from other small business owners.

NONDISCLOSURE AGREEMENT

Between [YOUR NAME] and [OTHER PERSON'S NAME]

This Agreement is entered into this [MONTH AND DAY] day of [YEAR], between [YOUR COMPANY] (herein "Disclosing Party") having an office at [ADDRESS] and [THE RECEIVING COMPANY] having an office at [ADDRESS].

The above parties contemplate discussions and analysis concerning [YOUR PRODUCT]. In order to facilitate such discussions, certain confidential and proprietary information may be disclosed.

Therefore, the parties agree to the following:

1. "Proprietary Information" is defined as information that the Disclosing Party possesses, which is not generally available to the public, and which the Disclosing Party desires to protect against unrestricted disclosure. Only that information specified by the Disclosing Party as proprietary shall be considered Proprietary Information by the parties.

2. All information that is protected as Proprietary Information of the Disclosing Party per this Agreement and which is to be disclosed to [THE OTHER COMPANY], shall be conspicuously labeled as Proprietary, Confidential, or the like in writing or other tangible form at the time of delivery.

3. The obligations imposed upon [THE RECEIVING COMPANY] per this Agreement shall not apply to Information, whether designated as Proprietary, or not that:

   a. is made public, other than through breach of this Agreement by [THE RECEIVING COMPANY];

   b. [THE RECEIVING COMPANY] already possesses and which is not subject to an existing agreement of confidence between the parties;

   c. is received from a third party, without restriction and without breach of this Agreement;

   d. [THE RECEIVING COMPANY] independently developed, as evidenced by its records;

   e. is disclosed pursuant to a valid order of a court or other governmental body or any political subdivision thereof.

4. This Agreement shall become effective on the date set forth above and shall continue until 24 (twenty-four) months thereafter or until terminated in writing by both parties, whichever comes sooner.

5. This Agreement shall be governed by the law of the state of [YOUR STATE].

[YOUR COMPANY]   [THE RECEIVING COMPANY]

Signature: _____   Signature: _____

Name: _____   Name: _____

Title: _____   Title: _____

Date: _____   Date: _____

COPYRIGHT

INTRODUCTION

A copyright is a form of protection for authors of original works of authorship, including visual arts (drawings, painting, and sculpture), audiovisual works (videos, films, and television), music, literary achievements (advertising, instructions, fiction, non-fiction, and poems), theatrical works, computer programs, choreography, and architecture. This protection is available to both published and unpublished works.

A copyright is an incident of the process of authorship. That means an artistic work immediately becomes the property of the author who created it. So whatever you write (or draw or film), belongs to you. You **do not** have to register your material with the U.S. Copyright Office to own a copyright. However, you do have to prove that it is your original idea if someone else tries to use it for commercial purposes.

A copyright eliminates the "I swear I didn't know he or she owned it; really!" plea (an "innocent infringement") in case of an infringement. It gives you, as the author, exclusive right to:

- Prepare derivative works based on your copyrighted work (e.g., a movie from a novel).
- Distribute and sell copies of your copyrighted work to the public.
- Display or perform your copyrighted work publicly.
- Sell or license these rights.
- Be identified as the owner, making it easier for people to contact you.

Registering a copyright is inexpensive and provides wonderful protection for your creative idea. The advantages of registering your copyright include:

- Establishing a public record of your copyright claim.
- Recording the registration with the U.S. Customs Service for protection against people importing copies of your work into the United States.
- Proving you are the true owner of artistic works.

THUMBS UP

Always use the proper copyright symbol on items you create. It notifies others that you are serious about protecting your work.

Length of Copyright

Works are automatically protected from the moment of creation and ordinarily endure for the author's life, plus an additional seventy years after the author's death. In the case of a joint work prepared by two or more authors, the term lasts for seventy years after the last surviving author's death.

International Copyright Protection

There is no such thing as an international copyright that will automatically protect an author's writings throughout the entire world. Even though some countries honor U.S. copyrighting, protection against unauthorized use in a particular country depends on the national laws of that country. The U.S. Copyright office has a list of countries that provide copyright protection.

TO DO

O U T C O M E

Copyright protection for your product.

1. In your Product Notebook, label a page "Copyright," and list all your copyrightable materials.

When you put an idea into a tangible form (e.g., write a story or an advertisement), it is immediately protected by copyright law, even if it has not been published. This step will provide you with peace of mind and help you determine whether there are items that you should formally copyright. Items may include your product statement or any advertisements you have developed or an instruction manual you have developed. The booklet *Copyright Basics* lists items that can be copyrighted. It is available by contacting the U.S. Copyright Office (or by going online):

> Call: 202-707-3000
> Write: Register of Copyrights
>   Library of Congress
>   Washington, DC 20559-6000
> Internet: http://lcweb.loc.gov/copyright/

2. Use the United States Post Office to protect your copyrightable works.

As discussed earlier, make a copy of your materials and put the copy in an envelope, sign across the seal, put stamps on it, and mail it to yourself. Include your product statement and any other items that may provide you with a competitive advantage. When you receive the package in the mail, do not open it!

The post office stamps a date on your envelope. This establishes a legal date for the existence of your product (reinforced by the date you recorded in your Product Notebook). If anyone copies your product, and you decide to sue them, you will take the envelope to court with you to establish the date you created your product.

3. Use the Notice of Copyright on all your copyrightable works.

Using the word "copyright" and/or the copyright symbol (©) is highly recommended because it informs the public that your work is protected by copyright, it identifies you as the copyright owner, and it shows the year of first creation. Using the copyright notice is your responsibility as the copyright owner and does not require advance permission from the Copyright Office.

- For published works, use Copyright (or the symbol ©), the current year, and your name or company name. For example: Copyright 2002 John Doe.
- For unpublished works, put the words "unpublished work" in front of the copyright symbol. For example: Unpublished work, Copyright 2002 John Doe.

4. Register the materials you feel should be officially copyrighted by following the steps detailed by the U.S. Copyright Office (e.g., forms, filing fee, and copies of your material).

You can obtain the necessary forms by contacting the Copyright Office and or by calling or visiting their web site. You mainly want to copyright materials that you or others can make money off of—materials that you will be reselling, such as film scripts, books, or computer code. Materials that you are using to sell your product or service, such as brochures or your 30-second commercial, will probably change over time and do not need to be formally registered.

NOTE

For something to "be published," copies of what you have developed have to be transferred or sold to the public. The material must exchange hands (e.g., by a sale, lease, rental, or transfer of ownership).

NOTE

As long as proper reference is used, other people can use portions of copyrighted material for criticism, comment, news reporting, education, scholarship, or research.

TRADEMARKS

INTRODUCTION

Trademarks are used to protect the items (logo, name, or slogan) that distinguish your product and will come to be associated with your company. Trademarks do not prevent others from making similar goods and selling them under a different name.

Trademarks protect consumers from confusing one brand with another. For instance, if you bought some McApple Pies, you would probably believe they were from McDonalds. So McDonalds has the right to sue anyone who uses "Mc" in their business or product name. They may not always win but due to the close association, they can sue.

Trademarks are based on the rule of "first usage." In other words, you do not need to register your trademark or service mark to establish nationwide rights to it. However, registering a trademark provides you with the legal right to sue another party if they use your trademark. And if someone else says that you infringed on his or her trademark, your registration will help you in court.

Trademarks last forever, as long as you continue to use the mark to identify your goods or services and update your registration as required. So protect your business by using the proper trademark.

TO DO

1. **In your Product Notebook, label a page "Trademarks," and write down the items that you think should be trademarked.**

   Look over the material you have created and determine which items should be trademarked. This list will also help you answer the question your mom, dad, or protective friend is bound to ask, "So . . . have you trademarked everything?" So do it now! Some items you currently have that could be trademarked are your name, slogan, and logo.

2. **Write down the various ways you will be using these distinctive items** (e.g., on letterhead, on packaging, or in television commercials).

   Writing down how you will use each item reminds you to focus on your identity—how your business will be seen in the public eye. You may decide that you really do not need a slogan or should change your logo. If you are going to use an item in many venues, the public will start recognizing it as yours and you will probably want to trademark it.

3. **Protect your "mark" during development by using the superscript TM.**

   The trademark symbol (^{TM}) shows people that you own that particular word, phrase, or logo. It acts as a warning. Remember, once you use your mark, it is yours. If you register your mark, you will place the registered symbol (®) next to your mark.

4. **Obtain the brochure called Basic Facts about Registering a Trademark and any relevant registration forms.**

   You can obtain this brochure and necessary forms by contacting the Patent and Trademark Office (or by going online):

   > Call: 703-308-5558
   > Write: U.S. Department of Commerce
   >   Patent and Trademark Office
   >   Washington, DC 20231
   > Internet: www.uspto.gov

GOAL

To gain an understanding of when and how to trademark.

OUTCOME

Trademark protection for your product slogans and icons.

NOTE

Always send all sensitive material via certified mail with a return receipt to ensure its arrival. Keep the receipt for your records.

When approving a trademark, the Patent and Trademark Office determines whether there would be likelihood of confusion by a consumer. The main factors considered are the similarity of marks and the commercial relationship between the goods and services identified by marks. This means businesses that are not competing in the same product category can both hold a trademark to the same business name. For instance, there can be a "Jammin' Java" recording studio and a "Jammin' Java" coffee shop in the same town.

5. **Conduct a trademark search online at www.uspto.gov or visit your local patent and trademark depository library; specific locations are listed at www.uspto.gov.**

Even if you are not going to register any items, conduct a search on your business name. It would be horrible if someone forced you to close your business or change your name because they already owned the trademark.

If you do not have the time to do it yourself, hire a professional trademark search firm to conduct the search for your business name. Trademark searches typically cost $150. If there are complications, the cost could go as high as $1,000.

6. **Register the items you feel you should trademark.**

Trademarking is easy, inexpensive, and invaluable, so consider doing it. You can discuss the items you are considering with a counselor at a local Small Business Development Center for a recommendation about registering them. To register your trademark, contact the Trademark Office for the appropriate paperwork, fill it out, and send it in. Don't forget to include your filing fee!

PATENTS

INTRODUCTION

Patents are like a legal contract between an inventor and the United States government. The inventor agrees to disclose his or her invention to the public so it can improve our way of life. In return, the government grants the inventor an exclusive right to sell or license the invention for a specified period of time. During this time, the inventor can charge whatever price he or she likes; it helps to recover research costs.

Patents protect a "fixed" (i.e., one that exists) discovery that changes the way people involved in a field would view their own field. It does not protect an idea, suggestion, or method of doing business.

I highly recommend using a lawyer or a patent agent to register a patent. It is a very complicated process, and the government requires specific language to issue a patent. And you might as well do it right the first time. Your patent application must include such exhaustive detail that someone reading the application could easily reproduce the procedure or invention that is being patented. Once your patent expires, others will be able to duplicate and sell your product (e.g., generic forms of drugs).

Patents protect your rights to manufacture or produce a product and your right to stop the production, use, and sale of your product. Patents are awarded in three categories: utility, design, and plant.

Utility patents are "functional" in nature and are good for twenty years from the date the patent is granted. The filing fee is approximately $300. Utility patents cover inventions that are useful and fit into at least one of the following five categories: a process, a machine, a manufacture, a composition of matter, or an improvement to an existing product, as long as the existing product falls into one of the previous categories.

THUMBS UP

If you decide to obtain a patent, do it right. Work with a registered patent agent or a lawyer to ensure that you complete the paperwork correctly.

Design patents protect "external appearances" and are good for fourteen years from the date the patent is granted. The filing fee is approximately $100. Design patents are granted for the invention of designs that are innovative or nonfunctional (not part of the mechanics of the item) but are part of a manufactured product. For example, a design for a new computer monitor that looks sleek and fits onto the corner of a desk (no change to the internal mechanics) is an external appearance aspect and can be awarded a design patent.

Plant patents protect new forms of vegetation derived from "asexual" (artificial) means. The filing fee is around $200. These patents protect such items as a pear-apple.

If you are anxious about someone stealing your invention, there are alternatives to obtaining a full patent on your product. For instance, your Product Notebook will hold up in court as a description of your product and the date you invented it.

There is also a program called the Disclosure Document Program that establishes a date of ownership for an invention. You send the Disclosure Document into the Patent and Trademark Office, and they keep it for two years. If you file for a patent during this two-year period, the document becomes part of your file. If you do not file for a patent within two years of submitting your disclosure form, your document is destroyed.

A Provisional Patent is an inexpensive way to start the patent process. A Provisional Patent establishes a patent date and allows you to say that you have a patent pending for your product. A Provisional Patent is good for only one year and can not be extended. If you do not file a regular patent within that year, you lose your patent date. This year allows you to do further research, find buyers, or secure financing for your product while being protected by a patent pending.

TO DO

1. **In your Product Notebook, label a page "Patents," and write a description of your invention and an explanation of how it works.**

   Since you will be working with a patent attorney (volunteered or paid), this precise description will save you time (and money) explaining the details of your product. Be specific and technical. For example, do not say, "It's a new medical device that helps people with asthma breath easier." Say, "This new asthma inhaler is made of clear plastic; it is 14 inches long and 2 inches wide. It has a 1-inch rubber tab at the top that is secured in place by 4-inch metal fasteners. The fasteners are made of . . ."

   Then describe exactly how it works, step by step. For example: "Step One: The device is placed plastic end down into the throat of the patient. Step Two: The rubber tab is pulled back till it locks in place . . ." Be as detailed as possible.

2. **To the best of your ability, draw the technical details of your invention.**

   Again, doing this step before you see an attorney will save you money. If you need help, hire a design student from a local college or university. They would love to draw your invention and use it in their portfolio.

3. **Obtain the booklet Basic Facts about Patents by contacting the United States Patent and Trademark Office. It is available online.**

   This booklet walks you through the patent process and explains the different types of patents. Reviewing it will help you understand the process. And understanding the process and completing as much as you can on your own will save you legal fees. The name of the booklet changes, so ask or search for the booklet that describes "general information concerning patents."

   Call: 703-308-5558
   Write: U.S. Department of Commerce
      Patent and Trademark Office
      Washington, DC 20231
   Internet: www.uspto.gov

NOTE

You can call Patent Assistance Center at 800-786-9199 for general assistance in obtaining your patent.

4. **Conduct a patent search.**

You can conduct a patent search by visiting the nearest patent and trademark depository (locations are listed online at www.uspto.gov). If you visit your local patent and trademark depository library, use the database called World Patents Index.

You can also conduct an online search at the Patent and Trademark Office home page, www.uspto.gov. This site changes frequently so look at the front page for "searchable databases," and follow the simple instructions. Be specific in your search terms. The search will show you whether a patent for a product like yours already exists.

5. **If you discover a product similar to yours has already been patented, stop and rethink your product.**

Ask yourself, "Can I change my product so it is significantly different from the patented products I found?" If not, a patent may not help you. In fact, if the patent is still valid—and you can't change your product to make it significantly different—you may be infringing on a patent if you manufacture and distribute your product. This can result in a lawsuit against you.

6. **If you want to protect your product immediately, send a Disclosure Package to the Patent and Trademark Office, or apply for a Provisional Patent.**

A Disclosure Package is another method to prove that you own your product if someone steals it. It does not affect your patent process. This package provides you with a legal source of evidence if someone copies your invention between now and the time you apply for your patent. You can find the necessary procedures at the Patent and Trademark Office home page, or call and have them sent to you.

As discussed earlier, another effective way to protect your product *and* to obtain the patent pending label is to file a Provisional Patent. Obtaining a Provisional Patent is much easier and less expensive than a regular patent. If filed properly, it establishes a legal patent date for your product. Be careful because a Provisional Patent is only good for one year and cannot be renewed.

There are many elements to filing a Provisional Patent. The most important information required is a written description and drawing of your product. This information and artwork must make it easy to understand how your product is made and how it works. You can check out the Patent and Trademark Office's web page or call them for further information and the proper filing procedures.

7. **Determine whether it is cost effective to obtain a patent.**

Obtaining a patent can cost between $2,600 and $8,000 (including lawyer and patent fees) and can be three times as much if you want a worldwide patent. If you feel that the money generated from your product sales will cover the patent costs, hire a patent attorney or a patent agent. If not, you can skip ahead to Chapter 5.

8. **Find at least three patent attorneys or agents to meet with, then choose one to work with.**

You should complete this step after completing the steps in this book and finalizing your product. You can create a list of attorneys by contacting your local Small Business Development Center or by asking other inventors. Always ask for a free initial consultation with any attorney or agent you hire. During your free consultation, present all the homework you completed (product description, product drawing, patent forms, and the results from your patent search). If you can barter for services (offer to do something for the lawyer in exchange for their help), do it!

Ask the attorney or agent whether your product is patentable, and if so, how much it will cost to obtain a patent. To find the best person to represent your product, it's a good idea to interview several lawyers and agents before making your decision. Choose someone who has a great reputation, whom you feel comfortable working with, and whose price is reasonable.

9. **Let your patent attorney or agent do their job, and assist them in any way you can.**

Your representative will conduct another patent search and prepare a patent package containing four items: a written specification (the product description and specific claims), a drawing (if applicable), a filing fee (the amount depends on the type of patent you are filing), and an oath. Your oath states

NOTE

If you apply for a Provisional Patent it is only good for twelve months. You must file for a regular patent within that year or risk losing the ownership rights to your invention.

that you are the original and first inventor of the product and must be signed in front of a notary public (check your local courthouse or the yellow pages).

10. **With the help of your representative, file your patent.**

Don't discuss your product with any corporations or manufacturers without the help of an attorney! If your product is patentable, you want to be sure you have the proper nondisclosure agreements in place.

Making It Better

This chapter encourages you to improve your idea by tapping deeper into the creative energies that are all around you. You have been asking your friends and family for help. However, this is the first time you will be formally seeking their advice to mold your product such that it engages the attention of a broader group of people.

STEP 14

FOCUS GROUP

INTRODUCTION

Now that you have a real-life example of your product, it's time to hear what people have to say about your idea. Find out by conducting an informal focus group party. Depending on your product, you may want to conduct more than one focus group.

A focus group is a group of people who examine your real-life example then offer their honest feedback. This step will provide you with fresh opinions while you can still improve on your product at a relatively low cost. So L-I-S-Ten to your focus group participants, write down their ideas, and use the ones that you think will improve your product.

Don't be shy about asking your friends and colleagues to participate in your focus group. This will be fun for them. After all, creating a new product is magical, and people love to be included in the process. Don't waste any opportunities for feedback. If anyone is shy about offering their opinion in front of a group, consider meeting with that person after the focus group session.

Treat the focus group as a business meeting. Use your 30-second commercial (Step 11, Product Statement) to tell participants about your idea, show them your real-life example, and ask them for honest feedback. Ask them to focus on attributes that can distinguish your product from the competition and on attributes you can change to make your product a best-seller.

Write down every idea they give you, even if you had already thought of it to keep the flow of ideas going. Later, you can privately analyze the ideas people suggested and decide which ones to use. Perhaps an idea you thought was silly when someone said it will now make sense.

During the focus group process, be patient and keep an open mind. It's difficult not to protest or defend your idea when people are critiquing it. However, if you

THUMBS UP

Turn your focus group into a fun, exciting event, and you will create an atmosphere conducive to generating useful feedback.

interrupt the process, you may inhibit the creativity and feedback that could help you develop a better product.

People trust what they see and experience. Those who are involved in your product development process are much more likely to help you or to invest in your product. So it might be a good idea to invite potential loan sources (your dentist or your mom and dad!) to one of your focus groups (preferably your second or third one).

GOAL

A coming-out party for your real-life example.

A focus group party provides you with the opportunity to promote your product, describe all the work you have accomplished, and share the results of any other focus group testing. Humor helps establish relationships. So why not, after getting an enthusiastic response from your mom or any other investor say, "So isn't this a better use for that money than a new car?"

TO DO

1. Plan your focus group party.

For the first focus group, you should concentrate on obtaining quick responses to your product from friends. The meeting should take no longer than an hour, so planning is extremely important. It does not matter how many friends par-

OUTCOME

Comments and ideas that will improve your product.

GAME, SET, MATCH!

After developing a new board game, a client held his first focus group with some friends. The game played well, but three hours into the game, no one had won yet. Instead of being disheartened, he asked the focus group participants for ideas to improve the speed of the game. He did not comment on any of the ideas; he just listened.

The group's suggestions led to changing a few of the game's rules and during the next focus group, a winner was declared in less than an hour. My client continued focus testing and refining the game until it consistently took about an hour to play. The game ended up being distributed internationally.

ticipate in your focus group. The idea is to obtain feedback on your product. You should:

- Find one friend who can record people's questions and reactions during the focus group. You could also use an audio- or videocassette tape to record the party. This will allow you to focus your energy on presenting your product.
- Schedule a day and time for the focus group to be held. Select a time when participants will be relaxed and unhurried. Talk to your friends to check that the day and time are convenient.
- Create invitations. Put in the date, time, and location for the activity. Make the invitation fun (e.g., call it a gathering for the birth of your brain child, and use baby shower invitations).

2. **Create a question board on a large piece of paper.**

Write down all the questions you would like your focus group to answer in large type that people can read easily. Participants will use the questions as a guide to providing you feedback. Sample questions (follow the outline of your product statement) might include:

- What do you think of the product's features? Are there any features missing that should be incorporated?
- What do you think of the name, logo, and slogan? Do you have any suggestions?
- Who do you think would buy the product?
- Where should the product be sold?
- Would you buy it? Why or why not?
- What price would you pay for it?
- What additional marketing ideas can you think of?
- If you had money to invest, would you invest in the product? Why or why not?

3. **Contact and invite your participants.**

Invite your participants and tell them that you need their help to make your product a reality. You can send out the invitations you developed in To Do number 1, meet with them in person, or invite them with a telephone call. Be energetic and acknowledge that you need their input. People love to help.

N O T E

Remember that some people may be shy about speaking in public. Don't be offended if they refuse your invitation. Consider inviting these people to come to the focus group, listen, and give you feedback later.

4. Conduct your focus group and create a professional yet fun environment. The environment sets the mood. You want people both to take the focus group seriously and to enjoy helping you develop your business. You can do this by being organized and speaking from your heart. On the day of the focus group:

- Put each participant's name on a seat and arrange the seats in a circle. This allows people to interact freely.

✸ A "LOAN"ER

As crazy as it sounds, a client of mine, Carla, invited a loan officer from a local bank to attend one of her focus groups. A loan officer?

Well, Carla didn't just invite the loan officer out of the blue, she did what I suggested earlier—she focused on benefit. She specifically focused on: "How could I make the loan officer's job easier?"

Carla knew a loan officer's job was to approve loans. She conducted some research at the local library and found an article that detailed a special loan program at a local bank. The bank had set aside a million dollars to "invest into the local small business community." The article spoke of the loan program's goals and listed the name of the person in charge.

Did Carla call him up and ask for a loan? No, she called up the loan officer and asked him for an initial meeting to understand their loan process. She told him that she wanted to make his job easier and his program successful by understanding how she could best prepare to meet his needs. She also said that once she understood the process, she would tell her other small business friends about the program.

A possible new client plus marketing help? The loan officer said he felt like he was in heaven! Most people only approached him to ask for money they needed immediately.

By asking for his input, Carla gained the loan officer's respect, confidence, and trust, which in turn inspired him to make a deal that worked for her. She invited him to her third focus group, and he has helped grow her business beyond her wildest dreams.

- Put a notepad and pen on each seat so they can take notes without interrupting the flow of conversation.
- Display your product in a fun, prominent manner.
- Have soft drinks and snacks available.
- Greet everyone who comes to the door, show them to their seats, and chat with them informally about your product.

Be friendly but remain in control. Your participants' time is valuable, make the most of the time they have given you. During the focus group:

- Start by thanking everyone for coming, and introduce your friend who will be helping you take notes and/or record the session.
- Explain that everyone is here to provide comments on your product, and they are welcome to express their ideas out loud or write them down on the notepads.
- Describe your product using the information you developed in Step 11, Product Statement, and present your real-life example.
- Answer questions the best you can. Your friend should record both the questions and the answers.
- Ask everyone to take a few minutes to write down any additional ideas they wish to suggest. Notepads can be left on the chairs.
- At the end, thank everyone and give your participants a party favor that will remind them of your product. For instance, a client of mine hand painted some T-shirts with the name of her product and handed them out at the end of her focus group party. The participants loved them, and the shirts became walking billboards for her product.

5. **After everyone leaves, look over all their suggestions.**
   Incorporate useful suggestions into your Product Statement, Step 11, in your Product Notebook. If no ideas are useful now, save them (in your 3-ring binder) for later.

6. **Conduct these focus groups as many times as you want.**
   Each focus group will give you new ideas on how to improve your product. I suggest you stop doing focus groups when there are no more suggestions for major changes. You have now developed a product that meets your focus group's needs.

INSPIRATION

Encourage the flow of ideas by recording every idea. This makes people feel valued and they are more willing to contribute. You can analyze the ideas later to determine which are feasible.

CREATOR CONTACT

INTRODUCTION

Your Product Notebook contains the names of other entrepreneurs, small business owners, and inventors (I call these wonderful people "creators") who have implemented products similar to yours. Your Information Center charts from Step 8 has provided you with a clear idea of your product, the competition, and what your "customers" think. Now it's a good idea to contact these other creators to discover how they brought their product to market.

Creators love to talk about their products. It is almost like a proud parent talking about their wonderful child. Just like your mom and dad, creators have advice and stories that can help you. Creators generally respond very positively to questions, but do not expect to learn everything you need from them. After all, there are some things you just have to learn the hard way.

L-I-S-Ten to everyone. After listening to their input, analyze it and decide whether or not to use it. Keep an open mind. You may be able to tweak an idea slightly and make your product that much better. L-I-S-Ten carefully, their ideas can save you frustration in achieving your dreams.

THUMBS UP

Use other creators' experience to your advantage by asking them for help and listening to their advice.

TO DO

1. **Call the creator (e.g., owners, founders, or inventors) contacts you have listed in your Product Statement, Step 11.**

   Just like in Step 5, Real-Life Investigation, it's a great idea to talk to creators in another town who have developed a similar business (such as the owner of a coffee shop in another city). They will not view you as the competition, but rather as another entrepreneur trying to realize the same passion. You can also talk to the creator of a similar product that does not compete for the same customers (e.g., a children's game, if yours is an adult game).

If a creator is reluctant to speak with you, do not force them. If the first creator you contact doesn't want to talk to you, try the second one on your list.

G O A L

To obtain information from someone who has already implemented a similar idea.

❊ IS THAT ANY WAY TO MAKE UP?

Stephanie was developing a new travel case for women's makeup. Her travel case made it simple for women to safely store and access the cosmetics they needed on the road. She had conducted her focus group party, and her friends loved her product.

She felt that she had done enough research, talked to enough people, and tested her product so much that it had to be a hit. When she got to this step, she felt that she really didn't need to contact any other creators. Thankfully, she did.

Stephanie contacted a creator of a makeup line for her target market, explained her product, and told the woman about all the research she had completed. The creator listened patiently. At the end of Stephanie's comments, she asked one simple question, "What materials are you using to make your cases out of?"

Stephanie told her about the plastic material she had found at a local supplier. The creator wondered whether Stephanie was aware that the plastic she had planned on using was actually very susceptible to heat. If one of her customers left the case near a heater or in a car, it could melt and be ruined.

Stephanie was shocked. She had never considered the fact that the plastic could melt. She thanked the creator and asked what material she recommended. The creator gave her the contact names of several suppliers who could help Stephanie out. Even if you test your product and people love it, those who have been through the process have valuable information they can share with you. Contact them.

O U T C O M E

A list of contacts, ideas, and risks from someone who has done it before.

Then try the third. It's better to ask for help now so you can avoid mistakes that could damage your business.

When a creator answers your call:

• Tell them you are familiar with their product and would like to talk to them to gain some insight into the marketplace. Be sure they know that you have done your homework and that you would just like to share information with them. Explain how your product is different from theirs or how it may complement theirs. This will establish your credibility, and they will more readily share their expertise with you.

• Praise their product or mention an article you read about their product. This is respectful and also establishes a common ground for your conversation.

• Always ask whether this is a good time to talk or whether you should call them back at a later time. If they ask you to call back, try to set a specific date and time.

During the call, be brief and specific. Creators have real-life information that will help your product meet the needs of your customers. The four major questions you should get answers to are:

• What are the pitfalls and unexpected problems they know about that should be avoided?

• Who are their best customers? What do their customers look for?

• What feature turned out to be an unexpected hit? Is there a feature they would add if they could create their product from scratch?

• How many items do they think you will sell and in what time frame? How many have they sold? What do they think your first couple months of sales will be?

Once you obtain answers to the four questions above, pause the conversation. Tell the creator that you know their time is valuable and you were wondering whether they would like to continue or whether it would be better for you to call them back at a later date. If the creator wants to talk more, let them. Some additional questions to ask now or later are:

• What marketing and sales strategies worked for them (e.g., direct sales or Internet)?

• How successful were they with the press? Do they have any good press leads?

- Where do they recommend you obtain current market and industry information?
- Are there any trade fairs or shows they recommend?
- What distributor contacts do they have?

2. **End the conversation by sharing any helpful information you may have that will help them expand their business.**

I'm not saying to give them information that will damage you, but there is information you can share that may assist them. This will build a foundation of sharing ideas and strategies. For instance, is there a store you found that would be interested in carrying both your products? Are there press contacts you can share with them?

3. **Contact any inventor associations or networks in your area and ask whether they have any information or programs that can help you develop your product.**

These associations and networks will put you face to face with other creators. People are more willing to discuss their experiences with you in person. And, of course, it is always fun to share your stories with other people who are working to achieve their dream business.

STOP!

WHAT IS THIS FEELING?

At this stage in developing their business, most of my clients are asking themselves—What is this feeling? Why can't anyone understand me? Have I changed? Why am I not as much fun as I used to be? Where does all the time go? Why doesn't anyone understand how important this is to me?

Take the time when you read this section to share it with a friend. You have accomplished a lot so far and are well on your way to developing your new business. In fact, it may have begun consuming your life.

You may be losing interest in things outside of your business that used to seem important. Welcome to the Entrepreneurial Zone. A place where only the few brave souls who start their own businesses dare venture, experience, and understand. A place that is full of energy, ideas, and frustration.

Fear not; your reaction is normal. That's right, normal! You have not changed physically or mentally, but the energy inside and around you has changed. You are no longer using energy; you are creating it.

You are vulnerable now because you are going after something you believe in, something that is part of your soul. You are also exhausted because creating energy is hard. It seems that every moment of your life is spent thinking about your business and what needs to be done.

You have cut the ropes that kept you where you were and created a space that is apart from your old world.

You've explored and discovered your true self, not what others perceive you to be. You've learned to listen to and believe in yourself. This is not easy. The things that used to keep your idea safely in your dreams (excuses about doing it later, feeling that no one will ever buy it, or explaining that you just don't know the next step to take) are gone; you are making your dream real and it matters very much.

You may have experienced difficulty expressing yourself as you try to align your head and your heart. You've had to learn a new vocabulary to present your dream business to other people. You might speak slower and more distinctly or search carefully to find the right words to describe something so powerful and huge!

It takes time to become comfortable and eloquent talking about something so important to you. Be patient. Soon you will speak with complete certainty and complete honesty. There is nothing more powerful!

Your energy has changed. You were searching for ways to make your dream come true and now you are finding them. And even more exciting than discovering your life goals, you are actually working to achieve them. Your steps are more confident, and people listen to you with greater interest. You have defined a purpose and are going after it.

By speaking from your heart, you will touch the hearts of other people, especially your friends. You will tickle a hidden place inside them. It is scary to talk about this place and the amount of energy stored there. Most people go through their lives looking for quick gratification (a new car, wearing the latest clothes) rather than a life reward (giving to others or improving people's lives).

You are beginning to live your life from the foundation of intent—to benefit yourself and others. Reward yourself and those who have helped you. By believing in yourself and working hard, you will create an energy that positively affects those around you; an energy from your heart.

At times, you may feel selfish. Perhaps you're not spending as much time with your family or friends as you used to. Ironically, your intention is to be less selfish, as attested to by your external intent. You will still have fun, but now your fun will be integrated into your dream. Keep speaking from your heart and as you begin to change peoples lives, you will recognize a pattern of benefit, not selfishness.

To survive in the Entrepreneurial Zone, accept where you are and know that, just like your idea, your life will continue to change. You have learned to L-I-S-Ten and take those who are important in your life along with you. You will create your own space in this new world. A space built around your goals. A space where you will freely use your heart and mind to learn and achieve.

Getting It Made

This chapter teaches you to effectively locate, communicate with, and negotiate with potential manufacturers. Tell manufacturers what you are going to create, what market you are targeting, and your targeted price range, then L-I-S-Ten to them. You will discover unique, economical ways to manufacture your product to meet the quality, price, and functionality your customers require.

STEP 16

MANUFACTURING IT

INTRODUCTION

Step 16 helps you discover companies that can make your product. These manufacturers will explain industry standards and production techniques and describe the actual material necessary to make your product real. Listen and learn from them; they have years of experience to share.

This step applies to people creating service business too. Every business needs something manufactured even if it's not a "product." A coffee shop owner can use this step to find printers to create their marketing collateral (such as brochures) or a menu. And don't forget the merchandise you may need. For example, if you open a restaurant, you have to order ovens, refrigerators, and some great tableware.

If you have positive experiences with any manufacturers, refer other clients to them. As your business grows, you will need to order additional products, and manufacturers love people who refer business to them. They may thank you by providing special discounts or by referring their customers to your business. Keep the circle of energy going, and it will come back to you. Besides, it's always fun to help other people achieve their dreams, too.

THUMBS UP

Don't reinvent the wheel. Always ask people in your industry for manufacturing leads and tips; their knowledge will save you time and money.

TO DO

1. **Review Step 8, Information Center, and list all the manufacturing contacts you found earlier.**

Your goal is to speak with as many manufacturers as you can. Each manufac-

OUTCOME

Top two manufacturers for your product and price estimates.

✳ REFLECTION IN A PLATE

Paul was opening a new restaurant and wanted everything to reflect his personality. He especially wanted whimsical plates that matched the unique presentation of his food and the atmosphere of his restaurant. He knew that the whole experience would help his restaurant stand out from the competition.

Paul searched large department stores, discount chains, and kitchen stores trying to find just the right plates. After two months, he hadn't found anything that reflected what he had imagined.

Paul was all set to buy some plates he liked (not loved) when I suggested that he develop a Request for Quotation ("RFQ"). He thought I was crazy. I explained that in an RFQ, he could specify the exact design he wanted and people would do his search for him. He agreed to give it a try. The plan was to send the RFQ to the stores and restaurant supply distributors he had discovered in his earlier research.

When developing his RFQ, Paul included his 30-second commercial, which explained his target market and his restaurant's theme. He even left a space on the form for additional ideas from the people responding to his RFQ.

One day after sending out his RFQ, Paul received a call from one of the distributors. The distributor enthusiastically explained that this was the first time anyone had asked him for a personal suggestion. He wondered whether Paul was only looking for plates or if he was interested in other ideas that would complement the theme of his restaurant. Remembering my advice, Paul said, "Of course," and listened to what the distributor had to say.

The distributor knew of a young artist (who turned out to be his son) who had just started designing complete table settings—plates, napkin holders, candleholders, and unusual salt and pepper shakers. The distributor felt that Paul's restaurant would be a perfect showcase for the artist's talents and was positive the artist would be willing to work at a discounted rate.

Paul was speechless. Personalized table settings that would help him stand out from the competition and, more importantly, create his dream?

"Yes!" was all that came out of Paul's mouth.

Paul ended up working with the artist (at a price equivalent to what he would have paid for the plates he "liked"). Even better, people loved the table settings so much that Paul sold them to his customers. This helped both Paul's and the artist's businesses.

turer has had different experiences, and if you L-I-S-Ten, you will discover hints on pricing, materials, order quantity, and manufacturing shortcuts.

Be honest with manufacturers. Tell them that you are getting prices for planning purposes and that you would like to call them with more questions as you develop your business. The manufacturers you want to work with are the ones who are willing to help you through the process.

2. **Act like you are a private investigator, and discover ways to expand your list of manufacturers. Sherlock Holmes, watch out!**

Various books list manufacturers, their reputations, and contact information. Specific resources include: Thomas Register of American Manufacturers, U.S. Industrial Directory, Moody's manuals, MacRae's Blue Books, and corporate annual reports.

Search the Internet to find companies that could help you. A great site to start with is www.yellowpages.com. The site lists all the companies that are in the yellow pages across the nation.

Associations are also a great resource. There are associations for everything under the sun. Go to the library or your local bookstore and ask for the *Encyclopedia of Associations.* Call the associations most closely linked to your product and ask for manufacturing references.

3. **Define and list all the components of your product.**

Create a table with a different row for each component. The table format makes it easy for you to track and evaluate responses.

If you have access to a computer, this is a great time to use it. You can create a table using a spreadsheet or word processing program, then add to it as you gather information.

N O T E

Most stores do not accept products without a UPC bar code, so include it as a component of your product. It is an inexpensive way to make your product appear professional. (See page 157 to learn how to obtain a UPC number.)

Packaging is the most important element of manufacturing your product; be sure to include it as a component. For example, for a board game, you would list the box top (packaging), box bottom, the box itself, the game board label, the game board, the cards, the rules, the pieces, and the dice.

4. **Determine your minimum production run and, using your list of components, develop a Request for Quote (RFQ). Pages 156 through 168 contain a sample RFQ.**

✳ GO TO THE SOURCE

Sherry was producing custom gift books commemorating weddings and other special events. Her books were like scrapbooks for special events. However, she was having trouble making a profit because the covers she was using were very expensive.

I mentioned that she could save money by sending an RFQ for the covers directly to manufacturers. She asked me where she should send the RFQ. I talked to her about finding manufacturers in the library and on the Internet, and then another idea came to me.

One block from my office was a great bookstore. I suggested she go to the bookstore, use her 30-second commercial to tell the staff about her product, and then ask for contacts for book cover manufactures. She went for it.

In less than an hour, a clerk provided her with a list of book cover manufacturers. After developing and sending out an RFQ, one of the manufacturers offered the exact covers she was using for half the price! She ended up saving over $6 per book just by asking for help.

However, Sherry did not stop there. She sent a nice thank-you flower bouquet to the bookstore clerk and mentioned that she was going to send her friends to the store. Guess what? The clerk offered to put her marketing materials in the bookstore, opening up a great marketing channel. Remember, what goes around, comes around.

You send an RFQ to manufactures to obtain production costs. Think of it as a grocery list. To make a fabulous dinner, you need certain ingredients. However, you have a limited amount of money to spend.

What do you do? You create a list of everything you need (e.g., salt, rice, beans, chicken, and tomatoes) then shop around for the best prices. To save time and money in evaluating the proposals that manufacturers send you, provide adequate space for them to respond completely to each component of your RFQ.

Use your past research and the manufacturer's experience to determine your minimum production run (the number of units you will produce). The manufacturers that you are contacting will have produced products similar to yours. Ask them what the minimum production run usually is for your type of product. Compare this recommended number to numbers you received during your research from other inventors or store owners and determine your minimum production run. Start with this minimum production run, and when you sell out, produce more.

Some helpful hints in developing your RFQ:

- Price: Specify that each component must be priced separately. This makes it easier for you to complete a detailed comparison of the different bids you receive. If a manufacturer outsources any items (has another company supply the component), have them indicate it. Firms generally charge a handling fee for items that are outsourced; you may save money by having these components made elsewhere and delivering them to the manufacturer.

- Material: Make sure you specify that materials meet necessary government requirements (e.g., nontoxic, fire resistant, or fireproof). The manufacturer should know what government requirements are necessary for your product.

- UPC number: Ask where the UPC bar code should be located and how much room it will require on your packaging.

- Guarantee: Ask the manufacturer to state their production guarantee. This is a written promise to deliver a quality product on time.

- Prototype: All companies should develop a prototype for your approval. For an actual product, it may not be your product exactly, but it will be close. Ask whether they will develop a prototype. If not, why not?

- Packaging: You will save money by sticking to standard sizes, shapes, and colors, so ask your manufacturer what the standards are and use them if you can.
- Printing costs: Ask the manufacturer whether there is a way to lower your printing costs (e.g., running two items on the same sheet of paper or changing colors).
- Film costs: In order to be printed, all artwork must be transferred to film. This is often outsourced. If it is, your manufacturer will help you save money by supplying you with transfer specifications and the necessary contacts. Just ask. Then you can shop around for the cheapest company to accomplish this.
- Inventory and shipping costs: Your manufacturer may have storage facilities and discounted prices with a shipping company. Ask the manufacturer to quote you costs for storage and shipping and/or recommend a fulfillment house (a storage and shipping facility).
- Shipping cartons: Ask how your product should be packaged for easy delivery, storage, and handling. Ask for the exact size and weight of individual and by-the-case shipping cartons. You will need this information to obtain prices from shippers like UPS. State that both should be "stock" shipping cartons (standard size boxes carried by regular carton companies).
- Payment terms: The industry standard is for the product owner to pay half of the production cost at the beginning of the production run and half upon completion. Another option is net 30; you pay 30 days after delivery. What are your manufacturer's payment terms?
- Delivery time frames: Ask the manufacturer to specify delivery time frames for the prototype and for the first run of your product. Ask how long additional orders will take to manufacture, just in case you have a hit on your hands.
- Delivery costs: What are the estimated costs for shipping your product from their factory to your storage facility?
- Insurance: What type of insurance coverage do they have for delivery and for storage of your product? Is there any additional insurance that you need to buy?
- Financial credibility: Ask for credit references from different suppliers the manufacturer uses or for an annual report. You are trying to determine

whether they pay their bills on time and whether they have a good reputation in the industry. Check the Better Business Bureau to see whether any complaints have been filed against them.

5. **Use your minimum production run number from To Do number 4 to determine how many of each component you need for your initial order.**

For your first run, use the recommended minimum production run you determined in To Do number 4. In order to compare prices at different quantities, you should request quotes for different production quantities in your RFQ. My clients usually ask for quotes for the recommended minimum production run and for half and double the recommended minimum product run. For example, if you have determined that your minimum production run should be 1,000 pieces, put 500, 1,000 and 2,000 pieces in your RFQ.

Usually the greater the quantity, the lower the per-unit manufacturing costs. The manufacturers' estimates will help you determine exactly how many units you should manufacture and what your quantity price breaks are.

Make sure you ask for the exact number of each component you require. For example, if you are producing 1,000 games and need two dice per game, you would order 1,000 box tops and 2,000 dice.

6. **After developing a draft of your RFQ, conduct a manufacturing focus group by sending out the RFQ for a trial run.**

To do a trial run, call one of the manufacturing contacts you have listed, ask to speak to a salesperson, and then pass your RFQ by them for suggestions. This allows you to test the manufacturing waters.

Manufacturers have a specific language that you need to learn. Don't be intimidated by them. Once you learn from the first manufacturer, update your RFQ so you sound knowledgeable when you contact other manufacturers. The more professional you sound to manufacturers, the more likely you will obtain great pricing.

To avoid feeling a novice in their professional relationships, most of my clients choose to conduct a trial run with a manufacturer that they are not likely to do business with (e.g., too far away or has a bad reputation). That way they can feel confident with the manufacturers they do work with.

INSPIRATION

Speak from your heart. Your passion may persuade a manufacturer to give you a great price.

On the telephone, describe your product in detail and walk through your RFQ with the salesperson. They will ask you questions and provide you with information (like "always use aqueous paper") that you may not have known to include. If the salesperson says that your product is not their specialty, ask them for a contact name—then call that person.

7. **Update your RFQ with the new information (especially the language) the manufacturer provided to you.**

You now have a good idea of all the components that are required for your product, and you speak the industry language. You are now an "insider," so use your knowledge to update your RFQ.

8. **Call the other manufacturing contacts you found, describe your product to them, and walk them through your updated RFQ.**

Speaking to manufacturers in person helps build a relationship. After your initial calls, fax your RFQ to all your contacts who are interested. Normal turnaround time for an answer to an RFQ is 48 hours. To save time in evaluating each proposal, state that responses must be in the same format as the RFQ. If you do not specify how manufacturers are supposed to respond, they may just give you a price, and you'll never know whether they can really meet all your requirements.

9. **Evaluate the proposals by first creating a list of "must haves."**

"Must haves" are things your manufacturer must do for your business to be a success. The most frequent "must haves" are:
- The price must not be above X dollars per unit.
- The manufacturer must deliver the total package to you with all the parts assembled.
- The manufacturer must deliver a prototype for your approval.
- The manufacturer must be financially sound.
- The manufacturer must have experience in manufacturing a product similar to yours. You do not want to be a guinea pig for any manufacturer; find one that has experience creating products such as yours.

10. Take each proposal and separate your responses into two piles: the manufacturers that meet your "must haves" and those that do not.

This step saves you time by focusing your attention on companies that meet your basic requirements.

11. Using the same format as your RFQ, create an evaluation chart that lists each product component and the prices you received from each manufacturer.

Only evaluate companies that meet your "must haves." Most of my clients add columns to their RFQ for each manufacturer that met their must haves. This chart makes comparisons between companies easy. Feel free to create a way that works for you.

12. Use a team to evaluate proposals.

Always have at least one person (perhaps a friend or a potential vendor) evaluate the proposals with you. This evaluation team helps keep the process nonbiased.

If a vendor you are interested in is missing a component in their proposal, call them and ask them about it. They may have missed the question, or that component may be incorporated into another part of the bid.

13. Select your top two vendors after considering their company's reputation and size (you want a company that can grow with you) and the quality and price they proposed.

Most importantly, choose a company you trust—that you know will make your product the best it can be. A small manufacturer may be a great partner. They have already been through the pains of starting a business and will see you as a peer. They may go out of their way to help you because they want to see you succeed too. Use your research and gut feelings to make a decision.

14. Obtain a Dun & Bradstreet financial report on your top two vendors to make sure they are financially sound.

This report tells the public about a corporation's ability to pay bills and whether they pay bills on time. Call Dun & Bradstreet at 800-234-3867 for the proper procedure and for payment terms for the financial search.

INSPIRATION

Keep an open mind. There is a world full of helpful hints for you to discover. Just because you have a great interaction with a salesperson or because the manufacturer is based in your hometown doesn't mean they are the best company for you. Stay unbiased, and see what develops.

15. Negotiate with your top two manufacturers. If you don't ask for a lower price or better delivery times, they will never provide it.

Specifically ask the manufacturers what you can do to lower the cost of manufacturing your product. You do not want to lower the quality of your product, just the cost.

Asking these questions is standard practice. You are just asking the manufacturer for their help. Manufacturers can recommend different materials, colors, run sizes, assembly procedures, or even outsourcing for parts of your product. Consider all the recommendations, list the impact on the price and quality of your product, and incorporate the ideas you like. If anything changes from your RFQ, always get the manufacturer to agree to the changes in writing.

This step applies to everyone. You may be shocked to find out that it only costs you $1.34 each to manufacture two thousand CDs (especially when you are used to paying the list price of $15.00 each). Just think, one phone call and you may find a way to manufacture them for $1.10 each, for a savings of $480!

✳ BILL ME

Sam came to me desperate for a solution. He had developed a calendar and had taken every precaution when he chose a print manufacturer; he had checked references, evaluated other calendars they had printed, and even visited the plant. However, he never checked the firm's financial history.

It turns out the company never paid their bills on time. And just when Sam's calendar was going to print, the manufacturer shut their doors because suppliers refused to sell them any more paper.

It was September and Sam had to deliver his product to stores before the New Year, otherwise people wouldn't buy it. Manufacturing time was critical to his success. We quickly developed an RFQ and sent it out to other printers. Unfortunately, no one had the capacity to take on Sam's project. Sam had to wait another year before manufacturing and selling his calendar.

16. **Determine your per-unit manufacturing cost.**

Your per-unit manufacturing cost is determined by dividing the higher of the two quotes by the number of units you are going to produce (for now, use the recommended minimum production run from To Do number 4).

Use the higher quote to estimate your per-unit manufacturing cost because prices are subject to change. The higher quote will ensure that you are using a reasonable number and will provide you with some leeway when setting the price of your product.

OBTAINING A UPC NUMBER AND BAR CODE FOR YOUR PRODUCT

Do not purchase your UPC code until you are certain that you are going to manufacture your product. Retailers are used to UPC bar codes being in specific locations, so follow the recommended UPC bar code placement guidelines for your product.

The Uniform Code Council, Inc. (UCC), is a not-for-profit membership organization that administers the Universal Product Code (UPC). A UPC number uniquely identifies your product, its description, and its cost. It helps retailers track their inventory and decreases the time consumers must spend at the cash register.

In order to obtain a UPC number for your product:

1. Contact the UCC to obtain your UPC number application by calling 937-435-3870, faxing 937-435-7317, or accessing their Internet site located at: www.uc-council.org.

2. Send your completed application and the appropriate filing fee to: UCC, P.O. Box 1244, Dayton, OH 45401-1244.

3. Processing time is approximately ten to fifteen business days from the date the UCC receives your completed UPC number application and the appropriate fee. They offer a "priority handling" service with a two to four business-day turnaround, but it requires an extra fee with your application.

4. After you receive your UPC number, your manufacturer can make a correct bar code and place it on your product.

NOTE

The most important part of negotiating is understanding the other party's goals. People often have a hard time communicating their goals, so L-I-S-Ten carefully, try to understand their goals, and develop a mutually agreeable solution.

Sample RFQ

BOARD GAME RFQ

This sample RFQ was developed to determine the price for different quantities of a board game. You can use this as a template for your own RFQ.

INSPIRATION

If a manufacturer says they can't make something for you, always ask for a recommendation of someone who can.

Dear Manufacturer,

As we discussed on the telephone, attached is a Request for Quote to manufacture a new board game. [Put your 30-second commercial here. For example: "This game will be used to teach children about different cultures and customs so they can develop friends from around the world."]

This is not a contract to do business. Please price each component of the game separately and respond in the same format as the RFQ. Also please note any items that will be outsourced to other vendors.

You may add any additional information in the space provided or as an appendix to your quote. If you have any questions, do not hesitate to contact us at 415-555-1234.

Sincerely,

Louis Kyer
Game Producer

GAME BOARD

Components	Price	Comments
Printing specifics: • 4-color process • Quark software ready for film		
Board Size: • 18" × 24" folded to 9" × 12" • 80-point chipboard • Backed with blue textured backer		

Game board label:
• 70# Cls Litho label
• Printed 4-color with
  aqueous coating
• Film ready for
  production		

Quantities: • 5,000 • 10,000 • 20,000		

N O T E

*Speak to manufac-
turers first. Then
incorporate their
language and ideas
into your RFQ.*

MASTER BOX

Components	Price	Comments

Size and material:
• Approx. $12\,^5/_{16}$" × $9\,^5/_{16}$" × $3\,^5/_{16}$"
  —should fit regular
  shipping cartons
• 40-point white chipboard		

Top label: • 70# Cls Litho Label • Printed 4-color process with aqueous coating • Film ready for production		
Bottom label: • 70# Cls Litho Label • Printed 1-one color (black) with aqueous coating • Film ready for production		
Quantities: • 5,000 • 10,000 • 20,000		

CARDS

Components	Price	Comments
Card Tray: • Approx. $4^1/_2" \times 3^5/_8" \times 2^1/_4"$ • No printing • No top • 32-point white lined chipboard		
Card deck: • Different printing (words) on the back of each card with 1-color icons on the front		
Cards: • Size: $2^1/_4" \times 3^1/_2"$ • 10-point Cls cover paper • Deck #1–204 cards • Side 1 (Icon Side) of Deck #1 prints pink ink only • Side 2 (Words) of all decks prints black ink only; no bleeds • Square corners: random collation • All cards inserted into card tray • Final film ready to print— press sheets are $28" \times 40"$		
Quantities: • 5,000 of each deck • 10,000 of each deck • 20,000 of each deck		

PLATFORM FOR INSIDE OF BOX

Components	Price	Comments
Size: • Approx. 12" × 9" × 2 $^1/_4$" with a 3 $^3/_4$" U-pocket • 40-point white lined chip-board • No stayed corners		
Quantities: • 5,000 • 10,000 • 20,000		

PARTS TRAY

Components	Price	Comments
Size: • 4 $^1/_2$" × 3 $^5/_8$" × 2 $^1/_4$" • 32-point white lined chipboard		
Quantities: • 5,000 • 10,000 • 20,000		

CARDBOARD MASTER SHIPPER

Components	Price	Comments
• Print name and address of company on top of box • Print item number on the side or top of the box • Two box sizes: One for 6 games and one for 12 games. Use standard box sizes.		

PIECES

Components	Price	Comments
• 8 standard pawns, each a different color • Above components to hot seal in 1 poly bag		
Quantities: • 30,000 • 80,000 • 160,000		

DICE

Components	Price	Comments
• 2 standard, square, 6-sided dice		

RULE SHEET

Components	Price	Comments
• 8 $1/2$" × 11" sheet folds to 8 $1/2$" × 5 $1/2$" • 50# white offset (1 per game) • Print black on both sides; no bleeds • Film ready to print		

PACKAGING

Components	Price	Comments
• Assemble and shrink-wrap individual games • Pack 6 units or more per case • 200# corrugated carton • Printed 1-color, 2 panels, common copy • Standard $1/2$–1" block type, 3 lines		

SHIPPING

Components	Price	Comments
If you provide fulfillment, please provide information on the following charges: • Paperwork required • Handling charges (for first case and additional cases) • Warehousing charges and requirements • Invoicing (paperwork provided or fulfillment house provides paperwork) • Packing list • Shipping labels for each carton • Bill of lading		
Please provide direct shipping information: • Shipping games from your factory to Orange County, California, USA • Recommendations for storage and fulfillment companies		
Put any additional comments or incentives here:		

SEVEN

Telling the World

The marketing events, delivery methods, and strategies you develop in this chapter will help you tell the right people about your product at the right time so they are motivated to buy it. Have fun, and don't underestimate the power of marketing and the spoken word.

TELLING THE WORLD

INTRODUCTION

Marketing. This one word frightens or inspires people. Some of my client's shudder when marketing is mentioned because their product means so much to them that they are worried someone might hate their idea or laugh at them. They're afraid they won't speak well, or will forget their 30-second commercial.

Don't be frightened. Your passion for your idea will come through loud and clear, and that is truly powerful. In fact, you have been marketing your product all along to your friends and family. Many people have already told you that you have a great idea. Some probably have already told you that they will help you market your product (or buy some after you produce it!).

When you hear the word *marketing*, replace it with *opportunity*. All you are really doing is expanding your message to a larger audience, an audience who will benefit from your idea. Start spreading the word. What fun, special opportunities are waiting for you to tap into?

Soon your marketing ideas will become so much fun that you will be anxious to implement them. "I could put hand-scribbled signs up (like "found kitten" signs) in the neighborhood to announce my product" or "A few friends and I could pass out free latté coupons for my coffee shop at the nearest bus stop." Become as inspired about your marketing efforts as you are about your product.

Hit the streets, speak from your heart, and form relationships to help you. The energy you generate by believing in yourself translates into your product and inspires others to help you.

What do others need in order to help you? They need three things to help you market your idea. First, they need to hear a concise marketing message that explains what your product does, who its customers are, and what benefit it provides

THUMBS UP

Treat your customers well. Referrals are the most powerful marketing tool a small business can develop.

(your external intent from Step 2). In essence, they need to hear the 30-second commercial you developed in Step 11, Product Statement.

Second, they need to understand your reason for undertaking this endeavor (your internal intent from Step 2) so they become inspired to deliver your message. Your intent helps personalize your business and provides people with a story they can share with others. People love to tell stories, let them tell yours.

Third, they need a reward, though not necessarily a monetary one. You can and should thank people that help you in special ways, such as taking them out to dinner, sending a thank-you card, or even quoting them in your marketing materials.

INSPIRATION

Speak from your heart, and others will help market your business for you.

AND SO ON . . .

Laverne created a seminar and book that helped people achieve their financial goals by following four easy steps. She hated the notion of marketing but loved helping people move forward with their lives.

She created a powerful 30-second commercial. So I suggested that an easy marketing step for her was to use her 30-second commercial whenever anyone asked her what she did for a living. Laverne felt comfortable with this suggestion and promised to try it at a party she was going to that night.

What happened next changed Laverne's perception of marketing. After telling one person, Sarah, her 30-second commercial, Sarah grabbed Laverne's arm and said, "I need that and so does my friend, Sam. Let's go find him."

Soon, Sam and Sarah were introducing Laverne to everyone at the party as the person who helped people achieve financial success. Laverne loved it! She realized that by speaking from her heart and providing benefit to others, people would help her business grow. She now has put her 30-second commercial at the top of her letterhead and loves to speak to everyone about her business.

STEP 17

MARKETING
STRATEGY

INTRODUCTION

Welcome to the world of marketing—a wonderful, wild world of opportunities. This step will teach you how to spend more time selling and promoting your product and less time worrying about what to do next.

You will accomplish this by developing a well-timed, effective marketing strategy. A strategy is a plan to help you achieve your goal. A marketing plan informs, educates, and entertains potential customers about your product's benefits. You create a viable strategy by testing your ideas and doing what works repeatedly and in various media.

The tool you use to create an effective marketing strategy is a simple tracking mechanism called a One-Page Marketing Strategy chart or as I call it, your One Pager. Your One Pager is a place to list your monthly marketing events, define your action steps, track associated costs, and highlight your outcomes so you can effectively evaluate your marketing activities. A marketing event is anything you do to promote your business. Some events are actual activities (speaking at a conference) and some are not (consistent use of your company's logo). Calling these opportunities "events" makes it easier for you to create steps and implement them.

Steps 19a–e, Marketing Events, your friends, and your research will help you generate lists of great marketing events to add to your One Pager. In fact, your dream junk drawer will be so full of ideas, it may not close!

Your strategy should emphasize the benefits of your product. You don't need to impress your customers with the idea that your product is from a large, established firm. In fact, it may be better to appeal to customers who have an affection for the

THUMBS UP

Plan your marketing events so you inform, educate, and entertain potential customers over and over again.

GOAL

To develop an efficient way to create, deliver, and track effective marketing events.

OUTCOME

A One Pager detailing monthly marketing events, costs, dates, and results.

✳ SPEAKING UP

Bruce, who owned a marketing consulting firm, was invited to become a member of a committee that was going to help revitalize a downtown neighborhood. Bruce joined the committee because he believed it was a great opportunity to give back to the community.

The committee developed some good ideas on how to attract small businesses and artists into the neighborhood. They felt that these enterprises would bring in new energy, money, and opportunities. However, the committee was unsure how the people in the neighborhood felt. So rather than impose their ideas, they decided to have a town meeting to discuss their suggestions.

The idea of the town meeting took off, and soon community leaders, residents, and even the mayor were all excited about the idea. To make the town meeting as effective as possible, the committee decided that they would have five small sessions where groups of people could discuss their ideas and make recommendations. Then at the end of the day, the committee chairman would announce all the recommendations. The city was buzzing about this event for weeks.

On the day of the event, the committee chairman got sick. Over 250 people (including the mayor and other officials) had assembled for the event. The committee asked if anyone would like to read the recommendations at the end of the day; Bruce volunteered.

Bruce nervously went up on stage, and as he looked out over the crowd an idea hit him. Here he was with an audience full of potential customers and the press. It was a perfect forum for him to get his marketing message to a large number of people.

After reading the recommendations, Bruce told the audience that his company could help them effectively implement the recommendations. He spoke from his heart and people listened. Neighborhood residents and city officials approached him right after his presentation, and Bruce was quoted in the local newspaper. An unplanned, simple, powerful event helped his business gain great attention.

little guy or who like to be different than everyone else. Corporations spend a lot of money trying to make their products seem homegrown; yours already is!

Creating your actual strategy is easy. First, you concentrate on developing fantastic promotional materials and events that you love doing. If you love doing something, you create an energy that attracts other people to you and your product.

Second, always make sure that everything you do focuses on your product's benefits, expands your customer base, and is memorable. Keep promoting your business and be as creative as you can—if you can get people talking about your product, you create a buzz.

Third, and most important, repeat successful marketing events that work. Don't keep reinventing the wheel. Save time and money by repeating successful activities. You have already learned from your mistakes and know what needs to be accomplished, use this to generate a great marketing strategy.

Life is full of surprises. Don't just rely on the events that you plan. Be ready to take advantage of any opportunities that present themselves without warning. You can't plan for everything.

T O D O

1. **Use your past research, your intuition, and your heart to set your product launch date.**

   Your launch date is the day you open your doors for business. When will you be ready to deliver your product? Get out a calendar (a large desktop calendar works great), choose a date, and write "Open for Business" on the date in big, fat letters.

   Setting your launch date now helps you effectively plan your marketing events. Do not worry too much about this date, but do select it carefully and thoughtfully. The coolest thing is (as I must state again) once you put something in writing—it takes on a life of its own. By writing down your launch date, you are creating a goal that you will strive to meet.

   You can always adjust your launch date as you further develop your product. If your date changes, you will not lose any of the work you have accomplished—you will simply adjust the dates of your marketing events to correspond.

N O T E

Make sure you create activities that you enjoy doing, will reach your target audience, and get the most bang for your buck (the most inexpensive and effective).

N O T E

Word-of-mouth advertising is very powerful. If one person tells their coworkers about your product, they may purchase it and tell others, and so on.

2. **Working back from the launch date, mark your calendar with any dates that will affect your marketing efforts.**

Mark any special dates by writing them in large letters. Such dates include major holidays, key buying times (e.g., back-to-school sales), and your own personal events (e.g., weddings or birthdays). Note these dates now so you don't plan a major marketing event when you or your customers will not be available.

You will be filling in actual marketing event dates on your calendar as you define your different marketing activities using Steps 19a–e, Marketing Events. Marking any special dates right now will help you solidify your marketing strategy as you develop your business.

3. **Review the sample monthly One Pager on page 178.**

Become familiar with the outline of the monthly One Pager so you can effectively track your progress as you generate marketing events in the future. Create a sample monthly One Pager as you go through the steps in Chapter 7.

4. **Put your 30-second commercial on top of your One Pager.**

Your 30-second commercial is the heart of your business and your marketing campaign. Put it at the top of your One Pager so you can always find it easily to refer to.

For instance, what do you do if someone from the press calls while you are in the middle of negotiating a new contract? Easy. Read your 30-second commercial to gain their interest, tell them you are speaking with a customer, and ask if you can call them back. They usually will give you a time to call them back.

5. **Follow Steps 19a–e, Marketing Events, and put one or more events into your first monthly One Pager.**

Read through Steps 19a–e to gain a familiarity with the different types of marketing events. Use this time to develop a draft of your first monthly One Pager. Go through the steps and add a couple of marketing events that you will complete to get your product noticed in the market.

Right now your primary marketing event is to use your 30-second commercial. Keep changing it until you get it just right, when it flows off your tongue smoothly. Depending on your stage of business, you may just list refining your 30-second commercial as your main marketing event for the first month.

The rest of your marketing strategy depends on the stage of your product development. For instance, as you get closer to your launch date, you should be planning your launch party—the event to announce your product. You will add activities to your One Pager as you gather more information, analyze your past activities, and discover new, unique marketing opportunities.

6. **Define the impact you want your marketing events to have on your business.**
At this point, many of my clients say, "How do I know what the impact will be?" That is exactly the point. You can't know exactly what the effect of certain marketing events will be—you can have a feeling or intuition for what the possible outcome will be.

If you never write down what you expect an event's impact to be and the actual results, you will never learn from your experiences. Use your intuition and your knowledge to define the expected impact of each event. As you gain experience, you will be able to more easily determine the potential outcome of different marketing events.

Determining actual results (e.g., sales by 360 units or added 24 names to my customer list) helps you define the most effective marketing events for your product.

Give it a try—use your heart and mind to define the impact you think a marketing event will have on your product. Soon you will be teaching other entrepreneurs how to define outcomes and effectively market their businesses.

7. **Define the steps, time, and costs required for implementing each event.**
Always develop a list of steps with associated time and costs for each of your planned marketing events. Breaking down each event by steps helps you flesh out the work involved. The amount of time and costs associated with each step provides you with a better idea of which activities you should implement.

Just like with the event's impact, your intuition will help you to define the steps and associated time for each marketing activity. Think about the actions you will have to undertake to make a marketing event successful. Write the steps down. You will continue to learn as you implement activities, but the steps you write down now will never help you build a solid foundation for planning marketing events.

If you are feeling anxious, just keep going. The more activities you plan and implement, the easier and more fun they become. They may lead to telephone calls from people asking when you are holding your next event.

INSPIRATION

Try it. If people could predict the future, everyone would be rich!

Tracking your costs and activities shows you where you are spending your money. Having your marketing costs in front of you saves time and aggravation when you are answering a question or preparing a report.

Try to calculate actual costs; they will help you determine the effectiveness of your marketing programs. Do a little research. Call different suppliers, ask other business owners, surf the Internet, use research books at the library, or talk to friends and family. Soon you will be able to quickly estimate your costs without spending too much time doing research.

Costing out each event also helps you decide exactly where and how to spend your money. For instance, you may want to create a brochure. After costing it out you can choose between a black-and-white brochure, a one-color brochure, or a multicolor brochure.

While you are determining which marketing events are the most effective, plan on keeping your marketing costs as low as you can. Be creative in reducing your costs. You can barter for services, hire students, or team with other small business owners to create effective, low-cost marketing events.

Try to obtain things for free. For instance, you could offer a free product to a startup graphic designer in exchange for helping you develop your product's packaging. If you are a great writer, trade services with a photographer—you can write a brochure for the photographer in exchange for some wonderful product photographs.

You do not need to develop deluxe brochures or ads; you just need to make it look like you did! And never assume that your competitors spent a lot of money on their marketing materials (unless you have firsthand information). Just because something looks expensive doesn't mean that the creator spent a lot of money on it. Throw out your temptations to splurge and assumptions and go with your heart—discover a way to develop marketing materials that stand out but do not break the bank.

8. **Review your marketing events, time frames, and costs with other business owners, a small business coach, or a counselor from your local Small Business Development Center.**

Each product has unique characteristics. After you develop your One Pager, review it with someone who has marketing experience. You want your events to reflect your product and have the customers flocking to you.

Questions to ask are: "Is there enough time to do these events well? Am I missing any important events? Am I targeting the right media sources?"

9. Develop your unique marketing strategy by reviewing your results at the end of each month.

Always track the results of each of your marketing events. Results help you analyze your past efforts, determining which events worked and which ones didn't. Your strategy is simple. Do more of the marketing events that work.

Create a successful strategy by concentrating on three high-impact marketing events you love to do (e.g., seminars, writing articles, or contacting the press). These are not necessarily the three activities you could accomplish most easily, but rather three different events (from different areas of Steps 19a–e) that will best sell your product. By doing an event over and over again, you build your confidence and save implementation time because it becomes part of your marketing routine. Find innovative ways to keep getting the word out rather than spending your entire marketing budget early on.

Create a special code to clearly mark marketing events that worked. My clients use a star or a highlighter to point out events that were fun to organize, helped increase sales, significantly expanded their customer lists, or achieved the impact they desired.

There is no set amount of time that you *should* allocate for marketing—it needs to become part of your everyday activities. Do what you have detailed on your One Pager, track your results, and repeat the activities that help your business.

Create your next monthly One Pager using the knowledge you have gained. Events that worked are events that met or exceeded the results you set. Keep those activities and add one new event a month.

You may not see the results of your marketing efforts immediately. Do not overwhelm yourself; a lot goes into running a business. It takes time for people to recognize your product, so try out your marketing events for at least four to six months. By then you should be able to obtain a true measure of your results. Don't forget that you are constantly marketing when you use your 30-second commercial.

N O T E

Since costs vary from region to region and from vendor to vendor, shop around. It may be cheaper to have your packaging printed in Kansas than in California.

MARKETING ONE PAGER

Marketing Events for [MONTH AND YEAR]

Yearly Sales Goals: _____   Monthly Sales Goals: _____

Next, add your 30-second commercial; it is the basis for your marketing program. You will use it every time you speak because it reflects your heart and announces your product's benefits.

30-Second Commercial
Briia helps people kick start their dream businesses. Step by step, our workshops and our personal coaching guide entrepreneurs through the process of creating a practical action plan for success.

List your monthly activities. Listing them will stop you from worrying about what you are going to do and lets you actually do it.

Marketing Events
In-store demonstration on March 27. (Use your 30-second commercial!)
Local press contacts by March 16, one solid story lead by April 4.

Explain how you expect your marketing events will impact your product. Determine the impact by using your intuition and the knowledge you have gained. Measure your results and choose activities that help you develop your business.

Product Impact
In-store demonstration
- Retail Contacts
- Product sales of $200

Press Story
- Increase product awareness
- Generate 44 inquiries
- Product sales of $400

INSPIRATION

Speak from your heart and energize others to help you achieve your dream.

Determine and list the steps, time, and money necessary to accomplish each event. List them so you can learn from them and not have to reinvent the wheel with each new event.

Local Press			
Success Steps	Date	Time	Cost
Internet search for local reporters	3/14	1 hour	0.00 (overhead)
Design media release	3/15	1 hour	0.00
Copy media release (15 copies)	3/15	1/2 hour	0.75
Call press contacts	3/15	1 hour	6.00
Send out media release	3/16	1/2 hour	5.40
Follow up after one week	3/20	1/2 hour	3.00
Conduct interview	4/2	1 hour	0.00
Total		5.5 hours	15.15

Always track your results to determine whether you are successfully promoting your product. Are your activities generating the impact you expected?

Monthly Results

March 16 One Press Article in Daily Reporter

Generated over 55 calls in two days

Sold 60 units on the phone and referred 4 customers to stores

STEP 18

PROMOTIONAL
TIE-INS

INTRODUCTION

THUMBS UP

Let other people market your business by teaming with organizations and businesses that already have the customers you want.

The key to promoting your business is to tell as many people as you can about your product's benefits. Concentrate on telling people who will actually benefit from purchasing your product or service. This can be your customers or someone who sells to your customers (i.e., a store owner).

This step concentrates on tying your product in with other companies, organizations, and charities. These partnerships help you access a larger audience by working through an organization that already reaches your target market. As a side benefit, your product may receive an endorsement from the organization you are helping or get some great free press.

These organizations make great partners for helping you implement many of your marketing events. They have mailing lists, locations, and newsletters you can use to get the word out about your product. As you develop your marketing events, think about ways you can incorporate other organizations into this step.

Always focus on benefit. Organizations exist to help fulfill their members' needs, and if you can help them do that, they will be happy to partner with you. Remember to dream like a child—events can be anything from donating your product to a silent auction or donating your time to organize a fundraiser.

Partnering is like dating—grab the attention of a potential partner by showing them your best stuff, establish a rapport with them, find out what they need, and then surprise them by offering them a beneficial relationship. For instance, meet with a charity and find out their goals. Then develop a fundraising event where the money raised benefits them. The charity will receive the money they need to continue their good works, and you will receive an opportunity for great publicity (and more sales!).

Promotional tie-ins also work with other noncompeting companies. Find a product that complements yours. You can help each other by referring qualified customers to each other. For instance, if you are a consultant who helps people

INSPIRATION

The worst any organization can do is say, "No!" If you never ask, you will never receive a positive response. So ask!

✳ A NEW KIND OF GAME

Tom developed a game that helped grade school students learn spelling skills in a fun, innovative manner. The game was designed to be played by the entire family so the child would feel supported by his or her parents.

Tom knew that schools would be a great marketing channel for his game, but was unsure of how to get his game into the schools. After speaking to him about promotional tie-ins, his eyes lit up. He knew exactly what to do.

Since his game helped educate students, he thought that a fundraising event for a grade school would be a great idea. He called the event a Family Game Night. The idea was to have families pay $5 per person to play his game in a school's gym. The money raised would be donated to the school's art or computer programs.

Tom approached a local grade school, and they loved the idea. The school sent out press releases about the event, sent invitations home with the students, and even arranged to have volunteers organize and implement the fundraiser. The outcome was overwhelming. The local newspapers and television stations mentioned the event, the school received thousands of dollars, and Tom received free publicity and increased sales.

Tom didn't stop there. He wrote down a step-by-step guide on how to develop Family Game Nights and sent it to other schools. They loved the idea and bought games (at a discount) to stage the events—increasing his sales and providing him with additional free press.

develop marketing strategies, perhaps you can partner with a graphic artist who creates brochures.

TO DO

GOAL

To develop marketing tie-ins or partnerships with organizations and companies.

1. **Brainstorm with friends on promotional tie-ins, and create a list in your Product Notebook.**

   Get crazy. Think of all the different partnerships you can develop to promote and sell your product. Some questions that will stimulate the creative juices are:

   • What charities or other organizations can benefit from your product? What types of promotional events can you stage with these organizations?

   • Is there another product or service that could be marketed or promoted with yours? If so, list the company's name. You can form a marketing partnership that will refer business to each other, helping both of you grow.

   • List ways you can barter (exchange your product or your time for free advertising) with event sponsors. For example, at festivals you could vol-

OUTCOME

A list of potential marketing partners.

❋ RENT-A-TOUR

Kristen worked with me to start a company that takes potential new corporate recruits on private city tours of San Francisco. Since she owned a small, two-door car, she frequently rented larger cars when she conducted her tours.

One day, while she was returning one of her rental cars, she decided to ask the owner whether he would mind putting up a flyer describing her tour. The owner said, "I'll tell you what. If you put our name and phone number on your flyer, I will put your name, phone number, and a description of your tour on the folders that hold our rental agreements." Without hesitation, Kristen shook the owners hand and said, "It's a deal!"

A simple idea turned into a marvelous partnership. Kristen and the car rental service both receive lots of referral clients who otherwise would not have heard about their businesses. This is the essence of grass roots marketing.

unteer to sell tickets or work at a food stand in exchange for a free booth or an ad in the festival program.

- Can your product be used in movies or television as a prop? If so, write to the producers about your product and explain how it can benefit their show.

2. **Take it a step further by adding special holidays and their sponsors to your list of events.**

Locate a yearly calendar and mark down all the national holidays (e.g., Halloween and Mother's Day) and local events (e.g., street festivals or major sporting events) on the appropriate dates. Then research what companies or charities (e.g., Hallmark or Budweiser) are associated with each event.

Look over the benefits that your product offers, and tie these benefits into one of the special dates on the calendar. Ask yourself, "Can the organizations or companies associated with the dates use my product to promote themselves?" The opportunities are endless. You could partner with stores to raise

❄ A LOVING MEMORY

A client of mine, Sherry, creates customized books from personal stories and photographs to help people celebrate and remember special occasions (e.g., weddings, birthdays, and anniversaries). Looking over her calendar, she wrote down Valentine's Day and Hallmark cards.

She is now developing a proposal for a contest, which she will send to Hallmark. The name of the contest is "Celebrate Your Own Love Story." During the contest, people will submit ideas for a new Valentine card based on a real-life experience. Contest winners will get some cash and a free personalized book to celebrate their love.

By participating in the contest, Hallmark will enhance its customer list and receive free publicity in newspapers, in their stores, and on the Internet. In return, Sherry will expand her business by having Hallmark advertise and sell her books in their chain of nationwide stores.

money for a local charity on a special holiday. Who knows, they may use your product as part of a holiday raffle with the proceeds going to a local charity.

3. **Present your product and proposal to the organizations and companies that can use your product as a tie-in.**

Contact potential sponsors by writing a brief proposal, sending it to them, then meeting to finalize the details. The worst they could say is, "Sorry, we are not interested." If one potential partner says no, approach the next one on your list.

Present your product to organizations before and after you launch your product. Before you launch your product, you want to meet with partners who reach a great number of your potential customers. You can show them your real-life example and see whether there are any changes they require to sponsor your product. If the organization requests changes to your product that don't cost a lot and improve your product, consider making the changes.

For instance, if you have developed a product that benefits the over-55 crowd, you may consider partnering with the American Association of Retired Persons (AARP). Arrange to meet with them, explain the benefits of your product (using your 30-second commercial), and ask them if they would be interested in working with you (e.g., selling your product directly to their members).

AARP may be interested on the condition that you make a minor change to your product, changing the handle to accommodate an elderly person's group. They know their members (and your target market) so the change probably will improve your product and your sales.

After your product is launched, you can approach other organizations to arrange special fundraising events. As long as you help the organization achieve its goals or benefit their members, they may appreciate partnering with you.

MARKETING EVENTS

INTRODUCTION

Opportunities to promote your product exist all around you: putting your 30-second commercial on your letterhead, putting your logo on your clothes or purse, or even writing the name of your business on your car. Each of these opportunities is a marketing event. Marketing events establish your identity, help you stand out from the competition, increase awareness of your product, and reach customers. Have fun creating and implementing your marketing events.

Starting and growing your business can become overwhelming, and you may feel that you don't have the time or money to market your business. You may discover that you love inventing new ideas, but absolutely hate marketing them. This is where your work in Step 2, Intent, proves its value. By focusing on your product's benefit, which comes from your heart, your marketing efforts become an expression of your passion. Use that passion to energize you and others.

Use all the ideas you and other people have already developed. In Step 4, Market Brainstorming, you and your friends developed some great marketing ideas. In Step 5, Real-Life Investigation, and Step 6, Researching the Foundation, you discovered articles and names of reporters. Now is the time to use them.

To save time, effort, and money, try to implement activities that have an "Octopus Effect"—that is, that target your efforts at people or organizations that can reach many of your customers.

Hit an octopus on top of the head and all its tentacles spread out as far as they can reach. Hit one organization with your message (and benefit), and it will be sent to all their members. The Octopus Effect may even extend so far that you receive an endorsement from an organization that people trust (e.g., AARP, Good Housekeeping).

INSPIRATION

Make your marketing events memorable, and always connect to people's emotions. People who care about your product, remember it.

Companies and other organizations (such as charities) that have already developed an extensive list of your potential customer names are great Octopus partners. For example, if you think of a contest that can bring recognition and money to a local charity, write up the idea and send it to them. If they like the idea, they may help promote your business for free by putting the name of the contest and your business in their newsletters and media releases.

Jay Conrad Levinson, author of *Guerrilla Marketing*, says, "MARKETING IS EVERYTHING you do to promote your business, from the moment you conceive of it to the point at which customers buy your product or service. . . ." I like to add a little twist and say MARKETING IS EVERYTHING you *and other people* do to get your idea noticed and sold! It's as simple as that.

Marketing events are not a one-time task. Remember people have to hear your message three to seven times before they will take advantage of it. Your 30-second commercial is the foundation of your marketing campaign. Use it everywhere—put it on your brochure and on your marketing materials and say it to everyone you meet. Use it on the phone, at cocktail parties, and in any of your correspondence. Start right now!

❊ ROLLING PUBLICITY

Stephan had just started a company that offered rollerblading lessons and group outings. He was having trouble attracting customers. I told him about the Octopus Effect.

Stephan decided to create a Learn to Skate Day by partnering with a local environmental group. After all, wasn't skating a great alternative to commuting by car? People would pay $10 for the class with all proceeds going to the environmental group.

The group had 4,500 members and loved Stephan's idea of teaching its members to skate safely while raising money for their cause. They wrote up descriptions of the event and Stephan's company and sent it out to their members and the local press. For free, Stephan reached a large new audience and got four stories in local papers.

STEP 19A

UNUSUAL MARKETING EVENTS

A great way to start your marketing campaign is by brainstorming on and conducting unusual marketing events. These events help your product stand out, provide a way to test your marketing message, and recruit people for your marketing team. The key is to develop low-cost, Octopus Effect events that put your name out in front of as many people as possible, over and over again.

Go crazy when you are brainstorming. Listen to all the ideas that are suggested and consider the possibilities. What seems unusual or even outlandish to one person will seem attractive and intriguing to the next. And the more unusual the event, the more likely it will get noticed and have high attendance.

THUMBS UP

Use the Octopus Effect to communicate your product's benefits, over and over again, to your target market.

TO DO

1. In your Product Notebook, title a page "Unusual Marketing Events."
List the unusual events that people suggest to you or that you discovered in your past research on this page. Transfer any marketing and sponsorship ideas you listed in Step 8, Information Center, and Step 11, Product Statement, to this page. This is an excellent opportunity to review the events you previously captured and to get your creative juices flowing.

Do not worry about the events you list. You will analyze them later. When you become serious about implementing an event (and when the time is right), you will add it to your monthly One Pager (Step 17, Marketing Strategy) so you can easily track your progress and success. As your market expands, you will monitor which events are working and which are not and do more of what works.

INSPIRATION

You never know what idea will work. Always write down any ideas people give you.

GOAL

To develop a cohesive list of unusual marketing events.

OUTCOME

A list of unusual Octopus Effect marketing events.

2. Add the development of your business card, logo, slogan, and letterhead to your One Pager.

Developing your image is very important when getting your product known. An image helps people recognize and remember you, understand your product's benefits and makes your company a reality. This should be the second marketing event you add to your One Pager (first is your 30-second commercial).

Many companies call this "branding," and they spend million of dollars on it. Your image sparks people's imagination and helps build trust in your product. Corporate identity items help you market your business, so they should have a consistent look and message. Branding helps deliver your message when you are not there to do it yourself.

If you have already developed these items, review them. Ask yourself whether there is anything you can do to make these items unusual so they

BATTER UP!

A store owner who sold sports equipment wanted to create some unique publicity for his business. At a brainstorming session, one of his friends suggested that he put up a sign at the local baseball stadium. The owner of the business knew he could never afford to advertise at a ballpark but wrote down the idea anyway.

The next day the owner reviewed his list of ideas for unusual marketing events. As he read them, he noticed that someone had suggested developing a mascot and walking around sporting events. An idea struck him!

He created a costume in the shape of large baseball, and made some large rubber magnets that had the name of his business, his 30-second commercial, and his contact information on them. He put the magnets on the side of his van and parked at the entrance of the local baseball stadium.

Wearing his costume, he stood by his van while handing out his business card (which included a 10 percent discount for first-time customers) to everyone who passed by. He was able to hit a large gathering of his target market by creating an unusual marketing event at a very low cost. He had fun, people remembered him, and his business took off.

stand out in the marketplace. Are there any special colors you can use? Is there an image you can incorporate that will tingle people's emotions?

3. **Expand your unusual marketing list by brainstorming with your friends.**
During your brainstorming session, read your 30-second commercial and then L-I-S-Ten. After you gain some new ideas, explain the Octopus Effect and ask your friends for ideas of organizations and companies you can "hit."

No event is too silly. A friend of one of my clients, who developed a new lipstick, suggested that she put her product on her clothes. My client made some T-shirts that had "Get Kissed Now, Ask Me How!" written on them in lipstick. She wore them all the time and became known as Lipstick Mama.

4. **Brainstorm on any personal networking events you can attend and add them to your list.**
Think of places you can attend or speak at. Speaking is a wonderful opportunity to use the Octopus Effect. Speaking once can spread your message to a group of a hundred or more people, who have a great opportunity to meet you in person. Don't forget to wear something (such as a button) that sells your product when you speak.

Consider speaking at seminars, conferences, or events that are related to your business. People in the audience are potential customers, and you will be using your valuable time wisely. Remember, since you are speaking from your heart; people will listen.

Can you be part of a panel discussion at a local university? How about attending a networking event at your local chamber of commerce?

5. **Brainstorm on ways to integrate the Internet into your marketing efforts.**
Think of the Internet as an extension of your marketing efforts. Try to incorporate it into your marketing efforts, even if it's only by obtaining an e-mail account to keep in contact with customers.

Don't be anxious about the Internet. An e-mail account is an easy way for people to contact you electronically. It also saves you money by allowing you to send information to potential customers and the press without having to print and mail your information. A web site is like an electronic brochure. It

N O T E

You can save money developing marketing items. Barter or ask a student at a local art school for help. Students would love to see their work on a real product (and it looks great on their résumé).

is an easy way for people who have Internet access to gain information about your product.

Every business is really an electronic business. You are probably already using a telephone or a computer (electronic machines). The Internet offers additional possibilities to aid your marketing efforts. Perhaps you want to start with an e-mail account and then, as your business grows, you can add a web site.

NOTE

Your 30-second commercial is the foundation for all your marketing activities. It should be part of every conversation you have.

The Internet is always changing, and there are books dedicated to getting your business online. Brainstorm on ways the Internet can help you market your business rather than deciding whether or not you should open an e-commerce company. Some ways to use the Internet as part of your marketing efforts are to:

- Start collecting e-mail addresses from everyone you meet. You can usually get addresses from people's business cards.
- Use your 30-second commercial as an e-mail signature (right after your name). This constantly reminds people of the benefits your business provides.

DOGGONE GOOD

Laurie loved dogs. She knew everything about them and felt that she could make a living by creating cards and other items especially for dogs. Thinking of the Octopus Effect and speaking engagements, someone suggested she develop a television talk show. A television show? Sound crazy? It wasn't!

Laurie learned that all she had to do is call up her local cable channel and say, "I want to be on TV." Every cable franchise must provide production facilities so the public can develop shows that will air on its public access channels. Laurie's show, *Devoted to Dogs,* is now on a Virginia cable channel, and she has become known as a person who is devoted to dogs.

Another client, a local accountant, started a show called *Tips to Grow Your Business.* He invited his customers on as guest speakers. Wouldn't it be great if you could say to your customers, "Thanks for all you've done for me; can I invite you to be on television? It will help promote both of us."

- Establish an e-mail account where customers can contact you. As your business grows, develop an e-mail relationship with your customers, the press, and stores that sell your product. You can send them articles about your product, about new trends, or about new uses for your product. (Baking soda used to be only for cooking. Now it's also used to deodorize and clean.) You can also send out order information without the printing, copying, and mailing expenses.

- Develop an e-mail newsletter that provides information on innovative ways to use your product and announces promotional specials. Invite your contacts to subscribe to the newsletter for free. This gives you a great way to keep them up to date on your progress.

- Create your own web site on the Internet. A web site is your own personal area on the Internet that you can customize. People can access this site and gain information on your business and your products. You might show a picture of your product, describe its benefits, and provide ordering and contact information. It's like having a multimedia brochure you can give to anyone, anywhere in the world.

NOTE

Using the Internet or creating a web site may seem like a significant project. It's really not that tough. Ask for help from your kids, a young neighbor, or a design student at a local college. They love this stuff!

STEP 19B

THE PRESS

THUMBS UP

Research! Do your homework and develop a story angle the reporters would love to write.

The press (television, magazines, the Internet, newspapers, and so on) is always looking for unique stories to print. Focus on how your product helps solve a problem, adds value to society in a unique way, or is part of a trend, and you will create great stories for the media.

Contact the press even if you think your story is not newsworthy; after going through these steps your story at least will be unique. Besides, the reporter's father may have had a store similar to yours (or loved playing games like the one you are developing), and your letter will spark an emotional response.

You might get lucky and hit a reporter with a timely, unique angle for a story currently being worked on. A reporter might be researching a story on a market trend, and your product could be used as a great example. Or maybe it is just a slow news week. You never know—so contact the press and get your name in lights.

Reporters are just people. Do not be afraid of them or hesitant to contact them. Like everyone else you speak with, talk to them from a point of benefit for them. They have a job to do, help make their job easier.

Just like a job interview, find out more about the reporter before you approach them and they are more likely to work with you. Research the topics each specific reporter has written about or expressed an interest in writing about. Then find out how your product can help them accomplish their goals.

Isn't life more pleasant when people express an interest in your work, in your passion? Provide reporters with the same respect, and they will help spread the news about your product.

TO DO

1. **Label a page in your Product Notebook, "Media Contacts."**

This is where you can put any reporters' names you found during your past research and add future names. Talk to people; they may volunteer additional names of contacts.

Some of my clients prefer to add reporters' names to their date books or to an electronic organizer such as a Palm Pilot. This is a great idea. However, you should at least list the reporters' names in your Product Notebook. It is a great way to backup your information.

2. **Write a media release that describes your product and its benefits.**

A media release is a one-page description of your product, written like a newspaper article, that communicates its unique aspects. Some people call this a press release. I prefer media release because "media" covers television, radio, and print; "press" only covers print.

Newsletters, Internet magazines, newspapers, radio, and television are constantly looking for newsworthy stories. All of these outlets use media releases as leads for possible stories. Your media release should be well written because smaller outlets may print your media release in their publications just as it is written.

You can follow the sample media release on page 200 to develop a release that reflects the unique attributes of your product. Right now you can develop a release that focuses on your product's launch. In the future, releases may focus on how your product has helped one of your customers or how it is part of a new trend. Whatever your write, always communicate your product's unique benefits by telling a simple, exciting story.

Some helpful tips on developing a great media release include:

- Think like a reporter by making your story unique. Review the stories that you gathered in Step 6, Researching the Foundation. Use themes or answer any questions the reporter poses in their articles as the basis for your media release. You may even consider using some of the reporter's favorite words, using buzz words (words that stand out), or imitating their style.

GOAL

To develop strategies with which to approach the press.

OUTCOME

A media release, a list of press contacts, and story ideas.

Whenever you are feeling down, look through your Product Notebook to review how much you have accomplished.

NOTE

Don't forget to continually refresh your reporter list by researching the Internet and the library to find additional contacts who write about products similar to yours.

- If you are having trouble coming up with a story for a media release, use one of the questions people always ask you about your business. If they have a question, the reporter's readers may also. The question may even make a wonderful headline for your media release.
- Write your story for as broad an audience as possible by focusing on trends (e.g., people have less time to cook) and listing other well-known or notable products that are part of the trend.
- Use facts. A media release is written from the point of fact, not fluff. It should not be an ad for your product, so do not use glowing adjectives. Use descriptive but objective adjectives, such as "first product to . . ." or "high-polished silver jewelry."

✳ SALE AWAY

Sherry had developed a special do-it-yourself keepsake kit for wedding albums. The albums were designed so the bride and groom could work on them together, forever keeping their memories alive. The kit included a special organic cover, decorative inside pages, and gold bindings.

Sherry sent out a media release on her product without any great luck. No one was interested in writing about her product. Then Sherry changed her strategy; she did her research. She went to the library and started reading bridal magazines and searching on the Internet for other magazines.

She found a wonderful national magazine that emphasized articles about how to make weddings memorable. She felt their theme was a perfect fit for her albums. She called one of their reporters and after speaking to him, sent him a cover letter, her media release, and a picture of her product. She knew the magazine was going to print an article about her product.

To her shock, the reporter decided not to write the story. Instead, he got the magazine to feature Sherry's do-it-yourself wedding albums (with a full-color picture) in their "Product of the Month" section. Sherry received a free ad in a national magazine! Do your homework; you never know what will happen.

- Provide examples of firsthand customer experiences with the product so people can easily relate to it. You might even add a quote from a satisfied customer so readers can visualize themselves using your product.

3. **Contact the press names you discovered when appropriate.**

If you decide to contact reporters, add their names to your One Pager so you can track your efforts with them. When you call your monthly contacts, introduce yourself and use your 30-second commercial to introduce your product.

You can start a conversation with a reporter by saying, "Are you the person I should send a media release to about a new product that . . . ?" At the end of your conversation ask, "Based on our conversation, will you be writing a story about my product?" If they say no, find out why and ask if they can recommend a different reporter who may be interested. Just ask; you will be surprised by the recommendations you receive.

Personal contact with the media is the best way to get your story in print. However, if you do not have the time to contact media outlets yourself, you can use a media distribution service. These services send your media release to a large number of publications for a set price. This saves you a lot of time but also takes the human touch out of the process. You know how much time you have, so decide whether it's worth the cost to use a distribution service. Two larger services are: Bacon's Media Distribution Services (800-621-0561) and PR Newswire (800-832-5522).

If possible, contact reporters by phone or in person before sending them a media release. However, some of my clients have had luck sending out "blind" media releases, that is, without a reporter's name. If you are going to do this, target a specific section of the publication by addressing your fax, e-mail, or letter to the editor of that section (e.g., New Products Editor).

Here are some tips for making your business stand out:

- Even if your contact says they are not interested, send them press items (which you will develop or collect in Step 20). Briefly, press items include a media release, a cover letter, faxable marketing information, a photograph (black and white, 5" x 7" or 8" x 10" format—a digital picture is wonderful!) of your product and, any press articles about your product that have already been written.

INSPIRATION

Focus on benefit when talking to reporters. Your 30-second commercial is a perfect tool to use if you feel uncomfortable.

*Photographs
showing your
product in use
(e.g., by customers
or at an event)
increase the chance
of your story
getting published.
On the back of
your photograph,
always identify
anyone in the pic-
ture and state your
name, phone num-
ber, and address.*

• If your product is inexpensive, offer a sample. To learn whether a reporter is interested, most of my clients send a postcard (with their address on the front and a place for the reporter's address on the back) that a reporter can return, which says, "Yes, send me a free sample."

• Thank the reporters, receptionists, and editors whom you came into contact with. A simple thank-you card or e-mail works wonders!

4. **Update your media release as your business grows.**

Keep your media release up to date. Change it when you discover new uses for your products, partner with a great organization, or obtain great customer stories. Keep sending your media release to appropriate reporters as you discover them.

If there is a significant change in your business (e.g., you found a new use for your product that benefits a special group of people), you can send out your new media release to reporters you contacted in the past. Reporters are busy people; they may have overlooked your first media release, or your story may now fit in with what they are covering.

5. **For the adventurous entrepreneur, you can gain free publicity by doing extra credit homework.**

Doing extra credit means doing more work. You might write an article about your product that specific (mainly national) publications would be interested in publishing.

It is very hard to get a product mentioned in national publications. Do your homework. A unique strategy that can work is to write an article that provides their readers with useful information, and submit it for their consideration.

The steps for researching and writing an article to submit to a publication are:

a. Choose a theme for your article. Use the benefits you defined in your 30-second commercial or a commonly asked question (e.g., the question your customers ask you the most) as your theme. For instance, if your product is natural makeup, you could write about how using natural ingredients in cosmetics eliminates the need for animal testing. Or you could answer the question, "How can we stop killing animals to test the safety of cosmetics?"

b. Select one national publication that reports on products such as yours. Choose the publication that you feel best fits with the benefits your product provides.

c. Look for articles written about similar products that have been printed in the last year. Review the articles you collected in Step 6, Researching the Foundation, or conduct a quick library search on your chosen publication. Check the publication's Internet site. If the publication maintains archives on the Internet, you can quickly review their previous articles. When you find new articles, print them out so you can analyze them later.

d. On the back of each article, list the publication's name and issue date, the section the article was printed in (e.g., Entertainment), the reporter's name, and the article's theme. Some short pieces don't list the reporter's name; in that case list the editor or managing editor's name.

e. Check to see whether the reporter works for the magazine or is a freelance writer. Most magazines use freelance writers almost exclusively. Editors are responsible for assigning articles to reporters or will assign reporters to write a full article based on an idea the reporter has pitched to the editor. You want to contact both the reporter and the editor if you can.

   A section at the front of the publication lists all the publication's personnel. If the reporter's name is listed as a staff writer, they work for the publication. If their name is not listed (or is listed as a "contributor"), the publication may accept articles from outside (freelance) sources in the section where the article was located.

f. Note common themes in the publication. Does your product expand on any of these themes? Does it answer any questions that past articles posed? If so, write down that particular theme or question, and define

NOTE

Don't forget to include Web magazines in your list of possible publications.

NOTE

Every publication has an editorial calendar that lists the topics the publication will cover for the next year. Call or visit the web site of the publication you want to submit your article to and obtain one.

N O T E

If you are afraid of writing, contact a journalism student at a local college to help you. They would love to see their name in print!

how your product will elaborate on it. For example, the articles you collected may talk about how animals are smarter than we think and should be protected. If your product relates to that theme, the publication will be more interested in telling your story.

g. Write an article identifying the benefits your product with the theme or question you discovered. The easiest way to write an article is to follow the style of articles already published in your target magazine. If they use flowery words or use bold headlines to break up the article, follow their example.

 Don't make your product the main emphasis of the article. In fact, try to include other products or services that are part of a trend you discovered; it makes your product seem appealing to a broader audience.

h. Contact the publication. If the reporter works for the publication, they will be your initial point of contact. If the reporter worked freelance, contact the appropriate section editor.

 When you contact the reporter or the editor, describe the research you have completed. Tell them you are familiar with the themes they have presented in the past year and that your article further explores one or more of those topics and provides fun and useful information to their readers.

 Ask the reporter or editor if you can send them a copy of your completed article for their review. If they don't like the way your story is written but they like your theme, they may follow up with you and find a way to publish your story. After all, their job is to write stories, and you have saved them a lot of time and effort.

 You can also contact a freelance writer directly. Freelance writers have relationships with editors and know what stories magazines are looking for. If they like your story, they will submit it to a variety of publications. Remember, publications are always looking for great stories of interest to their readers.

i. Always follow up with reporters and editors. Do not just send your story in or just send a letter—always check to see whether they liked your story and whether they would like to hear other ideas you have.

j. Don't stop with one publication. Look for other publications, including online publications, that cover similar themes. Now that you have your story written, it will be easy to modify for use in other publications.

k. Have fun. Just like your 30-second commercial, your article will take on a life of its own. You will discover new things about yourself and your product. Who knows, maybe you will become a freelance small-business reporter on the side!

N O T E

Constantly use your 30-second commercial. A reporter could be standing nearby, overhear the unique benefit you are offering, and realize it would make a great story.

SAMPLE MEDIA RELEASE

Refer to the next page for details on the following ten elements of a media release.

①

P. O. Box 108, Jupiter, Florida 33458

Media Release

②	③
For Immediate Release	**Contact:**
31 January 2002	Roland Sample: 561-555-2342

④ **PREPARE HEALTHY MEALS IN MINUTES**

⑤ *The Super Duper Cutter Saves Working Parents Time in the Kitchen*

⑥ JUPITER, Florida—Preparing a perfect Waldorf salad is now faster and safer than ever thanks to a new product that slices fruits and vegetables *not* fingers. According to a survey by the Food Experts of America, the Super Duper Cutter cuts food preparation time in half.

⑦ "The Super Duper Cutter saves families food preparation time, making the *dinner hour* a reality in today's fast-paced world," beams inventor, Roland Sample. Sample created the cutter after seeing both his grandmother and his wife nicking their fingers during simple tasks such as slicing tomatoes, dicing onions, and carving radish flowers.

⑧ "Thanks to the Super Duper Cutter, I have time to prepare fresh vegetables instead of using stale, frozen ones!" raves Ma Brown of Dubuque, Iowa. The Super Duper Cutter surrounds the sharp edges of the knife with pliable soft plastic that retracts when it comes into contact with the skin. At $12.95, it makes a perfect gift.

⑨ For further information on the Super Duper Cutter and retail locations please visit www.thesuperdupercutter.com or call Roland Sample at 561-555-2342.

⑩ ###

1. Always print a media release on your company's letterhead. If you haven't printed any letterhead yet, create some using a software program.

2. This is the date you want the information released to the public.

3. Connect an answering machine or service to any number you put in a media release. You don't want to miss any messages.

4. The headline is the topic of your media release. It usually concentrates on your product's main benefit or a question that a number of your customers have asked. Your headline is always in all caps.

5. The subtitle further explains your product's unique benefits. It is in sentence form (only capitalize the first letter of each main word and leave prepositions and articles in lowercase).

6. The opening paragraph attracts the reader's attention by concentrating on the unique problem your product solves. It must "sell" your product—so use your 30-second commercial to help your product's unique benefits stand out. Always use double spacing.

7. The next paragraph should use simple, exciting and emotional words to describe your business. Reporters are interested in facts, not fluff. For instance, instead of saying, "The Super Duper Cutter has helped bring families together at dinner so they can enjoy each other's heartfelt stories because they spend less time cooking," say, "The Super Duper Cutter saves families over an hour in food preparation, making the dinner hour a reality in today's fast-paced world."

8. The next paragraphs expand your story. You can discuss how your product helps solve a unique problem and how it affects your customers. You can also discuss trends in the market and explain how these trends affect a broad audience. Explain how your customers (and their readers) will benefit from buying your product. Customer quotes are always great to use. For example: "I now have time to prepare fresh vegetables instead of using frozen ones, thanks to the Super Duper Cutter—Ma Brown, Dubuque, Iowa."

9. The last paragraph lists your contact information and sales locations.

10. This symbol indicates the end of your media release.

TRADE SHOWS

Trade shows are events that showcase new products and the people who bring them to life. There are trade shows for almost every product, and they cover everything from steps it takes to manufacture and deliver a product to how to promote that product. For instance, if you want to own a restaurant, there are restaurant owner trade shows, kitchen product trade shows, food trade shows, and promotional trade shows you can attend.

This step helps you develop a trade show strategy that fits with your unique business needs. At this stage in your business development, you will be concentrating on determining which trade shows you should attend. Trade shows occur throughout the country. Look for the one nearest your home.

Trade shows are a fantastic way to gain market information quickly. The right trade show can give you great ideas or introduce you to potential distributors, reps, and store owners to sell your product.

Store owners, distributors, and reps attend trade shows to discover new products to sell. Even if you have not manufactured your product yet, you can talk to potential distributors and store owners, show them your prototype, test out your 30-second commercial, and obtain professional feedback on your product.

You will also be able to compare your product to other products in the market, including others that have not been released yet. By investigating these new products, you may find ways to enhance your product, develop new partners, or improve your packaging.

Exhibiting at a show is very expensive (ranging from $3,000 to $10,000 just for registering, plus paying to create and staff your booth) and time consuming. It is best at this stage of your business to consider just attending trade shows. Check them out, talk to people, and then decide whether it is worth it to actually exhibit at a trade show.

TO DO

1. **Label a page in your Product Notebook "Trade Shows."**

Record any trade show ideas you discover, including exhibit ideas and a list of possible trade show partners.

No matter what you decide to do, you should create a list of the trade shows that cover your industry. This creates a reference guide as you develop your business. As you meet distributors, retailers, and other inventors, you can help them by sharing your list with them; they will give you any feedback they have on the shows. You can obtain a good list of the national gift and trade shows online at www.expoguide.com.

2. **Obtain brochures for each show that seems appropriate for your business.**

You don't want to waste your time attending trade shows that don't meet your needs. Call the show's sponsor before attending the event and ask for an attendee brochure and an exhibitor brochure.

✱ SNOOPING

A client of mine attended a trade show thinking that she would just snoop around to see whether anyone was making a product similar to hers. Guess what—she found not one, but three products with themes similar to her product. Did Sue run away and pout? No. She remembered that her product was unique and decided to investigate further.

Sue went up and spoke to the inventors of each of the products. She used her 30-second commercial and even shared the things she had learned from her focus groups. She then asked for help.

To her amazement, the inventors liked her idea and told her that their products were actually quite different from hers. They gave her suggestions on pitfalls to avoid, recommended manufacturers, and offered some marketing tips. One inventor even asked her if she would like to share a booth at an upcoming trade show. Remember, speak from your heart, ask for help, write down ideas, and miracles will happen.

GOAL

To find trade shows that will help you develop and market your product.

OUTCOME

A list of useful trade shows you should attend.

Trade show brochures describe the show's main purpose, its demographics (types of exhibitors and attendees, such as store owners and distributors), a list of that year's exhibitors, total attendance numbers for previous years, associated costs to exhibit, and (if possible) a dollar amount of business generated from the previous show. Most trade shows will also have this information on the Internet. Make your research easier by going to their web site.

3. **Determine whether or not you should attend the trade shows that sent you brochures.**

There are so many trade shows out there that you will have to narrow down your choices. Otherwise you will spend all your time attending trade shows rather than developing your product. Once you receive a brochure, ask yourself:

- "Does it cover the industry I'm in?" If not, do not attend.
- "Does it promote itself to buyers of my product?" If so, it is probably worth attending just to meet potential customers face to face.
- "How many exhibitors will there be? Are many exhibitors returning from the last trade show?" If a high percentage of companies are returning to a trade show, it means they probably had some success at the show.
- "Is anyone carrying products similar to mine?: If so, you will be able to learn from other inventors as well as hit potential buyers.
- "Is it close to my home or a friend's home?" Save money on travel, hotel, and meals by attending trade shows where you can bunk for free.

4. **Create a chart in your Product Notebook detailing the trade shows you are strongly considering attending.**

If you answer "yes" to the questions in To Do number 3, add the trade show to your chart. Just because you do not attend a trade show this year doesn't mean that you won't attend it next year. If you decide not to attend a show, you can throw the brochure away or pass it onto another entrepreneur who may find it helpful.

TRADESHOW INFORMATION

Details: List the trade show's name, location, and date.

Audience: Who specifically is attending? Store owners? Distributors? Manufacturers? Inventors? Or a combination? Circle the people that can help your business.

Exhibitors: Obtain a list of last year's and this year's exhibitors. What general categories (e.g., buyers, store owners, or manufacturers) do the companies fall into? List the categories in this column.

Contact names: Identify the specific people that you would contact for information about attending the trade show.

Other information: Include items such as costs for attending and booth rentals, any comments people have made about the show, and whether or not you are interested in attending. Also list specific booths (customers) that you intend on visiting.

5. **Conduct real-life market research by calling or e-mailing small businesses that have exhibited at the shows in your chart.**

When you contact a small business owner, tell them that you are calling to ask them about their experience at the trade show. Always ask them whether this is a good time to talk. If it is not, try and schedule an acceptable time to speak with them.

Start your conversation by telling the small business owner about your product. Then ask them about their experience at the trade show. Use the information they provide to help you decide whether or not you should attend a specific show.

Sample questions to ask include: "How was the show?" "Did you make any great contacts or learn anything new?" "Did you exhibit? If so, did the number of sales or contacts you made during the show cover your costs?" "Would you have gotten just as much out of the show if you only attended the show, rather than exhibiting?"

6. **Decide whether you will attend the show or not.**

Use all the information you have gathered and listen to your gut feeling when determining whether or not to attend. Trust yourself. Bounce your choices off a friend or another business owner if it will help you decide.

If you decide to attend, find a way to attend the trade show for free. Look in the brochure you received and see whether they let inventors or distributors attend for free. If they do, go to the show with your business card, register, and get a free pass. Volunteering is also a great way to get a free pass. You will learn a lot from volunteering; you'll rub shoulders with the host companies who have lots of contacts that can help you.

Only exhibit at the show if you believe that you will generate enough sales at the show or create enough long-term buzz to cover your expenses. You are more likely to generate sales if your target customers are attending the show and if past attendees with similar products have told you that they were successful.

7. **Always make the most out your attendance by being memorable.**

For trade shows you decide to attend, use your 30-second commercial throughout the event so you make a lasting impression on the people you meet. You want them to remember you and your business.

And network, network, network. Carry plenty of business cards and other marketing materials to give to potential customers, distributors, and store owners. Always bring your real-life example with you; it will show you are serious.

Speak from your heart and L-I-S-Ten. Find out who is attending the show and why. Ask people who are selling items similar to yours how the show is going for them and whether or not it was worth having a booth. This will help you decide whether or not you should exhibit at the trade show in the future.

Stand out in the crowd. One way to do this is to create a walking booth. Have a friend wear a costume that represents your product (such as a giant lipstick), and walk around the show with this mascot. Or just hand people a small reminder of your product (e.g., a candy bar signed by you or a magnetic heart to illustrate your passion). A simple memento will give your product exposure without the expense of renting, setting up, and running a booth. It will also put a smile on people's faces.

8. **Always follow up with any contacts you make at the show.**

People love to be remembered. If you remember them, they will remember you and your product the next time you call them. A client of mine always thinks of ways she can help another person's business, then includes the idea with a personal card. The idea can be simple, like providing them with the name of a new store that might buy their product.

Other clients have created postcards that illustrate their product and sent them to contacts they made. Postcards are usually inexpensive to make; talk to a local copy shop and find out how you can make some for your business. Remember, even a simple thank-you note works great!

INSPIRATION

You will be amazed at the amount of business and referrals you can generate just by sending a thank-you note.

PAID ADVERTISING

THUMBS UP

To help your ads stand out in the crowded market, always dream like a child, decide as an adult. Be creative. Make your ad as unique as your product, and people will take notice.

Advertising is promoting your product in specific media outlets. Outlets include magazines, newspapers, television, local newsletters, trade show catalogs, and even church bulletins. Don't forget the Internet; there are many online sites and publications where you can advertise.

You are probably overflowing with ideas from friends, family, and other associates on how to advertise your business for free (or inexpensively). Investigate free possibilities before paying to advertise your product. Free or almost-free marketing events are generally more unusual than advertisements and will help your product (and you) stand out. These events help you clearly define your marketing message and differentiate your product's benefits.

Paid advertising is an extension of your marketing plans—alone it cannot create a miracle. In fact, most of my clients just break even (if they are lucky) when they use paid advertising. However, it is a great way to get your product into the minds of your customers. If they see your ad a couple of times and then receive a postcard telling them how to order your product, they may be primed and ready to place an order.

People have to see an ad about your product several times before they will respond to it. Therefore, paid advertising is a series of events, not a one-time action. The goal of paid advertising is simple—to put the name of your business and its benefits in front of people as often as you can.

People are bombarded with ads all the time, so much so that we have become conditioned to ignore them. If you decide to use paid advertising, be consistent in your design and the content of your ads so you don't confuse potential customers. Consistency familiarizes people with your product so they remember it and refer potential customers.

TO DO

1. **Ask yourself whether you should pay to advertise.**

When you are starting your business, do not use paid advertising as a primary vehicle to sell your product. Advertising is expensive and requires you to place a number of ads to achieve results. In the beginning, it is better to test the market through free marketing events or by bartering for ad space (e.g., helping sponsor a community event).

Ask yourself whether your product can be effectively described in an advertisement. Will your customers be able to understand your product's benefits in different formats, including print, video, or radio. For now, dismiss any formats that won't promote your product successfully.

2. **Label a page in your Product Notebook "Paid Advertising Outlets."**

Store any advertising ideas you develop for your product here. Review your Product Notebook and write down any outlets you discovered in your previous research.

Even if you have decided not to advertise right now, list these outlets. It will make the information easily accessible for when you need it, and you can share it with others.

3. **Add to your list of possible outlets by holding a brainstorming session with your friends and potential customers.**

Use your 30-second commercial to explain your product to the group and then L-I-S-Ten to their ideas. Discuss all types of outlets, including magazines, newspapers, trade magazines, web sites, and special events. A list of possible outlets in on page 216.

4. **Choose your top three advertising outlets, and create a Paid Advertising chart in your Product Notebook.**

When you decide to advertise, you will add the decision and the outlet to your One Pager as a marketing event. Your top three outlets are based on the outcomes of the following questions:

GOAL

To understand how to create and place an effective ad.

OUTCOME

Specific information on outlets through which you may advertise.

Speak from your heart to help your business stand out from the competition.

- Does the outlet you are considering reach the target market you defined earlier in Step 11, Product Statement? You want to advertise in outlets that best reach your target market. How many people or households will be exposed to the outlet during a specific time period? Be mindful of statistics. For example, many publications will include "pass-through" readers in their circulation totals. Pass-through readers are viewers who do not subscribe to the publication, but may read it secondhand. An outlet should provide you with specific information on their customers, how ads for other products have done, what results you should expect, and the best time of year or day of the week to place your ad. If the outlet doesn't reach your target customers or won't provide you with above information do not advertise in it.

- Can you afford multiple advertisements in the same outlet? Advertising is ongoing; it is not a one-time occasion. People must see an ad multiple times before they act. You may have to advertise in the same outlet three to seven times before a potential customer will pay attention to it.

- Are other products similar to yours advertised in the outlet? If not, ask why. If a similar product is advertised often, it may be a good indication that a previous ad was successful. It does not necessarily make it the right outlet for your product, but it does provide you with some assurance that you are on the right track.

- Will the outlet provide you with good placement? The upper right-hand corner is the best position for an ad (it is the spot most noticed by readers) in a magazine or newspaper. You should also position your ads near relevant editorials or high-interest issues. For instance, if you have a new entertainment product, place your ad near the television schedule. As people reference the schedule, they will continually see your ad.

PAID ADVERTISING

Advertising Outlet: Specify in which section you want to advertise (e.g. the *Yummy Post,* entertainment section).	Contact Information: List the names and numbers for the advertising departments of each outlet.	Audience and Circulation Numbers: Make sure that the outlet targets the same audience as your target market.	Reason and Results: This will help you learn where to place additional ads.	Comments: Put any additional comments here. Comments might include dates for special promotions or special inserts the outlet is developing.

5. **Continually add to your Paid Advertising Outlets list in your Product Notebook.**

Continually update your list as your business grows. Pay close attention to advertising venus that other small-business people recommend. An updated list saves you time and frustration locating contact names and finding the right outlets when you decide to advertise. You can also share your list with other small business owners.

6. **To the best of your ability, write an ad to sell your product.**

Write an ad even if you are not going to pay to advertise. You can always use that ad at free events or if you decide to barter for ad space. Start out by stating your purpose for creating the ad. As you write the ad, continually ask yourself whether it accomplishes your purpose.

What are you hoping to achieve by placing an ad? Do you want people to call you or visit a store that has your product (or both)? Do you want to improve your brand image? Or promote a special event?

A sample ad is on page 216. Glance over the ad to become familiar with it, but don't worry about the format of your ad yet. Let the message you want to deliver dictate format. You can develop your ad on a piece of paper or using word processing software, whichever you are more comfortable with.

7. **Create a headline for your ad.**

Announce the benefits of your product in your headline. Your ad becomes more believable when you state the problem your product solves. Review your 30-second commercial and answer the question: "What is your product's greatest benefit?" State it concisely in seven words or less.

Have fun! Catch the readers' attention and make your ad easier to remember by keeping the words to one syllable whenever possible (e.g., "We Make It Your Way").

You can develop a different headline for each benefit your product offers. Then use the one you like best (and that best fits with the outlet you are advertising in). Your headline can take the form of a question. For example: "Want to save $1,000 in heating expenses?" Is your product longer lasting, faster, easier to use? Questions make readers reflect on their lives and relate to your ad.

8. **Develop a second headline that expands the benefit you have chosen to promote.**

Make your product easy to remember by concentrating on one key benefit and repeating it throughout your advertisement. Your second headline simply reinforces your message.

9. **Write the rest of your ad copy (the text in the ad).**

Ad copy must support the headline and provide a solution to the problem you stated in the headlines. Your text should convince the reader that you have a great product. The language must also reflect the purpose of your ad.

10. **Make your ad credible by using real-life testimonials that prove your product works.**

Testimonials are powerful. Use actual customer testimonials; you will never be able to re-create the true feeling a customer has when they experience your product. Condense the testimonials to a few key words that support the benefit you stated in your headlines.

11. **State the action you want the reader to take.**

Suggesting actions such as calling your toll-free number or visiting a store may move your customers to purchase your product. You can add urgency to the action by putting a time frame on it. "Hurry. Visit our store today, as supplies are limited!"

12. **Try to include a photograph or a graphic.**

A picture is worth a thousand words. These items should grab the readers' attention and emphasize the benefits of your product. A great idea is to use a photograph that shows your product in use. You can ensure the quality of the photograph by submitting a digital photograph on a disk.

13. **Put a fun caption below your photograph or graphic.**

The caption below the picture is the most-read part of an ad. People's imaginations are sparked by the picture, and they want to know more. Your caption should explain your product's benefit or differentiate it from the competition.

N O T E

Your local copy shop can scan any photos you have and make them better!

14. **Design your ad.**

Keep in mind that the public only knows what you tell or show them—so show and tell them your best! Capturing a product's benefit in an ad is difficult. Work with a graphic artist or an art student to lay out your ad. Graphic artists often know how people react to certain aspects of ads and can help you generate greater sales. Some tips on hiring a graphic artist are:

- Meet with each graphic artist in person so you can see samples of their work. Ask them questions and evaluate their responses to decide who would work best with you. Ask yourself whether there is a personal fit. Will you like working with them? If not, don't. If you are uncomfortable at your first meeting, you will probably be uncomfortable throughout the process.

- Listen to the artist and see whether they understand your product and how it benefits your customers. If they don't understand your product's benefits, they might not be able to develop an ad that grabs your customer's attention.

- Discuss payment and the designer's process before you hire them. You will save a lot of heartache by stating exact prices and the process up front. Ask whether they get paid by the hour or for a fixed fee. If they get paid by the hour, how many hours do they estimate it will take to complete your project? How many revisions will you be able to make? How much will it cost to make additional revisions?

- Ask whether they will create new graphics for your ad or use graphics from existing databases. If they will be using an existing graphic, who else is using it and how will it affect the uniqueness of your ad? If your ad looks like others, your customers may become confused or disinterested. If you are going to spend money placing an ad, make sure it stands out from the competition.

- When there is a personal fit, concentrate on the quality of their past designs, their price, and their reputation to make your decision.

15. **Test your ad by following the To Dos in Step 14, Focus Group, and hold a focus group party.**

Create a couple of ads and ask people to comment on each ad. L-I-S-Ten to their responses. Some questions to ask include:

- Did the ad immediately attract their attention?
- Does the ad prompt them to buy your product (or achieve other goals you set)?
- Do they understand what the product is?
- How would they make the ad more effective?
- Which ad do they like best and why?

16. **Incorporate any changes that improve your ad.**

Ask yourself whether any of the ideas improve your ad. If so, change your ad accordingly. If not, do not make the changes—you are in charge.

If you make significant changes to your ad, you can use another focus group to test your ad again. After a couple of rounds with a designer, you may have lost perspective on how effective your ad really is. You are going to spend a lot of money if you decide to use paid advertising—make it the best ad you can.

17. **Test your ad and evaluate customer response.**

You can relate purchases to a specific ad by putting a code number in the action item of the ad. For example: "Call now! Mention code MRQ for 10% off." Or put a code on the ad and tell the customer to "Bring in this ad for 10% off." List the code when you add an advertising outlet to your One Pager (Step 17) so you effectively track results.

A great way to test your ad is by placing it in a low-cost or no-cost outlet that specifically targets your market (such as a trade journal) for a couple of weeks. If the ad generates satisfactory results, continue. If not, rethink your strategy and ask others for help. You may want to change some aspect of your ad, such as the headline.

18. **Advertise in your chosen outlets and sell, sell, sell!**

Update your ad as your circumstances change. For instance, if someone from a well-known entity (such as your local paper) writes an article about your product, update your press information and ad to include: "As seen in the *Oregonian*."

POSSIBLE ADVERTISING OUTLETS

Always test your ads by showing them to potential customers before placing them in any outlet.

- Industry-specific magazines, newspapers, and trade journals. These outlets are great advertising resources because they are usually lower in cost than national editions and they target specific audiences.
- Newspapers, classified section of papers, magazines, programs for plays (and other special events that your target market might attend), billboards, buses, inside taxis and the yellow pages. These outlets are all great places to reach a large audience.
- The Internet, especially on sites that target your customers. The Internet is growing as an advertising medium because people can control what sites they visit. People visiting a certain site are interested in the specific information that site offers.
- Radio ads are usually inexpensive to create and can be very effective. Stations can sell you a set number of spots during an hour, so your customers will hear your ad more than once.

DIRECT MAIL

Direct mail is sending your ad in the mail (or over the Internet) directly to your customers. Direct mail pieces are specific items (e.g., coupons or postcards) that inform your customers about your product. The more personal (and brief) you can make your direct mail piece, the better.

For a startup business, direct mail is probably too expensive to do on a large scale. However, it is a wonderful way to follow up with customers who have expressed an interest in your product. Remember, people have to be reminded about your product's benefits over and over again before they act. If you know someone is interested in purchasing your product, a postcard in the mail may be all they need to actually buy it.

No matter why you are sending a direct mail piece, always include a unique offer to spur your customers to take action (e.g., 10 percent off the regular price if they call now). You can test different offers on different direct mail pieces to see what works best.

THUMBS UP

Your direct mail piece represents your product. Make it special.

TO DO

1. **Ask yourself whether you have the time and patience to conduct a large direct mail campaign.**

Direct mail is time consuming. Most entrepreneurs find that they have to conduct their first direct mail campaign themselves. This means that you or friends who you recruit have to do the manual labor.

You may have to collate and/or fold marketing materials. You have to stuff, seal, and address envelopes and place stamps on all the direct mail pieces you send out. It also takes time to track responses and follow up on questions that customers pose to you about your product. Plus, you may have to call the people to whom you sent mailers to prompt them to order.

Even if you are sending a direct mail piece via the Internet, you still have to create the piece and find a great e-mail list. It is not as expensive because you eliminate postage and paper costs, but it takes a great deal of time to do it right.

If you feel a direct mail campaign will benefit your product right now, try to partner with an organization that sends out direct mail pieces to their members. Remember to specifically target specific Octopus organizations (hit a large number of your customers).

2. **Label a page in your Product Notebook "Direct Mail."**

List any wonderful direct mail ideas on this page. The ideas will be handy whenever you decide to send a direct mail piece.

Hold a brainstorming session with your friends and other colleagues to develop a list of possible direct mail ideas. To save time, you can combine this session with your advertising brainstorming session. Have fun and remember to L-I-S-Ten.

3. **Determine whether you need to purchase additional names from a mailing list company.**

If you are going to conduct a direct mailing, you need names to send your direct mail piece to. Creating a database of potential customers takes a long time. Mailing list companies specialize in developing lists of names from specific target markets. They can help you increase the effectiveness of your direct mail piece.

Since you are just starting out, you probably will have to purchase names from a mailing list company. Things to consider when purchasing a mailing list include:

- **The list of names.** Make sure that the characteristics of the people on the list match your target market requirements. Direct mail houses should provide you with the demographics (unique characteristics) of their audience and the results of other direct mail campaigns. If the direct mail house does not have this information, do not buy its list.
- **Accuracy.** How recently was the list created or updated? People move

To understand how direct mail can benefit your marketing efforts.

O U T C O M E

A direct mail plan.

often. Customer lists should be updated at least every six months. You do not want an outdated list that will waste your efforts and your money.

- **Frequency.** How frequently do the names on the list purchase products via direct mail? The mailing list company should give you statistics about the buying habits of people on their mailing lists in writing.
- **Refunds.** Direct mail houses should give you a refund in the event that you receive more than a given percentage of returns (10 to 15 percent is common).

4. **Simplify your mailing procedures by locating a direct mail house to help you.** Direct mail houses help you simplify your procedures by creating a database of the names (and e-mail addresses) who will receive your direct mail piece, putting names on envelopes, stuffing the envelopes, putting stamps on the envelopes, and mailing out your pieces. If you can afford to use one, do it.

You can find direct mail houses by asking other entrepreneurs, searching the Internet, using the yellow pages, or conducting research at the library. Ask around, you will find an inexpensive direct mail house to help you. Choose your direct mail house by reviewing the services they provide, their costs, and their reputation.

5. **Calculate the costs associated with conducting a direct mail campaign.** Calculating these costs now will help you develop a marketing campaign that works for you. Determining the actual costs of a direct mail campaign helps you decide whether or not it is worth conducting one. If you do not calculate the costs, you may assume it is too expensive for you to do. Costs can include:

- **Purchase of mailing lists.** Depending on the number of names you purchase and the degree to which the names fit your target market, your list can cost between $350 and $5,000 (or more).
- **Stationery and mailing.** Costs can include postcards, paper, envelopes, and response cards. Don't forget you have to put postage on each piece. Depending on the quantity you print, prices can run from $1 to $2 per piece for black-and-white items and $5 per piece for color items.
- **Phone calls.** These include follow-up calls to your mailing list recipients and calls to stimulate sales. You probably will have to conduct telephone calls even if you use e-mail.

N O T E

Two reputable direct mailing list companies are: Hugo Dunhill Mailing Lists (800-223-6454) and SRDS (800-851-SRDS).

6. **Estimate the sales a direct mail campaign will generate.**

An average response rate is in the range of 1.5 to 3 percent, providing you (or your mail house) have done a good job of targeting your customers.

To estimate your sales, use an average response rate of 2 percent. Multiply the number of direct mail pieces you will send out by 2 percent; then multiply that number by the minimum quantity order and the price per piece.

For example, a client of mine has a product that sells for $5 wholesale with a minimum order of six. He is considering sending out 1,000 direct mail pieces. In this example, his direct mail costs would have to be less than $600 for him to break even. The calculation is: 2 percent of 1,000 pieces sent out = 20; 20 × 6 pieces minimum order × $5 per piece = $600 in sales generated from the direct mail piece.

7. **Determine whether conducting a large direct mail campaign is cost effective for you.**

Subtract your estimated costs from your estimated sales. If you think you will make money (to cover both your time and costs), consider using direct mail as a marketing event. Do not forget to include your time in this calculation. Time you spend sending out and following up on direct mailings is time taken away from other activities.

8. **If you decide to use direct mail, develop your direct mail piece.**

Have I persuaded you not to conduct a large direct mailing right now? It is a lot of work. However, each product is unique, so after going through these steps, if you feel that direct mail is the best way to advertise your product—it probably is.

Your direct mail piece is an advertising piece. You are basically creating an ad that you will mail (or e-mail) to specific people. So review the hints provided in the Step 19d, Paid Advertising, to make your direct mail piece as effective as possible. Get people energized to buy your product!

Postcards are a great direct mail piece. Not only are they cheap and fun to design, but the amount of information that will fit on a postcard is just the amount of information your customers will actually read. Your customers don't have to open anything to read a postcard; the information is right in front of them.

NOTE

Put something (such as a graphic or a headline) on your envelope so people will open your direct mail piece. One effective and cost-efficient alternative is to send a postcard. You can also send an e-mail designed as a postcard.

Some other hints on helping your direct mail piece stand out in the market are:

- Review your past research. Did you find any direct mail pieces that you loved? If so, incorporate those ideas into your piece.
- Use testimonials to provide proof that your product works.
- Include a unique incentive that will spur the reader to action. Can you offer them a special savings or a free gift if they respond by a certain date?
- Develop a unique way to deliver your direct mail message. If you are sending a letter, can you send it in a special envelope, on a CD, as a postcard that acts like a mirror (which my makeup client used), or as a hologram that shows your product and its benefits (e.g., the name of your business and money)? If you are sending an e-mail postcard, can you add music or make it interactive?

9. **Add punch to your direct mail piece by adding a postscript (p.s.).**

People do not have a lot of time to read details. Restate your product's benefits and the action you want people to take at the bottom of your direct mail piece as a postscript. People are more likely to read your p.s. than any other words on your direct mail piece. And if you catch their interest in the p.s., they will probably read the rest of the information. Use it to make your piece more effective.

10. **Test your direct mail package.**

Send your package to friends and other potential customers and see how they respond. Mail (or e-mail) 150 direct mail pieces to the people you think are most likely to order and see what happens. You can follow up with a phone call to this test group to obtain any suggestions they may have. L-I-S-Ten to them and then decide what suggestions to incorporate.

Some of my clients print more direct mail pieces than they will use to conduct their test. This is because (especially for postcards) there is not much difference in cost at different quantities. If you print more direct mail pieces than you send out, you can use them for something else later. For example, you can hand out postcards as a unique business card. After all, they have all your pertinent information on them.

11. **Once your test mailing works well, send out your revised direct mail pieces.**
After making sure your direct mail piece really works, send your revised direct mail piece to the remaining names on your list. Track any direct mail pieces you decide to send using your marketing One Pager (Step 17, Marketing Strategy). Add your direct mailing as a marketing event and track the results. Now you will learn what really works and what doesn't.

Be ready to process any questions or orders that your direct mail campaign generates. You do not want to lose any customers by having poor customer service.

SALES KIT

INTRODUCTION

This step helps you develop your Sales Kit—the place where you store your marketing materials and tools. Your Sales Kit holds such items as your media release, pricing information, ordering procedures, and any press you have generated. It also holds direct mail pieces or flyers that you will use to promote your product.

A Sales Kit keeps all your sales and marketing information in one place for easy reference. If a reporter calls, you can quickly send them your latest press release. If one of your sponsors asks for a description of your product for their newsletter, you can read it to them right then. If you want to evaluate your promotional success so far, you can pull out your latest marketing strategy One Pager.

Promotional items in your Sales Kit (e.g., press releases and advertisements) represent your product when you cannot present it personally. Remember, you want to help your product stand out from the competition by reflecting your product's benefits in everything you write.

Many of my clients find that selling their product is difficult because it is so personal. They often say that it hurts when someone responds negatively to their product. They know it shouldn't, but it does.

A friendly warning: It may hurt so much that you want to stop selling your product altogether. You may think to yourself, "Enough is enough, I don't want to do this anymore" or "Why can't people just be nice?"

Don't quit now! My clients have discovered that all they need to do is to remember to L-I-S-Ten. When you receive a negative comment, think: "This person is trying to help me somehow. It's up to me to figure out how." Relax, keep an open mind, and let the person explain their position. L-I-S-Ten for ideas and ask questions. You may be surprised at what you discover.

THUMBS UP

Consider negative comments just as you do positive ones. Listen to them and find a way to use the comment to improve your product.

Listening applies to your whole life, not just to your business. If you make it a practice to listen, you will discover opportunities where none seem to exist. These opportunities will help you defy the odds and create solutions to what seemed like impossible problems.

G O A L

To design or collect items that you will place in your Sales Kit.

O U T C O M E

An easily accessible storage place for your marketing materials and tools.

T O D O

1. **Buy a 3-ring binder and label it "[Your Product Name] Sales Kit."**

The next To Do outlines the items you will develop or collect to put into your binder. This binder allows you to easily update and add new information. You can use any type of system (file folders or a briefcase) you want to store your marketing materials, just make it easy to access.

Your Sales Kit provides you a central location for your promotional materials and tools. It has saved my clients hundreds of hours (and lots of frustration) hunting for information when someone asks them to send them something describing their product.

Since you will be writing a lot during this step, here are some successful writing hints:

- Make sure each item you develop focuses on benefit.
- Write as if you are speaking directly to your audience.
- Always write to inform, not to impress. Most people just throw away hyped-up promotional ads.
- If you get stuck, start at the end. It may stimulate some ideas.
- Use plain, simple, short words that everyone will understand.
- Proofread your work; you never know what you may have missed.

2. **Create a section in your Sales Kit titled "Cover Letter."**

Develop and put a sample cover letter in this section. A cover letter is a simple story; it tells people who you are, what you do, who your customer is, and what problem you solve. A cover letter sells your product. The letter goes on top of your Sales Kit. If anyone calls and asks about your product, you can open your Sales Kit and read directly from the letter.

A client had just moved to San Francisco. During our second meeting, she broke down in tears. I asked her what was wrong, and she told me that her mom was going to put her cats to sleep. "What?" was all that came out of my mouth.

When Abbey decided to move to San Francisco, her mother (who was very allergic to cats) had agreed to watch her two cats for one month. Unfortunately, the rental market was so competitive in San Francisco that property owners did not take any tenants with pets. Abbey read newspapers, searched online resources, and walked through neighborhoods for over two months and couldn't find a place to live.

At the same time, Abbey's mother was trying to find a good home for the cats. Nothing worked. Finally, in desperation for a place to live, Abbey took an apartment that would not allow pets. The morning of our meeting, her mother had called and said she had no choice but to put the cats to sleep. Abbey was devastated.

We discussed options for Abbey. How could we promote her cats to people who would adopt them? We decided that she could put up adoption flyers around her neighborhood discussing how friendly and loving her cats were.

An hour after she put up the flyers, the telephone rang. Abbey thought someone had come to her rescue but she was wrong. The caller began to yell and scream at her. She told Abbey that she was a horrible person for giving up her cats.

Abbey wanted to slam down the telephone, but then remembered that she should L-I-S-Ten. So she did, and after the caller stopped yelling, Abbey asked her, "When was the last time you rented an apartment in the city?" The woman answered, "Twelve years ago." Abbey replied, "Things have changed!"

Speaking from her heart, Abbey proceeded to tell the woman about her struggles trying to find an apartment, her heartbreak at having to leave her cats, and her desperation to find a place for them to live.

This time it was the caller's turn to listen—to realize there is always more to the story. After Abbey finished, the woman was so moved that she

Promotional items need to attract people's attention. Rouse your readers to action and get them excited about your product.

agreed to adopt the two cats. Abbey's cats now live right down the street from her, and she has full visitation rights.

Some would say Abbey was extremely lucky. I say that she created her own luck. By listening first, she was able to get someone to help her achieve her goals. Guess what? Abbey did not receive any other calls. Had she hung up the telephone, she may have lost her cats.

The cover letter you develop now is just a sample. Whenever you send out information about your product, you will personalize each letter (including the name of the recipient and the purpose of the letter). You can use parts of the media release you developed in Step 19b, The Press, in your letter. A great cover letter includes:

- An opening paragraph that sets the tone of your letter. You want to recognize the reader and entice them to keep reading.
- A paragraph explaining your product and its benefits in one or two sentences. Your 30-second commercial is perfect here.
- A paragraph that explains how the person reading the letter can benefit from your product. This paragraph can be based on a common need you found during your research. It may help to start writing as though you are directly addressing a reporter, a distributor, and a store owner.
- A closing paragraph that asks your reader to contact you to set up a meeting or a telephone conversation to discuss your product.

SAMPLE COVER LETTER

You are selling your product's benefits, not just the product itself.

January 21, 2002

Kim Dryer
Puno Services
999 Wolter Street
New York, NY 10036

Dear Kim,

Thank you for the great telephone conversation about Briia. How fortunate to meet another person whose soul is lit by helping small businesses grow. I know that working together we can help grow Puno Services and the customers it serves.

Briia helps people kick start their dream businesses. Step by step, our workshops and personal coaching guide entrepreneurs through the process of creating a practical action plan for success.

I know that Puno strives to provide great computers to entrepreneurs to save them time and money and to move their ideas forward. Briia's programs and services are targeted toward the same customer base. By partnering with Briia, Puno will gain educated customers, build customer loyalty, and increase sales.

I have attached an overview of our workshops, several personal recommendations, and a copy of my book, *Kick Start Your Dream Business*. Please contact me at (415) 555-1234 or at romanus@briia.com to discuss sponsoring workshops and using my book as a free gift to attract new customers. I look forward to the possibilities.

Sincerely,

Romanus Wolter
Founder, Briia

INSPIRATION

Always focus on customer benefit. It will enhance your business in amazing ways.

3. **Create a section in your Sales Kit called "Product Description."**

Write a product description page and put it in this section. Your product description explains your product by focusing on the benefits it provides. If you offer one product, this is simply your product's name and your 30-second commercial. If you offer more than one product, list each product and its corresponding 30-second commercial.

Add one-sentence quotes from customers who have used your product to your product description page. These references can restate your product benefits or provide an endorsement for your product.

4. **Create a section in your Sales Kit called "Real-Life Stories."**

Write at least two real-life stories that describe your product benefiting customers and put them in this section. These success stories detail situations where a customer uses your product to solve a problem.

People remember the benefits your product provides when they visualize your product in actual use. These stories help investors, customers, and reporters relate your product to an actual situation. Limit these stories to one page; that's all your audience will want to read.

5. **Create a section in your Sales Kit called "Pricing and Delivery."**

Your pricing and delivery sheet details your ordering information, pricing, suggested retail price, payment terms, and shipping information. You have your preliminary pricing completed. Use it here.

As discussed in Chapter 8, Setting the Price, you will offer a different price to a store owner who buys a few products directly from you than you would to a distributor who buys hundreds of units. Develop separate sheets for different pricing situations rather than putting them all on the same sheet. This allows you to send out appropriate information about your product quickly.

6. **Create a fax cover template so you can easily send your "Faxable Marketing Information."**

Your cover letter, product description, real-life stories, and pricing and delivery sheet are all you need to sell your product to potential customers, distributors, reps, or store owners. These four pages are your Faxable Marketing Information.

These four pages act as a brochure for your product by quickly explaining your product, its benefits, and how to order it. These sheets should make people so excited about your product that they pick up the telephone to make a purchase.

Create a fax cover template so you are ready to send this information to people when they request it. A fax cover page is simple to create and includes your company's logo, address, and phone number; the individual's name and the company you are sending the fax to; your name and contact information; the number of pages being faxed; and a short message describing the content of the fax.

As you generate publicity about your product, you can expand your Faxable Marketing Information by adding a media release or copies of articles written about your business. Articles written about your product add legitimacy to the benefits it provides.

7. **Review your Faxable Marketing Information to make sure it is easy to read and reflects the benefits your product provides.**
All your marketing materials should be easy to read. Newspapers and advertisements are written so that a sixth grader can understand them. Everyone who reads your stories should be able to understand them, regardless of their educational background. Review your cover letter, product description, real-life stories, and pricing and delivery sheet by asking yourself: "Could a thirteen-year-old understand what I have written?"

Even better, have a young person (maybe the son or daughter of a friend) read your Faxable Marketing Information and comment on it. If you need to, rewrite your materials using simpler words so everyone can relate to your product and the benefits it provides.

8. **Set your Faxable Marketing Information aside for one day, and come back to read it when you're fresh.**
This is the time to proofread your work and be sure that what you wrote attracts the reader's attention. Be as concise and exciting as you can. You may even replace your longer stories with short real-life testimonials that explain the benefits your product offers.

N O T E

Your product is continually evolving, so keep your Faxable Marketing Information updated.

9. **Fax your Faxable Marketing Information to a friend.**

Fax these pages to a friend, and ask them to give you feedback. Did they like the way you worded your information? Did the sheets make them want to call you and place an order? What information was missing, or was there too much information? Did the fax come through cleanly? Were all the items easily readable even though they were faxed?

L-I-S-Ten to your friend and change any information you feel will improve your Faxable Marketing Information. You want it to be the best it can be.

10. **Create a section in your Sales Kit called "Marketing Tools."**

Marketing tools help you sell your product. Adding marketing tools to your Sales Kit makes it easier to evaluate and update your marketing efforts.

Use your marketing tools to position your product so that it is desirable to your customers. Positioning is creating an image of your product that helps prospective buyers see your product as beneficial to them. There are many marketing tools available to help you position your product to make it memorable and to stand out from the competition.

Store these tools in your binder so you don't lose them and so you remember to change them when you update your Faxable Marketing Information. This section is a great reference area if you decide to develop new marketing tools. Just look through this section, determine what wording, colors, or graphics you like best, and use them to create the new marketing tool.

Some marketing tools include:

- **An ad.** Put the ad you created in Step 19d, Paid Advertising, in this section. If you haven't created an ad yet, use your 30-second commercial and put your contact information on it. It will act as a placeholder until you create an ad.
- **Displays.** Describe where you want your product placed in stores and any display ideas you have generated (e.g., posters or display holders). You can include a draft copy of a poster or a drawing of an effective in-store display.
- **Direct mail.** If you decided to develop a direct mail piece (Step 19e), include a copy here.
- **Flyers.** If you design any flyers to hand out during events, put them in this section.

- **Additional marketing tools.** Put samples of any additional marketing tools you develop (e.g., coupons or event announcements) in this section so you can reference them in the future.

11. **Create a section in your Sales Kit called "Product Sales Areas."**

List the ways (e.g., via stores, reps, or distributors) you are going to sell your product. As people suggest new avenues for selling your product, add them here. You can copy the sales area page (Step 8, Information Center) you developed in your Product Notebook and put it in your Sales Kit.

12. **Create a section in your Sales Kit called "Promotional Tie-Ins."**

List your potential sponsors and events (Step 18, Promotional Tie-Ins) in this section. Add other ideas as they arise. Again, you can copy the promotional tie-in page you developed in your Product Notebook and put it in your Sales Kit.

13. **Create a section in your Sales Kit called "Marketing Strategy."**

Put your monthly One Pagers (Step 17, Marketing Strategy) in this section. Having these pages near your promotional materials makes it easier to review what you have accomplished and what worked in the past. It's a lot of fun to flip through your One Pagers and acknowledge your progress.

14. **Create a section in your Sales Kit called "Press Recognition."**

Put copies of all the press that your business receives here. If someone asks you a question about the press you have received or what other people think about your product, you can quickly pull out an article and send it to them. When your parents or friends come to visit, be sure to show off this section of your Sales Kit. They will be proud of what you have accomplished.

EIGHT

Setting the Price

This chapter helps you determine the right price for your product. To be successful, you have to provide the public with a product they can afford, while still making a profit. Base your price on your research and all you have learned so far and on your gut feelings.

PRICE ESTIMATE

INTRODUCTION

This step helps you determine an estimated price for your product. Pricing your product right the first time is important because changes to your price always have to be justified to your customers. Determine the best price you can by L-I-S-Tening to other people and making a decision based on their suggestions and your research, calculations, and gut feelings.

Everyone, whether you like it or not, is a consumer—be they frugal, extravagant, skeptical, or impulsive. Talk with people who say they can't wait for your product to hit the market and ask other entrepreneurs what they think is the right price for your product.

Talk to store owners and reps who have firsthand customer knowledge of what your customers are willing to pay. Everyone has different knowledge and experiences to share with you, so L-I-S-Ten to them all! L-I-S-Ten, learn, and apply what you've learned to your pricing efforts.

Learn how to set a price for your product by designing a system that incorporates your past research and any new information you receive. Look over the research you have completed so far and see what your competition is charging for their product. Your product may have some extra benefits that the competition doesn't. These unique benefits may provide your product or service with a higher perceived value, and you may be able to charge a higher price than the competition does. Or maybe your product has less frills but the essential benefits and you can offer a lower price.

You know your product better than anyone, so listen to your intuition. If you have a number of products to offer, you may want to attract people's attention by setting a low price for your first product and then charging a higher price for future products as your reputation and experience grows.

THUMBS UP

Setting a price is like a game. Play fair, watch your competitors, and develop different strategies to win.

You could also offer a free sample to entice people to try your product. For example, software game makers often give away samples of their games to pique people's interest and create grass roots, word-of-mouth publicity.

TO DO

1. **Label a page in your Product Notebook "Pricing."**

Keep all your pricing information on this page and use it to conduct your pricing calculations. It is fun to go back later and see how you determined your price.

2. **Finalize the amount of product you will produce and record the number in your Product Notebook.**

The initial amount of product you produce is called your initial inventory. Any products you do not sell have to be stored somewhere. Leftover product is called your remaining inventory.

Determining your initial inventory is a science and can't be answered here. It depends on your product, your costs, your pre-orders, estimated sales, and the amount of money you are able to raise.

However, pricing and inventory are based both on science *and* your gut. You have a great deal of knowledge about your market right now; ask your gut what your estimated initial inventory number should be. Review the numbers recommended by manufacturers, store owners, distributors, other inventors, and the minimum production run you determined in To Do number 4 in Step 16, Manufacturing It. Recommendations from professionals can be quite apt because their years of experience have given them firsthand knowledge of your customers' buying habits. Go for it, and trust yourself!

In later steps, you will use this initial inventory number to calculate your production, storage, and fulfillment costs. Of course, the best-case scenario is to produce only as many items as you know you can sell.

✳ MOVING ON UP

A client of mine, Taylor, wanted to break into the web design market but was having trouble pricing his services correctly. His customers wanted to know what price he would charge before he started working with them. Taylor felt he did not have enough experience to tell them.

Taylor was uncertain how to price his various offerings (and his clients kept requesting new things every day). For example, one of his clients only wanted a one-page web site without any graphics and another one wanted a twelve-page site with graphics, an area for people to chat, and a way for people to pay for products online.

Taylor wanted to charge enough to cover his living expenses plus make a small profit. Time was his biggest expense. Due to his low overhead, he could afford to charge a lower rate than most of the competition.

I suggested Taylor do two simple things. One, charge a lower rate (that covered his time plus a small profit to cover living expenses) to break into the market and gain client referrals. Two, create a historical pricing chart.

In his historical pricing chart, Taylor tracked his jobs, listing different elements he created and how much he charged per element. He kept this chart near his computer so he could also track the time spent on each item. This recorded information would help him decide how much to charge for his services in the future.

For instance, if a client asked for graphics and one-page web site, Taylor would do an estimate for each element, not for the total package. He would then fill in the information on his pricing chart. As he tracked his progress, he quickly learned from past work. He knew how much time (and, therefore, how much he should charge) each individual element took on average and could charge his new clients appropriately.

After breaking into the market, building his reputation, and creating wonderful client samples, Taylor raised his price to market rates. As he gained experience, he even started telling his clients what they needed on their web sites. Write down your achievements, track your success, and you will properly develop your business.

3. **Establish a working sales price for your product.**

Your working sales price should be in line with the competition. Set your price by using the pricing information you have found so far (i.e., use the price of a real product or a price suggested by a store owner).

People who sell products similar to yours have spent a lot of time setting their price so benefit from all their hard work (and their mistakes). They may have priced their products too high or too low in the past and had sales suffer as a result. By adjusting their prices, they discovered what their customers are willing to pay—so their prices are a good indication of what you should charge.

You can choose one of the prices you found or take an average of all the prices you found. Your working sales price will be used as a pricing reference point in subsequent To Dos in this step.

4. **Review the information you gathered during your focus groups and list attributes that people loved about your product.**

Underneath your working sales price, list attributes that your focus groups told you helped your product stand out in the market. Make a special note of attributes that your product has and the competition does not. You can use the Information Center you created in Step 8 to complete this To Do.

The price you charge for your product may end up higher or lower than your competition's. That is OK. You can explain the difference in price to your customers by describing your product's attributes. As your business grows, you will use this list to justify your price or to raise or lower it.

Consumer perception plays a large role in pricing decisions. For example, if a card can record a voice and play it back rather than just play a prerecorded song, a consumer may value it more. These cards might cost the same amount of money to produce, but the creator could charge more for their special attribute. The reason is complex, but it boils down to consumer perception—what the consumer thinks and feels about the product. Consumers are willing to pay more for products they perceive to have benefits they want.

N O T E

Pricing is personal to you. Always keep your strategy and your target market in mind.

N O T E

Prices are set according to personal goals, competition, costs, demand, and the benefit your product provides.

*Pricing a service has its own unique formula. Go to To Do
number 11 if you are pricing a service.*

N O T E

*Profit is the money
left over after
you collect from
sales and pay all
your expenses.*

5. **Use a simple formula to calculate your product's wholesale price.**

You sell your product to store owners at the wholesale price. Store owners then increase your wholesale price to cover all their expenses and to make a profit. This increase in price is called a markup.

Most store owners mark up a product's price by at least 100 percent. If you sell your product to a store for one dollar, they probably will sell it to their customers for two dollars.

There is a simple formula for calculating your product's wholesale price. Divide your working sales price by two. This becomes your wholesale price.

6. **Use a simple formula to calculate your product's working capital percentage.**

For this exercise, we will assume that you are not opening your own store and that a majority of your sales will take place on the wholesale level. Your working capital percentage is the percentage of income you will use to cover your profit and all your expenses except manufacturing. Simply put, it helps you decide whether you are charging enough money to make a living.

Subtract your per-unit manufacturing cost (Step 16, Manufacturing It) from your wholesale price. This is your gross margin—how much money is left over for you to cover your other expenses.

Divide your gross margin by your wholesale price. This number is your working capital percentage. While this formula isn't as accurate as it could be were you to cost out each component of your business, it does give you an approximate price you could charge. Your working capital percentage usually needs to be between 55 and 65 percent of the wholesale price for you to cover all your expenses and still make a profit. For example:

$$\frac{\$30.00 \text{ (Working Sales Price)}}{2} = \$15.00 \text{ (Wholesale Price)}$$

$15.00 (Wholesale Price) – $6.56 (Manufacturing cost per unit) = **$8.44 (Gross Margin)**

$8.44 divided by $15.00 = 56 percent. This is the working capital percentage. This means that you will be able to use 56 percent of the income you generate to cover your expenses (not including manufacturing) and make a profit.

7. **Establish your calculated sales price.**

Your calculated sales price helps you determine how much you (or stores) should actually charge your end customers. If necessary, change your wholesale price so you are within an acceptable working capital percentage range. Fifty-five percent is the lowest you want to go. Anything higher is great!

Multiply your new wholesale price by two. Congratulations, this is your calculated sales price. Compare this price to the working sales price you set in To Do number 3.

Your calculated sales price can point out potential areas of concern. For example, if your calculated sales price is higher than your working sales price (the competition), you had better be ready to convince your customers that your product is worth it! Or maybe your manufacturing costs are just too high. Therefore, you want to do some more manufacturing research to find the best price for producing your product.

8. **Use an alternative method to create a comparison sales price.**

It is always a good idea to compare your pricing using a couple of different formulas. That way you will be confident that you are covering your expenses and making a profit. Besides, it is a lot of fun to see the range you could charge for your product.

An alternative method for determining your product's sales price is to divide the number of units you plan to produce by all of your estimated expenses, manufacturing costs, and desired profit. This method is an excellent tool to use once you have all your business processes established and expenses estimated. You will be coming back to this step later.

In order to determine your appropriate costs, you will be referring to Step 16, Manufacturing It, Step 17, Marketing Strategy, and Step 30, Financial Analysis (for overhead costs). The formula for establishing a comparison sales price is:

Expenses can be fixed (i.e., they do not change with increases or decreases in sales), such as insurance, or variable (they change with increases or decreases in sales), such as production costs.

$$\text{Sales Price} = \frac{\left(\begin{array}{c} \text{Number of} \\ \text{Units Produced} \\ \text{per year} \end{array} \times \begin{array}{c} \text{Cost of labor} \\ \text{and materials} \\ \text{for one unit} \end{array} \right) + \begin{array}{c} \text{Estimated} \\ \text{annual} \\ \text{overhead} \end{array} + \begin{array}{c} \text{Desired} \\ \text{annual profit} \end{array}}{\text{Numbers of units produced per year}}$$

N O T E

It is harder to raise the price after you launch your product, so take your time setting your sales price.

9. **Compare your comparison sales price (To Do number 8) to your calculated sales price (To Do number 7).**

Are these prices similar? If not, find out why not. Are your costs in your comparison sales price all actual, or are you making some of them up? Use the most accurate information you can. Explain the difference between the two prices so you really know whether you are charging enough to cover your expenses and make a living.

10. **Choose one of the prices you developed as your real sales price. Highlight this real sales price in your Product Notebook.**

Use the explanations you developed and your gut feeling to pick the most appropriate real sales price you can. You will be selling your product to consumers at this real sales price.

Your real sales price will be used throughout the rest of this book. Mark your real sales price by highlighting it on a page in your Product Notebook. Some of my clients put huge dollar signs around their real sales price so it is easy to find. Your real sales price is also called the going-rate price or your product price point.

Underneath your highlighted real sales price explain how you calculated it. If you used the above formulas or if you used a competitor's price, record that. You can write, "I'm charging what the competition is charging because I'm uncertain of what my exact expenses will be. As I develop these expenses, I will reevaluate my real sales price." This statement will help you explain your pricing strategy to potential investors and buyers.

If your real sales price is higher or lower than a competitor's price, state your reasons why. This will help you tell your pricing story. "I know that this is what the competition is charging, but due to this list of great attributes, I am charging this [higher or lower] price." Again, if your real sales price is higher than your working sales price, be sure your product's unique benefits can sustain the higher price.

N O T E

Compare your charges to what others in the industry are charging. If you are over the competition's price, you may want to charge a lower price in the beginning and then raise your price as your reputation builds.

11. **If you provide a service, establish your initial hourly rate.**

Pricing a service is different from pricing a product. Use your past research, ask other professionals what they charge, or use annual salary surveys (from the Internet, local trade associations, or the library) to find a comparable yearly salary for the type of service you offer.

Once you have determined your desired annual salary, use the following formula to obtain your hourly pay:

$$\frac{\text{Desired Annual Salary} / (52 - X \ [X \text{ is weeks of vacation per year}])}{40 \ (\text{hours a week})} = \textbf{Hourly Pay}$$

Then multiply your hourly pay by three to determine an hourly rate that will cover your indirect expenses and expected profit. Most independents hope to make a 20 percent profit. The hourly rate formula is:

$$\text{Hourly Pay} \times 3 = \textbf{Hourly Rate}$$

Your hourly rate does not include any extra expenses so make sure you always charge your client for all direct expenses (e.g., phone, photocopying, or travel).

If your client wants a total cost per project, base it on your hourly rate. First, estimate how much time the project will take, then multiply that time by your hourly rate.

12. **Make sure your pricing works for you.**

Your pricing strategy has to work for you. The above steps help build a solid pricing foundation, but you have to change your price according to any marketing strategies you've developed. For instance, if you have multiple products and have decided to enter the market at a low price with the first one to attract attention and sales, do it.

In the beginning, it's a great idea to make sure your price is in line with the competition. Keep investigating different pricing strategies. Once you get close to your product launch date, set a real sales price that works for you.

13. **Establish your product discount schedule.**

Retailers, distributors, and reps (and anyone else who helps you sell your product) expect a discount off your sales price. People who help sell your product use money generated by their profits (e.g., 15 percent for reps) to pay their expenses and advertise your product.

In your Product Notebook, list your product discounts using the following information:

- **Wholesale discount.** If a store orders from you directly, the standard discount is 50 percent off the real sales price. You can offer additional discounts if they order a larger number of items. Items are not usually returnable. Books sold to bookstores are an exception; bookstores are allowed to return any unsold copies.
- **Internet discount.** An Internet storefront receives a discount of 25 to 40 percent off the product's real sales price. The item is not usually returnable.
- **Rep discount.** They receive 15 percent off of the wholesale price for all the products they sell (the store receives the wholesale price). You receive a lower percentage but obtain expanded product sales. Since you are shipping the products, they are only returnable if it is your policy to accept returns.
- **Catalog and distributor discount.** Catalogs and other distributors receive a 55 to 60 percent off the real sales price to cover shipping and additional marketing costs. They only pay you if the product sells and can usually return any unsold product to you at their expense.

14. **Define your payment plan (when you expect stores and distributors to pay you for your product).**

There are many different payment plans. Create one that works for you and your customers. Your specific industry probably has set payment guidelines; use them if you can. Always provide your price and payment plan in writing before shipping any product.

Options include cash on delivery (COD), which means stores pay you when your product is delivered and net 30, which means that the stores have 30 days after your product is delivered to pay you. It is standard practice to ship goods out COD if you are not familiar with the store. For stores that reorder your product, you can usually use a net 30 payment plan.

15. **Review your pricing every couple of months.**

It is always a good idea to review your pricing strategy every couple of months or when there is a significant change in your business. For instance, if your sales skyrocket you may be able to charge more. If your sales are stagnant or if you find a cheaper manufacturing method, maybe you should lower your price. There is no magical formula to determine when you should change your price—it depends on the market, your competition, and your customers. Talk with the people selling your product (and other professionals) and use your intuition to continually monitor your product pricing.

N O T E

In the beginning, you may consider not putting a permanent price on your product's packaging. You can put price stickers on your product, so after you test the market you can change your price easily.

NINE

Delivering It

A key to running a successful small business is to provide personalized and superior customer support to everyone with whom you do business. This chapter helps you develop procedures that will effectively support the delivery of your product or service. It provides tips and techniques that enable your business to stand out from the competition, attract new customers, and generate repeat business.

CUSTOMER SUPPORT

INTRODUCTION

Customer support is everything you do from making contact and generating the sale to following up with customers. It is the first thing people remember after they do business with you, so make it special. Your customer support plan accomplishes three things: it will help differentiate you in the marketplace, build customer loyalty, and expand your business through referrals. You want to stand out by offering exceptional customer support.

In marketing, your goal is to get your message out to as many people as you can. Once you make contact with these people, the relationships you develop with them are a key to your success. Satisfied customers come back for more and spread the word about your product. Customer support is an integral part of building relationships and driving future customers to your business.

For instance, a coffee shop owner I know not only serves great coffee, has comfy couches, and offers free Internet access, but also provides free refills, enthusiastic recommendations of Internet sites, tips for brewing great coffee at home, and even a dating referral service. Talk about building relationships! It's become the hottest place in town for a coffee date.

Your customers are an indispensable source of good ideas. Buried inside the meanest customer or the most absurd customer complaint is a wonderful idea to help your business. L-I-S-Ten to them and implement any great ideas they generate; you will be able to refine your products or services to better meet their needs.

It's easy to become lost in day-to-day business activities and forget your external intent—you are here to benefit your customers. You have to pay suppliers, send marketing materials to distributors, answer that annoying accounting question, ship product, eat, and then find time to sleep—if you are lucky.

THUMBS UP

Stand out by offering unexpected customer support. When people are surprised, they tell everyone about it.

Customer support reminds you customer benefit should always be at the top of your To Do list.

Remember, without satisfied customers, you do not have a business. Customer support is like a muscle. If you stop exercising it, it stops supporting you.

G O A L

To create a plan that will make doing business with you memorable.

O U T C O M E

A customer support plan that will help your product stand out in the market.

T O   D O

1. **Label a page in your Product Notebook "My Customer Support Plan."**
Use this area to write down ideas you develop in this step. You can also add to this page as you discover new, superior customer support ideas.

2. **With friends, brainstorm on some unexpected customer support programs for all your customers (i.e., store owners and distributors as well as end users).**
Use your 30-second commercial and then ask people: "How can I make it easy and fun to do business with me?" Enhance your list by having them share stories about any great customer support they received in the past.

For example, you can send a thank-you card or a small gift to customers that place large orders. Some businesses go even further. A dry cleaners in my neighborhood offered to sign for and hold any express packages that were to be delivered to a customer's home. Their customers could pick them up from the store at their convenience (and of course drop off their dry cleaning). Another client always sends an e-mail to customers after they order, telling them when they can expect their product. A simple act builds loyalty and generates great word-of-mouth advertising. L-I-S-Ten to your friends and potential customers.

3. **Define a process for asking your customers questions, listening to their answers, and implementing any feasible ideas they may generate.**
Don't forget to reward customers who come up with a great idea. Some ideas that my clients have used to survey their customers are installing a suggestion box, mailing postcard surveys, e-mailing satisfaction questionnaires, and conducting in-store surveys.

You could even hold a "best suggestion" contest, and give the winner a prize or put their photo on a wall. The best question you can ask customers is: "What ideas do you have to help me improve my business?" This question shows people that you are open to suggestions. Remember, when you ask for help, you will receive it.

4. **Develop a step-by-step guide that explains the processes for providing marketing materials to and following up with customers who request information on your business.**

These procedures provide specific information so all customers are treated equally. Once you develop a process, you have something to update.

Be sure to include procedures for: answering the telephone and responding to frequently asked questions (write a script everyone can use to describe

N O T E

Always treat customers as if they were the most important marketing resource you have—they are.

✳ A LITTLE WHINE?

A new restaurant with superior food, great service, and inexpensive prices opened in my neighborhood. As word of mouth spread, people began to flock to the restaurant. The owners thought they had a gold mine until a week later when they started hearing complaints from customers.

The complaints spread through the neighborhood faster than the news about their great food. "The lines are too long." "You have to wait over an hour to get in." "Let's go someplace else." The owners were concerned but had no idea what to do. One of my clients suggested they ask their customers for help and listen to their ideas.

After returning from a weekend trip, I decided to see how the restaurant was doing. It was Monday and there was a long line. To my surprise, everyone in line was happy!

I walked over to the owner and asked him what had happened. Smiling, he said that listening to his customers had worked wonders for his business. The first idea a customer suggested was that he offer free wine to people who were waiting in line. He thought the idea was crazy but decided to try it. Happily, he pointed to a sign above him. It read, "If there is a line, don't whine—just sip some free wine!"

your business), customer data entry, mailings, and follow up. People love to receive exact information quickly. If you can accomplish this, you are way ahead of the game.

5. **Develop simple ways for individuals, stores—both brick- and click-and-mortar (Internet)—distributors, and catalogs to order and pay for your product.** You can make these procedures a step-by-step process so your customers always know the status of their orders. Put these procedures in writing so anyone can refer to them. Some suggestions include:

   - **Phone orders.** Establish a toll-free number and attach an answering machine to it. A toll-free number is approximately $5 per month with a charge of about $.35 a minute. Any telephone company can hook you up with a toll-free number that will ring on your regular line.

   - **Fax orders.** Obtain a fax machine so people can fax in their orders. You could also consider a combination fax/phone/answering machine or purchase a computer that has fax/answering machine software already installed.

   - **Internet orders.** If you have decided to take advantage of the Internet, develop customer support procedures. Internet ordering can be as simple as having people send an order request to a distinct e-mail address (an electronic mailbox) and have a sales person call the customer back. Or it can be as complicated as taking credit card orders over the Internet. Attend a training course or speak to an Internet Service Provider (you can find one in the yellow pages under "Internet") about the best way to accomplish this. Make sure you understand how to make any ordering process secure so your customers' personal and payment information is safe.

   - **Credit card orders.** Shop around for special small business rates from credit card firms. Obtaining a credit card machine is hard for a small business because most banks require you to connect electronically, which is expensive. Many of my clients join a trade organization that has a credit card authorization process already set up with a bank. Since they are part of a larger organization, they save money and obtain better customer service from the bank. Banks usually charge a percentage of your total sales price to process credit card orders. This percentage ranges from 1.45 to 3 percent of the total sales price per order.

6. **Develop a process for updating your customers with new information.**

Develop a way to keep in contact with your customers. They would love to hear about new products or lower prices. An e-mail newsletter is a fantastic tool for keeping in touch with your customers. For example, if you hear of any new uses for your product or service, pass this information on to store owners— it helps their businesses and yours—or e-mail new product information to customers who have signed up for updates.

7. **Create a unique customer complaint policy.**

Your customer complaint policy defines how you do business with your customers. It is like a motto, something you define and attempt to follow. You should try and satisfy every reasonable customer request. "Reasonable" can be defined as a legitimate request that will not strain your business' finances or time. The key to a great policy is to be up-front and honest with your customers and expect the same from them.

Clearly define your return policy. As a small business owner, I recommend that you do not accept returns even from customers you sell to directly. Your life is going to be complicated enough without having to worry about refunding someone's money because they did not like your product. If there is a defect, however, you should replace the product.

Your complaint policy should define your policy for replacing defective or damaged products. It's always good customer service to replace any damaged or defective products free of charge, usually within the first thirty days of purchase. If your product is expensive, you may request that the customer exchange the old product for a new one rather than just refunding their money.

If you decide not to take returns, always tell your customers this fact in advance. In fact, you can declare "No Returns" on sales receipts you generate. If a store wants to return your product because it's not selling, it is not reasonable to accept the return (unless you told the store you would).

8. **If required, determine repair procedures.**

Depending on your product, you have the option of offering no repair services, on-site repair, or replacement for a defective product. Develop repair procedures that meet the needs of your customers and your product.

Include your manufacturing and shipping partners in your repair procedures. If a product is damaged, it is most likely because of the manufacturing or shipping process. If one factory manufactures all your product, you may be able to negotiate with them to handle fixing (or replacing for free) defective products. This is especially true if your manufacturer also ships your product to your customers.

If you decide to use an outside entity to replace defective products, make sure you receive a report about how many items are fixed (or replaced) because you want to keep the quality of your product high. Investigate what your competition is doing. Adding free replacements for damaged items (up to thirty days) may be an opportunity to distinguish yourself from other products on the market.

STEP 23

FULFILLMENT

INTRODUCTION

Fulfillment is your plan to store, track, and deliver any products you develop. Tracking is the process of determining where your product is at all times, starting with your initial inventory and ending with customer acceptance. All three aspects of fulfillment are important. If you find a cheap place to store your product, but have no way of delivering it—you can't sell anything.

Fulfillment also provides you with an excellent opportunity to show your customers that you care (and to help your product stand out). Efficiently fulfill orders and keep your customers up to date on the status of their orders and they will appreciate your business even more.

In your fulfillment procedures, you can also include information on promotions ($10 off your next order!) or get paid by other businesses to include their promotional flyers (like newspaper inserts). Your customers may appreciate information on complementary products.

Always ask for help. An effective fulfillment plan will save you time, money, and heartache. For instance, you may be able to limit your storage expenses by asking other people for ideas. A friend or local business owner may have an empty office or room that you can use temporarily. Tell the world what you need and see what it delivers to you.

Inventory and storage are very expensive. As we discussed in Step 16, Manufacturing It, try to produce the minimum quantity you can when testing the market. However, if you limit your inventory, be sure you know exactly how long it will take and how much it will cost to produce more of your product quickly in case you have a hit!

THUMBS UP

Make fulfillment easy. If the price is right, find one company that can store, ship, and track your product.

G O A L

*To find a place
to store and
ship any products
you develop.*

1. **Label one of the pages in your Product Notebook "Product Fulfillment Plan."** The following steps will help you create your fulfillment policy by outlining, step by step, your storage, ordering, delivery, and tracking procedures. By placing this information on one page, you develop an easy reference guide.

2. **Using your initial inventory number (from To Do number 2 in Step 21, Price Estimate), ask your chosen manufacturer (Step 16, Manufacturing It) how much space is required to store your product.**
   This will give you an idea of how much room you will need to store any product delivered to you. Also ask whether there are any special storage requirements for your product (e.g., air conditioning or pallets). If so, plan for them.

3. **Brainstorm on different places to store your product.**
   Look at your garage or basement, your neighbor's basement, a friend's extra bedroom, an attic, or even a doghouse to determine whether you can store all or part of your product in any of these places. If so, do it and save money. If you decide to use a private area (e.g., your home or a friend's home) for storage in the long run, always clear it with the rest of your family or other people who have access to the area.

   Delivery services (e.g., UPS or FedEx) treat your home like a small business and will pick up directly from you. If you decide to store your inventory yourself, you will spend more time completing the delivery paperwork, but you may save a lot of money on storage fees.

O U T C O M E

*Locations,
methods, and
costs associated
with storing and
shipping your
products.*

---

*If you are storing all your inventory in your home,
you can skip to To Do number 7.*

---

4. **In your Product Notebook, create a contact list of storage facilities and fulfillment houses.**

This list will help you discover the best place to store your product and to fulfill your orders. You can create your list using the following:

- The facilities you found in Step 16, Manufacturing It.
- Your local yellow pages. Look for facilities close to your home or office.
- The *Toll-Free Directory* (available at a library or on the Internet).
- The Internet. Use key words (e.g., warehousing, shipping, or fulfillment) and different search engines to find possible locations.
- Business resources at the library. Reference librarians can save you a lot of time; ask for help.

5. **Call each facility on your list to confirm the services they provide (e.g., storage or shipping) and their prices.**

Save time by interviewing each company as you call them. Trust, rapport, and respect all factor into the gut feeling you will develop about each company. Turn on your "good vibe sensor"; it is one of the most important factors in determining who to work with. In your Product Notebook, answer the following questions for companies you are considering working with:

- What is the cost per month for storing your initial inventory? As you sell more units, your storage cost should decrease because your inventory is taking up less space. A typical storage cost is $10 per pallet of space. A pallet is a wooden platform that keeps your product off the floor.
- What is the cost for fulfilling each order (prepare paperwork, ship, and track orders)? A typical cost is $3 for the first case shipped (as long as the case is approximately 18 × 12 inches or smaller) and $.25 for each additional case going to the same location.
- What is the cost for breaking open a case? Your product will most likely be stored in cases containing several units. You may have to break open a case to fulfill small orders. Determine what that cost is up front so you can decide what to charge your customers who do not order a case.
- How much will it cost to deliver a case of your product to different parts of the United States? Are there any special discounts available to you through an association?

N O T E

To save time accessing small quantities of your inventory, you may be able to store the inventory you need in your home on a weekly or monthly basis.

N O T E

Ask for help. Your manufacturer may have a storage facility or have a relationship with someone who does.

- How long does it take the company to ship after they receive an order from you? How long to different areas of the country?
- To make sure the company is sound, ask to see a credit reference or a credit report.
- What kind of insurance does the company have? What happens if a fire or any other disaster destroys your product? What happens if goods are delivered damaged?
- Ask for some customers' names. Contact these customers, and ask them about the fulfillment house's service.

✳ BACK ME UP

Anna is a physical therapist who worked with me to develop a new back-pack designed for women. After testing and developing her product, she attended a trade show to show it off. After the show, she received lots of small orders. At first she was excited and then she became discouraged.

Since Anna had a full-time job, she did not have the time to fulfill all the small orders she received in a timely manner. She knew she had to do something because she was offering horrible customer support. She had found a couple of great fulfillment houses, but they were too expensive for small orders. It just did not make sense to use them until she was selling greater quantities of her product.

What a dilemma. Anna did not want to alienate any potential customers by not promptly delivering her product. What did she do? Anna asked ask for help. Anna called the fulfillment house she liked best and told them about her situation. She asked the owner if he could help her out by providing a reasonable price on smaller initial orders.

The fulfillment house owner listened to her and said he would help as long as she signed a contract with him for future orders once her sales picked up. Even though she would not make any money on her first orders (at least she would not lose any!), Anna took him up on his offer. By asking for help, she limited her financial risk while being able to satisfy her customers.

6. **Evaluate and rank each fulfillment house.**

If any of the companies do not offer a service you need (such as tracking), cross it off your list. Circle the attributes of each company that stand out from the others. For instance, if one company offers free shipping for damaged items and the others don't, circle it. Rank each company on each of the attributes you listed. For instance, put a number one by the company with the lowest price. Select your top two vendors considering quality, price, reputation, size, and most importantly, your gut feeling.

7. **In your Product Notebook, define your storage, order processing, payment tracking, and delivery procedures.**

Now that you have selected your top two companies, develop your fulfillment procedures. Even if you decide to do it all yourself, put it down in writing. Include the following for each of the procedures:

Storage

- Decide where you will store your inventory. If you can store part of your inventory near your office or home, do it. This inventory can be used in case of an emergency, during a product demonstration, or to replace a defective item.
- Define any special requirements your product has and how your storage area meets these requirements.

Order and Payment Tracking

- Put the ordering methods you developed in Step 22, Customer Support, in this section.
- Develop an invoice that you can send to stores. You can buy blank invoices at a business bookstore or create your own using software such as Microsoft Excel or QuickBooks. Invoices save time tracking delivery and payment dates.
- Create a large-customer chart (customers that order cases) separated by state (and if necessary, city) that you can use as an easy reference tool. If individuals call and ask where they can buy your product, you can refer to this chart. Your large-customer chart should contain store names, con-

Always inform your customers of any shipping delays. If you treat them as if they are a part of the team, they will not feel neglected.

tact names, addresses, phone and fax numbers, and e-mail addresses. Additional columns can be used to track orders, payments, and reorders.

SAMPLE LARGE-CUSTOMER CHART

San Francisco, California			
Customer Name	**Phone/Fax**	**E-Mail**	**Order/Shipping/ Payment**
Rich Kwan, A Store, 108 Quart Avenue, San Francisco, CA 94114	P 415-555-1234 F 415-555-1235	rich@astore.com	• 12/4 – 4 hats, prepay • 12/5 – shipped • 12/14 – 8 hats, prepay

Delivery and Delivery Tracking

- Establish a business account with a delivery service such as UPS (800-742-5877) or FedEx (800-762-3725). After you call them, an account representative will visit you to discuss your shipping requirements, calculate estimated costs, and set up your account.
- Ask each service whether there is an association you can join to obtain a discount. If there is, get the information so you can consider joining.
- Ask each service about packing requirements. Make sure you share the packing requirements with your manufacturer so you can keep your shipping costs low.

• Ask each service about insurance coverage. The first $100 in merchandise shipped should be insured for free. If there is any additional expense to insure your product, add it to your shipping price.

• Choose a service or, even better, set up an account with more than one service. That way you always have a backup option (in case one service goes on strike).

• Set up a cash on delivery (COD) system with the service you choose. If you use COD, the delivery service will collect the money from your customer before delivering your product.

8. **Purchase a software program to help you track your orders.**

I highly recommended this if you can afford it. It takes an awful lot of time to track deliveries, inventory, orders, payments, and delinquent accounts. You should spend your time on marketing and selling your product rather than tracking it.

It is critical to keep accurate and timely records. You want to be prepared to answer any questions that store owners or customers ask you (e.g., When did my product ship? At what stores can I purchase your product?).

An accounting software package can track your sales, accounts, and inventory. A great software package that is not too expensive is Intuit's QuickBooks or QuickBooks Pro. These software packages are easy to use and allow you to create purchase orders, track payments, and create customer lists.

If your resources are limited, you may want to swap some product for an old computer, buy an older version of the software (it works pretty well!), or borrow a computer once a week to track your sales. Of course, you can track all these items manually too.

DISTRIBUTION

INTRODUCTION

It's time to sell! The next three steps help you find and hire other businesses that will help you deliver your product to customers. Remember the Octopus Effect (market to one place that hits many customers). Stores, reps, and distributors all help you target a large group of customers. You are going to have a great time watching these professionals become mesmerized by your product and the benefits it delivers.

All my clients have found that great reps and distributors are worth the expense. The thing they do best is save you time and money distributing your product. For instance, you can tell one rep about your product, and they will show it to over 100 stores—without you having to call, set up an appointment, or travel to each store location.

It can be difficult to convince people to sell your product. The key to persuading people is to think about how you can help their businesses, not just how they can help you. Before approaching a rep about your product, do your homework! Find out what product lines they carry and how your product fills a hole in their line or how your product is already selling to the rep's target market. You want to develop partners for the lifetime of your product, not just for a one-time shot.

Even if you use a rep or distributor, continue to sell your product yourself. There is no better salesperson for your product than you. If you walk into a store, tell them about your product (people love to speak to inventors!), then call your rep or distributor (per your contract) in that territory to follow up with the potential new customer. The store owner and your rep will love you.

When selling something, a small, inexpensive gesture can go a long way. Ask a store owner or your rep how you can make their jobs easier, and then follow through on their ideas. For example, always provide them with good, solid sales

THUMBS UP

Harness the power of businesses around you by focusing on how you can help them increase their sales.

materials (which you developed in Step 20, Sales Kit) so they can easily explain your product's benefits, keep them up to date on any new product features, and fax them any new press coverage your product receives.

Most importantly, if you provide great materials (and business cards) to people, they will pass them on to others. A friend of mine is always on the lookout for neat stuff for her aunt's gift store. When she finds it, she asks the store owner or sales person for the artist's business card and forwards it to her aunt. If there is no card or handy information, she often passes it by. People lack time; make it easy for them to market your business.

❋ DO UNTO OTHERS

Sue, who made decorative desk calendars, was frustrated because no reps or distributors would return her calls. I asked her a simple question: "Did you tell them how you can help their businesses grow?" Confused she answered, "No."

I explained to Sue that the best way to get someone to call you back is to offer them a benefit. We decided to find a way we could help each of these potential business partners.

Sue looked over her past research and found two stores that could easily sell her product. She approached these stores (using her 30-second commercial), told them about her research, and explained why their customers would love her product. The stores really appreciated the research she had done and bought some of her calendars.

Now that she was in a few stores, Sue decided to approach a rep from her area. She called the rep and said, "I have a product that complements the lines you sell. In fact, it is already in some stores you visit. I know your business will profit by working with me." The rep listened, picked up her product, and helped both of their businesses grow.

The best part is that after one rep picked up her product, reps from other areas of the country called her. She had made a name for her product simply by focusing on the needs of the other businesses. Do the same thing with yours!

REPRESENTATIVES

("REPS")

GOAL

To understand how representatives can help your business grow.

OUTCOME

A list of possible representatives and a plan to partner with them.

TO DO

1. **Label the top of a page in your Product Notebook "Reps."**

This page is your easy reference guide to reps with whom you can partner. Write down the names and contact information for any reps you come across. Start by locating local reps so you can practice selling your product to them. Once you have local representation, expand your search nationally (and internationally). Some ideas for finding possible reps:

- Write down any reps you found in Step 8, Information Center.
- Ask store owners and other inventors about their suggestions for possible reps.
- Visit your local library and ask the librarian for books listing product reps.
- Surf the Internet.
- Attend trade shows and ask exhibitors for the names of great reps.

2. **Call each rep that you feel will help your business grow.**

Start with your local area and test the market. Use your 30-second commercial and the information from your Faxable Marketing Pages (which you created in Step 20, Sales Kit) to describe your product. Tell them when you expect to have the product ready and the estimated price you developed in Step 21, Price Estimate.

Ask them if they would be interested in working with you before you launch your product. A good rep may be able to get you preorders based on your real-life example. This is wonderful because it helps limit your risk! If they are not interested in working with you now, ask them if you can contact them after your product is manufactured.

3. Ask reps to help you refine the pricing and marketing strategies you developed in previous steps.

Reps are on the front line every day. They know your customers, what works, and what doesn't, so ask them to share their experiences with you. L-I-S-Ten to them and learn.

Don't forget that reps are salespeople. They may have a tendency to steer the conversation. Be strong and try to get complete answers. Think of these calls as test runs. The calls are an opportunity to see the rep in action, but instead of selling your product, they're selling themselves. Some great questions to ask include:

Rep Questions

- Have they sold similar products? If so, what was their success rate? If the response has been low, ask what can be done differently to make your product a success.
- How many stores do they have as clients? In what geographic territory?
- What are their sales projections (quantity, dollar amount, and time frame) for your product?
- What is their preferred ordering and payment process? It is typical to pay representatives 30 days after you receive payment from the retail store.
- How often will they check to see whether your product needs to be restocked? Do they automatically place reorders with you at certain stock levels?
- Do they know of any other reps, outside their geographic area, that may be interested in picking up your product?

Product Questions

- Is your price reasonable? Is your price below or above average for a product like yours?
- Do they know of any similar products? If so, does yours stand out?
- Do they know of any special marketing strategies that can help promote your product? What in-store promotional materials do the stores they represent prefer (such as posters or displays)?
- Do they know any manufacturers (domestic or international) that may be able to lower your production costs?

N O T E

If you get a good vibe from the rep, they may become part of your business family. You need to feel comfortable with anyone you work with.

INSPIRATION

Build great relationships by discovering stores that want to buy your product and referring them to one of your reps.

NOTE

Reps take a standard commission of 15 percent (of your wholesale price) for products sold and delivered.

4. **Send your top choice of reps (in each geographical area) a letter that asks them to represent your product.**

Show your passion! Don't be afraid to get creative with your query letter. For example, the inventor of a women's investment workshop designed a query letter that looked like the front page of a newspaper. Attach a copy of your Faxable Marketing Information (Step 20, Sales Kit) to your letter. The letter should:

- Request representation and include your contact information.
- Talk about your product, its benefits, and why it will fill a space on the shelf. (Use your 30-second commercial.)
- Thank them for considering your product.
- Close by telling them you will call to follow up on the possibility of them representing your product.

6. **Always sign an agreement before you work with a rep.**

Reps have a standard agreement that outlines their responsibilities, your responsibilities, and payment terms. Most people sign a rep's agreement after they ensure that the terms and conditions cover what they agreed to. It is a good idea to have an attorney review any vague terms and conditions.

Most reps will ask for exclusive representation of your product. Exclusivity gives a rep the sole right to sell your product in a specific geographic area. This is standard practice. However, always make sure you have an "out clause" if the rep fails to produce. Keep your rep agreements in a safe place for easy reference.

7. **In your Product Notebook, highlight the reps you have agreed to work with.**

Use a highlighter to mark the reps you have agreed to work with. You might arrange your reps by territory so, you can make quick referrals when customers call you. Don't forget, even if you use a rep, continue to market your product yourself. You are its best salesperson.

STEP 24B

STORES

- -

TO DO

1. **Label the top of a page in your Product Notebook "Stores."**

Create an easy reference guide to stores with whom you can partner. Write down the names and contact information of stores you are interested in. To create a potential store list:

- Write down the contact information for any stores you found in Step 8, Information Center, and from contacting other inventors.
- Ask store owners for the names of stores in other locations (other geographic areas) that may be interested in selling your product.
- Contact catalogs and distributors about buying their lists of stores. Call and ask them how much their lists cost.
- Surf the Internet to find appropriate stores, including online stores. Try online business reference sites such as www.bigyellow.com.

2. **Visit stores in your local area to determine their potential interest in your product and secure pre-orders.**

Walk into local stores and talk to salespeople or call and make an appointment with the store manager. When calling, ask for the store manager or owner to be sure that you are reaching a person with the power to make decisions about your product. Describe your product, tell them you are going to manufacture it, explain how it benefits their customers, and ask if you can meet with them.

Store owners are small-business people just like you. They need to watch their expenses, and your product is an expense. Your job is to convince the store manager that your product will sell. When you meet with the store man-

GOAL

To understand how and why retail stores purchase products.

OUTCOME

A list of stores that will help expand your sales efforts.

N O T E

When you call or e-mail a large store (or one with multiple locations), ask whether they have open house days where they evaluate products and place orders. If they do, plan on attending!

ager or salesperson, describe your research and the sales potential of your product. Use your 30-second commercial to tell them about your product.

Your real-life example and Faxable Marketing Pages are great tools for securing an advance purchase order. An advance purchase order is a written guarantee that the store will purchase so many units of your product once it's produced. These advanced orders lower your risk when producing your product.

When you work with a rep, you should forward any orders you produce yourself to them. Your initiative will inspire your rep to work even harder for you. The rep (instead of you) will stop in, see how sales are going, and follow up with reorders.

3. **If a store places an order, always get a purchase order number (smaller stores primarily use the date of the order).**

A purchase order number provides you with a reference when you speak to a store owner in the future. It also shows that they are serious about ordering your product. To ensure that you get paid, tell them that the first order will be COD (cash on delivery) and ask for credit references for future orders. Also ask your contact at the store about:

- **Conducting in-store promotions.** Can you conduct an in-store demonstration of your product? Can you place flyers or postcards about your product near the cash register? Can you get your product into a window display?
- **Additional locations.** Does the store have any other locations that would be interested in carrying your product? Do they have an online presence that can advertise your product?
- **Reordering.** What is the best time to contact the store for reorders? This is an important question because a store may not automatically reorder when they sell out of your product. You must be proactive and call stores periodically.

4. **Always follow up with stores after your product is launched.**

Call stores that ordered your product, thank them for ordering, and let them know your product will be shipping soon. After your product ships, call to see if they need any marketing assistance or additional products.

N O T E

Don't be discouraged if you do not receive any preorders for your product. Keep stores up to date on your progress, focus on benefit, and you will get orders.

Persistence pays off. For stores that did not order earlier, call them again. Tell the manager that your product has been launched and is doing well in stores just like theirs. Describe your product again and ask for an order. A lot of people say they are going to manufacture a product, but never do. The fact that you actually made your product a reality may change their minds.

5. **Send stores that purchase your product any press about your product.**
Press always makes people excited about products. Stores may even display news items about your product next to it, which will attract attention to your product.

6. **In your Product Notebook, highlight the stores that have placed orders.**
Use a highlighter to mark the stores who have placed orders with you. You can also arrange stores by territory so their contact and ordering information is easily accessible.

N O T E

You are your product's best salesperson; don't be afraid to contact stores yourself. Store owners like to hear about new products and their inventors. Be nice and have fun!

N O T E

When someone does something nice for you, don't forget to send them a thank-you card.

DISTRIBUTORS

GOAL

To understand more about distributors and distribution.

OUTCOME

A list of possible distributors.

TO DO

1. Label the top of a page in your Product Notebook "Distributors."

This page is your easy reference guide to distributors. Write down names and contact information for distributors. My clients also include catalog sales on their distribution page because catalogs work much like distributors; you ship them a quantity of products, and they advertise and try to sell them. To create a potential distributor list:

- Write down the contact information for any distributors you found in Step 8, Information Center, and from contacting store owners and reps.
- Visit your local library and ask for books that list distributors and catalogs that sell products similar to yours. Helpful catalog resources are *Oxbridge Communications National Directory of Catalogs* (800-955-0231) and the *Catalog of Catalogs* (800-843-7323).
- Search the Internet for appropriate distributors and catalogs (both brick- and click-and-mortar).

2. Add to your list of distributors by obtaining a directory issue of a trade magazine (an issue that lists the people and firms in your industry).

Trade magazines cover industry-specific topics. Find one for your particular industry (e.g., children's toys or educational items) and look through the classified section and advertisements to find potential distributors. To save money, you can ask trade magazines for an advertiser's check copy, which is a free issue. When you receive your issue, add the names of any appropriate distributors you find to your list.

3. **Using the same techniques you did with representatives in Step 24a, contact your list of distributors.**

Following the techniques and questions in Step 24a, Reps, call the distributors on your list and ask whether they would be interested in working with you. If they are not interested in working with you, ask them if they know a distribution company that might be interested in working with you. This is a great strategy because not only will you gain additional information but distributors may think twice about representing you (because you are such a go-getter!).

4. **If a distributor you want to work with becomes interested in your product, put all terms and conditions in writing.**

As long as distributors do not cross into each other's territory, you are free to test them out. If they sell your product, keep them. If not, find new distributors who can help you. Remember, if you get bad vibes from a distributor or do not feel you can trust them, do not work with them. Step 25 talks about self-distribution, which is always a possibility.

Distributors will have a standard distribution agreement that you can review. Ensure that the terms and conditions cover what you agreed to before signing the agreement. It is a good idea to have an attorney review any vague terms and conditions.

Everything is negotiable. For example, if you do not ask for a discount, you will never receive one. Items you can negotiate with a distributor are:

- **Commission.** Distributors receive 55 to 60 percent of the real sales price for selling your product. Their percentage is higher than a rep's because they carry inventory, advertise your product in their catalogs, and ship your product to their customers.
- **Frequency of checking stock.** Biweekly calls or visits to stores is wonderful, but their response is dependent upon your product's sales.
- **Ads and ad placement.** Ask if you can be listed in their product catalog and/or on their Internet site.
- **Customer returns.** Are they allowed? Customer returns should not be allowed unless the product is damaged.

N O T E

Most distributors and catalogs will only pick up your product after it is manufactured.

Make sure any agreement you sign:

- Clearly states who supplies and pays for marketing materials (e.g., product samples, poster design, printing, study guides, or instructions).
- Provides you with a monthly sales report of how many units of your product the distributor has sold. If possible, it should include a list of buyers.
- Is not an exclusive contract. Distributors sell many different products and may not spend a great deal of time selling yours. A large order can justify their request for exclusivity. Use your gut feeling and the advice of other small business owners to decide whether or not to grant a distributor exclusivity. It depends on your product, your goals, and how great the distributor is.

5. **In your Product Notebook, highlight the distributors and catalogs you have agreed to work with.**

Use a highlighter to mark the businesses you have agreed to work with. Track the date of orders and how many units each of the distributors and catalog companies order from you.

SELF-DISTRIBUTION

INTRODUCTION

Self-distribution is anything you do to sell your product. It includes talking to friends, making public appearances, writing articles, and visiting stores. It can be setting up booths at local fairs or distributing postcards with your ordering information on them. If you self-distribute your product, you will have to take orders and collect payment yourself.

No matter how many distributors or reps are working with you, you have to be involved in getting the word out about your product. You are your product's best spokesperson. You have the energy, the love, and the knowledge to inspire other people to purchase your product.

If you do not want anything to do with taking and fulfilling orders, read this step anyway. The more you know, the better understanding you will have of what it takes to sell a product. In fact, reading this step may even trigger some great ideas that you can share with your representatives, stores, and distributors.

The United States Post Office and Federal Express provide free mailing boxes. These boxes are limited in size, usually on the small side, but free! Check out the boxes and use them if you can. Think how much money you could save even if you only used them to ship single orders of your product.

If you decide to distribute all of your product yourself, it will be a lot of hard work, but it will also be a lot of fun. There is nothing quite like the feeling you get when you witness someone actually agreeing to buy your product. It is magical, and it motivates you to keep going during the hard times.

The key to self-distribution is to have fun, tell everyone about your business, and of course, always speak from your heart!

THUMBS UP

No matter with whom you partner, always continue to market your product yourself. You are your greatest spokesperson.

G O A L

*To include your-
self in the distribu-
tion process.*

1. **Determine whether or not you should use self-distribution as your primary sales method.**

As the inventor, you always have to market your product, but distributing it may be a different story. Self-distribution takes a lot of time and effort. If you rely solely on self-distribution, you may not have time to market your product.

Most of my clients love the process of developing their business but hate the details of calling stores, shipping product, and following up on payment. They almost always partner with professionals to handle a majority of the distribution process. This partnership saves them money in the long run because someone else is visiting and calling thousands of stores. However, your product may be best distributed directly and primarily by you. To determine whether self-distribution is for you, ask yourself the following questions:

- "Do I enjoy speaking to people about my product?" The answer to this should be "Of course I do!" However, distribution is more than talking to people about your product; it also involves actually selling and shipping it.
- "Do I have time to call stores, distributors, and wholesalers about my product?" Do you like speaking on the telephone to complete strangers? If you do not, then work with a rep or distributor to help sell your product.
- "Am I organized enough to keep track of orders, shipments, and late payments?"
- "Do I have the time to fulfill and ship orders?" Or the question I ask my clients is, "Do you want to spend time fulfilling orders?" Most of them answer no. Their skills and interest are geared more toward the creative side rather than the technical side of the business.

O U T C O M E

*A refined
distribution plan
that includes
the efforts you
will personally
undertake.*

2. **Review your answers to the above questions.**

If you answered "no" to any of these questions—STOP—and think about your product and what you are getting yourself into. Selling and distributing a product is difficult! If you would rather spend your time developing and marketing new products, then develop distribution partnerships sooner than later.

If you are low on funds, you may want to save commission expenses and distribute your product yourself. In my experience, the opposite is true—a professional saves you time and money so you can develop your business. The key is to pick the right professionals for the job—people who have great contacts and who believe in your product.

You can also bring in a person to help sell and distribute your product. This person might be a friend who loves to sell, a retired salesperson who still wants to work, or a student who wants sales experience. If you decide to hire someone, always have a signed agreement in place (detailing their salary or commission) before you begin to work together. And do not forget, if they are not doing their job, you can let them go and find someone else.

3. **Include yourself in the selling process by personally creating answers to the To Dos in Steps 24a, Representatives; 24b, Stores; 24c, Distributors; and this step.** Even if you decide not to sell your product yourself, answering these questions will provide you with an overview of the distribution process. You will also develop some new distribution ideas that you can share with your distributors, reps, or stores.

4. **Review Step 23, Fulfillment, and change your fulfillment process if required.** Completing this step (and most likely Step 24) may have triggered some great storage or fulfillment ideas. Go back through Step 23 and update your procedures as required. Celebrate! You have just finished creating a fantastic fulfillment and distribution plan for your product.

TEN

Making It Legal

This chapter provides the information you need
to choose the proper legal structure for your business. You will
learn how to protect yourself, your business,
and your investors by obtaining the proper contracts,
licenses, and insurance coverage.

STEP 26

YOUR LEGAL STRUCTURE

INTRODUCTION

This chapter describes the steps necessary to form a legal structure that will protect you, your investors, and your business. You know what your product is, how you are going to deliver it, and what price to charge. It's time to make your company legal so you can concentrate on marketing your product rather than looking over your shoulder.

First, realize that "you" are a business. That's right! You have been working on developing a product that you are going to sell. You are a sole proprietor—a person who is going to make a profit by selling a product you believe in. There is nothing you have to do (no legal formalities) to call yourself a sole proprietor; you just have to be in business.

Your job now is to decide whether or not you should remain a sole proprietor or form a different legal structure. The big question to ask yourself is: "Is personal liability a big worry for me and my business?"

In other words, are you likely to be sued or are you going to be borrowing a lot of money that you may not be able to pay back? As a sole proprietor, your personal assets (e.g., your house, car, and savings) are inseparable from your business. If you fail to pay an obligation, people can take your personal assets. Forming a corporation protects your personal assets if your business gets into any trouble.

Forming a legal structure is a very personal decision. It can be a difficult, intense decision, especially if other people are involved. You are taking a step that will affect the way you do business.

THUMBS UP

Always protect yourself in case of liability from use of your product. There is no reason to increase your stress by always having to look over your shoulder.

GOAL

To understand
the steps to estab-
lishing a legal
business structure.

OUTCOME

A legal structure
to help you sell
your product and
protect your assets.

This chapter does not contain legal advice, but provides you with general guidelines to consider when choosing a legal structure. It is difficult to give specific advice because every situation is unique. There is no right or wrong choice. You need to understand each legal structure then pick the one that best meets your needs.

During this process, consider yourself an architect, designing the future of your enterprise. One of the greatest modern architects, Frank Lloyd Wright, had a motto he carried into every design meeting he attended: "Form follows function."

You have figured out what you want to create and how it will be used (function); now you will design a legal structure to fit your goals (form). Build your business structure (i.e., contracts, licenses, and insurance) with your intent in mind; it will enhance and support your goals.

Your legal structure will affect your ability to raise funds, sell stock, obtain loans, attract employees, and sell your product. You should discuss your plans with an attorney and your accountant before making a final decision. So read, learn, ask for help, and decide.

TO DO

1. **Familiarize yourself with the various types of legal structures.**

   Review the different types of legal structures, and become familiar with each one. This will relieve some of the anxiety associated with making legal decisions. A description (with advantages and disadvantages) of the different types of legal structures follows.

   Regulations affecting each of the different structures may change, but the basic principles behind them will not. It is a good idea to obtain the latest information by visiting your local Small Business Development Center, asking a lawyer for help, or searching the Internet for specific information.

   ### Sole Proprietorship

   A sole proprietorship is the easiest form of legal structure. Once you start your business, you are a sole proprietor. In essence, you and your business are the same structure. Strongly consider staying a sole proprietorship if you have a limited amount of financial exposure and liability and will be managing your business yourself. Financial exposure means that there is a high likelihood that someone can sue you for a monetary reward.

In other words, a sole proprietorship is a good business structure if you will not have high debt and will not have a high likelihood of being sued by anyone (e.g., if your product harms them). "Sole" means only one owner. As the sole owner of all the company's assets, you are entitled to all the profits, but you must also bear all liabilities and losses. This means that if you are sued, your personal property (e.g., house, car, or savings) is at risk.

There is no need to file any legal paperwork with the federal or state government to become a sole proprietor. However, you may have to submit a fictitious business name registration with your local government (and some state governments). Reporting taxes is also easy. You simply complete a Schedule C and attach it to your tax return.

N O T E

Use other creators' experience to your advantage by asking them for help and listening to their advice.

Advantages

- **Minimal legal paperwork.** Sole proprietorships are simple to start. Depending on the state, the most you will have to do is register a fictitious name filing with the county clerk and obtain the necessary tax filings. There is no need to file a statement with the federal government.

- **Simpler taxes.** No separate income tax returns are necessary for a sole proprietorship. You deduct all business expenses, and report your income or loss on Schedule C of your 1040 tax form.

- **Management freedom.** You are in charge!

- **Low investor risk.** Investors in your business are making a personal loan to you. It is comparable to making a loan to a friend. Investor risk is low because your personal assets (e.g., your home, car, or future income) are not separated from the loan. This may make it easier for you to obtain loans for your business.

Disadvantages

- **High liability risk.** Creditors and investors can go after your personal property, bank accounts, cars, and other assets.

- **Increased risk of mixing personal and business finances.** Personal finances can easily be mixed in with business finances. Keep the two separate. You might open a different bank account for your business and/or maintain accurate records of all your business income and expenditures.
- **Fewer tax benefits.** Sole proprietors can't write off many of the expenses on their tax returns that corporations can. Once you make money as a sole proprietor, it is income and you have to pay tax on it. A corporation is a separate structure for income tax purposes. As a shareholder, you don't pay tax on money earned by the corporation until you are paid. If you wanted to buy some new equipment, as a sole proprietor you would have to buy it from income that you already paid taxes on. A corporation can buy the equipment before paying taxable wages to its employees. A corporation can also pay for 100 percent of an employee's health insurance and take it as a business deduction while a sole proprietor (at this time) *may* be able to deduct 60 percent of his or her health insurance costs. (Contact your accountant or visit www.irs.gov for the latest regulations
- **Greater difficulty selling your business.** A sole proprietorship usually exists because of the reputation and skills of its owner. If the owner decides to terminate the business, its most valuable asset (its owner) usually does not transfer; this makes it difficult to sell a sole proprietorship.
- **Limited ability to raise capital.** A sole proprietor can't sell stock to raise funds for his or her business.

Partnership

A partnership is a legal structure that is easy to establish. You should consider forming a partnership if two or more individuals are acting as co-owners and you have limited liability exposure. There is no need to file any paperwork with the federal or state government, and taxes are reported with each partner's personal income tax statement. A partnership can be created by formal agreement, an oral agreement, or "implied through actions."

Sharing management control can be an enormous benefit or a serious detriment to your business. Make sure both partners are committed to the business. Partnerships are all about clearly defining the business and each person's role in it. Clearly state in writing what strengths and weaknesses each partner brings to the business, their passion for the business, and both person's roles in the business.

There is no test to determine whether you and your partner are compatible. You have to form the relationship and trust that you will be there for each other. Like a marriage, a partnership can turn into a catastrophe if goals diverge. The best thing to do is to agree to always tell each other the truth, listen to the other partner, and put everything in writing (including your personal goals). That way if conflicts arise, both of you will be ready to handle them!

Most of my clients only form partnerships if they created their business idea with another person or if they are weak at a certain business skill. If you can leverage the skills of both partners, you will create a great success. For example, if you love creating but hate selling, it might be a good idea to partner with someone who believes in your product and loves sales (and collecting money from vendors after the sale).

Advantages

- **Limited investor risk.** In a partnership, each partner is liable for any losses or other company liabilities. As opposed to a sole proprietorship, you can limit the financial risk of investors by creating a special kind of partnership called a "limited partnership." If you create a Limited Partnership Agreement, it will legally limit the liability of investors to the extent of their capital contribution. In other words, the amount each investor puts into the venture is all he or she can lose (rather than all their personal assets!). This option provides people an opportunity to invest in your company while limiting their risk.
- **Simple legal forms.** The process is a little more difficult than a sole proprietorship but still quite simple. A partnership must secure a Federal Employee Identification Number from the IRS using Form SS-4. Then you must file Form 1065 each year with your tax return, and send a Schedule K-1 to each business partner. But unlike a corporation, there is no requirement to have board meetings or to keep minutes.
- **Simple taxes.** Partnership taxes are easy. Each partner reports his or her share of the partnership's profit or loss on his or her individual tax returns.

N O T E

You must file federal self-employment taxes if you choose to form a partnership. Call the IRS at 800-829-1040 or visit their Web site www.irs.gov for more information.

Disadvantages

- **Being bound by acts of other partner.** A partnership can be thought of as a legal marriage. You are fiscally responsible for each other's actions and liabilities in the business.
- **High liability risk.** Just like sole proprietorships, general partnerships carry unlimited liability. Since you are running the business, you automatically are a general partner (unlike investors who could be limited partners) and, therefore, personally liable for all debt—including any incurred by your partner. If your partner skips town, you are liable.
- **No income splitting and no tax-free fringe benefits.** A partnership can't write off some of the fringe benefits (such as health benefits) that a corporation can.

Limited Liability Company

Limited Liability Companies (LLCs) are a slightly more complicated form of business than a partnership. The primary benefit of an LLC is that it protects the owners from personal liability for business debts and claims. People cannot come after your personal assets for business debts or court judgments against the business. LLCs can range in size from one person to an unlimited number of owners. I suggest that my clients consider forming an LLC if they are a sole proprietor or a partnership and require a limitation of personal liability.

Currently, if a small business decides to protect themselves from liability, most owners favor LLCs over S corporations (a type of corporation that protects personal assets) because of their simplicity. Like partnerships, LLC owners report the profits (or losses) they receive on their individual income tax returns. But unlike S corporations, there can be an unlimited number of owners, and a single person can form an LLC except in two states, the District of Columbia and Massachusetts. It is expected that these two states will change their laws soon.

Legally, LLC owners are known as "members." Members can manage the organization informally unless they decide to hire a management team. A member may be an individual or a separate legal structure, such as a partnership or corporation. Members invest in the LLC and receive a percentage ownership interest in return and a percentage of voting rights.

Unlike a corporation, an LLC allows its members to decide what share of the LLC profits and losses each member will receive. Instead of being restricted to dividing up profits proportionate to the members' capital contributions, you may split up LLC profits and losses any way you wish (just like a partnership).

Advantages

- **Limited liability.** All members are limited in their exposure to lawsuits filing for company assets. No one can go after a member's personal assets. However, this does increase investor risk because they no longer can come after your personal assets. So it is an advantage to you but a disadvantage to your investors.
- **Raising funds.** LLCs do allow for the sale of multiple classes of stock (voting and nonvoting), but it is complicated. The issuance of stock can help you raise funds for your business.
- **Simple taxes.** Owners report all income and losses on their own individual tax forms.
- **Profit sharing.** Members of an LLC can decide how to distribute profits rather than relying upon who owns shares in the business.

Disadvantages

- **Increased legal paperwork.** Owners have to file Articles of Organization with the Secretary of State. Most states have a fill-in-the-blank form that takes just a few minutes to prepare and usually can be obtained on the Internet (at your state's home page). It is recommended that you also execute an Operating Agreement that defines the relationship between your company and its members.
- **Poor tax treatment on fringe benefits.** Compared to corporations, LLCs are not able to write off as many benefits.
- **Limited ability to transfer stock.** The transfer of stock is a disadvantage because of the paperwork involved. As compared to a corporation, there are tight restrictions on stock transfers. You can research these issues online at www.nolo.com. Just conduct a search on Limited Liability Company.

Corporation

A corporation is the most complicated form of business. Besides developing Articles of Incorporation (legal explanation of the business), the owners have to file company paperwork including an annual report and separate tax forms with the federal and state governments. Strongly consider forming a corporation if you have a hot product, are going to hire over ten employees (you can offer them before-tax benefits), and expect to grow substantially.

It is also a good idea to form a corporation if you want to issue stock or stock options to employees who are not owners of the business. You may also consider forming a corporation if your business is so profitable that you can save tax dollars by keeping profits in the corporation rather than paying them out.

A corporation is considered a distinct legal structure separate from any of the people who own, control, manage, or operate it. The law views a corporation as a legal "person." A corporation enters into contracts, incurs debts, and pays taxes separately from its owners.

A corporation is the most difficult type of business to form and maintain but has numerous advantages when it comes to raising money and paying taxes. For instance, it can issue stock to reward loyal employees or to raise money from the public, and it can use its profits to pay for health benefits, while other legal structures cannot.

Advantages

- **No personal liability risk.** A corporation is separate and distinct from its owners. As a separate entity, it can acquire, hold, and convey property, sue and be sued, and act in its own name. Creditors cannot look outside the corporation for settlement of debt.
- **Credibility.** When you incorporate your business, you can put "Inc." after your business's name. This suggests to your customers and suppliers that you are a large and stable structure. Some businesses will only do business with corporations because of liability issues.
- **Financial flexibility.** Corporations can issue voting and nonvoting stock to raise money or reward employees. They can also use this stock to buy other businesses.
- **Employee satisfaction.** Corporations can purchase employee health benefits and life insurance policies with pretax dollars (and at discounted rates), which saves their employees money.

Disadvantages

- **Loss of ownership due to centralized management.** Your decision-making ability is diminished with a corporation. The corporation's rights come from its Articles of Incorporation (which explain the business) and its bylaws (which explain how the corporation will conduct business, such as electing officials and making decisions). If you do not have a majority of voting stock, you could actually lose control of your business.
- **Complicated legal issues.** Corporations are expensive to maintain. Your legal fees will increase substantially. For example, in addition to an annual report, a corporation has to file incorporation papers and bylaws.
- **Complicated taxes.** The biggest disadvantage is double taxation. The corporation pays taxes on its profits. It then distributes these profits to individuals in the form of dividends or pay. Then each individual pays individual income taxes on the money they received from the corporation. In essence, you are paying the government twice.

S Corporation

S corporations are corporations and carry all the requirements and protections granted to corporations. An S corporation is the same as a regular corporation except when it comes to taxes. An S corporation does not pay taxes because it is able to pass income (and losses) through to its shareholders. The shareholders then pay their individual tax on the amount they received from the S corporation.

There is a lot of information available on what (IRS Form 2553) the shareholders of an S corporation must file to be exempt from paying taxes. Search the Internet or go to the library for more information.

S corporations are also similar to LLCs in that they provide owners with liability protection, and taxes can be passed through to individual shareholders. However, S corporations are much more restrictive than LLCs. In fact, LLCs were formed to help small business owners obtain the same liability protection as corporations but without the restrictions of an S corporation.

Recommendations from experts indicate that as a small business owner, it is preferable to form an LLC rather than an S corporation. Investigate this yourself and determine which is the best solution for your unique situation.

Advantages

Review the advantages of a corporation and an LLC to obtain an overview of the advantages of an S corporation. The main difference between an LLC and an S corporation is that it is easier to sell stock in an S corporation than in an LLC. The pass through of taxes to individual shareholders is the main advantages of an S corporation over a regular corporation.

Disadvantages

The same disadvantages that apply for a corporation apply to an S corporation. In particular, the disadvantages to a small business owner are:

- **Number of shareholders.** Sole proprietors cannot create an S corporation. Two or more individuals (limited to thirty-five shareholders and naturalized U.S. citizens) have to form an S corporation.
- **Compensation.** Owners are compensated by the proportion of stock they own, not by a split the company determines.
- **High investor risk.** Investors cannot go after the shareholders' personal assets if the business fails to pay its liabilities. In a partnership, investors can go after the owners' personal assets. This may make it harder or more expensive to find investors.

2. **In your Product Notebook, label the top of a page "Legal Structure" and beneath it develop a list of pros and cons for each type of legal structure.**

Your list of pros and cons will help you choose a legal structure that makes the best sense for you, your investors, and your company. There is no right or wrong choice; it really depends on your situation. Reflect on each legal structure and imagine how it will help your business grow. Highlight how each form of business will affect you, your goals, and your investors.

For many small businesses, the best initial choice is either a sole proprietorship or, if more than one owner is involved, a partnership. Either of these structures makes especially good sense in a business where personal liability isn't a big worry. An example is a small service business in which you are unlikely to be sued and for which you won't be borrowing much money. If liability risk is high, most of my clients seem to choose to become a LLC.

The following questions can help you develop your list:

- Is there going to be more than one owner? If so, you cannot choose to be a sole proprietor.
- Is there a significant possibility for legal action against your business? If so, an LLC may be your best choice because it protects your personal assets.
- Do you have the time to ensure that you are meeting all governmental regulations? For instance, an S corporation requires you to produce corporate minutes and have an annual corporation meeting. A sole proprietorship does not require any documentation.
- Do you want to relinquish total control? If not, either keep your company a sole proprietorship or make sure that over 50 percent of the company's ownership is in your name. The greater percentage of the company you own, the better.

N O T E

Sole proprietors can protect themselves from injury by obtaining the proper insurance (see To Do number 6).

3. **Develop a list of any liabilities that you think may harm you or your business.**
Take the time to really consider any liabilities your business may encounter in the future. This is a list of worries you have about how your product could harm other people (and for which they would sue you for damages). For instance, are there any small pieces on which a baby could choke? Are you providing advice that will affect a business's performance?

If you do have substantial financial exposure, it would be beneficial for you to choose a legal structure that protects your personal assets, such as an LLC.

4. **In your Product Notebook write down the legal structure that best fits with your needs.**
Specifically state why you believe this is the best legal structure for your business. To make their decision stand out, my clients often draw a big box around the legal structure they have chosen.

Keep in mind that your initial choice of business structure doesn't have to be a permanent one. Most of my clients grow into a legal structure. You can start out as sole proprietorship or partnership and later, as your business grows or the risks of personal liability increase, you can convert your business to an LLC or a corporation.

5. **Investigate the different state regulations that affect your top choice.**

Different states treat businesses differently. There may be specific business taxes, resale licenses, or other issues particular to your state. Call your state's tax department or clerk's office and ask them to fax you details on your top legal choice.

This is a good time to obtain any appropriate legal paperwork that you need to make your business legal. You can obtain the necessary paperwork from your state office, visiting your local SBDC, searching the Internet, or reading a small-business legal guide. A guide some of my clients recommend is the *Legal Guide for Starting and Growing a Small Business* by Fred S. Steingold.

6. **Determine the proper insurance you need to protect you and your business.**

The best way to discover what insurance you need is to talk to a small business insurance broker or someone at a Small Business Development Center. You can find either of these by looking in your local yellow pages directory. Share your list of liabilities with your contact, and ask him or her about other liabilities associated with your top choice and the costs to insure against such liabilities. There may be a blanket policy that can cover both your business and your personal liability, especially if you choose to be a sole proprietor.

The most prominent types of insurance include:

- **General liability.** This insurance protects you or your business from financial loss due to lawsuits that claim bodily injury or property damage. This is known as "fall-down insurance."
- **Product liability.** This insurance protects you from any liabilities associated with the use of your product. It covers any financial losses you may incur if your product harms anyone.
- **Professional liability.** If you are offering professional advice, this insurance protects you if you are sued from any outcome of that advice.
- **Property and fire insurance.** This insurance protects your inventory against damage or loss caused by fire, windstorm, theft, vandalism, explosion, or riot. Your fulfillment house and manufacturer probably have this type of insurance, but if you are storing your product yourself, you will need it.
- **Medical insurance.** This is not required by law, but do not go into business without it. If you get sick, who is going to run your business?

7. **Choose an insurance agent.**

An insurance agent will help you choose the proper insurance and provide you with the associated costs. Choose an agent by evaluating the services they offer, their personality, cost, customer service, and whether they were referred by someone you trust.

8. **Review your choice of legal structure and your insurance coverage with an attorney and an accountant.**

As a sole proprietor or partnership you do not have to work with these professionals. However, it is a great idea to review your choice with them to ensure that you have thought of everything. They will have ideas on how to make your business more efficient and will be able to point out any hidden liabilities. You do not want to expose yourself to any surprise liabilities.

Your local Small Business Development Center and other small business owners are good sources for referrals. Choose professionals who specialize in small business, provide great customer service, charge reasonable prices, and have great referrals.

Present these professionals with your criteria for making your decision, and ask them whether you have missed anything. Keep moving forward.

Complete To Do number 9 only after you have made a final decision to go into business and sell your product or service.

9. **Make your business legal by completing any required paperwork.**

After making a decision on the legal structure for your business, try to prepare any of the required legal paperwork yourself. This process saves you money since experts bill by the hour.

If you complete the paperwork, your attorney can review your goals, help you resolve any complicated issues, and finalize all the required legal paperwork. By completing your paperwork yourself, you also gain a better understanding of situations that can affect your business.

There are wonderful, easy-to-understand books in the library and in bookstores that describe the forms required to establish your business legally, so use them. If you have decided to become a type of corporation, file the appropriate legal paperwork before you start selling your product.

No matter what type of business structure you choose, always:

- Obtain a Federal EIN (Employer Identification Number) by calling 800-829-1040, or have your attorney fill out form SS-4 and send it to the IRS. This number identifies your business with the IRS and is your business tax number. If you are a sole proprietor, you can use your Social Security Number.
- Register with your city or state tax collection office. Registration rates vary by location.
- Open a separate bank account for your business. This will keep your personal and business finances separate and make it much easier for you at tax time.

LEGAL PAPERWORK HINTS

Sole Proprietor

If you choose to become a sole proprietor, file a fictitious business name statement with your local government. Since you are basically doing business under an assumed name, the registration helps track the rightful owner of your business. The fictitious business name registration is also known as "doing business as" (dba).

Consider the following registration information:

- Your local bank will probably have information on obtaining a dba.
- Registration procedures vary by state, but the most common procedure is to register with the county clerk or the city tax collector's office and pay a registration fee. Fees are generally between $10 and $100.
- Some states require that you place an ad in the newspaper to declare you are doing business under your new name.

Partnership

Always develop a written agreement outlining the terms and conditions of your partnership. You should have a lawyer review any agreements you and your partner develop. Be sure your agreement includes the following:

- Sharing profits. Define the distribution of profits (or losses).
- Responsibility. Define each partner's specific daily and company responsibilities.
- Dissolving the partnership. What happens if a partner dies or a partner wants to leave the business? Who has the right to purchase the departed partner's stock? How will the purchase price be established? What is the payment method?
- Selling the business. Always include language pertaining to the sale of either partner's share of the business. You do not want to be in a situation where you are forced to work with a new individual not chosen by you because your partner sold his or her share to someone else. Ideally, you will have first right to buy the stock or approve the sale of the other partner's share.
- Capital contributions and ownership percentages. Specifically state how much each partner will contribute to the partnership and how much of the partnership each partner will own. Ownership of a partnership does not have to be 50–50.
- Subsequent investments. Always include details on how subsequent investments in the partnership will be made. Subsequent investments can help expand the business or possibly continue operations. If one partner contributes more money later, does he or she increase their ownership share of the business?
- Voting rights. Explain in writing the formal process for making decisions. This should be a documented process so it can help settle any disputes and should include the allocation of each partner's voting rights.
- Signature authority. Define who has signing authority for bank accounts and for orders. Also specify the dollar amount a partner can spend without oral and/or written permission from the other partner(s). You may not mind if your partner buys some stationery, but you may get upset if he or she purchases a new car using the company's money.

N O T E

No matter what legal structure you choose, a lawyer should review any agreements that are developed for your business.

Corporations

Make sure you define all the areas described in the partnership area above, and also do the following:

- Obtain a copy of your state's standard incorporation and bylaw documents and fill them in to the best of your ability.

- Write down what you believe the agreement between you and your investors should be. For example, I am willing to give up 20 percent of my company to bring in outside investors. Do not worry about dollar amounts yet.

- Determine how the company's stock will be split among the owners. Remember, stock is equal to voting privileges. Make sure you own a majority share of the voting stock. You do not want to give up control of a company you worked hard to develop! Have your lawyer specifically explain the voting rights for each shareholder.

Money Sources

This chapter lays the groundwork for an investor
meeting you will hold later. You will develop a list of great investors
for your business. Then you will develop answers to the
questions investors most typically ask. Preparation is the key to
a successful presentation.

STEP 27

INVESTOR BRAINSTORMING

INTRODUCTION

You have come a long way. You have developed your product, found a manufacturer, located outlets to sell your product, and made your business legal. Now is the time to think about how to raise the funds necessary for you to produce, distribute, and promote your product. It's time to find investors. Not meet with them, just find them. (Step 33, Investor Meeting, explains how to present your idea to investors.)

An investor is defined as any person, institution, or organization that you team with to make your idea a reality. Investors provide you with the capital and/or knowledge (contacts and technical expertise) you need to get your product off the ground. This step sets you on your way to raising the money you need by helping you develop a list of possible investors for your business.

THUMBS UP

List and pursue any ideas that your friends, family, or coworkers suggest. You never know who will turn out to be an investor.

TO DO

1. **Label a page in your Product Notebook "Potential Investors."**
Write down any investor ideas you develop. Make sure you include their contact information such as e-mail, phone, and fax number.

2. **Brainstorm on potential investors.**
List as many potential investors in your Product Notebook as you can. Look through your past research for names of any potential investors. You can also

G O A L

*To develop alter-
native financing
ideas for your
business.*

invite some friends over for a brainstorming party. That way you involve other people in your search.

When brainstorming, focus on your product's benefits and go wild. Would a store owner invest in your product? Did the articles that you read include any potential investor names? Would someone in the local government like to see your product developed (and therefore provide you with a loan)? When an investor decides to invest in your business, they often tell other investors about it. It may take just one investor who believes in you and your product to obtain the money you need. Do not be intimidated by the thought of meeting an investor—include everyone on your list. Some ideas to help you create your investor list include:

Personal Funds

You can invest in your own business. Using personal funds is a good way to finance your product because you remain in charge and you get to keep all the profits. However, you also run the risk of losing all your money and accruing a large amount of debt. Potential personal fund sources include:

- Your savings, credit card cash advances, second mortgages on your home, bank loans, or obtaining a loan from the economic development office of your city.
- Loans backed by collateral borrowed from people close to you. For instance, if your parents or a friend has two cars, you might be able to use one as collateral. Your parents can cosign and serve as a guarantor on a loan to help you obtain the funds you need.

Working Partners

Are there any suppliers, distributors, or other organizations that would benefit from investing in your business? If you are opening a coffee shop, would the supplier of your coffee, cups, or machines be interested in giving you a low-interest loan? Or would a supplier of non-coffee items (such as juice) provide you with funds if you put their name on your door (e.g., "Sunny Juice available inside")? Possible working partners include:

- Local firms wanting a special promotion
- Other inventors with products they could sell at your location or with your product

- Store owners that will make money from your product
- Suppliers of goods that you are going to sell

Private Investors

These potential investors are people with money to invest. They usually want a good return on their investments because a startup company is a high risk. Potential sources include:

- Wealthy individuals, venture capitalists (people who invest money for a stake in your business), coworkers, or even enthusiastic customers of stores where your product will be sold
- Local investment or entrepreneurial clubs
- Investor names you find in articles
- Store owners

✳ A DOG'S LIFE

Ben and I worked together to develop a line of greeting cards featuring his dog, Bernie. Ben used his home computer to make prototype cards and sold some to local gift stores. At a trade show, he picked up more orders. So many orders, in fact, that the time had come for him to raise money so he could get a large quantity of cards printed professionally.

What did he do? He listed everyone he knew who might be interested in helping him launch his business. About the same time, Bernie became ill. It was in the vet's waiting room that an idea popped into Ben's head.

Ben decided to donate one percent of his profits to the local animal shelter. After Bernie's visit, Ben handed his vet one of his unique greeting cards and told him about his business. Instead of just asking for money, Ben mentioned that he already had sales and that a percentage of profits would benefit lost dogs and cats.

Ben's passion (and the cards' designs) touched the vet. He not only invested in the company, but also told others about Ben's business and agreed to sell the cards at his clinic. By focusing on benefits and asking for help, Ben raised the money he needed to develop his business.

Banks

Banks are not usually the best source for startup capital. Their loan requirements do not allow them to invest in businesses that are less than two years old. However, you can obtain a credit card from a bank and use the cash withdrawal option to obtain some funds. Warning: These carry very high interest rates! But if you don't ask for an investment loan, a bank will never lend you money. Here are some things to keep in mind:

- Relationships are a key to conducting your business. Banks and credit unions can be good sources of loans if you have an existing business. So meet with possible lenders now and say that you may be approaching them in the future.

- Before making a loan, banks usually like to see two to three years of financial records and look at the five Cs. (1) Character. You must have a good credit history; (2) Capability. Do you have the skills necessary to run your business? Does your product reach a wide audience? A great business plan helps you prove your capability; (3) Collateral. You will need something (a home or securities) to ensure repayment of the loan; (4) Capital. You must also put some money into the business yourself. Banks usually require 30 to 35 percent investment in the company be from you. Do you have cash reserves or other assets that can be made available in case of an economic downturn?; (5) Condition. What is the possibility of your business growing? How does your gross profit compare to other companies in your industry? Will you have the cash flow to pay back the debt?

Other Investment Resources

Your local government or a local bank may offer many programs that can help you obtain funds for starting your business. This is especially true if you are locating your business in a low-income neighborhood that needs economic assistance or if you are hiring or training people with special needs (e.g., welfare to work, handicapped, or low income) to help in your business. The criteria for these loans are specific to your local community, so ask and find out what is available to you. For example:

- Call your local economic development office. Your local government may provide a loan guarantee program that helps reduce a bank's risk of loaning money to you. This reduction in risk provides an incentive for banks to loan you money because they are guaranteed a good portion of their loan back.

- Investigate to see whether there are any special programs for minorities or women. There may be economic development dollars available from your local government, especially if you are a woman or a minority person starting a business. These programs still charge you interest but have fewer restrictions placed on them.

- Explore special government commissions and foundations. Depending on your product, there may be additional government money available that can be used to develop your idea. This is especially true if your product improves the environment or is an advanced technology. Check at the local, state, and federal levels. For example, the Department of Energy provides money for the development of energy-related inventions. You can contact them at the National Institute of Standards and Technology, Building 411, Room A115, Gaithersburg, Maryland 20899.

3. **Expand your investor list by searching the Internet.**

Search on the Internet to locate potential investors, loan programs, or grants that may help you make your product a reality. Use specific words during your search (e.g., "financing board games"). Be creative.

You may even find a web site where an investor states his criteria for investing in a business. Most investors and companies listed on the Internet are usually interested in high-technology companies or in products that benefit the community. In other words, they want to hear your 30-second commercial. Search—you never know what you will find.

4. **Think of people who could help you market your business by associating their name or expertise with your product.**

A person can also invest his or her name or knowledge to help you market your business. Concentrate on people that really believe in the benefit you are providing. If you are helping a cause they believe in, people are more likely to help you. For instance, if your product makes it easier for women to obtain a breast exam for cancer, there are many celebrities who may help you. Don't forget to include the names of any endorsers you listed in Step 8, Information Center.

The instant recognition a person brings with them can be worth a lot of money in sales. For example, Planet Hollywood gave movie stars ownership shares in the company in exchange for use of their names in company advertisements. Being associated with the stars gave Planet Hollywood a lot of free publicity and other investment money.

Your endorser does not have to be a star. Is there a local celebrity who would say wonderful things about your product or write something special? Anything helps. Your local doctor, dentist, or an association might endorse your product. These people are not celebrities but have the confidence of a great number of people. Make sure you receive written permission before using anyone's name; you do not want to open yourself up to any lawsuits.

If you ask someone to associate themselves with your product, you will probably have to reward them in some way. You can agree to give them a certain percentage of profits or provide a certain percentage of profits to one of their favorite charities. You can even create a celebrity. For instance, a coffee shop in my neighborhood takes pictures of their customers, blows them up, and puts funny captions (and their names) under them. These pictures act as endorsements and make local celebrities out of the coffee shop customers.

STEP 28

INVESTOR

QUESTIONS

INTRODUCTION

This step is all about preparation for your investor meeting (Step 33). You will familiarize yourself with and prepare answers to the basic questions people have when they invest in a business. When you meet with investors, your answers will knock their socks off, they won't be able to say "no," and you will build solid investor relationships.

Feel free to include others in developing answers to the questions in this step. But remember, this is your business—so any answers must resonate with you. Be true to yourself and your business will prosper.

Your answers to these preparatory questions will continue to evolve as you complete your financial analysis (Step 30) and your business action plan (Step 31). The key is to start.

By developing your answers to these typical questions now, you will always have them in the back of your mind as you progress with your business. You will be thinking of your investors as you finalize your packaging, as you contact stores, and as you tell people about your business. And what better way to develop your business than by keeping in mind why people would invest in your business?

THUMBS UP

Take time to prepare answers to questions before they are raised; it puts you in control of your business.

*To become familiar
with questions
investors may ask.*

1. **Define why you want to bring in investors.**

Bringing in investors is a personal decision. Most of my clients actually do not need investors but feel like they should have them because everyone says so. If you grow your business with smart enthusiasm, you may avoid the need for investors.

Your reasons for talking to investors may change as you develop your financial analysis and business action plan. However you need to start somewhere, so take the time now to ask yourself, "Why do I want to bring in investors?"

Do you need to expand your business quickly and therefore need investors now? Do you need help manufacturing your product? Do you need money to develop marketing materials? Do you not want to risk all of your retirement money?

During this process you may find out that you do not need investors. Maybe you have enough money (if you squeeze your personal spending) to get your business started. Giving up a portion of your business to an investor is a tough decision. Be clear about why you want to do it. Write your answer in your Product Notebook.

*Knowledge of
what investors are
looking for in a
business and in
a business owner.*

2. **Create a list in your Product Notebook of your top ten potential investors.**

Look over the list of investors you created in Step 27, Investor Brainstorming, and choose your top ten. Even if you have decided not to bring in investors, create your top ten list so it's handy if you need it later.

Your list is based on your gut feeling, possible investor interest, the investors' access to capital, and your relationship to each investor. You are starting with the top ten prospects so you can focus your efforts and treat each potential investor with personal attention. Do not forget to include personal investors who will contribute their name or expertise rather than money.

3. **Create a list of potential customers for your business.**

The first question investors always ask is: "Will this product sell?" Answer this question before you meet with investors by generating customers for your product right now. After completing previous steps in this book, you probably have preorders from individuals, stores, or distributors. Or you may have letters from people who can't wait for your product to become available. List these people and stores. This will build your investors' confidence.

Investors love a business that has a proven product and needs capital for expansion. Who knows, maybe one of those enthusiastic customers will become an investor. If you never ask a person to invest, they never will.

4. **Develop answers to the typical investor questions listed below.**

Having answers to typical questions prepared or addressed in your materials will make you appear organized and confident. Investors will believe that you can run a successful business. Even if investors do not ask these questions aloud, they are probably wondering about them. Develop a solid explanation for each question so you can turn any skepticism into enthusiasm for your product.

You won't meet with any investors until after you develop your financial analysis (Step 30) and your business action plan (Step 31). These items will provide additional information for some of the following questions. Expand on your answers as you continue in this book. You are selling yourself and your business. Answer the following personal and business questions to the best of your ability:

Personal Questions
- What is your intent for starting this business?
- Are you trustworthy? Have you paid off other loans or kept your promises?
- Are you putting up any of your own money? If so, how much?
- Do you have experience marketing this type of product?
- Does your family support you? What dependents do you have and how will you support them?

Product Questions
- What are the product's social, emotional, or spiritual values?
- Who is the target audience for your product? Can you or a third party (a distributor) reach the audience easily?
- Is your product unique with growth potential?

You are in charge. Ask for help, but make decisions based on your research, intent, and gut feeling.

- Is your product better than the competitions'?
- Do you have a business action plan that demonstrates your knowledge of the industry, the competition, and how to market your product?

Financial Questions

- How much money are you asking for?
- What will the money be used for?
- What is the return on the investment? How long will it take?
- Will your business make money? What proof can you provide?
- What is your credit history? Do you pay your financial obligations on time?

Participation Questions

- Is there a team that believes in your product and will be able to deliver it to the market, or is this a solo venture? If it's solo, will you have to hire people?
- Can I help design or market the product?
- What business areas can I participate in?

Control Questions

- These will partially depend on the entity you choose in Step 26, Legal Structure.
- How much control are you willing to give up?
- How much control will I have during production and after the product reaches the market?

TWELVE

Keeping It Straight

Maintaining the financial strength of your business will keep your stress level low and your sanity level high. This chapter helps you develop a simple system for tracking all of your payments, expenditures, and income. You will save time preparing taxes and making financial decisions. This chapter also discusses financial analysis steps you can take to keep your business strong.

RECORD KEEPING

INTRODUCTION

Don't freak out when you think about record keeping. Let go of any negative thoughts you are harboring about record keeping; "I hate numbers," "I do not have any money to spend," "I hate organizing," "There are more important things to do." This step provides you with an easy solution that has worked wonderfully for my clients.

I like to think of record keeping as keeping track of the "ins" and "outs" of your business. The "ins" are primarily your sales, and the "outs" are any expenses you incur. By tracking these items, you can easily calculate your revenue, costs, and profits. Develop it now so you can stop worrying about finances and get on with selling your product.

Record keeping is one of the most important logistical aspects of selling your own product. Financial records help you discern problems and make decisions that will help your business grow. If you do not keep track of your money, it can easily fly out the door.

Keeping your customers happy and tracking their shipments is important, but if you fail to collect payment or pay your taxes, you could be out of business. Great record keeping also helps you analyze the health of your business.

In order for any record keeping system to work, it must become part of your daily life. You know your business and your personal quirks ("I can only look at numbers in the late afternoon"). So develop a system that works for you by integrating the needs of your business and your personality into it.

THUMBS UP

Keep your financial systems simple. Otherwise you won't use them!

To develop a simple process that will keep track of your financial responsibilities.

OUTCOME

Respect for the importance of basic financial tracking procedures.

TO DO

1. **Label a page in your Product Notebook "Record Keeping."**

This page will become a quick reference guide to your financial records. Write down any accounts you open for your business or any major decisions you make that will affect your record keeping process.

2. **Open a separate bank account for your business.**

You must keep your business and personal finances separate. The best way to accomplish this is to open a bank account under the name of your business and conduct all business financial transactions through that account. If you are a sole proprietor, this bank account does not need to be in the name of

❄ PERSONAL NUMBERS

A client of mine, Brian, despised finances. In fact, he never balanced his checkbook and always had to check with his bank to see if he had enough money in his account to pay his bills. When we arrived at this stage in developing his business, Brian froze.

He was sure there was no way that he could keep track of the money flowing in and out of his business. He was afraid that a full-time accountant would exhaust any money he made. I told him to relax. All he really needed to do was develop a simple system and keep to it.

Brian breathed a sigh of relief and followed the steps in this chapter. He discovered that if he developed a system he liked, he would actually use it.

Not only did he develop a wonderful accounting system, but he was so excited by it that he developed a similar system for his personal finances. Brian no longer has to scramble at the end of each month. With the click of button, he can tell you where his business and his personal life stand financially. Instead of panicking over finances, he now says, "Numbers are my friends. At least when I have them under control."

your business. It can be a second personal bank account that you only use for business. For easy reference, record the name of the bank and your account number in your Product Notebook.

3. In your Product Notebook, report which accounting method you will use to record your cash flow.

Do not be intimidated by accounting terms; just try to learn how they affect your business. Cash flow, for example, is simply the movement of money in and out of your business over a certain period of time (a day, a week, or a month).

There are two methods for tracking your cash flow—cash basis and accrual basis accounting. Read the following descriptions, choose one for your business, and use that method to track your income and expenditures.

The two methods for tracking cash flow are:

- **Cash basis accounting.** In cash basis accounting, you keep your records and pay taxes based on the amount of actual cash that flows through your business. Income and expenses are counted in and charged to the period in which they are received or paid. You record any sales the day you are paid, and you record any expenses the day you pay them. This method is great for businesses that do not carry any inventory.
- **Accrual basis accounting.** In accrual basis accounting, you charge expenses and apply income to the period in which they originate (e.g., dates on invoices), regardless of whether or not you have received or paid the money. For example, if you make a sale and deliver your product in March, you will count the sale price as income in March, even if you receive payment in April. The accrual method is mandatory if you use inventory in your business.

When you choose a method, write it in your Product Notebook under record keeping and circle it. No matter which one you choose, follow it consistently. If you decide to change it later, you will have accurate records to start work from.

4. Create safe, easily accessible places to keep your receipts and financial documentation.

Most of my clients have a special place for receipts in their wallets, backpacks, or purses. Every night they transfer all receipts (cash and credit card), sales

Make financial record keeping part of your routine by picking a specific time each week that you will update your financial records.

records (income generated), and expense records to an expanding file folder. The file folder is separated by month and by category to make it easy to track expenses and income.

Deductible expenses are expenses that reduce the amount of tax you owe the government. Track every expense; you never know what you or your accountant will find to be deductible. Some deductible expenses you should track include:

- **Administrative expenses.** This includes telephone, Internet access, rent, and utilities; legal and accounting expenses; and dues and subscriptions for business publications. If you are working from home, consult with an accountant (or the IRS at 800-829-1040; it's free) to determine how much (if any) of your household expenses are deductible.

- **Travel expenses.** Travel expenses include hotels, gas, meals, and public transportation expenses you incur in running your business. Keep all your receipts, and write on the back of each what the expense was for. You also have to track all the mileage you put on your car for business reasons. To make this process painless, most of my clients keep a travel logbook in their car to record the name of the client, purpose of travel, beginning miles, and ending miles. The amount you can deduct is a formula generated by the federal government that changes each year. Check with the IRS at 800-829-1040 to determine the current mileage formula.

- **Entertainment expenses.** When deducting entertainment expenses, you must record who attended the event or dinner, what business was conducted, the name of the establishment, and the amount spent. Most of my clients write this information on the back of each receipt. Even though you cannot totally write off these expenses, keep track of them; they add up quickly.

- **Equipment purchases.** Keep all of your receipts for equipment used in your office. When you prepare your taxes, you can deduct these expenses from your income.

- **Supplies.** Supplies you purchase to run your business are deductible.

- **Shipping and mailing.** All expenses associated with mailing your product or promotional materials are legitimate expenses.

- **Printing.** Any expenses incurred in printing marketing materials, letters, or business cards are deductible expenses.

5. **Develop a simple method for tracking cash flow weekly.**

This method has to fit with the needs of your business and with your personality. Below is an easy system I developed to get my clients started. Feel free to modify it to meet your specific requirements. As discussed in Step 22, Customer Support, you can use software programs, such as QuickBooks or Microsoft Excel, to help track your income, expenses, sales, and deliveries. Your simple tracking system should include two items:

- A mechanism to track and record all your income, expenses, deposits, and expenditures. Many of my clients record their activities on Friday morning. It becomes a ritual and you feel like you forgot something if you don't do it. A sample chart for tracking payments and income is on page 312.
- The ability to summarize your records on a monthly basis. This is called tracking the cash flow (the ins and outs) of your business. It can be as simple as creating a chart where you log activities, just as you would in your checkbook. A sample cash flow chart is on page 313 and includes:

    a. Starting Cash: Cash at the beginning of the month.

    b. Total Cash in: Cash that came in during the month.

    c. Total Cash out: Cash that went out during the month.

    d. Ending Cash: How much you have left at the end of the month.

6. **If you decide to use the sample cash flow chart, modify it so the cash out and cash in categories match your business.**

Make sure your cash flow chart is useful by modifying it for your specific business. Put in the expense categories that you now have. Remember to update it as your business grows.

7. **Keep all business papers that affect your taxes for at least seven years.**

The IRS may conduct an audit (review) of your taxes and your business for up to seven years from the date you filed your taxes. Keep all your information in a safe place for at least that long. Information to keep includes insurance records, payroll records, income tax withholding records, Social Security and federal unemployment taxes, invoices, sales slips, canceled checks, cash receipts, credit card receipts, and cash register tapes.

N O T E

Whenever you or any of your employees pay for a business expense, always get a receipt. On the back of the receipt, write what the expense was for and who spent the money. This makes it easy to record and file the expense in your simple tracking system.

If you can't find an accountant to work with, consider taking a course at your local community college. These classes are inexpensive and are taught by wonderful teachers.

8. **Ask for help.**

Find a local teacher, an accountant, or a qualified financial analyst to review your financial procedures before you open your business. Listen and learn from them.

Ask your friends or other small business owners for recommendations. A local accounting teacher may look over your procedures for free. Review your financial tracking system with them and ask for suggestions to improve it. Find out whether or not you need a full-time bookkeeper, an outside accounting service, or a once-a-year accounting and tax-preparation service. Be diligent about following their recommendations; they will save you time and money.

Remember to thank everyone who helps you start your business. They are an important part of your success. Send these financial gurus a thank-you card or a free product after you launch your business.

SAMPLE DAILY RECORD KEEPING CHART

Date	Amount Paid Out	Amount Paid In	Purpose	Paid To	Check #/ Credit Card #	Balance

SAMPLE MONTHLY RECORD KEEPING CHART

Cash Flow Statement

Cash Flow Areas	Month 1	Month 2	Month 3	Month 4
Starting Cash				
Cash In				
1) Cash Sales				
2) Invoice Collections				
Total Cash In				
Cash Out				
1) Cash Purchases				
2) Marketing				
3) Production Costs				
4) Loans Paid				
Total Cash Out				
Ending Cash (Starting Cash + Cash In – Cash Out)				
Growth Divide ending cash for the month by the prior month's ending cash				

STEP 30

FINANCIAL ANALYSIS

INTRODUCTION

You have defined your record keeping procedures. This step provides you with simple tools that will help you easily communicate financial information about your business. Financial statements tell a story of what has happened to your business in the past, what is going on in the present, and what you expect to happen in the future.

This is a lot of work! You are going to create a lot of reports during this step. Most of my clients set aside two days a month to conduct their financial analysis. The first day they prepare all the required statements, and the second day they review their work.

Consider completing this step with a friend, especially the first time through. They do not have to be a financial expert; they just have to be someone to bounce ideas off of and who can provide encouragement. Of course, if they are a financial expert—congratulations!

The results achieved in this step are amazing (and worth all the work). You will establish a clear financial picture of where your business is now and where it is headed. In the future you will create these financial statements on a monthly basis to determine the health of your business. These statements are important; they help you create a budget for your business and minimize your exposure to financial risk.

If you have any trouble in this step, ask for help. There are many inexpensive workshops (at community colleges or Small Business Development Centers) that can provide you with guidance and knowledge.

THUMBS UP

Set aside a specific time to conduct a financial analysis. Make it part of your routine.

TO DO

1. **Label a page "Financial Position" in your Product Notebook.**

   Use this page to prepare your first financial position for your business. This will be included in your business action plan and shared with other people (including investors). This is a financial snapshot of your business. It answers the question: "Where is your business right now, and where is it headed?"

2. **Define the key items that will affect your financial calculations.**

   Several financial terms need to be defined so everyone starts with the same assumptions. It is helpful to let people know where you stand on items that affect your financial analysis. Underneath the Financial Position heading in your Product Notebook, define the following:

   - **Inflation trends.** Estimating inflation trends is an occupation in itself. I recommend that you do not include inflation in your first set of financial calculations. If you do not, record this decision. If you wish to include inflation, have an accountant help you develop the appropriate financial analysis.
   - **Retail price.** State the expected retail price for your product. This is the real sales price that you developed in Step 21, Price Estimate.
   - **Sales projections.** State how much of your product you expect to sell. State it per month for the first year. You have a lot of information you can use to determine your anticipated sales. Start with the initial sales projections you developed in Step 23, Fulfillment. Your other research, information acquired from experts, and marketing plans and your gut feeling will also help you develop your sales projections.

3. **Calculate your product development costs.**

   Every month you will review the costs associated with running your business. Since you are not officially open yet, it's a great idea to estimate your development costs now. This step provides a picture of how much it will cost you to bring your product to the market. Add the expenses you have incurred and the costs you expect to incur until you open your doors for business. Product development expenses include:

GOAL

To develop tools that can help you plan wisely.

OUTCOME

Your first financial analysis statement.

- Real-life example development (materials and labor), Step 12.
- Focus group, Step 14.
- Legal costs, Step 26.
- Accounting costs, Chapter 12.
- Investor meeting expenses, Step 33.
- Any other startup costs you incurred (e.g., consultant fees, equipment, or software).

4. **Estimate your monthly marketing costs.**

A good target is usually 10 to 15 percent of your expected gross (before tax) sales for the first year. Once a product becomes established, average marketing costs will probably be around 5 percent of yearly gross sales.

To calculate your monthly marketing costs, calculate your gross sales by multiplying your estimated total unit sales by your estimated price per unit (Step 21, Price Estimate). Then multiply your gross sales by the percentage of sales you want to spend on marketing (.15 if you choose 15 percent of gross sales). You are left with your yearly marketing costs. For monthly marketing costs, simply divide your yearly marketing costs by twelve (twelve months in a year).

5. **Define your monthly overhead expenses.**

Overhead expenses relate to items that are associated with the daily running of your business. These expenses are usually necessary to your business. However, you do have some control over them. In the future, you will be looking at these expenses with the intent of lowering them. For instance, you may be able to save money by negotiating with a new telephone company.

A sample of monthly overhead expenses include:

- **Wages and salaries.** What will you pay yourself and any staff you may hire?
- **Social Security and unemployment compensation.** If you pay anyone a salary, you also have to pay the Social Security and unemployment taxes required by law. You may want to hire people as independent contractors; then they are responsible for their own taxes and Social Security payments.
- **Office rental, supplies, and equipment.** What is your monthly rent? What equipment do you need to run your business?

- **Storage and shipping (Step 23, Fulfillment).** How much will it cost per month to store and ship your product?
- **Accounting, legal, and other professional fees.** How much will it cost to consult with these experts?
- **Insurance premiums (Step 26, Your Legal Structure).** How much is the monthly premium (if any) for your liability, property, and health insurance?

6. **To determine how much money you need to raise, calculate your total start-up costs.**

It's common practice to raise enough money to keep yourself in business for the first three months. This money gives you time to collect enough income to begin paying your monthly expenses out of the money you earn. Your startup costs are your total development costs (To Do number 3) plus other expenses for running your business.

This exercise also helps you describe how you will use money obtained from investors. You can show this to both your employees and potential investors. In the future, you can use this step to determine whether you need to raise any additional money for your business.

Calculate your total startup costs by adding the following expenses:

- Your development costs.
- Your total cost to manufacture your product's first run.
- Your monthly marketing expenses multiplied by three.
- Your monthly overhead expenses multiplied by three.
- The cost for any fees or business licenses.
- The cost for any office supplies.
- A contingency fund of approximately 10 percent of your manufacturing costs. This is money for emergency situations..

7. **On a monthly basis, review your cash flow statement (from Step 29, Record Keeping) to determine the growth of your business.**

Most of my clients review their cash flow statements on the last Friday of the month. By looking at a larger picture (trends), you can use this monthly review to measure the growth (or shrinkage) of your business. Growth is the percentage increase in your ending cash amount each month.

The money you spend now builds a solid foundation for your business. Spend smart and reap great rewards.

This monthly review of your cash flow statements can work as a warning system for your business. Use it to spot any trouble areas before they hurt your business. Are you growing as fast as you thought you would? Are you spending too much money mailing items? Look for any areas of concern, write them down, and then develop an action plan to correct them.

8. **Calculate your break-even point.**

A break-even point is the number at which your total revenue from sales equals your total costs. It helps you predict how changing your costs or sales level will affect your income. This serves as a good reality check for your business. It also provides information for your marketing efforts.

You determine your break-even point by:

$$\frac{\text{Total Fixed Expenses}}{\text{Sales Price per Unit} - \text{Variable Cost per Unit}} = \begin{array}{l}\textbf{Break-even Point}\\\textbf{(in number of units)}\end{array}$$

9. **Figure out your monthly net profit by developing your income statement.**

A sample statement format is on page 320. An income statement helps you discover how you are spending your money for a set time period. Income statements track your profits and losses for a given period (usually monthly). They can also be called profit and loss statements (a P&L statement).

Income statements help you determine what happens to your income if you lower your expenses, reduce your cost of goods sold, or raise your price. Do not be intimidated, you need only enter information you have already developed in a format that is easy to understand (once you get used to it).

Customize your income statement to meet the requirements of your business. It can be an effective tool in managing your business. If you are developing a business that has inventory, the law stipulates that you have to record your sales and expenses on an accrual basis (when transactions occur), rather than on a cash basis (when cash is actually received or paid out). Specifically, your income statement can help you:

- **Calculate your cost of goods sold (COGS).** The COGS is the direct cost of any products you sell. The COGS formula can help you determine if you have too much money invested in inventory. It can be quickly estimated with the following formula:

$$\text{COGS} = \frac{\text{Beginning Inventory Costs (Amount} \times \text{Price)} + \text{Inventory Purchases}}{\text{Costs (Amount} \times \text{Price)} - \text{Ending Inventory Costs (what is left)}}$$

If you buy inventory at various prices, you have a choice of how you value your inventory and items sold. For example, you can choose to: assign an average cost to your remaining inventory, indicate that the first inventory items in are the first to go out (FIFO), or that the last items in are the last out (LIFO). Most of my clients use an average inventory cost because they are just looking for a snapshot of where their business is right now.

• **Summarize your profit.** Profit is the money you have left after you have paid all your expenses. Your income statement can help you determine whether or not you will create a profitable business. Different profit calculations include:

    a. **Gross Profit** = net sales (gross sales minus any returned items) – COGS. This shows how much money you made before including any of your expenses except inventory.

    b. **Operating Profit** = Gross Profit – Operating Expenses (all other expenses except interest expense and income taxes). This shows how much money you made after deducting expenses directly related to producing your product.

    c. **Net Profit** = Operating Profit – Other Expenses. This calculation shows how much you made after deducting both your fixed and variable expenses such as production, marketing, promotion, distribution, and taxes.

• **Determine your tax liability.** Your income statement summarizes how much you have made in income and, therefore, you can use it to approximate the amount of tax you owe.

INCOME STATEMENT

NOTE

If you are developing a business that has inventory, the law stipulates that you have to record your sales and expenses on an accrual basis (when transactions occur), rather than on a cash basis (when cash is actually received or paid out).

Sales	Subtract	Add	Month 1
Gross Sales			
Returns and Allowances			
Bad Debt			
Net Sales			
			Subtract
Cost of Goods Sold			
Manufacturing Cost for Units Sold = (Beginning Inventory + Purchases – Ending Inventory)			
Shipping Costs			
Gross Profit			
			Subtract
Operating Expenses			
Marketing			
Operating Profit or Loss			
			Subtract
Loan Expenses			
Interest Paid			
			Equals

Income (Loss) or Net Profit (before taxes and salary)

10. **Create a balance sheet for your business.**

A sample balance sheet is on page 323. A balance sheet shows the financial stability of your business at a particular moment in time. It is a table of assets (stuff you own) and liabilities (money you owe). For small businesses, it is primarily prepared at the end of the year.

It is called a balance sheet because the two sides of the financial statement balance out. For example: If you borrow $10,000, you owe the bank $10,000 (a liability), but you have $10,000 in cash (an asset).

The primary formula for a balance sheet is:

$$\text{Assets} = \text{Liabilities} + \text{Owner's Equity}$$

Assets are what you own; they show how you use your cash (e.g., buying inventory). Assets include such things as cash, securities, accounts receivable, equipment, and inventory. Inventory is calculated using the price you paid to manufacture your product, not the price you sell it for.

Liabilities are what you owe to outside entities, such as shipping companies, banks and suppliers. Liabilities show where you obtained the cash to run your business (e.g., a loan or stores).

Equity is money left in the company (its value) after all the liabilities are paid. It usually reflects how much money you have put into your business.

The steps to completing your balance sheet are:

1. List your current assets on the left-hand side of your balance sheet. These are assets that can be easily converted into cash within a year.

2. Below your current assets, list your fixed assets. These are long-term assets that can not be converted into cash within a year (e.g., heavy machinery).

3. List your short- and long-term liabilities on the right-hand side of your balance sheet. Short-term liabilities are due in less than a year, and long-term liabilities are due in over a year.

4. Below your liabilities, list your company's equity position. This part of your statement will change when people invest in your business.

NOTE

Most businesses only create a balance sheet once a year.

11. **Gain an understanding of depreciation so you can use it in your business planning process.**

Depreciation is used to allocate fixed costs over the expected life of an asset. It represents a decrease in the asset's value.

You will primarily use depreciation at tax time. You can write off the depreciation value of some office equipment and other physical assets. If you spend money on buying fixed assets, the IRS allows you to deduct a certain amount of the purchase price each year from your tax bill. This depreciation is allowed because it is assumed that fixed assets wear out, and you will eventually have to spend more money to replace them.

Your fixed assets should be listed in your financial records at their depreciated value (subtract depreciation from actual costs). This is tricky because different assets are depreciated at different rates over time. List your fixed assets at the price you paid for them, then get help from an accountant, a friend, a teacher, or the IRS.

As an example, say you buy a $100,000 piece of equipment and according to the IRS's depreciation schedule it lasts five years. You can write off $20,000 in equipment depreciation for each of the next five years. After you have written off the equipment's purchase price, you can no longer take tax deductions on the equipment because it no longer has any value (at least in the eyes of the government).

SAMPLE BALANCE SHEET

Assets

Current Assets	Amount
Cash	
Inventory	
Accounts Receivable	
Other Prepaid Accounts: Insurance	
Total Current Assets	

Add

Fixed Assets	Amount
Equipment	
Real Estate	
Furniture	
Car	
Total Fixed Assets	

Equals

Total Assets	

Liabilities

Current Liabilities	Amount
Taxes Payable	
Loans Payable This Year	
Accounts Payable	
Salaries Payable	
Utilities Payable	
Total Current Liabilities	

Add

Long-Term Liabilities	Amount
Mortgage Payable	
Loan Payable Future	
Total Fixed Assets	

Add

Capital/Equity	
Common Stock (Owners Equity)	
Paid In by Owners	

Equals

Total Liabilities and Owner's Equity	

THIRTEEN

Focusing Your Information

This chapter helps you summarize your business, document the research you have completed, and declare the action steps you will take in a business action plan. This plan helps tie all the work you have completed back to your passion. Write from your heart, and people will be inspired to help you succeed.

STEP 31

BUSINESS ACTION
PLAN

- -

INTRODUCTION

Your first step in *Kick Start Your Dream Business* was to clearly define your passion.
Your business action plan provides you with a way to formally communicate your
passion to everyone in the world. It tells a story about everything you have accomplished so far and of where you are headed into the future. It puts all the ideas and
strategies you developed in your Product Notebook into paragraph form that is
easy to read and understand. It is exciting to see everything all in one place.

Some people call this document a business plan. I call it a business action plan
because it reminds you to keep going after you complete your business plan. I
have witnessed many people who hold out their plan to show what they have
accomplished but never take the next step.

You have to *take action* to implement your dream, not just talk about what you
have accomplished. A business action plan is not an end product. It continually
evolves as your business matures and grows.

Like a personal road map, it helps you track where your business is and evaluate what has worked to date so you can plan for continued success. Your plan
incorporates all your research, ideas, and conclusions in one place. A business
action plan combines all the elements of success; it:

- Speaks from your heart, motivating you and exciting others.
- Provides something others can respond to so you can L-I-S-Ten to their ideas.
- Is written down so you have a clear path to follow.

Your business action plan focuses on how developing your product will benefit
you, your customers, and your investors. However, it is primarily for you. The

THUMBS UP

*Write a great busi-
ness action plan
by tying your
action steps back
to the benefits your
product provides.*

focus of your business action plan should not be to attract investors, but rather to solidify your goals. If your goals and plans are well grounded, you will naturally attract investors.

As a small business owner you will soon discover it is easy to get pulled in numerous directions. You may be taking a sales call when a press call comes in, or you may be paying bills when a customer calls to complain. Your business action plan helps you maintain your sanity and figure out what to do next. It is something you can refer to when you get frustrated, and it reminds you of your goals so you don't get lost in day-to-day details.

Each business action plan is unique; it reflects your personality and the benefits of your products. Don't just fill in a template you find in a book or on a web site. Customize your plan so it reflects your passion.

There is no typical length for a business action plan. The To Dos in this step serve as topic suggestions and guidance for you to create your plan. Be sure to add action steps at the end of each section. They remind you about and show others your next steps to success.

Your business action plan is a testament to all the hard work you have accomplished and the benefits your product will provide. Keep your business action plan up to date by writing down any new processes you develop. Have fun and tell a great story.

TO DO

1. **Label a page in your Product Notebook "My Business Action Plan."**
   This area of your Product Notebook is used to put any additional ideas and strategies you develop as you develop your business. You will use all the information stored in your Product Notebook to create your business action plan. Most of my clients create their business action plan using a computer and word processing software (e.g., using MS Word or WordPerfect). If you would like to, you can also store your immediate next action steps in your Product Notebook and check them off as you achieve them.

2. Explain why you are creating your business action plan.

Do not just create a business action plan because someone told you to. State how creating it will help make your business a success. Your business action plan is your story. It can help you focus your efforts, discover new opportunities, or obtain investment money for your business. Keep these goals in mind as you finalize your action steps and strategies.

3. Review all you have accomplished to refresh your memory.

Review all the information you have gathered, in your Product Notebook and elsewhere, to refresh your memory of everything you have accomplished so far. What a great feeling! Congratulations. Celebrate the pride you feel in your work.

4. Create your business action plan.

Now is the time to put your information into a logical format that tells your story. The following To Dos serve as great section topics for your business action plan. Use them and add your own, if necessary, to develop your plan. Be creative, and always focus on the benefits you provide to your customers.

✳ UNEXPECTED SURPRISES

Jackie not only wrote a wonderful business action plan, she went a step further. After completing her plan, she created a "To Do" book that included all the actions steps she was going to take to make her business successful.

Jackie put her To Do book on her coffee table as a reminder of her goals. A friend who was visiting picked up the book and skimmed through it. Unexpectedly, the friend asked Jackie whether she needed help implementing any of the action items. "Are you kidding?" Jackie responded immediately.

Jackie's friend (and others later on) helped her accomplish some of her action items. Her friends were delighted to help Jackie realize her dream. Be specific in developing your next action steps and share them with others; you never know what will result.

Be as concise as you can because you do not have an abundance of time. Nor do you want to lose people's interest in your plan by putting in useless information.

Always end each section with any action steps you are taking to advance your business. This demonstrates your commitment to sticking with it and moving your business forward.

5. **Describe your business and its purpose.**

Use the information you developed in Step 11, Product Statement, to complete this section. Describe your business and the benefits it provides by focusing on your passion. This section needs to hook your readers so they will want to read the rest of your plan.

  a. Start by writing down your 30-second commercial. Update and revise your original 30-second commercial to include any information you have learned since creating it, and to reflect any additional benefits your product now offers.

  b. Tell the story of why you started this business as it relates to your passion.

  c. Describe the location of your business, and state whether the space is leased or owned. Include a description of other businesses in the area if applicable.

6. **Describe your objectives.**

Objectives are the goals you hope to accomplish with your business. Review and expand on the objectives you developed in Step 11, Product Statement.

  a. State your personal objectives.

  b. State your specific business objectives (e.g., to sell over 10,000 units in the first year with a 22 percent return on investment). These are your business goals. Make sure they are specific and measurable.

7. **Describe your competition and why your product will be a success.**

Use the information from Step 11, Product Statement; Step 12, Real-Life Example; and Step 21, Price Estimate, to complete this section. Focus on what makes your product stand out from the competition and why people will purchase it. The goal of this section is to get your readers excited enough to want to buy your product.

a. List your competitors. List the prices, benefits, features, and customers for your product and for your competitors. State your product's strengths. A table might be a great way to show and compare your product to the competition.

b. Include how your product is (or will be) legally protected (e.g., by copyright, trademark, or patent).

c. State your product's price and how you determined it. For example, "Our price of $14 was determined by investigating the competition and factoring in our manufacturing, distribution, and marketing costs." Show the action steps you have completed by including your pricing formula if you used one.

d. Describe how you have tested your product in the market. Include information on the results of your product's focus group, interviews, and retailer and distributor reactions.

e. Include a picture or drawing of your real-life example.

8. **Define your business's legal structure.**

Use information from Chapter 10 to complete this section. Describe how your business's legal structure fits in with your overall plans. Explain to the reader how you, your business, and your investors will be protected from potential liabilities.

a. Describe in one or two sentences the legal form you chose for your business and the reason for your choice. Include any insurance you will purchase to cover any known liabilities.

b. Name the owners and any key team members of your business and list their responsibilities. If you have a board of directors or advisors, describe their areas of expertise and how they will help the company grow.

c. If applicable, list the allocation of stock to your team members.

d. Define your communications program. Show how key players in your business will be informed of your progress. People reading your plan will know they will be updated as you move forward.

   • How will key team members be updated on product status?

   • How will investors be updated?

   • What is the process for making changes to your business action plan?

INSPIRATION

Look back at the heart you created in Step 2, Your Intent, if you need inspiration.

Create focus and energy by tying everything you develop back to the benefits that your product provides.

9. **Describe your product's packaging.**

Use information from Step 11, Product Statement, Step 16, Manufacturing It, and Step 20, Sales Kit, to complete this section. Describe your product's packaging so it really wows them. Provide real-life examples or pictures if you can.

    a. Describe (or draw) your product's packaging, and indicate how it meets the needs of distributors, retailers, and your customers. Indicate that you will have a UPC code on your product to facilitate product ordering and sales.

    b. Explain how your packaging will be consistent with your marketing materials to create a unified company image.

    c. If applicable, describe any items that will promote your product in stores, such as posters, flyers, or videos.

10. **Define your target market.**

Use information from Step 11, Product Statement; and Step 15, Creator Contact, to complete this section. State why you choose this target market and define what benefits you are providing to your target market. Try to include a real-life story to show actual benefits of your product.

    a. Describe your customers and their unmet needs. Be as specific as possible so your readers understand why people will buy your product. Update your customer information with any ideas that inventors, store owners, or reps provided to you.

    b. Describe the research you completed to determine your customers.

    c. Describe reactions from prospective buyers, customers, distributors, and salespeople with whom you have spoken.

11. **Describe your marketing and promotional campaigns.**

Use information from Step 11, Product Statement; Step 17, Marketing Strategy; Step 18, Promotional Tie-Ins; Steps 19a–e, Marketing Events; and Step 20, Sales Kit, to complete this section. Inspire your readers by telling them about your unique marketing strategies.

    a. Describe your research techniques, including the results of any focus groups you conducted. Don't forget to report that you spoke directly to inventors, stores, and representatives.

b. Describe or draw your logo and state your slogan. Explain how they will help your product stand out from the competition.

c. Using information you obtained from retailers and other inventors, describe how the seasons or other time-specific events (e.g., Easter) will affect your product sales. Tell readers how you will time your campaign to coincide with or avoid these dates.

d. State the top three marketing activities with which you will launch your business. In addition, record the top two events you created for each of the unusual marketing and press events you developed in Chapter 7, Telling the World.

e. List the top three organizations and/or corporations you will target for product tie-ins, and explain how they will help you get your product to your target market.

f. Specifically state the conferences or trade shows you will be attending and how they will help you achieve your objectives.

g. Describe the Sales Kit you developed in Step 20. Include copies of any promotional and advertising materials you developed as appendices if they are ready for viewing. Refer readers to the appropriate appendices.

h. State the yearly and monthly marketing costs you developed in Step 30, Financial Analysis.

N O T E

Show people that you have done your homework by describing the research you completed for each section of your business action plan. This shows that you are serious about being successful.

12. Describe your manufacturer and the manufacturing process.

Use information from Step 16, Manufacturing It, to complete this section. Make your manufacturer part of the team. Explain their commitment to quality and to making your product the best it can be. If you are not manufacturing any products, skip this section.

a. Describe the manufacturer or manufacturers you chose and the specific reasons why you chose them (e.g., price or reputation). List their contact information and their areas of expertise. If you sent bids out to a number of manufacturers, include them in an appendix for comparison.

b. Describe or make a chart of the key steps in manufacturing your product. Keep it to no more than ten steps. You can show this in a timeline and include a list of suppliers, production costs, and information on each supplier's quality-control programs. This information ensures investors that you will develop a quality product.

c. State how many units you will produce and why you chose that number (e.g., it was the most economical, your research suggested it, it's the industry average production run, or pre-orders determined it).

d. Describe the process and timeline for ordering additional products. This shows investors that if you have a hit, you are prepared to meet demand.

13. Describe you customer support systems.

Use information from Step 22, Customer Support, and Step 25, Self-Distribution, to complete this section. State that customers are what will make you a success. Tell your readers how you will L-I-S-Ten and learn from your customers.

a. Use one or two sentences to describe how important customer support is to you and how your customer support plans will make it easy for your customers to do business with you.

b. Describe any unusual tactics you will use to build customer loyalty.

c. State the process you will have in place to listen to your customers, solve any complaints they may have, and incorporate any great ideas they may provide.

d. Describe the telephone, fax, Internet, and credit card ordering procedures you developed. Specify how it will be convenient for all of your customers, distributors, and stores to order and reorder from you.

e. Record your policy on replacing or repairing defective or damaged products.

14. Describe your fulfillment procedures.

Use the information you developed in Step 23, Fulfillment, to complete this section. Make this section a continuation of your customer service programs. Declare how you will keep your customers up to date on their shipments and make it easy for them to reorder.

a. Explain your fulfillment procedures (how you will store, deliver, and track product delivery and payment). Include the name and reputation of any facilities you will use and all associated costs. If your storage facility is the same as your order fulfillment house, explain how this reduces potential handling problems.

b. Explain your plans to monitor your product inventory. For example, will you be using QuickBooks, a manual system, or reports from stores and reps to track inventory levels?

15. **Name the retail outlets you have targeted or are planning to target.**

Use the information you developed in Step 8, Information Center, and Step 24, Distribution, to complete this section. Make your retail outlets part of your team. Mention any retailers who are excited about carrying your product.

    a. Describe the retail outlets that have agreed to carry your product and whether they are a large, medium, or small outlet. Provide copies of any purchase orders you have already received in an appendix.

    b. List additional outlets that you are planning to approach.

    c. Explain your plans for informing retailers about your product (e.g., direct mail, distributors, or walking into stores).

    d. Explain your product pricing structure for retail outlets, including any discounts.

16. **List your possible distribution channels.**

Use the information you developed in Step 8, Information Center, Step 24, Distribution, and Step 25, Self-Distribution, to complete this section. Describe how you interviewed and chose the greatest reps and distributors you could find. They are an integral part of your team and your success.

    a. List the representatives (Step 24a) and distributors (Step 24c) you have already decided to work with and those you will target in the future. Add any rep or distributor résumés as an appendix and refer readers to it.

    b. Describe the payment options you will be offering to your representatives (usually 15 percent off of wholesale price) and distributors (usually 55 percent off of the sales price).

    c. Explain the self-distribution plans you developed in Step 25.

    d. Explain how will you integrate reps and distributors into your promotional efforts.

N O T E

If a section of your plan is incomplete, write down the specific action steps you need to take to complete that section.

17. **Explain your implementation strategy.**

This section explains the steps you will take to succeed. In detail, outline the action steps you need to take to ensure the success of your business.

  a. Provide a general overview of how you plan to maintain a balance between your work and your personal life. People do not want you to stress out and fail.

  b. State how you will ensure that production schedules will be met (e.g., with contracts, by visiting the plant, or through weekly updates). Include your time lines for testing, producing, and shipping your product.

  c. Describe how your marketing plans will be implemented. Your marketing time lines can be built from the One Pagers you created in Step 17, Marketing Strategy.

  d. Explain how your distribution plans will be implemented. Provide time lines for launching your business and for delivering your product to stores, reps, and distributors.

18. **Describe your human resource plans.**

This section provides people with an understanding of who is associated with your business, their specific roles, and how you will reward them. What associates will help you make your business a success?

  a. List all company team members and their salaries. If some or all do not get paid, but share in the company's profits, include that.

  b. Develop an organizational chart and list the names of individuals who will be responsible for day-to-day activities, including answering the phone, taking orders, checking inventory, and contacting retail locations, suppliers, and distributors. It's fine if your name is in most of the boxes right now.

  c. State the incentive people will have to complete their work conscientiously (e.g., profit sharing, part ownership, or accountability).

  d. List the physical resources (e.g., desks, computers, a fax machine, or a copier) that are available for team members to use.

19. Describe your business's financial situation and strategy.

Use the information you developed in Step 29, Record Keeping; and Step 30, Financial Analysis, to complete this section. Explain your development costs and discuss whether or not anyone (including yourself) has invested in your business. Conclude by discussing how you will continually monitor the health of your business.

   a. Describe the funds required now and how you will use those funds (for startup costs). You can use a table to summarize the costs for each step necessary to produce, market, and distribute your product.

   b. State the funds raised to date (include your own money).

   c. Describe the benefits of investing in your product (e.g., a short loan repayment time frame or a high rate of return on their investment). Do not forget to include the nonmonetary benefits such as being associated with a great product that will help your customers.

   d. Describe any requirements for subsequent investment (e.g., money for a second or third production run), and state whether or not first-time investors will have priority over new investors when further funds are needed.

   e. Describe your operations plan by explaining your record keeping and financial analysis procedures. Tell how these procedures will help you track the financial progress of your business, allow for accurate financial reporting, and prepare your taxes. You can also define your accounting controls.

20. Provide sample financial data information.

Use the information you developed in Step 30, Financial Analysis, to complete this section. This information shows that you have completed your financial homework and understand the realities of running a business.

   a. State when you expect to reach your break-even point (the point at which your costs and revenue are equal), and declare your expected yearly profits.

   b. Provide a cash flow chart for your first six months of business.

   c. Develop a one-year income statement based on your sales estimates.

   d. Develop a sample balance sheet for your business.

21. **Report any business issues that will help or hinder your success.**

Use the information from Step 9, Opportunities and Threats; Step 11, Product Statement; and Step 30, Financial Analysis, to complete this section. This section shows that you know the risks involved in starting your own business but are willing and able to conquer those risks.

   a. List your critical success factors (i.e., your Rules to Live By from Step 9, Opportunities and Threats).

   b. List any threats to your business, and tell how you plan to counter them (from Step 9, Opportunities and Threats).

   c. List any key assumptions you have made in your business action plan (e.g., you will be able to raise a certain amount of money by a certain date, or a national distributor will pick you up).

22. **Develop Your Appendices.**

Your appendices contain any additional information that you want to present. This information includes any charts you reference in your business action plan. Possible items to include in your appendices are:

   a. Résumés for all team members, consultants, and other key players

   b. Marketing materials you have developed (e.g., Faxable Marketing Pages, any media releases, direct mail pieces, or articles written about your business)

   c. Your personal credit reports—if you are asking investors for money

   d. Copies of any leases or distribution or manufacturing agreements

   e. Any customer letters supporting your product

23. **Develop an executive summary for your business action plan.**

An executive summary is just that, a summary of your business action plan. Write this part last after having completed all the sections of your plan. The executive summary goes at the beginning of your business action plan.

Your executive summary is an extremely important document. If investors ask to see a business action plan, they may only read the executive summary. The executive summary should capture the reader's attention, be one to two pages in length, and describe each section of your business action plan in two to three sentences. The language should be concise and should make an impact. Here are the steps to creating a great executive summary.

a. Product description:

- Use your 30-second commercial to describe your product's features, the problems it solves, and the benefits it provides. As in all your written materials, always link back to the benefits your business provides.
- Define your target market.
- Explain your product's key features, including the name and reputation of your manufacturer if applicable.
- State who owns the idea for your product and whether or not it has been copyrighted, trademarked, or patented.

b. Company description. Provide a brief description of your management team and each of their major accomplishments. State the legal form of your business and why you chose that form.

c. Investment opportunity. Declare the amount of money you need to raise, how the funds will be used, how much the owners are personally contributing to the product, and what the return on investment will be (e.g., a percentage of the company's profit, or a 15 percent return on their money). Specifically state your ability to pay the loan back.

d. Marketing plan. Briefly describe how you plan to let people know about your product, and state your expected sales.

e. Distribution plan. Briefly describe your distribution plans and what key players will be involved.

f. Current status. State the current status of your product (e.g., ready to manufacture).

24. **Create your business action plan cover and table of contents.**

These pages announce your product name, provide contact information, and tell the reader where important information is located. They go before your executive summary.

a. Develop a cover that includes the name of your business, the names of the product's principals (people with a vested interest or ownership in the product), your company's address, your company's phone number, and the date. To help protect your information, at the bottom of the cover, write: "Business Action Plan Copy Number [Number]" and "This document contains confidential information that belongs to [Your Company Name]. Do not copy or distribute without prior written approval of [Your Company Name]." Number the copies of your business action plan so you can track the copies you send out.

b. Create a table of contents. List the sections of your business action plan with corresponding page numbers. Include your executive summary and your appendices.

25. **Review your business action plan with someone else.**

After you have developed your business action plan, review it with a friend, a store owner, another small-business person, or a counselor at a local Small Business Development Center. L-I-S-Ten and learn. These people can help discern whether you have overlooked anything. Make any changes that you agree with.

26. **Complete you business action plan by adding the final touches.**

Copy your business action plan onto nice paper and have it ready to present to possible partners, investors, or distributors. A great way to bind your plan is to go to a copy store and have them spiral bind it with a clear cover. This protects your plan and looks professional. Make your plan look great; it represents all the hard work you have put into your dream business.

FOURTEEN

Convincing Others

This chapter helps you create a tightly packaged overview of your business, highlighting key information. People will quickly understand your business and why it will be a success. You will also learn how to present your information in a smartly enthusiastic manner that will persuade others to work with you.

STEP 32

PROSPECTUS

INTRODUCTION

This step helps you focus on what investors need and want to hear. A prospectus is a tightly packaged version of your business action plan that is specifically prepared for investors. It is a sales tool that attracts and convinces investors to review your business action plan or to meet with you personally. Usually no more than six pages in length, it covers information about you, your business, and your business's profit potential.

Contact investors personally and talk to them about your business and the benefits it will provide to your customers. At the end of each conversation, you will ask whether the investor would like to see a prospectus. If so, send them one. After reviewing your prospectus, investors may be so excited that they will not even need to read your business action plan.

Investors want to know that the business they are investing in will be successful. Guess what? They also know that the success of the business depends on the *person* behind the business—your commitment and passion play a huge part. How do you bring this commitment to the forefront? Focus on your intent and always tie your presentation back to the benefits your business provides.

Your goal is to create the most positive picture of your business possible. Your prospectus should be honest and thoroughly convincing—a professional image of your passion and hard work. Every sentence should cause the reader to think: "Who do I make the check out to?" or "I can't wait to read the business action plan." People only know what you tell them, so pack a punch, and let them know about all your wonderful work.

Go for it. This is the time to get the money you need to develop your dream business. People live for passion, let yours jump off the page. Create a prospectus

THUMBS UP

Write from your heart! Your positive energy will attract people who will help you become a success.

that will grab reader's hearts as well as answer their questions. Share the story of your greatest success—your own business.

To instill your passion and knowledge into a concise package that carries a lot of weight.

OUTCOME

A tightly packaged, enthusiastic version of your business action plan.

TO DO

1. Label a page in your Product Notebook "My Prospectus."

This area of your Product Notebook is used to store any ideas you generate that can be included in your prospectus. Most of my clients create their prospectus using a computer and word processing software (e.g., using MS Word or WordPerfect). Now get ready to wow your investors!

2. Keep a copy of your business action plan next to you as you work.

Use the information you developed in Step 31, Business Action Plan (especially the executive summary), as you develop the To Dos below. Separate your sections with headings so readers can quickly skim your prospectus. Each To Do can serve as a section topic for your prospectus.

3. Describe your company and product.

Start with your 30-second commercial. Then state your company's legal structure and describe your management team to show that your company has a solid foundation. Describe your product's packaging and include a picture of your real-life example. Graphics are a wonderful sales tool. You can scan in images at your local copy shop and put them into the body of your prospectus so readers do not have to flip to the appendices (see To Do number 11).

4. Create your statement of purpose.

State your intent to produce and market your product. Express your enthusiasm and let readers know you will do whatever it takes to make your business a success. Use bullets to highlight your top three or four objectives, including raising capital.

5. **Declare the opportunity to invest in your business.**

Describe the investment opportunity in your company, including the amount of investment required, rate of return on the investment, and ownership percentage of the business that you are offering (if any). State the minimum amount you will accept from individual investors. Your accountant, other entrepreneurs, or a counselor at the Small Business Development Center can help you decide what the minimum amount should be from each investor. You do not want a large number of investors because it will be more difficult to manage them. Specifically describe how the funds will be used to develop your business.

6. **Highlight the results of all your research.**

State the size and demographics of your target audience, and briefly describe the research you undertook to verify these numbers. Use charts to summarize any relevant trends and the effect they will have on your business. You can add quotes from experts who talk about the unique qualities of your product, its benefits, or even about your special skills. A great quote from one of my clients is, "*Kick Start* helped me find what set my heart on fire, and now I'm doing it for a living."

7. **Describe your progress to date.**

Provide a progress report for your readers. Create a chart of the steps (with associated costs) it takes to bring your product to the market (e.g., finding distributors, producing the product, or leasing office space). Indicate the work you have already accomplished and the steps you need to complete to launch your business.

8. **Highlight your planned marketing activities.**

State the top six marketing and promotional events you will implement to tell others about your product. Include any marketing materials you have developed as appendices. For a service, this could be your brochure. These real-life activities make your plans come to life for the investor.

N O T E

Go wild with your prospectus. Thrill readers with your product by presenting your information creatively (e.g., with charts, pictures, or cartoons).

Think of investors as your first customers; they want to be assured that you understand your product and how to market it.

9. **State your distribution plans.**

Highlight your ordering and fulfillment policies by concentrating on items that will help your business stand out from the competition. State the number of stores, reps, or distributors who have agreed to sell your product: include any well-known names.

10. **Summarize your startup costs.**

Use the information you developed in the financial analysis section of your business action plan to state your startup costs and your monthly overhead expenses. Invite the reader to request cash flow statements, income statements, and balance sheets if they need them. You should have a copy of the financial statements with you when you meet with investors.

11. **Include any important appendices.**

Attach relevant documents here including your key team member's résumés. This shows the investor you have assembled a competent team. You may also consider attaching congratulatory customer letters and any purchase orders you have already received. Always enclose an investor response form that lets you know whether or not someone wishes to invest. This item moves your readers to action. A sample investor response form is on page 348.

12. **Get a few friends (the more the better—shoot for five) to read and comment on your prospectus.**

Bring some friends together and have them read through your prospectus. They can write down any comments they have as they read it. After they have finished reading your prospectus, L-I-S-Ten to their ideas, and make any changes that improve it.

13. **Create an engaging cover.**

Get creative with your cover. Entice readers to open your prospectus and read what's inside. For example, scan a picture of your real-life example (at a local copy shop) and put it on the cover. Always label your prospectus with "Prospectus Copy Number [Number]" so you can track who receives a copy of your prospectus. To protect yourself, at the bottom of the cover put "This document contains confidential information that belongs to [Your Company Name]. Do not copy or distribute without prior written approval of [Your Company Name]."

14. **Bind no more than ten copies of your prospectus.**

Take your prospectus to your local copy shop (support another small business!) and have them make six to ten copies of it. Have them spiral bind the copies (it makes it easier to flip the pages) with a clear front and a colored back. These are your emergency copies. If you meet someone who is interested in your business, you have a prospectus ready to send to them. You do not want to make too many copies of your prospectus because as you continue to review it, you are bound to make changes. Once you get down to two copies, make five more so you always have a copy on hand.

15. **Hand your prospectus to potential investors and key team members.**

Do not get nervous and just toss your prospectus in the mail—always hand it out to people yourself. You are the power behind your product. Your presence infuses your document with an equally energetic personality. Your investors will appreciate your personal touch.

Present your prospectus to the key people working with or supporting you. It will help them understand your business so they can better help you. Besides, you never know who will come into contact with a potential investor.

N O T E

Use both visuals and words to add zest to your presentation. Some people understand things best after they see visuals, and others respond to words, and numbers.

SAMPLE INVESTOR RESPONSE FORM

[YOUR COMPANY NAME]
Investor Response Form

[DATE]

[NAME]
[STREET ADDRESS]
[CITY], [STATE] [ZIP]

I have read your prospectus with great interest and wish to invest in [YOUR COMPANY NAME] that will [30-SECOND COMMERCIAL].
Amount: $_____

I support your efforts but do not wish to invest at this time.
Initials: _____

I would like further information about [COMPANY NAME], or I have the name of a contact who can help you and your business.
Please call me at _____ to set up an appointment.

Sincerely,

[INVESTOR PRINTED NAME]

STEP 33

INVESTOR MEETING

INTRODUCTION

You have completed your business action plan, your prospectus is ready, and your energy is high. Now is the time to get the money you need to launch your business. Speak from your heart and energize others to help you succeed.

During investor meetings, you are selling yourself as much as your product. The investors must believe in you before they invest in your product. In fact, most studies have shown that when you are speaking about your product to potential investors, what they hear is 85 percent smart enthusiasm and only 15 percent content. Personality sells.

Knock your investors' socks off from day one. The more you believe in and are passionate about your product, the more investors will believe in it too. No one can predict the future, but a smart, passionate entrepreneur (that's you!) will surely create a way to handle any obstacles thrown in his or her path.

Don't be intimidated by investors. You know in your heart that your product will be successful, so always speak with confidence. You have a great product, and for every person who says "no" there are a dozen others who will say "yes". If an investor is rude or tells you that you cannot succeed, just let it go. You have a great product; the right investor will come along.

There is no typical investor. Some want money, while others are most interested in the benefits your product provides. There are many different ways people can invest in your business. An investment can be as simple as a loan or as complicated as obtaining an ownership stake in the business. Some people only want a reasonable return on their investment (say 15 percent), rather than a piece of your business. The key is to speak from your heart about your product, L-I-S-Ten to what the investor needs or wants, then write down how your relationship will work.

THUMBS UP

Treat potential investors as partners. Keep them up to date on your progress and achievements.

To infuse your presentation with energy, focus on telling a story rather than on trying to sell your product. Begin your story by describing your business and its benefits, then walk the investors through your strategies for success, and end with the outcomes you expect. People (including investors) will respond to a story told in a dramatic way much more than to a review of the nuts and bolts of a business.

O U T C O M E

A fantastic investor meeting.

T O D O

1. **Review a copy of your prospectus and pick out key points to present.**

   Highlight the key points in an unbound copy of your prospectus. You will usu-ally meet with investors one-on-one. During this meeting, investors will not want to read your prospectus—they will want to hear about it.

   An investor meeting has two simple goals. First, you want to give the investor enough information to become excited about reading your prospec-tus (and, therefore, your business action plan). Second, you want them to relate to your passion and understand that you will make your business a success.

2. **Use the highlighted words in your prospectus to write a 10-minute script for your investor meeting.**

   During your investor meetings, you want to tell a story about your product and why it will succeed. Personalize your story by telling how you came up with your idea and how it will benefit others. People love to help other people realize their dreams, and your product is a physical representation of your passion, a dream come true.

   An investor meeting is informal and should not last more than ten min-utes. Your goal is to leave the investor ready and raring to read your prospec-tus (and invest in your company). Your prospectus and business action plan have the facts; you provide the excitement and motivation.

   The beginning of your presentation should focus on your product's bene-fits. Then you want to expand the investors' understanding of your product. All your remarks should link back to the benefits your product provides.

Include testimonials and expert opinions in your presentation. They lend credibility. At the end of your personal presentation, review memorable points and remind people why they should invest. Your 10-minute personal presentation should:

- Begin with the name of your product, and tell the story of how you came up with your idea. This adds an emotional connection between your business and your investors.
- Describe your product's benefits. Your product is so good that you will succeed.
- Summarize your accomplishments to date. For example: "I have been working on it for ten months and have accomplished the following (e.g., developed a real-life example and found manufacturers) . . . My product will be out in the market by (March 8) . . . and distributed by (forty local toy stores)."
- State how much money you need to raise, how it will be spent, and what you are offering in return for the investment.
- Answer any questions.
- End with a statement that asks them to read your business action plan and invest in your product. If you don't ask, they may not invest.

3. Practice. Practice. Practice.

Once you have outlined your 10-minute personal presentation, practice it. Rehearse your presentation in front of friends and, if possible, someone who has invested in other startup businesses.

When you practice, try to get all the way through without stopping, even if you make mistakes. After you do it a couple of times, it will seem more natural. Try to maintain eye contact because your eyes (and the investor's eyes) reveal a great deal. Eye contact also makes the presentation more personal. Don't forget to smile. A smile expresses goodwill and relaxes you and your audience.

Have your trial audience ask you some of the tough questions you may get from potential investors. This will help you iron out the kinks in your presentation and prepare you for hard questions from actual investors. Don't forget to L-I-S-Ten to their suggestions.

INSPIRATION

Investors invest in people, not just businesses. So speak from your heart, and you will discover a way to finance your business.

If you believe in your product and know that it benefits others— whether commercially, emotionally, politically, or spiritually—you will find someone to invest.

Create energy by focusing on your internal and external intents and speaking from your heart.

4. **Create your list of top ten possible investors.**

Review the names and organizations you developed in Step 27, Investor Brainstorming. In your Product Notebook, rank these investors using your gut feelings. Which investors do you believe are more likely to give you money and why? Remember to include investors who may contribute their names or expertise.

5. **Find a creative, comfortable place to host your investor meetings.**

You will be meeting with investors one-on-one unless otherwise requested. Find a place where you can comfortably present your business and yourself. Ideally your location will reflect some aspect of your product. Can you hold the meeting at your production facility, in your offices, or at a customer location? If necessary, reserve a location for your investor meeting.

It is exciting for investors to experience the environment where your product will be produced or sold. Make sure the location for your meeting is clean, comfortable, and safe. And do not forget that it should have great parking. There is nothing more frustrating for an investor than having difficulty getting to your meeting.

If an investor is very busy, it is OK to meet at their home or office. However, these personal sites can be distracting (e.g., phones ringing or children playing). It is better to get investors away from their environment and show them yours.

6. **Invite potential investors to your investor meeting and meet with them.**

Invite investors to meet with you in person. This adds personality to your product and makes it harder to say no to you. Schedule meeting times that are convenient for your potential investors, not just for you.

Start with an investor who is down your list a ways (maybe even number ten). You will practice and learn from your first couple of meetings. When you invite your top investor, you will be confident and ready. A word of caution: When you invite investors to your meeting, they may start asking you questions right away. Be ready to present your 10-minute script!

When you invite investors, tell them:

• The purpose of the meeting is for you to tell them about your product, its benefits, and how it will blow the market away.

- What will happen at the meeting. "During the meeting, I will discuss what the product is, how I plan to market it, and why I know it will succeed."
- The meeting will take less than one hour. And make sure it does!
- The date, time, and location of the meeting.

7. **Be prepared for questions from investors.**

Be ready for investor questions. Questions are good things. The more potential investors know about you and your business, the more comfortable they will be in loaning you the funds you require.

When an investor asks a question, listen carefully. Then answer the question to the best of your ability. Don't feel that you have to provide additional information; answer the question and then be quiet. If the investor needs to know more, they will ask you additional questions. Investors will also share their ideas, concerns, and experiences with you.

8. **Conclude your investor meeting.**

Thank the investor for taking the time to meet with you. Hand them your prospectus and invite them to call you with any questions. If appropriate, ask investors the following questions:

- "Are you interested in seeing a product like mine in the market?"
- "How long do you typically take to decide on investing in a business?"
- "What size of investment do you typically make?"
- "Is there anything I can do to make your decision easier?"

9. **Always follow up with investors.**

Treat everyone with respect. You never know who may be interested in investing in your business in the future. Send personalized, handwritten thank-you cards to every investor. Even if an investor said they were not interested in investing, send them a thank-you.

Send responses to any lingering unanswered questions via fax or e-mail. You should also keep all potential investors up to date on your business progress. A bit of good news (e.g., getting your product manufactured) may just spark someone to invest in your business.

NOTE

Make sure your investor meeting reflects your product. For instance, if your product is international, meet at an international café and use a picture of the world with pins in the locations where you will be marketing your product.

INSPIRATION

Be honest. If you don't have an answer to a question, tell the investor you will find the answer and get back to them as soon as you can.

10. **Sign an investor agreement with investors you agree to do business with.**

You are in charge. Just because an investor says he or she wants to invest in your business does not mean you have to accept their offer. You need to be as comfortable with your investors as they are with you. If you feel uncomfortable with any particular investor, consider declining their offer to invest.

If you decide to partner with investors, be prepared for suggestions on how to run your business. It is hard to keep investors, even silent ones (who are guaranteed a return on their investment, but have no say in the running of your business), silent!

For any investor you agree to partner with, have a lawyer prepare your final investor agreement. You can prepare a draft of your investor agreement by using a sample agreement from a legal book. However, you want to make sure your agreements are valid, and you must have a small business lawyer review them. You can find a great lawyer by asking other small business owners or by visiting your local Small Business Development Center.

FIFTEEN

Getting It Going

Measure your life in heartbeats. Each beat represents
a new opportunity. This chapter provides you with techniques
to launch your business. These ideas keep you focused,
energized, and moving forward.

STEP 34:

IMPLEMENTATION

INTRODUCTION

If you haven't realized it yet, you are in business. That's right. You have your product, you know how to market it, and you may have people ready to invest in it.
People around you are undoubtedly amazed at how much you have accomplished
in a short period of time. They may even consider you an overnight success.

There's no need to describe the heartache and sweat that went into making
your dream a reality. Enjoy the moment, nod your head, and say, "I am very proud
to be here!"

You and those around you have probably changed during this process. Your
friends and family have become more supportive of your business, and you have
met other entrepreneurs who can give you advice. You have discovered confidence that you never knew you had. You have created an energy that keeps you
on track, conquering obstacles and succeeding.

Enjoy the ride as your business continues to expand and grow. Your work is an
expression of yourself. As you implement your idea, you are improving your life—
make sure it's fun, exciting, and most of all, rewarding.

THUMBS UP

*Accomplish
something every
day and your
business will
continue to grow.*

TO DO

1. Take action.

By reading *Kick Start Your Dream Business,* you now have a great overview
of what it takes to start your own business. Now is the time to implement
your plans.

Return to the chapters where you created action steps for implementing your plans (e.g., Chapter 7, Telling the World, Chapter 9, Delivering It, and Chapter 10, Making It Legal). Start doing the activities you developed. Accomplish something every day and you will obtain impressive results. Don't over complicate things. Follow your plans, stay true to your heart, and ask for help when you need it.

2. Have a product launch party.

When you are ready, unveil your product with a unique product launch party. This is a day of celebration for you—a day to thank the people who have helped you make your product a reality.

You may feel nervous, like having stage fright. But stand strong. It's time to show everyone who believed in you (and those who didn't) that your product is a fact. It's time to reap praise for your dream product and to benefit from all your hard work. You have realized your internal intent. Congratulations!

Remember to focus on your product's benefit to others—your external intent—so the message you send energizes you and the people listening to you. Some hints on creating a successful launch party include:

- Brainstorm on fun ways to launch your product. Can you have a party at one of your Octopus Effect organizations (e.g., make it a fundraiser)? Can you create a contest to give away your product on the radio? You might present your product as having just been born (which it has) and hold a baby shower.

- Invite people who have supported your efforts. This is an opportunity to thank people who have helped you. Invite your friends and family, distributors, store owners, and other people you have met while developing your product. The party can be as small or as large as you want it to be. Don't forget the press!

- Have your product and sales materials ready to present. Set up a table to display your product and your Faxable Marketing Pages.

- Demonstrate your product. Show it to your guests as part of the launch party (e.g., if you developed a new dessert, give people samples) or have one of your friends tell a story about how it has benefited them.

3. **Make sure you stay in touch with any outside firms you are using to bring your product to the market.**

Do not forget that any outside vendors will affect your product distribution and marketing plans. Stay in contact with them. Make sure you have signed agreements with each outside vendor that states the actions (with timelines) they will take for you. Call at least once a week to determine the status of your orders. This shows that you care about the work they are doing and points out any trouble spots before they become catastrophes.

4. **Sell your product based on its benefits.**

One of the hardest activities my clients have is closing a sale. They are so attached to their businesses that they have a hard time selling their products. Since their product is an expression of their passion, their feelings are often hurt when someone does not immediately purchase their product.

Don't take any negative feedback about your product personally. Let it go. Sometimes people just need a little time before they make a purchase. Remember people have to hear about a product at least five times before they purchase it. Tips to closing a sale include:

- Speak passionately! Share your dream. Tell people how your product benefits them, and they will be more inclined to buy it.
- Visualize your success. If you see your product selling, you will approach each meeting with a positive attitude, encouraging other people to agree with you.
- Think like your customers. Remember your research. If you know what your customers want and your product meets these needs, people will purchase your product.
- Close with an action statement. Sometimes all you have to do is ask. End every meeting with a question or statement that moves people to buy your product. For example, you might end with: "Most of my stores your size usually purchase twelve. Is that how many you would like to order today?" If you own a restaurant, you might say, "Would you like fries with that?"

INSPIRATION

You were dreaming; now you are achieving.

INSPIRATION

Speak from your heart. Your energy will include everyone in your dream.

5. **L-I-S-Ten to your customers, suppliers, distributors, representatives, and store owners.**

Always L-I-S-Ten to people out in the marketplace. These people are in contact with customers every day. They know the market. If you keep an open line of communication, you can learn about new market trends, marketing strategies, or what the competition is up to. Analyze the information they give you, decide whether it affects your business, and take action (even if the action is to do nothing at this time).

6. **Keep your stress low by staying organized.**

Each morning, take a deep breath and prepare yourself for a great day. You have proven your commitment to your product, now keep going!

Prepare a To Do list that states everything you hope to accomplish the next day. As you accomplish the tasks, cross them off the list. To stay focused on the positive, make crossing off your accomplishments a ritual and remember things always change.

Most of my clients cross off completed items and make a new list before they go to bed. This allows them to take a breath, dump all the "stuff" from their brains, and get a good night's sleep. As a friend of mine says, "Measure your life in heartbeats." Each heartbeat represents a new idea, new moment, a new day. Look forward to each day as an opportunity to achieve your goals.

7. **Take time to exercise your mind, body, and soul.**

Include personal objectives in your nightly To Do list. Keeping your dream going is stressful, and stress is a very demanding animal. In the short term, it may help you accomplish your goals. But if you maintain stress too long, it can sneak up on you and cause great harm.

If you love taking a walk every morning, keep doing it. If attending a religious service calms you, go for it. There is a reason you enjoy these things. If your family wants to see a movie, challenge them to a race to the car and go! Your body, mind, and soul need these activities; don't neglect them. These activities lessen your anxiety and keep you in touch with the "real world" outside your business.

8. **Spend time with others who are achieving their goals.**

    Becoming an entrepreneur can be lonely at times. It is a great idea to join a professional small business organization or to meet with other small business owners for an occasion cup of coffee. These meetings remind you that you are not alone, and they are great ways to learn more and to socialize. You can learn a lot from other people's mistakes and successes. Even better, you may make some new friends who will always ask you, "How is your business going?"

9. **Most importantly, don't isolate yourself during this process.**

    Always keep your loved ones up to date on your progress. Make them a part of the process. They will help in whatever way they can, offering moral support when you need it. Knowing that people love and support you will help get you through a tough day.

SIXTEEN

Keeping It Going

STEP 35: POSTLAUNCH .... *Page 365*

*This chapter provides you with techniques to
keep your business growing. Keep your creativity alive and your
energy flowing so running your own business remains fun.*

STEP 35

POSTLAUNCH

INTRODUCTION

You are using all of your abilities, skills, knowledge, and passion to keep your business going. You may not have the time or energy to accomplish everything you need to do. Guess what? This is natural. Every small-business person I know has a long list of things they hope to accomplish. Your job is to continue working, not to beat yourself up.

Keep thinking long-term. It is easy to get caught up in the day-to-day needs of your business. Today may be horrible, but tomorrow's results may be magical. Keep your business going (and growing) by staying on top of the market and continually keeping the big picture (why you are doing this) in the forefront of your mind. When faced with new challenges, replenish your energy by going back to your heart—your intent, from Step 2.

As your business grows, you will follow the same steps outlined in this book. Speaking from your heart, L-I-S-Tening to others, and writing down new ideas are the three most important things you can do. Always dream like a child, decide as an adult. The steps you have completed—focus groups, surveys, competitor research—are not over. You will continue to do these things so you can revise your business and find new partners.

You are human. You will make mistakes. There will be tough days. But give yourself a break; you are doing your best. Your passion is a key ingredient to your business success.

People are there to help, let them! You don't have to do everything yourself. Let other people share in your dream. It will give you a boost and add creative juice to your business.

THUMBS UP

Listen to others and to your heart. Both will tell you what actions you must take to keep your momentum going.

GOAL

To solve all new challenges with the same energy and dedication as the day you began reading Kick Start Your Dream Business.

OUTCOME

Congratulations! A business that is a reflection of your passion.

✳ AN ENTREPRENEUR

A friend of mine, Lois, who owned her own medical consulting business for over seven years called me up one day and asked if I had time to talk. Before I could say anything, she started crying.

She explained to me that for the first time ever, she was not able to book the business she needed. She said, "I'm going to have to get a job. Isn't that sad?"

Instead of agreeing with her I said, "Lois, just wait, things will change. You are working from your heart; keep going. Life is not about getting a job, but about working from your passion. You have been through this before; you know tomorrow will bring something marvelous into your life."

Lois replied, "It's frustrating. You work all these years and you still don't know where the next dollar will come from."

I agreed with her and said, "Ah, the life of an entrepreneur!"

I heard a giggle of acknowledgment on the other end of the line. Continuing I said, "That's the joy of having your own business. It's all up to you. You decide the next actions you will take. Remember you are not alone. Think of all the people who have helped you and are looking for ways to help right now. Ask for help, work from your passion, and you will find a way to succeed." I heard a sigh of relief.

Lois then added, "And I have the passion, don't I? I know. Speak from your heart and great things will happen. OK, I'm going to call my friend, Jon, down at a hospital group in Texas. He may have something for me." Lois told me thanks and hung up the telephone.

Three days later Lois called back and exclaimed, "I'm booked for the rest of the year. Can you believe it? Jon was just about to call me. It's incredible. I must be doing something right. I wouldn't change anything. I love having my own business!"

For me, that is what "it" (and this book) is all about, hearing the words "I love having my own business."

1. **Take a moment to reflect on how your business has changed your life.**

   This is why you started your own business. There was a need to change your life and the lives of others. Remember this every day. How different your life is! You are more passionate. Your actions affect much more than just you. Acknowledge and appreciate everything you have accomplished.

2. **Continually monitor your industry and record your findings in your Product Notebook.**

   Your work has only just begun. Your business must evolve along with your industry. Keep an eye on the market; it will help keep you and your product fresh.

   Monitor your industry by using the Internet, reading new articles, and conducting in-person market research at least once a month. Key market information influences your business and your profits by helping you stay on top of new trends and new ways to expand your business (e.g., via new stores, new packaging ideas, new uses for your product, or changes in production schedules). You may even discover cool product spin-offs (related products with slightly different functions). Things to monitor include:

   - **Description.** Do people understand your product and its features? What information can you display near your product (such as a fact sheet) to increase customer awareness and understanding?
   - **Pricing.** Is your pricing effective, or have any similar new products come out with lower or higher pricing?
   - **Usage.** Have any new uses for your product been discovered? If so, develop new marketing materials that describe them.
   - **Press.** What new press contacts can you discover? What new story ideas can you develop (such as new uses)? Maximize free publicity by developing and sending out interesting stories about your business.
   - **Promotion.** Is your point-of-display marketing effort working? Are there any special sales or holidays you can tap into?
   - **Distribution.** Are there any new distributors in the market? Are your distributors successful? If some are, ask them what are they doing to

N O T E

Tell people about significant product developments. It may be just the thing they need to buy or write about your product.

increase sales and then share the information with other distributors. If they are not effective, brainstorm on other distribution avenues.

- **Sponsorship.** If an organization begins to use your product, announce it to the world! Send personal announcements to similar organizations that might want to use your product.
- **Customer support.** Are any customers complaining? If so, what are you doing to resolve the issues? What unexpected customer support activities are you conducting? Do you need to train your store owners, reps, or distributors about your business so they can more effectively sell your product?

3. **Keep up to date on what your competition is doing by researching them.**

Let reporters do your research for you (after all, that is their job). There are many industry-specific trade magazines, organizational newsletters, and Internet groups that showcase new products and developments. Subscribe to one or more that monitors your industry so you can follow key events.

Trade shows are an excellent way to find out information on products before they are released into the market. When you find similar products, create a list of the new product's attributes (e.g., sales strategy, selling points, product attributes, or price) so you can analyze how they will affect your business later.

4. **In your Product Notebook, develop specific strategies to improve your product or counter any threats you found in To Dos number 2 and number 3.**

Take time to reflect on how the competition and industry changes may affect your product. If necessary, develop new strategies that incorporate these issues. This does not mean you have to change your product. However, if you want to make a change and the timing is right, do it.

You still have to run your business so don't overwhelm yourself with new strategies. I recommend that you choose one or two top strategies a month to implement. If possible, incorporate these strategies into your everyday activities. For example, just because a new competitive product is launched does not mean you immediately have to modify your product. Instead of worrying about how you can beat the competition, make your product's unique characteristics stand out more clearly. You may only need to change the perception of your product by modifying your marketing materials.

5. **Establish processes to free up your time so you can update your product or develop new ones.**

No matter how great your product is, consumer attention spans are short. Every day someone is starting a new business. So continually be on the lookout for new ways to make money or to attract new customers to your product. Keep your product fresh in the minds of consumers.

Manage your time wisely. Develop processes for your business that limit your management time, especially at night. This is hard because it means giving some control to someone else.

For instance, if you open a restaurant and establish an excellent training program for your staff (including a manager), you might only have to check the books in the morning and can spend the majority of your time marketing your restaurant and developing new products.

You might develop take-out or delivery services. Or you could develop unique cocktails, sell T-shirts, or create special events (e.g., murder mystery nights, theme parties, or offering special rates for corporate functions) that will delight clientele at your established restaurant.

6. **Pursue debt collection with vigor.**

Make sure that people pay you the money they owe you. Do not be nice if people do not pay you. You have provided them with a product or service, and they need to honor that. You do not want to endanger your business (or go bankrupt) just because people do not pay you. Usually this only takes a telephone call to remind them. Some more drastic measures may include:

- Speaking to the manager or owner, telling them that their late payment is affecting your business. Ask them to pay you according to the terms and conditions you agreed on.
- Sending a follow-up invoice that states "Late Payment Notice."
- Using a collection agency for large bills. You can tell the store, "If we do not have the check by the agreed date, I have no other choice but to turn this delinquent account over to a collection agency. Your cooperation is appreciated."
- If all else fails, going to them in person and staying until they write you a check.

7. **Pay all your bills on time.**

Do not waste time looking over your shoulder. Pay people who provide you with products or services. Your reputation will help your business stand out in a crowded marketplace. And you want to show the same courtesy to other businesses that you would have them show to you.

8. **Take time out to be with your friends and family.**

Balance in your life is extremely important. You are not only creating a business, you are creating a new life for yourself (and those who are important to you). Life is not complete without other people. You will need their energy and support to keep going. Have fun with people you care for. Invite them over for dinner, send them thank-you cards, and involve them in your business by telling them about your successes, asking them for help, and listening to them. Life is about relationships; keep them strong.

9. **Celebrate!**

Tell everyone about your accomplishments and let them be part of your joy. Take a moment each week (or each evening while creating your nightly To Do lists) to smile and pat yourself on the back.

Conclusion

Congratulations! You have graduated. You have completed *Kick Start Your Dream Business*. And you have created a business and a life based on your passion. It's exciting, frightening, and frustrating all at the same time. You have created something wonderful, magical. Some days you will shake your head with wonder and say, "Wow. This is real. I created it. How incredible." Pat yourself on your back. Don't be shy—kiss your Product Notebook. Celebrate!

In the process of working through *Kick Start Your Dream Business*, you have learned a lot about how to start and grow a business, but you have learned even more about yourself. You now know how to focus your enthusiasm and achieve your goals, rather than just imagine them. Relish your new world. Your energy will continue to grow along with your business and will help you overcome any hurdles you may encounter along the way.

Don't forget the *Kick Start* steps. Use them to enhance your new business, develop additional products or services, or to help others.

Make a difference in the world by sharing what you have learned. If you know someone who has a dream, tell them that achieving it is possible. If an entrepreneur is struggling, offer them support. You know the right steps to take because you are a *Kick Start* graduate. Teach others to speak from their hearts, L-I-S-Ten, and write down ideas for their business.

People will marvel at your achievements. Thank them and ask how you can help them achieve their goals. Can you imagine helping others achieve their dreams? I already know your answer to that question. Your answer is, "Yes I can!"

Your business will touch people's lives every day. You can help other people create businesses that provide a benefit. The joy you felt in creating your own business is magnified untold times when you help others do the same. There is no greater experience than seeing someone's eyes sparkle when they realize that they too can achieve their dreams. A world filled with people achieving their dreams—what a joy. You are now living with that joy and energy. Congratulations.

THUMBS UP

People are there to help you succeed. Always speak from your heart, listen to others, and ask for help when you need it.

INDEX

About the Author

For as long as he can remember, Romanus Wolter has dreamt of helping people make a living from whatever they are passionate about. Growing up in Taipei, Taiwan, from age four to eighteen, he watched the country grow and the people prosper. He saw the roads, factories, and homes being built. Movie theaters, stores, and restaurants sprung up on every corner. All this activity sparked something inside of young Romanus—the realization that the imagination is limitless. Any idea can become a reality.

After returning to the United States, Romanus obtained a master's degree in international marketing. As a marketing consultant in London and Hong Kong, he gained product development experience by helping small businesses expand their markets beyond their geographic barriers to other countries. This experience led Romanus to developing practical steps to ensure small business success.

Romanus has received a Trainer of the Year award from the San Francisco office of the U.S. Small Business Administration. He has been a small business advice columnist providing answers to questions commonly asked by entrepreneurs on national and local Internet sites. As a workshop leader, an instructor at City College of San Francisco, and an independent consultant, he has helped hundreds of people create business action plans for success.

As the director of the San Francisco Small Business Development Center, Romanus provided the proven tools and real-life information people need to be successful in a variety of industries. Romanus currently leads "Kick Start" workshops to inspire people to bring their ideas into reality, to help business owners boost their sales, and to energize teams to achieve business goals. He is also a consultant to numerous economic development organizations.

Romanus lives in San Francisco, California, where, besides always being on the lookout to help another passionate entrepreneur, he enjoys yoga, collecting Asian art, eating ice cream, and hanging out with anyone who contributes a unique perspective to life.